SEARCH

America has lost its soul.
Will "We the People"?

Written by
Richard H. Coller

Publishing

Published by
Innovo Publishing LLC
www.innovopublishing.com
1-888-546-2111

Providing Full-Service Publishing Services for
Christian Authors, Artists & Organizations: Hardbacks, Paperbacks,
eBooks, Audiobooks, Music & Videos.

SEARCH

Biblical quotes are from the Scripture taken from the NEW AMERICAN STANDARD BIBLE®, Copyright © 1960,1962,1963,1968,1971,1972,1973,1975,1977,1995 by The Lockman Foundation. Used by permission.

ISBN 13: 978-1-936076-54-3
ISBN 10: 1-936076-54-3

Cover Design & Interior Layout: Innovo Publishing LLC

Printed in the United States of America
U.S. Printing History

First Edition: January 2011

To my Lord Jesus who knows me better than anyone
and loves me just the same.

And to my wife Marilyn who is most instrumental in my understanding
of Jesus. Marilyn emulates the Lord's wisdom and empathy better than
anyone I know. Thank you—with all my love.

In Memory of

Eva (Judy) Coller—My mother who always encouraged me.
She would proudly promote this endeavor to one and all.
I hear you now, Mom. I love you.

Dear Abbie and Mickenzie,

It's almost time for me to keep my promise about my research on the Network. I know you want to understand my research and my past, so I'm sharing my story and years of investigation with you. I write this not only for your enjoyment, but with the hope that you learn of our Lord and Savior in a more personal way.

Love, Grandpa Ryker Cuff
December 14th, 2129

Table of Contents

PART ONE

"I the LORD search the heart
and examine the mind,
to reward a man according to his conduct,
according to what his deeds deserve."
Jeremiah 17:10

"All have turned away,
they have together become worthless;
there is no one who does good, not even one."
Romans 3:12

PROLOGUE

The cobalt blue beam missed his head by a hair's width. He saw the thin, blue ray before he heard it. The energy beam splashed against the brick wall ten feet in front of him and then flashed out. The irradiate brilliance was magnified by the twilight hour. Buzzing, sizzling sounds preceded the acidic, ozone smell. The beleaguered man ducked seconds after it would have done any good. Spurred on at break-neck speed, the man reached the black opening in the wall and lunged through to the darkness beyond.

Seconds later two black-uniformed pursuers came to a sudden halt at the opened doorway. One quickly peered in. The pair of black figures held small stunners poised at the dark maw. One pushed the other through and followed quickly. Inky black. The only thing visible was the thin, blue band of light that ran across the helmet visors of the dark-suited pair.

As their helmets automatically initiated infrared vision assist, the pair noticed two doorways down the long, dark hallway and ran toward them. They split up, one running into the first doorway; the other, racing for the second. When the second man entered, he saw a bright, thin light flash in one corner of the room.

"Simon, in here!"

Finding a light switch, he touched it on as his partner entered the room. His visor adjusted and he could see the room was as vacant as the rest of the building except for the teleport in the corner. Swearing and rushing to the controls, Simon punched the keypad with perceptive fingers. After seeing the results, he slammed the keyboard. In a swearing rage he shouted, "He's done it again! How'd he find his way in this dump with no lights? And how'd he rig this thing so we can't trace'm?"

The other agent shook his head negatively, and the band of light on his helmet shimmered. "I don't know, Si, but we've got some information on this one. I think we can reach him before he goes underground and starts spreading that Christian crap. This Cuff character needs to be stopped. It shouldn't take long for us to figure where to look next." -

Simon nodded in agreement but was concerned. "We'd better be careful with this one. I don't think Mr. Hawkins is going to like that we missed Cuff again."

"Yeah, I've got some ideas about that."

They captured the teleport logs and reset the controls. Moments later they teleported back to the NMA Eyrie so they could analyze the information they hoped would lead them to the evasive, newest member of the recently created underground organization called the Network.

THE SEARCH BEGINS

"Today marks an historic event for the NMA. Legislation passed, which provides us with the power to halt or curtail any Network actions without waiting for the red tape that has previously bogged us down. We owe it all to Sly Hawkins. We wish him good luck in his new position, which will help us accelerate our organization's charter."

James Rice, *Eyrie Standard*, an NMA communications publication, 09/18/2076

The Visit
Saturday, September 19, 2076

A horse? No. It's definitely a duck. Not just any duck but one that drives a vehicle like Grandpa used to drive. It looks something like a lazy duck driving a fluffy car into the bright blue sky.

"Ry y y y y y y y y ker. Come in the house. It's almost time."

I hate it when Mom does that to me. Now the cloud looks like a dumb old cloud again.

"Be right there." Ryker stood under the apple tree to survey the view of his backyard. He savored the feeling of contentment in knowing that all he could see was his to explore and enjoy. Below him lay rolling hills peppered with cultivated meadows and deciduous forests. Situated at the bottom of the hill was a family cemetery. Contentment slipped away as a foreboding thought crept in. *So what? Does it really matter?*

"Ryker. Get in here! Now!"

The young man trotted across the yard, sullenly plodded through the doorway, and into the family room. "Just in time, son. Come here and sit next to me," Homer said as he directed his eldest child to the footstool in front of him.

The rest of the family waited also. Judy stood behind her husband and gently massaged his shoulders. Sarah tended to her younger, wiggling sister, attempting placement of a ribbon in her hair. The last-minute adjustment developed into a wrestling match. Ray shoved back on the pair crowding in on him.

"Mom! Tell'm to knock it off. Joanne almost kicked my drink down the front of me." The youngest male, Cuff, often seemed to be in the wrong place at the right time.

Homer settled it all. "OK kids, that's enough. Here they come."

All heads turned to the teleport in the corner of the room. It resembled a small stage, about six feet by four feet wide with a glass wall that slid in front when activated. A keyboard and small visual display were recessed in the wall next to it. The glass wall moved into place, turned black, and obscured the view behind it. For milliseconds a bright light shimmered behind the wall then quickly faded away. The black panel paled in hue and slowly became transparent again. An elderly couple dressed in fine clothes of noble distinction stood smiling at the family.

As the glass wall retracted into the adjoining wall, Homer tripped over Ryker to get to the couple. "Uncle Vern and Aunt Rose! How're you doing?"

The older man greeted Homer, "Just fine, my boy. Just fine." Vernon shook Homer's hand then gave him a hug. The quaint couple greeted the rest of the family with warmth and genuine pleasure. They took time to greet each family member with sincere interest, to Ryker's amusement.

I wonder if these people are really Dad's relatives. They look rich enough to be in a palace or something. I like Uncle Vern. He seems able to look right into my head and understand me, and I don't even know him.

"Ryker. Don't just stand there gaping. Run and turn the meal maker on so we can feed our guests," Judy directed.

"OK, Mom."

"And leave it where I've set it. We don't need to feed Uncle Vern and Aunt Rose dessert first."

"Aw, Mom. I wouldn't do that."

Vernon gently halted Ryker just before he left the room and whispered to him, "I still like dessert first sometimes, too." With that intimate insight and a slow wink, Vernon Cuff won a place in Ryker's heart that had been reserved for his grandfather.

Judy slowly trudged the hallway from the children's rooms and plunked down on the couch next to Homer with a familiar bedtime expression. "I didn't think they'd ever settle down."

Rose giggled politely, covering her mouth to help conceal the spontaneous reaction. Her long, thin, lined face gave the impression worry was a normal countenance. She wore the appearance gracefully, as a trophy. Her dancing, dark bronze eyes betrayed the rest of her face. "Judy, I don't mean to laugh at you. It just brings back memories."

Vernon smiled at the younger couple. "You've such a nice family here. Thanks for letting us barge in on you this way." His gratefulness echoed the seriousness in his voice.

Homer took the cue and reassured his relatives. "Uncle Vern and Aunt Rose, you know you're welcome, but why all this cloak-and-dagger stuff?"

Vernon looked at Homer solemnly. "Homer, we need to explain something to you and Judy. I hope you will understand." Rose looked down in a moment of contemplation as Vernon continued, "Rose and I are wanted by the NMA."

Judy's usual bright face went pale. The mark on her left cheek seemed florescent blue against the chalk white skin. She had a blood tumor just below her left eye. People who didn't know her mistook it for a bruise. Homer had received suspicious looks more than once. The news was such a blow, she wouldn't have argued the point with anyone just then. Finding her voice, Judy blurted her concern, "But why? Surely you haven't gone against the Policies?"

Rose lifted her head and piously looked at the younger couple to confirm what Vernon explained: "Rose and I are what some people call RCs. That's their name for us. I see it differently."

Shaking himself out of his stupor, Homer reluctantly asked, "Uncle Vern! A Rigid Christian is a person with ancient moral concepts, right?"

Vernon smiled at his brother's son and replied, "I wouldn't use the term ancient. I believe the concepts to be relevant and true for today, not gone and lost long ago."

Judy anxiously exclaimed, "No wonder the Neutral Morals Agency is looking for you! My goodness, what do you think you're doing?"

Recovering from the initial shock, Homer gently laid a calloused hand on Judy's shoulder. "Now, calm down, dear. I'm sure they've a good reason for feeling the way they do. Let's hear them out." The four sat silently for a moment. Homer could now calmly and confidently address the subject. "We're Christians also, but we wouldn't dream of going against the NMA Policies."

Homer studied Vernon's face and noticed true compassion. It reminded him of a work of art he once saw. The painting pictured Jesus on the cross looking down upon the soldiers who had just crucified Him. The caption under the painting read, "Father, forgive them for they know not what they do." Homer wondered why Vernon had compassion for him when it was he who was in the wrong.

Vernon saw his nephew's confusion and told him, "Homer, my boy, you and Judy are good people. I understand your dismay. Rose and I don't want to cause you two any problems. That's why we'll be leaving tomorrow night. Now, I know you don't understand our contrary position related to the NMA, and I'm more than willing to explain myself. But it's late and we've all day tomorrow for explanations. What do you say we just go to bed and let you sleep on it? In the morning you may have more you want to talk about."

No one argued with the logic. Judy settled her guests down for the night and drifted off to sleep immediately. Homer lay in bed only half-awake, contemplating the evening's events. As he slept, a picture frozen in his mind troubled him and affected his dreams throughout the night. It was the face of his uncle, superimposed over a picture of Jesus on the cross. What could it mean?

Something New

Ryker's room faced the early morning sun. Golden fingers of warmth caressed his face, beckoning him to wake up. The eleven-year-old needed little encouragement to get up and explore another day. Stealthily he dressed so no one would discover his early morning departure. *I got to make sure Ray or no one else finds out about the cave Buck and I found the day before yesterday. I just want to make sure I can still find it. We didn't get a chance yesterday with all the stupid company.*

As Ryker made his way out the back door, a sight caught his attention making him forget his mission. Under the apple tree, almost hidden from view by the mock orange bush, Uncle Vernon sat on a large rock with his head bowed and hands over his face. Ryker thought he heard whispering or mumbling. Curiosity got the better of him, and he decided to sneak closer behind the bush and spy on Uncle Vern.

Listening closely, Ryker could hear, ". . . because I've a burden on my heart, Lord. May You open hearts and clear minds before it's too late. Not only are souls lost but blinded to a better life here and now. Oh, Father . . . and why must . . . for it seems maybe I should . . . but Your will, not mine." Though he strained to eavesdrop further, he couldn't understand all the words being spoken.

He looks like he's praying or something. Why would he bother doing that?

Carefully moving in to hear better, Ryker stepped on a plastic cup Sarah had left behind. It cracked with a resounding snap. Vernon whipped his head around to detect the source of intrusion. There in front of him was a slender-built boy half hidden behind a bush. His eyes were so big and round they filled the large frames of his glasses. Never had Vernon noticed such large, green, owl-like eyes on anyone. Adding to the appearance of an owl were two tufts of dark, sandy-colored hair sticking up and out on each side. In his haste to get about the day's business, Ryker hadn't used a comb. His mouth was agape at his mistake, making him look even more like a great horned owl ready to let out a hoot.

Vern couldn't contain the laughter that welled up from his belly. "Oh, for goodness sake, son," Vernon managed to say in between the chuckles, "you look like you just swallowed some currant wine and you're surprised it tasted so good."

When Ryker sensed Vernon's good mood, he relaxed and wiped the silly look off his face. Vernon motioned him a little closer. "What's a young fella like you doing pussy-footin' around this time of morning?"

With a quizzical gaze, Ryker slowly moved in and answered, "I woke up and came outside to fool around. Uncle Vern, what's currant wine?"

Vernon became immediately serious as he sensed this little "owl" might be a wise one. Even an off-the-cuff statement didn't escape his inquisitive mind. "Well, it's a sweet-tasting but strong wine made from a certain kind of shrub berry."

Sandy-colored eyebrows went up in awe. "I didn't think someone like you'd know anything about wine. Does it taste good? I heard Dad say it's evil stuff."

Vernon had the boy sit down next to him. "Have you ever heard of a mouse trap?"

"Sure. You catch mice with'm."

"Why would the mouse go into the trap?"

"They put food on the trap so the mouse'd come and eat it."

"What kind of food?"

"I don't know."

"Cheese, peanut butter, or anything else a mouse would like to eat. How would that trap work if you placed a piece of dirt on it?"

"He'd have to be a pretty stupid mouse to get caught."

Vernon gave another wide smile and a low chuckle at the statement. Ryker smiled, too. First, because he got a laugh from his uncle and second, because he understood what Vern was driving at. "I get it! People wouldn't get hooked on evil things if they weren't fun in some way. Right?"

"You're a sharp lad. I can truly see your dad in you. Tell me, Ryker, what're you going to be when you grow up?"

Ryker looked down at his feet. "I don't know. I don't think it matters."

Feeling Ryker's sense of hopelessness, Vernon questioned him. "Why do you think that?" Ryker could see the compassion in Vernon's eyes.

"We're all just going to die anyway. So what's it matter what we do in this dumb old life?"

The anger was obvious, and Vernon realized where it was coming from. "You miss your grandpa, don't you?"

Tears welled up in Ryker's eyes. He didn't like to think about losing such an important part of his life. Hanging his head, Ryker softly said, "I'll never see him again."

Then the tears came, which prompted Vernon to reply, "That's not true. You may or may not see Grandpa again, but that's up to you."

His words created such a shock that the tears stopped almost before they started. Ryker took off his glasses, used his sleeve, and wiped his eyes dry. "What'd ya mean?"

Vernon put a hand on Ryker's shoulder. "Everyone's going to spend eternity somewhere, either with God or without Him. In heaven or in hell. The choice is up to you. Jesus is the only way to get to heaven. I happen to know my brother, your grandpa, chose to follow Jesus and is in heaven."

It was the first time Ryker had ever heard such a thing.

Rose hollered out the back door. "Vern, where are you?"

"Right here, dear."

"Come on inside. Judy has breakfast ready."

"Be right there."

Turning to Ryker, Vernon continued, "Remember, Jesus is the Way. Come on and have breakfast with me." Ryker had no choice. Vernon had captured his attention just as Grandpa had.

***

Sly Hawkins glared at the pair of Search Squad (SS) agents with a visage difficult to decipher. His rise within the agency had been extraordinary, and the pair standing before him was definitely not augmenting his early success. They stood outside on the roof of an NMA building. The view of Washington, DC was impressive, even with the impending storm which threatened to drench the men at any moment. The roof was unique—made of glass—but they stood on the edge, out of sight of anyone below who might venture to look up. Few people knew of the supervisors' tactics involving a place out of reach for surveillance.

Chris and Simon were nervous. They had discussed the different actions Sly might take because of problems they had encountered over the last few months. The pair of SS agents had contrived to eliminate their supervisor if he proved to upset their careers. Holding their helmets under their arms, they stood with their backs to the view, only feet from the edge. Chris would speak for the two, and Simon would react if needed. Chris was the most physically impressive (about twice the size of Sly), but Simon had little regard for life and could kill without reservation.

Sly's voice was deep and resounding, demanding attention. He began the conversation with a neutral smile. "You boys have been a disappointment to me."

The term "boys" irked Chris. He answered Sly sarcastically, emphasizing Sly's implied superiority. "We understand your disappointment, *sir*, but Cuff has some connections we didn't expect."

It was the response Sly had expected as evidenced by his thin, wide smile. "I see you understand your precarious career situation." He held the grin while settling his hands behind his back. Simon moved his hand closer to his weapon. The supervisor didn't miss the reposition. "A truly foolish move by you two. But it proves my intuition to suspect you both of rebellion. The next move by either of you had better be well calculated."

17

Both men sensed their mistake when they noticed how calm Sly seemed. Chris slowly glanced around and stopped staring off to the pair's far left. Simon gradually followed his partner's lead and casually moved his gun hand away from his firearm. A large SS agent stood poised, holding a stunner on the pair.

Sly's smile increased. "Maybe you both are smarter than you look. Devon's itching to pull that trigger, and it's not set to stun either. No one would ever know where you two have gone. I'll make a deal with you *boys*." He purposely used the debasing term. "Walk carefully away from here, finish the job you started, and if you complete it satisfactorily, I'll not remember this small insurrection. Of course, if you're not successful, we'll worry about that then."

The rain began to pound as Sly and Devon watched the other two walk toward the roof entrance. The torrent couldn't wash the satisfied smile off Sly's face.

The Visit Ends

After dinner, Judy and Rose sat at the dining room table engrossed in deep discussion. The conversation was so intense that Joanne couldn't get her mother's attention, even when she lay on the table between the two women. Judy simply scooped the five-year-old up and sat her on her lap while still listening to Rose. Even the consistent "Mom . . . Mom . . . Mom . . ." was mute to Judy's ears.

Homer and Vernon watched the scene while settling down on the couch in the next room. Vernon smiled with a nod. "Those two younger ones of yours can sure be corkers at times. Do you ever wonder why you went through the trouble you did for the last two?"

Homer felt like a dog on a leash. He was being taken for a walk, didn't know where, and that bothered him. But he responded cordially. "At times we wondered, but as you know, we wouldn't give them up for anything. When we were sent here, we thought at first the penalty was too great. We've since learned that being separated from most of society has its own rewards. We have what we need, and we don't miss our old friends like we thought we would."

Vernon relaxed, giving the impression his attention waned. His eyes were half closed and focused elsewhere. Not a word got by him as he informed his nephew, "They're not giving permits out for extended families anymore. Did you know that?"

Homer crossed his arms and shrugged his shoulders. "No, but I'm not surprised. We were treated awful when Judy and I applied for ours. It looked like we might not get it at first. The man at the NMA Family Center said he thought it should be illegal to have more than two children."

Vernon relaxed totally, closed his eyes, and stretched his legs out in front while crossing his arms over his pudgy little belly and asked, "Did anyone ever explain to you why they put you and your family here away from most others?"

Homer's thoughts could be read on his face. He wasn't sure he liked the direction of the dialogue. The answer to Vernon's question involved moral convictions that went against the NMA. He replied simply, "It was necessary because what Judy and I wanted leaned heavily toward an old-fashioned, traditional-style family, which many think is against the policies of the Neutral Morals Agency."

Vernon bolted from the couch and spun around to face Homer. His face glowed pink and his eyes, sparkling like two sapphire jewels, were wide with amazement. Vernon's reaction was so sudden that Homer almost missed his words. "Can you sit there and honestly tell me that you see nothing wrong with that logic?"

Numb shock. And then the only response he could give, learned from society: "We shouldn't force our personal moral convictions on other people."

Vern relaxed a little but held his ground. "Who says?"

"The NMA."

"On what do they base their decisions when it comes to what's neutral and what's not?"

Silence. Vernon continued.

"Answer this for me. Is it wrong to steal?"

"Why . . . yes."

"Is it wrong if your family's starving and you steal only to feed them?"

"Now that'd be a little more understandable . . ."

Vernon didn't want to lose momentum so he pressed the issue before Homer could get off track. "Yes, it would be more understandable, but the question remains, is it wrong to steal?"

Homer glared at his uncle in disdain. He was beginning to see why some called his aunt and uncle "rigid" Christians. They saw things

19

so black-and-white, and the world just didn't seem to operate that way. Homer's answer made perfect sense to him. "In that situation I'd say it would NOT be wrong for a person to steal—if it meant saving his family."

Vernon relaxed and sat back down. "An answer I'd expect from someone whose philosophy is based on situation ethics. I thought you'd see it that way. The idea of neutral morals is ludicrous. Look at a man's head. If it's bald, does he have a neutral head? No, he has no hair. A head either has hair or it doesn't have hair. Granted the amount of hair may vary, but you either have it or you don't." The older gentleman smiled.

Homer was just as stunned by Vernon's relaxed attitude as he was by the sudden outburst just seconds earlier. "What other answer could there possibly be?" Vernon calmly faced his nephew. "Only the correct answer, as I see it. Stealing is stealing, and stealing is wrong. The key to understanding this law depends on who you believe gave it to us. If it came from man, then it can't be absolute. It'd change from one situation to the next depending on who's judging the circumstances. My goodness, people debate whether stealing something is a misdemeanor or a felony, and they ignore the true question." Vern received an eyebrow lift for the comment and so continued, "But if the law came from God, He IS an absolute—never changing, the same yesterday, today, and forever. If He says stealing is wrong then there are no ifs, ands, or buts. Now I may forgive the man for stealing to feed his family. I may help him through the situation, but I do so because God says He'll forgive the man if he'll repent and turn from his evil ways."

It was the first time Homer had ever heard such an argument. He had never realized there might be another way to view the issue. He wasn't alone either. Judy stood in the kitchen doorway. She had listened since Vern's flight from the couch. The next minute was quiet as each looked at one another until the alarm went off on the teleport.

Ryker had been at the top of the stairs listening to his father and uncle the whole time. *Uncle Vern and Aunt Rose have to leave now. I can't stand the thought. He's not any better than Grandpa. Why do all the people I like end up leaving me just when I get to know them?*

The elderly couple took a few minutes to gather their luggage and stood at the teleport ready for their next destination. Homer's family said their goodbyes. Ryker didn't look much like Vernon's wise little owl at the moment but rather a little rejected puppy. Not wanting to look his great uncle in the eyes, Ryker peered over the top of his glasses so he couldn't focus on Vernon's face. "Why won't you tell us where you're going, Uncle Vern?"

Vern squatted to make eye contact with Ryker before he replied. "You see, it's this way, son. The government has changed its governing policies over the last one hundred years. They say things contrary to what this country was originally based upon and what I still believe to be true. Aunt Rose and I think our country has changed for the worse and we want other people to know why we think that. The government doesn't want us to tell other people this so they're trying to stop us. It's better for you, your mom and dad, and everyone if you don't know where we are. It's for your protection and ours, too. OK?" Ryker wasn't really sure he understood but he felt better after his uncle had talked to him about it.

Vernon stood and faced Homer and Judy. "That's why we prearranged this departure with our other contacts. They'll transport us to their location so there'll be no records punched in through your teleport computer system. That way if anyone does come around to investigate just tell them the truth, and they won't be able to track us."

As if on cue, the teleport signaled for a one-minute countdown before transmission. Vern and Rose stepped up on the translator pad. The whole Cuff family looked on as the couple left the same way they had arrived.

The NMA

In his repair shop in the basement of his home, Homer struggled to revamp his handheld plant growth analyzer. It was harvest time, and he needed the information gathered by the unit to improve his production for next year. It was the few families like Homer's—those under the extended family plan—who were required by the government to supply food for the entire country.

Nine-year-old Sarah and seven-year-old Ray played near their father. As a rule, Ray had very little to do with his older sister, but since Ryker had disappeared somewhere during the morning, pestering Sarah was the next best thing.

Frustration over his task caused Homer to scold the two. "Sarah and Ray! If you're going to argue over everything, go do it somewhere out of my way!"

Judy hollered down to Homer. "Homer, get up here! Someone just bypassed the security clearance on the teleport, and whoever it is will here in two minutes."

Homer, Judy, and the three younger children stood waiting when Ryker came through the back door. "Hey, Mom and Dad, guess what I found over by the—." He stopped in mid-sentence and queried, "What's going on?"

His father answered, "Someone's giving us an unexpected visit."

Ryker noticed the countdown on the teleport. *Maybe it's Uncle Vern and Aunt Rose coming back!*

The teleport screen became opaque but quickly faded, revealing a sight the children had never seen before. On the pad stood two figures wearing slick, black uniforms and matching black helmets with dark visors. The only other colors were a dark band of blue light that ran around the visors where eyes should be and the red-and-yellow emblems on the left breast of their uniforms. The emblem drew Ryker's attention. A red patch emblazoned with bright, yellow letters: NMA. Only days earlier it would have meant nothing to him, but now he knew without a doubt why these visitors were here.

The smallest of the pair directed his attention to Homer. "Are you Homer R. Cuff?"

"Yes."

"Do you know a Vernon W. Cuff?"

"Yes."

"Is Vernon here now?"

"No."

"Has he been here within the last three days?"

"Yesterday and the day before."

"Would you please inform us where we may now reach Mr. Vernon Cuff?"

"I don't know."

While one NMA agent interrogated Homer, the other keyed through the teleport controls. "Simon, there's been no record of any destinational transport from this terminal for months."

Agent Simon turned away and mumbled a disturbed reply. "Typical. These RCs know what they're doing."

Fingering an unseen control on his belt the second agent contacted his superiors. "This is Chris Hasselman from Search Squad 217, to the Eagles' Nest. We've followed the suspects to New York, section B-352, port 2371. As per normal MO of RCs, there's no immediate sign of the fugitives, and again they've left no trace of their next destination. We'll further interrogate the last known contacts, but initial discussion indicates no fruitful information will be available." Hasselman stood motionless for several moments listening for further instructions. "Affirmative. We'll do what we can. Expect to return in about fifteen minutes. Hasselman out."

Turning to Simon, he continued with strict protocol and procedures. "Si, I'll finish questioning these people. You go search the rest of the premises." Simon pulled one of three palm-sized devices from his belt and left the living room scanning the area as he went. The action instantly intrigued Ray, and he started following the agent.

"Ray, stay here. You don't need to be following him around." Homer wanted to keep track of all his family. Frustrated, Ray grumpily sat down with the rest of the family seated in the living room.

Chris stood before them. Not being able to see his face through the dark helmet was intimidating. "What was the purpose of Vernon and Rose Cuff's visit here for the last two days?"

Judy revealed her nervousness by gathering the children a bit closer as Homer answered questions. "Vernon is my uncle on my father's side. He was here for a personal visit."

"Did either of them spread propaganda concerning strict moral standards adhered to by the radical movement known as Rigid Christians?"

Homer felt comfortable answering the question. So far all he needed to do was tell the truth. The answer came swift with no hint of deception, something the SS member was trained to detect. "No. It was a family visit only. They made no contact with others while here."

No surprises for Chris so far. This was all normal procedure whenever RCs visited family. The agent knew that hesitation with the next question would not be out of character. "Did Mr. or Mrs. Cuff in any way try to convince you or any of your family that NMA policies are wrong?"

The father glanced away looking out a window to gather his thoughts before turning back to answer. His answer was crisp and to the point. "Yes."

"Does anyone in the family plan on making a request to visit friends, family, or any other business sometime in the near future?"

"No."

"Thank you for your cooperation. I need to inform you that all communication and teleport transmissions will be monitored for the next nine months, at which time we will re-evaluate to determine whether the procedure needs to continue."

Simon came in when he knew the interrogation was over. As the two agents stepped up on the teleport, Simon keyed in their destination as Chris triggered his communication device. "Search Squad 217 reporting the end of search sequence 23. Results negative. Procedure watch W-15 is now activated and in effect for Cuff residence, area NY-352, P2371. SS team 217 destination, the Nest."

The two men left as quickly as they had arrived. The younger children were yet unaware of the purpose of the unannounced visit. "Mom," Ray said, shaking his mother's elbow, "can I get a helmet like that?"

Homer, Judy, and Ryker, on the other hand, were very well aware, and they realized the impact Vernon and Rose had on their lives. *They can search and search for Uncle Vern, but they won't find him. He's too smart for them. When I grow up, I want to be like Uncle Vern.*

Ryker's motives were good, but over time most of the convictions ingrained by Uncle Vern were erased . . . until many years later.

***

Chris and Simon had no plans of returning to headquarters. Their hope was to succeed in nabbing Vernon before he made his final move to hide within the Network. Forces dictated otherwise, and the pair reaped the bitter results of their failure. Simon keyed the teleport for a destination the pair decided would give them opportunity to run.

At the Washington, DC NMA teleport station, Sly anticipated the action of the team. The boss would follow through on his threat. Looking over the nervous shoulder of the technician, Sly saw the move by the pair. "Intercept them now!"

The technician cringed under the force of Hawkins' voice but reacted in time to comply. As the teleport effect diminished, Chris and Simon blanched at their destination. They had failed to save themselves, and Sly beamed at his success. When the glass retracted into the wall, Sly turned to SS agent Devon who had his weapon on the pair. "These two will be a fine test for our new level sixteen."

ON HIS OWN

"The term tolerance has been overused and abused. It was successfully used to elevate lenience of ideas contrary to unsophisticated Christian conviction. But it was turned upon progressive philosophies in like manner. The term we need is something that matches our goals of tolerance but only supports neutral reactions. The term neutral should be integrated into the idea of freedom."

Morgan Tanner, New American Bill of Rights taskforce leader – 8/18/2022

Reunion

He gazed at the shiny, midnight blue 2038 Ford Finally. It was the last car on exhibit before exiting the museum and the one where he spent most of his time. Except for the color it could have been the very one in which Grandpa had given him a ride when Ryker was only ten years old. It was the last car Ford ever made. Ryker later heard that was just the reason his grandfather had bought one. Henry Cuff hadn't cared much for the newfangled teleport transmitters, and he couldn't get his wife Carrie on one of the things. This made it that much easier for Ryker's grandpa to decide to buy what the Ford Company had had trouble selling during its last year as a car company.

"Ford started it. Ford finished it. That's a virtue worth copying." Ryker heard him say it more than once. *Grandpa, what would you think of your grandson now? I wish I could ask you. I believe you'd see it my way. Mom and Dad just don't listen to me like you used to. It'd be fun to take for a spin, wouldn't it?*

His meditative state caused the intruding voice to surprise Ryker. He vaulted up from leaning on the railing and turned to see a friendly face—a person Ryker didn't think he would see for many more years. "Buck! What're you doing here?"

The visitor leaned on the railing. "I could ask you the same thing."

They gave each other a hearty handshake and hug. Unknown to Ryker, an NMA agent casually looked on. As a member of the Watch Squad, he appeared as one of the regular patrons. He observed two young men standing toe-to-toe, glad to see each other. Ryker had long, light brown hair. He seemed to be about six feet tall, give or take an inch, and wore stylish, wire-rim glasses. Buck was a few inches shorter; had dark, wavy hair cut in traditional, military style; and didn't wear glasses— so the two were very different in appearance.

Ryker gladly informed his friend on his current status. "I'm working at Conklin's Construction. I've been there about two weeks. We're waiting for some materials so Jim gave me the afternoon off. I heard there was an antique car exhibit here so I stopped in to check it out. What about you? You're supposed to be training in Texas somewhere. What're you doing here?"

Before answering, Buck surveyed the area and inadvertently noticed the WS agent. He respectfully grabbed Ryker's arm and calmly meandered out of the building before answering the question. "I graduated and came home for a two-week vacation. You know how I like old artillery, guns, ammo, and that kind of stuff. I came here to get some information on a couple of old army rifles I have a chance to purchase. I can tell the fella knows nothing of their true value. I believe the guns are from the Iraq Civil War of 2018. That makes them sixty-six years old! My gain if I can talk him into the sale." Before Ryker had an opportunity to respond, Buck continued, "Where ya going? I've got nowhere special to go. By the way, where're you staying?"

Ryker laughed. It was so out of character for Buck to ask more than one question at a time. Ryker took the opportunity to pick on his old friend. "Forgive me, but do you know who you sound like?"

Buck gave him a blank look. Slowly he painted his face with a smile, and then a knowing smirk when he realized to whom Ryker was alluding. "You're not going to start calling me Red, are you?"

They both laughed while giving each other a friendly punch on the shoulder. Buck effectively steered his friend from any suspicion. "OK. So I'm not entirely myself. I'm just excited to see you. It's been three years."

Ryker kicked at a rock on the sidewalk and replied. "Yeah, I know. To answer one of your questions, I'm living with my grandmother Mogie."

The two ambled casually down the city sidewalk. Above them hung a sign that read, "Freedom is a treasured gift. Do you know someone who would take that from you? Inform NMA Statistics Officer Theodore Burnap. Earn fifty credits while protecting your rights." A flashing arrow pointed to Burnap's office door.

An idea came to Ryker. With a big smile and wide eyes he said, "To answer your other question, we could stop here, turn Red in, and use the money to party."

For a moment, Buck didn't react. For a half-second fear glazed his eyes, but the pair's hubbub kept Ryker from noticing. Buck recovered and put on a congenial face, realizing Ryker was only joking. "You never quit, do ya?"

The two playfully batted one another faster along the sidewalk until Buck regained his directive. "Hey! Does Mogie still make some of her meals the old-fashioned way?" Ryker knew what he was fishing for. "You bet. Why do you think I came here when I left home? Come on. She'll be glad to meet you and maybe you'll get a Lucky Lunch."

The two approached a teleport on the corner street. As they stepped onto the translator pad, Ryker made an announcement. "Scottie, beam us up." Buck chuckled as Ryker keyed in the destination. "You're still reading those old books of your grandfather's, aren't you?"

The teleport immediately snatched the pair from the street. The NMA WS agent turned from studying their departure and went into the office of Ted Burnap.

***

Ryker's grandmother loved entertaining company. "It's ready, but you have to give payment first," Mogie spoke pointing to her cheek. She was a small woman, quick on her feet and always busy. She would stand statue-like until payment was made in full. Ryker had to stoop down well over a foot to give her a peck on the cheek.

"You too, young man," Mogie said as she pointed to her other cheek.

"His name is Buck, Mogie."

"I know, but he's a young man also."

27

Buck graciously performed his duty with anticipation of the treat to follow. The pair sat down and chatted as Mogie put things on the table. Buck asked an obvious question about the woman. "Why does everyone call your grandmother Mogie?"

Ryker eyed his grandmother busy in the kitchen and then turned back to answer. "I don't know the whole story, but it's something to do with the oldest granddaughter. When Cathy was very young, her attempt to say grandma in Dutch faltered. Her father's a Dutchman. The closest she came to the pronunciation was something like Mogie. The name's stuck with her ever since."

Mogie set before them a meal of baked ham, mashed potatoes with gravy, fruit salad, and Ryker's favorite vegetable, peas. As good as the meal before them was, Buck still eyed the homemade apple pie on the counter, which prompted his appreciation. "This is only the third time I've ever had a meal made this way. It's really great, Mogie. Thanks for welcoming me into your home."

The little woman showed her pleasure with a smile. "You're welcome. I don't do this as often as I used to. It's harder to find the ingredients. Not many people use stoves and refrigerators these days. I found these at an old antique shop on the corner of Maple and Market Street. I remember my grandmother teaching me how to cook on them." The comment incited a faraway look in Mogie's eyes. There was a short time of little conversation as they savored the food.

After the meal, Ryker and Buck relaxed in the living room while Mogie cleaned up the kitchen. Buck studied a picture near him and asked, "Why're you living with your grandmother?"

Furrows developed between Ryker's eyes as he considered the question. "I don't know. It just seemed too difficult tolerating Mom and Dad's advice constantly. They had issues with my exercising my NMA juvenile rights. You'd have thought it's against the law or something the way they bucked my practicing freedoms the government gives me." A smile appeared when Ryker recognized something he just said. "No pun intended there on your name."

Buck grinned. It almost looked evil. "You may not've intended it, but it was punny."

Ryker rolled his eyes then gave Buck a serious look in reflection. "I don't believe I know what your real name is."

Buck sat up regal-like and boldly made his announcement. "Alanson. My full name's Alanson Samuel Shanach." He dropped his voice level and continued with a catty smile. "I don't use my full initials." He beamed with self-satisfaction.

"I should hope not!" Mogie loudly proclaimed as she came into the room.

Ryker laughed hysterically. Buck forgot he was in the home of a strict HM. He knew the concept of Home Moralists, those who lived a home life of harsh traditional moral values, but never had to conduct himself in such a constricting social environment. He stammered and stuttered trying to be very apologetic.

Mogie let her guest off the hook. "That's OK, Buck. Ryker shouldn't be in such hysterics over it though. He knows better." Glaring at Ryker, Mogie set the tone. Attempting a serious attitude, Ryker explained himself but it looked like holding back a sneeze. "It's just that you had such a funny look on your face, Mogie. I'm sorry. It's really not that funny." Snorting out the last few words didn't help him sound any more convincing. Mogie silently waited until he had complete control and then reassured him. "OK, but remember you're in my home, and I don't like that kind of talk." She sat down in her favorite chair and busied herself tatting a stand scarf for her niece's birthday present.

Ryker and Buck reminisced much of the afternoon about the good old times as young boys. They had been very close friends, which was a by-product of their childhood circumstances. Both parents had elected a lifestyle requiring them to farm for a living. This left them separated from the majority of society. It was a solution reached by the government in the spring of 2043. The process killed two birds with one stone. There were problems with conventional farmers staying in business because more profitable and meaningful enterprises lured them from the trade. Another quandary involved those who attacked the new Neutral Morals Agency's ethics and policies for the United States. It was President Kathryn Guildsman who formulated the plan that got her re-elected in 2040. It became a consensus by both sides of the political arena. The needed farming tradition continued, and those struggling with the new society would do it. In return the farmers were given some freedom in living their religious or political beliefs, but were not to interfere with the rest of society. Besides family, Ryker and Buck were almost the only friends each had. Farm kids could only play with other farm kids. They used teleports to connect because of distances between them. By law each farm had to be a minimum of ten miles apart.

As the two young men conversed, the subject came back around to Buck's original question. "What was it that made you leave home in the first place?" Ryker gave an interpretive, thoughtful look at the question, meditating on the questioner.

Buck seems very interested in why I left home. He should know already. He left for the same reasons and at the same age of eighteen.

Ryker re-settled himself in his chair before answering. "It all started when I found out my parents were censoring some of my school material. I never realized until I was sixteen that the government had given me certain rights as a minor. When I questioned them about it, they tried to tell me they were protecting me from myself."

Mogie looked up over her glasses and calmly commented. "They thought they were doing the best thing."

Ryker turned to his grandmother and apologetically replied, "I know, Mogie. It's just the principle of the thing. That they couldn't trust me with the information was kind of belittling."

Mogie went back to her work with a short, indeterminate remark. "Umm."

Turning back to his friend, Ryker finished. "Anyway, it kinda blew up a few months ago when I wanted to go see a LIFE counselor. I'd never seen one, and most kids visit them from the age of three, as you know."

In a sympathetic response Buck arched his eyebrows. "Yeah. I saw one only two times before I was eighteen. That's still only about a tenth as much as most kids."

Ryker stood up and paced around the room seemingly stretching his legs and said, "I mean, what's so bad about wanting to know what one of those Living is for Everyone counselors might have to tell me?"

Click. It was just like hitting a start button. Buck sat up on the edge of the couch, grinned from ear to ear, and joyfully announced his next idea. "Nothing! As a matter of fact, why don't we go out tonight and investigate that idea on our own?"

Mogie put her work down on the end table. She watched as the two gleefully made their plans. Ryker noticed her out of the corner of his eye. "Don't worry, Mogie. We're not going to get in any trouble or do anything illegal."

She stood up, shook a kink out of her back, and walked down the hall to the bathroom. "Your mother, father, and I are counting on that."

The two young men looked at each other. When she disappeared, Ryker defended his grandmother. "She really cares about me, but she won't stop me either. Mogie's pretty cosmic that way. She keeps me in line AND still lets me think for myself."

It wasn't long 'til the spruced-up couple transported to a busy section of town.

The Fall

"How about it, young man? You'll never regret it." The speaker had long, golden, curly hair, but it was the face that grabbed Ryker's attention. The eyelids were like shadow patties from a compact. His lips were a bright ruby red, very much out of place within the rich, bronze beard that encircled the mouth covering the lower part of his face.

"Let go of me!" Ryker slurred while shaking out of the man's grip on his elbow.

I might be out of it some, but I haven't gone that far yet!

It all started when Ryker staggered accidentally into the wrong booth. Buck rolled with laughter. As Ryker recovered his sense of direction and maneuvered into the opposing seat from Buck, he reprimanded him for his behavior. "It's not that funny . . . ALANSON."

Buck feigned a slap on the face but held his wily smile. "You don't need to get mad. I was just keying your board."

As a waiter walked by, Buck stopped him. "Give this guy another Honolulu Highball. He needs the fuel if he's going to keep going around in circles all night," he blurted out with a laugh.

Ryker reacted with a sarcastic, sour-looking face then downed the last of his drink.

The place was one Buck frequented often—the Tiki. Being it was Ryker's first time ever in a place like this, he carefully surveyed his surroundings. A social life was foreign to his upbringing.

The room had low lighting and lots of novelties and trinkets setting around to give it a Polynesian feel. There were alcoves leading from the two main rooms—sanctuaries of varying communal preferences—which served most societal appetites. As Ryker scanned the room, he observed behaviors his parents and grandmother would never have given their permission to view. He felt guilty being there, but others

31

had told him he would feel that way because he had never had the opportunity to assimilate alternate values.

Buck reinforced this logic. "Don't worry about it. When you get used to it, you'll wonder why you ever thought it was odd."

The waiter arrived with a tall, frosty glass containing an orange-colored liquid topped with an umbrella. He set it next to the six empty ones, which he picked up and carried away. Ryker saluted Buck's comment with his new full glass, sloshing some on the table. "Hey. One or two more of these and I'd care less about anything." Discarding the small umbrella, Ryker swallowed two quick gulps.

Buck sipped his drink, studying Ryker, then set his glass down. He came to a conclusion about the situation. Now was his time. "Have you had a good time tonight? Those girls seemed to enjoy teaching you to dance."

Ryker appeared focused on other things rather than the question. Slowly he comprehended what Buck said and turned to face him. "Oh, yeah. I was kinda nervous at first, but I'm having a great time now." He raised his eyebrows and squinted his eyes, studying his next question before asking it. "Where'd the girls go?"

"They said they had to get up early in the morning. I'm supposed to tell you goodnight for them."

"Oh, yeah. You told me that once, didn't ya?"

Buck smiled. "Remember when we found that cave near the ledges?"

Shifting gears in his thought process gave Ryker some trouble, but he caught on after a minute. "Yes! That was great, wasn't it? We had a grand time in that old place. I don't think anyone else ever did discover where it was." Ryker put his elbows on the table and cradled his head in his hands.

Buck glanced around, moving his head a little and stated, "If I remember right, you had company that weekend when we first found that cave."

Tightening his face up in deep thought, Ryker replied, "I remember that. Dad's aunt and uncle had come to visit. They're nice people."

Buck smiled as Ryker stared off into space trying hard to recall the visit.

"That's right. You told me the day after they left. Didn't your uncle talk to you about how he thought the NMA was wrong and destructive?"

Ryker relaxed so completely in deep thought that it appeared he didn't hear the question. Suddenly his elbow slipped off the table causing his head to dive for the edge. Buck reacted with reflex action to stop the inevitable, catching him by the chin. Ryker sat up and answered the question as if nothing had happened. "Sort of. I don't know if he said they were destructive, but you're right. He didn't think very highly of the organization. Boy, he'd make you see things another way though. He was pretty clever. I liked him."

Ryker lost himself reminiscing, and Buck felt compelled to press him. He didn't want to lose the opportunity before him. "Tell me, Ryker, did your uncle ask you to believe in some religious idea?"

Ryker's head nodded slightly with sleepy eyes. Buck reached over and shook him to get his attention. "Ryker! Tell me. Did he get you to believe in a radical religious idea?"

Coherency was almost beyond Ryker, but his last sentence would forever change his life. "Uncle Vern told me I'd see Grandpa if I believed in Jesus." Everything went black.

Ryker never recalled the rest of that night but dealt with the consequences for years to come.

Morning

He was cold and his right arm ached. He wanted to move but could not. Opening an eye in the dim morning light caused his head to pound. When his eyes focused, the first thing he saw was the coffee table—sideways! Lifting his head to rectify the disorienting scene caused even more pounding behind his eyes. He felt something run down his cheek and drip off his chin. All of a sudden, he bolted straight up. The shock from his pounding head, the realization of where he was, and the trickling down his face had sobered him instantly. He was sitting in the teleport at Mogie's place. He had vomited all over the translator pad and was lying in it. The longer he was conscious, the more he realized how sick he felt.

Oh man, this is awful. I've never felt this bad before. What a mess! Mogie's going to kill me. She must not be up yet. If I hurry and get moving, maybe she'll never know.

Ryker floundered to his feet and gripped his head as if it would fall apart like a shattered eggshell if he didn't hold it together. He snatched some paper towels from the kitchen and cleaned himself up. With the paper towels he smeared his mess up into one pile on the teleport thinking he might add to it in the process.

What am I going to do with this? I've got to make sure Mogie never finds out.

An idea came to him that changed his outlook momentarily. Stepping up to the teleport controls, he keyed in some information and stood back to watch the machine do its work. The unit was as clean as new.

That'll be a two hundred credit fine if I'm caught, but it'll beat facing Mogie. I hope Buck steps in it!

Ryker left a message for his boss explaining he was ill and wouldn't be coming in for work. He went to his room, took off his clothes, and put them in the regenerator. After taking a quick shower, he went to bed and immediately fell asleep.

Mogie was working around the house when the teleport signaled. She attended to the controls and activated the view phone. The glass partition slid into place and darkened. In seconds the screen lightened to focus on a life size image of Judy Cuff sitting in her living room.

"Hi, Mom. How're you doing?"

"Fine, dear. To what do I owe this long-distance visual?"

"An e-mail would've been cheaper, but I wanted to talk to you face to face for a change. Just wondering how Ryker's doing."

"He's still in bed," Mogie said, slightly displeased. The quizzical look on her daughter's face amused her, making the visual worth the credits.

"I thought he had a job."

"He does—or at least this morning he did. I assume he called in today. He probably didn't feel well."

"Is he ill, Mom?"

"If he is, it was self-induced," Mogie said with disgust.

Sudden revelation prompted Judy. "Has Buck Shanach been there?"

Mogie mirrored her daughter's surprise only moments earlier. "Yes. How'd you know?"

With slight agitation in her voice, Judy informed her mother, "Buck was here a few days ago looking for Ryker. I thought it funny then and wondered why he showed up without calling ahead. He asked if Ryker had taken everything with him or had left some stuff behind. When I asked why, he told me Ryker had something of his. He was polite enough, but when he found out Ryker didn't leave anything, he seemed pretty anxious to go."

"Did he say what he was looking for?"

"Not directly. He did mention something about a book. I didn't pay much attention to it then but now that I think about it, I believe that's what he was interested in."

Standing in the hallway, Ryker had heard the conversation from the time Judy mentioned Buck's visit. As he walked into the living room, he had a question of his own. With fear in his voice, he asked, "Mom, did he say what kind of book he was looking for?"

Judy changed her focus from her mother to her son. "Why aren't you at work today? Did you and Buck go out on a weeknight?"

Ryker turned his back to the teleport then quickly faced it again. "Mom, don't start harping first thing. Did he say what book he's looking for?"

Judy struggled for a second but resolved to treat her son like the adult he wanted to be. She simply answered, "No. He did not."

Ryker stood next to Mogie with his arms crossed. Judy gave a puzzled look and leaned forward studying something on the viewer. Suddenly she jumped up from her seat with a shocked look on her face and franticly questioned Ryker. "What's that you have?"

Glancing over at Mogie, Ryker shrugged his shoulders. Mogie asked her daughter, "What on earth are you talking about?"

Judy no longer tried to hide her excitement. "His hand! What's that on the back of Ryker's hand?"

Ryker and his grandmother both looked startled as he brought his hands up to look at them. Mogie grabbed the left one and examined it. There it was, tattooed for the world to see; a small, dark-colored emblem. It was the symbol of a cross, encircled with a large capital R. Mogie gasped. Ryker tried to rub it off. Judy sounded like a broken recording. "Is it a ross? . . . Is it a ross? . . . Is it a ross? . . ."

Mogie looked to her daughter. "Yes, Judy. Calm down a minute."

35

Surprised as the other two, Ryker tried to explain, "I've no idea where it came from. I don't remember getting it. Honest."

Judy struggled to gain composure while asking, "Why would the NMA want to mark you, Ryker? What've you been doing since you left home?"

Mogie turned to the screen and scolded her daughter. "He hasn't been doing anything like that. Give the boy some credit."

Ryker was more than willing to reply. "Honest, Mom. I didn't even know I had it until now." He continued sheepishly, "I don't remember much that happened last night after I passed out."

Judy didn't want to focus on what her son had just confessed so she ignored it. "What I don't understand is why Buck would let you get into that situation. He's two years older than you and should know better."

Mogie added, "He seems like such a nice boy. I don't doubt he likes to have a good time, but I find it hard to believe he'd let Ryker get himself into this kind of trouble."

Ryker wasn't listening to either of them. Recalling his last words from the night before, coupled with what he had just learned, gave him a sick feeling in the pit of his stomach.

I don't think Buck is the same person I remember. That son-of-a-gun had me marked! I hope the credits he earned choke him. I know one thing. He's never going to get his hands on that book he gave to me years ago.

Church

Ryker studied his suit and tie critically in the mirror as he adjusted his long ponytail. He looked as comfortable as an Eskimo nudist, and wasn't above complaining—even in Mogie's home. "Do I have to wear the tie? It feels like I'm going to choke to death."

Mogie approached him and adjusted the knot. "No one goes to church unless he's properly attired, physically and spiritually."

Ryker pulled on his tie hoping the effect would stop the choking. He turned away from his grandmother and mumbled to himself, "Who wants to go to church?"

Mogie was a grandmother but there was nothing wrong with her hearing. "I believe YOU do, young man." She stared at him sternly. Ryker could read her like a book.

"I'm sorry, Mogie. You're right. I need to do this to prove my mark was a mistake. I'm not a Rigid Christian. I'll do whatever I need to do."

Mogie softened and continued in a reassuring way. "It was your idea, and I believe you need to follow through with it."

"I'm going to. I'm just nervous, that's all."

"Well, let's go then. This won't be as bad as you think."

She keyed information on the teleport and the two stepped up on the pad. In a few seconds, Mogie's home was vacant—or at least they thought it was.

Leaving the corner teleport, grandmother and grandson casually walked down the sidewalk to church. It was a cloudy day but very warm with a sweet smelling breeze softly rearranging the loose ends of their hair. Ryker asked, "Mogie, I've heard the government may not grant you a permit to continue the moral stand you take in your home. Is that true?"

She thought a minute before answering. The question brought strong feelings she wanted to control in front of her grandson. "That's true. My church is fighting the proposal. But convictions seem to have changed over the last several years. The church doesn't have the clout it used to. I'm not sure they see it the same way they did at one time. I believe the government's going to get its way very soon. I personally don't understand what harm can come from someone living the way they wish in their own home."

Ryker reacted to the comment. "It's funny you say that. I just remembered something Buck said the other night. He told me that when young children visit homes like yours, it affects them psychologically. He quoted some government report. I argued with him because I used to visit you often when I was little. He laughed and said, 'See what I mean.' I laughed with him at the time. But when I think about it now—he wasn't joking!"

Mogie developed a stone-hard look. "He's the kind of people I'm fighting."

They reached their destination in front of a small, brown building. Only one thing distinguished it from the surrounding structures. Over the door hung a bold sign that read, "First Church of Living Truths." In small letters below, almost illegible, were the words "NMA approved."

As they walked inside, a few heads turned to see who had entered. Most recognized and greeted Mogie, but Ryker received blank stares and a cool reception. Mogie took her regular place—left side, fourth pew from the front, inside aisle.

As they sat down, Ryker noted about thirty people in a place that could easily house eighty or more. He was nervous so to occupy himself, he focused on items in the pew rack. There was a hymnal, which he thumbed through. He found only one song he thought he recognized. When he picked up the Bible, he realized it was only half as thick as the other book he had handled. As he set it back in the rack, he read the small letters in the corner: NMA approved.

The preacher began reading from the pulpit. "Today we're gathered together in this place of God to hear from Him."

The whole congregation replied in unison causing Ryker to jump. "Teach us, Lord, the way we should live." The girl sitting behind him stifled a giggle.

The minister continued, "Lord God, always shine Your Light on the paths of Your Word that we may know the truths of human living."

Ryker thought he managed better the second time, but the girl behind him still chuckled at his reaction. "Teach us, Lord, the way we should live." He realized the pattern developing and knew to look to the pulpit for the next words. "Open our eyes, our ears, and our hearts to the Word as it is given to us this day." The giggle came before the entire reply this time. Ryker was a word ahead of everyone. "Teach us, Lord, the way we should live."

Stepping down, the minister stood in front of the pulpit. He was a young man, maybe in his thirties but probably in his late twenties. He was rather large with curly blonde hair that cradled his balding crown. His jowls jiggled as he announced the next part of the service. "Open your hymnals to page thirty-five and lift your voice in praise to our God." Ryker nervously thumbed the hymnal assuming it was not the song he had noticed earlier.

I feel rather silly in this place. I hope I don't have to face that giggling girl behind me. She must think I'm some kind of idiot or something. Please, Mogie, don't make me do this every Sunday.

Ryker readied himself for anything and didn't react in such a way as to draw attention again. The rest of the service went smoothly, but preoccupation with his conduct had caused the message of the sermon, based on one of the Seven Commandments, to elude him.

When the service had ended, Ryker stood to leave with everyone else. Ahead of Mogie, he turned to go up the aisle and there she was. She looked him in the eyes and gave a quaint little smile. Her rich brown hair was long—down to the middle of her back—and full of curls. Her smile matched the twinkle in her deep blue eyes. Mogie nudged Ryker in the center of his back. He snapped out of his trance long enough to react to the girl. "Oh, excuse me. After you, please," he said as he graciously motioned the young lady to step ahead of him

Looking back once before going through the doors, she smiled. Mogie had to nudge him again. "You like this place so well you're going to stay here all day or what?"

He turned and addressed his grandmother without registering her question. "Who was that?"

"That's Harold and Rena Jones. I don't know what the kids' names are. Now get going before they lock us in here."

People stood out on the lawn chatting. Ryker noticed the girl standing by the gate leading to the sidewalk. She was waiting for her parents. He puffed up and pseudo-confidently but nonchalantly wandered out to the sidewalk. He might have walked right past and kept going if she hadn't been bold enough to greet him. "Hi."

"Oh. Hi."

"Nice day, huh?"

"Yeah, cosmic."

They stood there, neither one knowing what else to say. Then she couldn't help herself. She had to ask the obvious. "You've never been to church before, have you?"

Ryker wished he had kept going. Looking down, he kicked at pebbles on the ground then looked up into those eyes. He stalled, thought for a moment, drew on false assurance, then answered with a smile, "I've been caught. You can't hide a fox in a hen house."

The young woman gave him a warm, inviting smile. "Cute. My name's Monica."

Her tender, rich voice helped him to gain the confidence to continue. "I'm called many things, but I prefer Ryker."

She displayed a coy smile. Ryker liked it. Monica wore the expression as an alluring veil and quipped, "Well, until I know you better I guess I'll call you Ryker."

It was his turn to smile and acknowledge a winsome remark. "Touché." Ryker brought his left hand up, touched his head with a salute and added a little bow. Monica noticed the ross on his left hand. She leaned back slightly with a puzzled look. Ryker realized she had noticed the mark, which until that point he had kept secret. He scrambled to assure her, "I'm not an RC unless you want to use my initials. Someone I thought was a good friend gave me this. It happened when I didn't know what was going on. It's the reason why I'm here. I want to prove it's untrue."

"It looks like you have trouble choosing friends. You must've done something he could've used against you."

"He must've recorded a conversation we were having. I believe he finally manipulated the discussion so I said what he wanted. I'm ashamed to say I don't really remember."

She looked at him, studying his thoughts. Ryker felt this kind of probing once before—when he was eleven. After a minute, she gave him a reassuring smile. "I believe you."

He hadn't realized his tension until his jaw started aching when he relaxed. "Thanks. That means a lot to me."

Mogie meandered down the sidewalk about a hundred feet then stalled, waiting for Ryker.

"I gotta go. My grandmother's waiting for me. Nice meeting you. Maybe I'll see you again sometime."

She lowered her eyes and smiled. "Maybe. Have a nice day."

He trotted to catch up with his grandmother and stopped beside her. She looked up with raised eyebrows and a little smirk on her face. Ryker felt a need to defend himself. "Don't say anything, Mogie. I know what you're thinking."

The two walked in silence back to the teleport. Mogie continued to look at Ryker with a smile. He ignored her. When they reached the corner, Mogie keyed the coordinates to her home along with the password. As they entered the teleport, she had one thing to say before it activated. "I think the next guest you bring home may be more appealing than the last one."

Ryker gave her a stern look as the teleport whisked them away.

As the teleport glass partition lightened and slid back out of the way, Mogie and Ryker immediately noticed trouble. A china closet was opened with many of its contents lying about. Mogie ran over to investigate. Ryker ran to his room. It was as he expected—torn all apart. Someone had been searching for something. Mogie came into his room to report and gasped as she saw the condition of his room.

"Whoever did this only searched a few things of mine and nothing seems missing. It looks like they searched every inch of your room though."

"They made a mess of my room all right, but I don't believe anything is missing. It must be they were looking for something in particular."

"What would that be?"

Ryker thought he had a good idea but didn't want Mogie to know about it. So he lied. "I don't know."

Mogie turned to leave the room and reported, "I'm going to call the police."

Ryker wasn't sure he liked the idea but he wasn't going to stop her.

A few minutes later, an officer graced Mogie's teleport screen. She gave him the information requested. "Alice Rodgood, 214 Sisson Street, apartment 4B. My home's been broken into."

The man keyed the facts and studied the screen a moment before looking up to give an answer. "Yes, Ms. Rodgood. I have data on that incident. There was an NMA search warrant issued this morning."

Mogie looked stunned, but Ryker developed a comprehending gaze as Mogie questioned, "Who issued that?!"

The officer looked at his screen again then stated, "NMA Apprentice SS Agent Alanson Shanach."

I don't understand why a search was put on a person such as me. What could be so important about a book Buck and I found in a cave so many years ago?

THE BEGINNING—1992

"This page has been made, so that everyone who don't(sic) know the bacis(sic) of Satanism (mainly you younger caracters(sic)) can get into what it's all about. You need to get the book, *The Satanic Bible* by Anton LaVey."

Youth for Satanism: Carl Hawkins' Web page, October 31, 1992

Thanksgiving Dream

Eight men sat around the dining room table casually discussing random subjects. Children played in the living room while moms cleaned up the kitchen after a hearty Thanksgiving dinner. Occasionally one of the women would invade the dining room to pick up or put something away, and naturally, she would comment on the discussion the men were having.

As Ann sat some dishes on the sideboard to put away later, she stopped to hear the conclusion of her husband's discourse on the current political situation. She couldn't resist. "Don't forget, dear. It doesn't matter who the president is. God's still in charge."

Lee Jinkens was a big man—not tall, but wide at the shoulders and squarely built. His profession helped to keep him in shape. Handling cement blocks all day was hard work. As his square chin dropped for a grin you could see a tooth missing on the bottom toward the back as he said, "You're right. I'm not saying we need to fall apart or tremble. I'm just saying that if all the people in this country who claim to be Christians had voted their conscience instead of being directed by their pocketbooks, the man voted into office this time would not have stood a chance."

Ann's father was the patriarch of the gathering in the Tarbell home on the Saint Lawrence River near Massena, New York. He couldn't hold back a comment. Roger ran his hand over his graying brush-cut a couple of times before saying anything. "That's right. But you know, I don't think many people really know what it means to be a Christian."

Roger was convinced that his sons-in-law knew what it meant to be a Christian, so he wasn't surprised when one of them spoke up on the subject. Algie Eton commonly let others speak, but when something was worth saying, he would certainly put in his two cents. "I agree. This country has come so far from what our founding fathers envisioned that I'm not sure how many Christians even know what it means to be a Christian."

The next few hours went much the same—some serious discussion, some playful. When most everyone had left, Alice Tarbell Eton came into the living room and asked, "Algie, where are Carol and Louise? We should get going. We've still got to go to your mother and father's for dessert." Algie rose from the couch. "They're in the playroom. I'll get them."

The evening news anchor on television announced President-Elect Clinton's intention to lift the ban on gays in the military. Roger sat in his favorite chair shaking his head. His mouth drew into a tight line. The hand went over his hair a couple of times. "I don't really agree with that at all."

Lee agreed. "I know what ya mean, and this is only the beginning. It looks like things are going to be really different before his term's up. First it was prayer in the schools, then legal abortions, and now this. Once these things become policies of the government, it's almost impossible to change them. In fact, just a few months ago, the U.S. Supreme Court made a decision that'll set this country tumbling toward moral chaos. In the case *Planned Parenthood vs. Casey* they decided *Roe vs. Wade* implied a personal liberty. It's now the right for all to decide what's right or wrong. I wonder if it'll ever be reversed."

Algie came back into the room followed by his fourteen- and ten-year-old daughters. "If what will be reversed?"

Lee turned to face his brother-in-law. The two valued each other's opinions. Algie had come to know Jesus first, and Lee had quickly come to the same convictions, and they often shared common insights. "The next president's influence on our country's moral fabric. There are many people out there who'd do much to dilute the Christian influence, and now they have a person in power again who'll give them an ear."

Algie helped Louise to get her coat and boots on. He gave her a peck on the cheek and a smile before he replied to Lee. "You're right. I wonder what it'll be like for these kids—or worse yet, for our grandchildren and their children. We're lucky we live so far north in New York. This North Country doesn't see half the effects of our country's moral decline as the big cities do. We have to remember what the Bible tells us—"

Alice was impatient and wouldn't let him finish. "You guys can talk about this at Tuesday night Bible study."

Algie smiled as he shrugged his shoulders. "OK. Well, we'll see you people later. Goodnight." Everyone said their goodbyes as Alice, Algie, and the girls left through the back door.

Within the hour, Algie's family had arrived at his parents' home, which was next door to them in the heart of Saint Lawrence County. Before the door to his father's home was opened, Algie saw his father lounging in a Lazy-Boy chair. His mouth was wide, and the noise that came from it sounded like a small engine. His hair, graying and usually parted deeply on the right side, had fallen to reveal the bald spot he usually kept well concealed. Algie signaled to his mother and family to be quiet. An impish grin graced his face. As the family stealthily walked in, Algie crept over to stand above his father. With a Kleenex he had found on the counter, Algie was poised to tickle Leland's nose. Just as he was about to do the deed, it backfired.

"BOO!"

Algie jumped a foot off the floor and landed with a wombat expression. Laughter filled the room as Leland questioned his eldest son, "You thought I was asleep, didn't ya?"

His son's smile gave away the real sense of his heart. "Dad, that wasn't fair." Algie held his hand over his chest and stared at his father with a half-smirk. Leland merely sat with a "gotcha" grin on his face. Algie couldn't help giving in. "OK, Dad. You win again. When am I ever going to get one over on you?"

"Well Al, you gotta get up earlier in the morning than your old man."

"No way, Dad. Four-thirty in the morning is too early for me."

Leland sat up in his chair as everyone settled in the living room. Leland and Eva Eton had had their new home for only a few years and they took pride in it. The family had moved around for years renting one place and then another. They might have owned a home before but they lacked the discipline it required. Jesus had been the center of their lives for the last six years, and it was He Who made the difference. (They liked to brag about their son being their spiritual father.)

45

Eva put things back on track by asking if everyone was ready for dessert. Carol nodded her head; Louise stated, "Sure."

Eva invitingly turned to her daughter in-law. "How about you, Alice?"

Alice followed her mother-in-law into the kitchen. "I'll have a small piece. Let me help you with it." She tossed her long, black hair behind her shoulders and followed Eva. Alice was the only Native American in this family but accepted the genuine love Algie's Irish family freely gave.

In the background, the two women chattered about their day. Algie turned to his father with a question. "Who showed up for your dinner today?"

"We went over and picked up Marie at her place. John and Liz came just in time to eat."

"So all you had this year were numbers three and four, huh?"

"Yup. Janet called from Ohio. She and her family were staying home this year. I can't put my finger on it, but something doesn't seem right with them. Janet doesn't act like her old self."

Louise entered the conversation. "I was glad to see Aunt Janet and Linda last summer. Linda and I are pen pals now."

Leland offered a paternal smile and said, "That's great, sweetheart. Seeing how your Aunt Janet never writes, maybe we can find out through you how things are going in the big city of Columbus." Louise beamed. She could talk with the grownups and be included.

The discussion sparked an inquiry from Carol. "Poppy, why'd Aunt Janet come to visit for the first time in—how long? Ten years?"

Eva came in with her hands full, heard the question, and responded, "Well honey, we don't know but it was nice to see them, huh?" Passing the dessert around ended the discussion.

After dessert, Leland set his empty plate down and fashioned a serious look. "Did you catch any of the news tonight?"

Alice piped right up. "Not all of it, but Al and the boys were discussing it before I ushered us off to come here. They were talking about the ban on gays in the military being lifted."

Leland's mouth made a tight short line as his daughter-in-law conveyed the information. He was primed for a vocal response. "Yes. That's part of it. They even had an interview with a soldier at Fort Drum. He claimed to be gay and was forming a task force to speak for the rights of gays in the military."

Algie valued his father's knowledge and discernment when it came to current events. It was natural for him to question his father. "What do ya think about that, Dad?" Algie knew he was in for a lengthy response and so settled back in his recliner.

Leland loved to get up on his soapbox once in a while. This was something about which he had given much thought. "Time has proven that this alternative lifestyle hasn't saved people in any way. Rather it's wreaked havoc. Gays have a right to believe what they wish. Never should they be mistreated or abused simply for having an opposing sexual preference. They need the help and support of society the same as everyone else. The thing I struggle with is how we Christians should react to that. We don't have laws protecting an employee from being fired if he's drunk or high on the job. Nor is a compulsive gambler's job protected if he decides to be absent from work for weeks to go on a gambling binge. I say that because the Bible tells us these things are wrong. Should we accept and allow the results of a kleptomaniac as an alternative lifestyle because they can't help it—they were born that way? If not, then why the gay lifestyle? They are on the same moral compass.

"These acts erode and undermine the basis of our American society, and it is the Bible that teaches us this. Yes, gays have rights, but no more than what was given to all of us when this country was founded. This means no special or equal family status, military standing, or any other special privileges that they're now striving to achieve. The Bible says it's wrong.

"I know the Lord teaches us to love one another and we should, but we need to show that love in the context of His Word. Sometimes love is very tough, just as Jesus was with people at times. Remember when the Pharisees brought the woman to Him to be stoned? He directed those who had no sin to throw the first stone. They all walked away because they had to. Then He told the woman to sin no more. Jesus gave her a chance to understand her plight, but then He expected her to break the cycle she was in because it was sinful."

Leland finished with a determined expression. The room was very quiet. Algie remained thoughtful for a minute, giving Alice time to comment. She gave her head one definitive nod with a smile on her face. "There. Does it feel better to get that off your chest?"

Leland sat back in his chair, gave Alice a big smile, and replied, "Yes, it does. That's been boiling up for a long time. Now you know how I feel about it."

Algie sat back in his seat also. He had followed his father's reaction as Leland gave his dissertation by sitting forward on the edge of his chair. "Some things you've said at Bible study led me to believe you had something to say about that. Why's it been on your mind so much?"

Leland gave a big sigh, looked up at the ceiling for half a minute, then told them about his dream. "I don't know. But I've had this recurring dream the last six months or so. I'm in church—not one I recognize—but a church. And I'm listening to a sermon. The preacher's a young gentleman, maybe thirty. He's wearing a ceremonial robe. I notice the lights reflecting off his curly blonde, balding head as he moves around.

"I don't pay much attention to him until he mentions something about the Seven Commandments. I look all around but nobody seems to mind what he's just said. I want to jump up and remind him that there are Ten Commandments, but I can't; all I can do is observe. He goes on with his three-point sermon, which is really only a good speech on human acceptance of one another.

"I always look at the Bible in the pew rack. It amazes me that it's so thin. It has some writing in the corner, but I can never read it. It's a blur of some symbols I can't understand. Until recently in these dreams, I couldn't open the book to read any of it. But the last three times, I've been able to examine some of the scriptures. The New Testament has only one Gospel. It's headed "The Combined Gospels." It seems to be mostly Jesus' teachings and parables. It records His death, but says nothing about the Resurrection.

"The dream always ends the same way. Behind the minister is a large, stained-glass window. On it is a picture of Jesus on the cross. He's looking right at me. I see the compassion in His eyes as He begins to cry. No one else sees this but me. Everything begins to go black and I hear a voice before I wake up saying, 'They must have a chance to hear the whole message.' At this point, I always wake up."

To the surprise of everyone, Carol was the first one to comment. "Poppy, is there a little red-headed boy whose father is always trying to keep him quiet?"

Astonishment embellished Leland's face. The rest of the family watched him. His answer was slow and low. "I don't believe it! Carol, sweetheart, you're right. It's always the first thing I notice in these dreams. How'd you know about it?"

Carol was a pretty, fourteen-year-old girl. The blush that came to her face only added to the vision of a maturing young lady. She looked her grandfather in the eyes and told him something she had never before revealed to anyone. "I have the same dream, Poppy. And I noticed that the Sunday school paper the young boy is reading has a date on it—Sunday, July 22, 2085."

A Christmas Gift for the Future

There was very little snow on the ground, which made Carol and Louise anxious. Christmas was only a few days away and more than anything it was a white Christmas they wanted. The girls concentrated on a mini play they planned to perform for their parents. Algie labored over his computer as the phone rang. Louise beat Carol to the phone.

"Dad, it's for you."

Algie annoyingly murmured exasperation but took the phone. "Hullo."

"Hi, Al. This is your cousin Jean. How're you doing?"

"Well, hi. I'm kind of surprised to hear from you. What can I do for ya, Jean?"

"Al, this isn't a very pleasant call. But I've been concerned about how you and your family might find out the news. Have you heard anything from Janet lately?"

"No. Not since she returned to Columbus back in July. Is she OK?"

"Oh, she's not sick or anything like that. You know my brother Dale is out there and sees Janet and Rob often. Dale didn't want me to say anything to you guys. He's afraid he might get himself in trouble for tattling. I told him I didn't believe he needs to worry about that."

"That's right. We're not going to blame him for anything."

"Al," Jean paused and then said, "Janet's left her family."

There was a moment of silence until Algie responded, "We figured something was wrong. Do you know what's happened?"

"Yes, I do. That's why I'm calling you rather than your parents. I think someone like you should tell them. I hate to have them hear it later and second-hand."

"Well, thanks, Jean. Is she living with another man?"

"That's the hard part. She's living with another woman."

Stunned, all Algie could do was thank Jean for her concern and finish the conversation.

Carol inquired about the call. "Who was that?"

49

Algie explained to his girls what he had learned. Afterwards he told them to behave themselves until their mother came home. He then went to his parents to break the news to them.

Carol and Louise continued working on their play. A small argument ensued and Carol was adamant. "Joseph did have a dream one night when an angel told him to go ahead and take Mary as his wife."

Her sister scrunched her eyebrows together. "I don't remember that."

Carol picked up her father's Bible from the end table, thought for a moment, then asked, "What Gospel is the Christmas story in?"

Louise had a sharp mind for memorizing certain facts. "I think one of them is in Matthew. We were reading in that one last Sunday."

Carol leafed through the pages until she found what she was looking for. "Ha! See, it's right here in Matthew chapter one, verse twenty."

Carol read it as her younger sister listened, "But while he thought on these things, behold, the angel of the Lord appeared to him in a dream saying, 'Joseph, son of David, fear not to take Mary as your wife: for that which is conceived in her is of the Holy Spirit.'"

The younger sibling frowned, ignoring her sister's questioning stare. "That's interesting. I don't remember seeing or hearing that before." A thought flashed to her and she spun around to face Carol. "Are you still having your dream?"

Caught off guard, Carol blinked a few times. She had no idea why Louise asked. "Yes, I am. As a matter of fact, I'm having it more often since Poppy and I talked about it." As she explained, she began to understand why her sister had asked. Carol's face lit up. "Hey! Do you think God's trying to tell us something?"

"That's what I was thinking. I don't know what it might be though."

The two sat down on the couch and held their heads in their hands. They had something very interesting to think about. After a minute, Carol sat up. "I don't understand how I could, but I think I know what God's trying to say."

"What?" Louise asked.

Carol scrunched her face in a thoughtful pose as she told her sister, "The people in the dream don't understand Jesus fully—how He came, died for our sins, and rose again. That's why the message at the end says they should have a chance to hear the whole message. But how can I tell them? Especially if it's people in the future?"

Louise shrugged her shoulders until they touched her ears. Thoughtful for a second more, she beamed with an idea. It was so obvious Carol could see the inspiration. "What? What'd you think of? How can I tell'm?"

Louise poked her palm with a finger as she explained, "We're studying in school about time capsules. We could make our own time capsule and hide it somewhere."

Carol's eyes grew large with excitement. "That's a great idea and I know one thing we can put in it. Remember that Bible Dad gave me when he got this new one?"

Louise nodded her head. "Yeah, and we can put some tracts and other stuff in it also."

The girls ecstatically made their plans. While gathering things for their project, Alice came home from work.

"Hi, girls. Whatcha up to?"

They had agreed the scheme would be their own little secret, so Carol's reply was natural: "Just working on a project for you and Dad."

Alice placed a bag of groceries on the table. "Where's your father?"

Carol told her about Aunt Janet and concluded, "So Dad's at Grandma and Grandpa's telling them the bad news."

Alice could hardly believe it and sat down to meditate on it. "It's hard to imagine. Janet and I were the best of friends in school. I never would have guessed she'd do such a thing."

Alice began doing some of her housework, but was too preoccupied thinking about Janet to be effective. Carol and Louise finished gathering and carefully placing items in a metal box they had found out back in an old dump the summer before. The items were wrapped, put in plastic bags, and sealed. When they were through, Carol approached her mother. "Mom, can Louise and I go out back for a while to play?"

Alice looked out the window before she replied, "OK, but dress warmly and stay within hollering distance."

Louise hurried her sister along as Carol tried to be polite. "Thanks, Mom."

It was still sunny. The few snowflakes present sparkled on the pine trees as the girls walked out through the backyard. When they made some distance from the house, Louise questioned, "Where we going to put this? The ground's still frozen."

Carol assumed a proud look. "Remember that small cave by the big hill across the fence?"

Louise shook her head yes. "Oh, yeah. No one else knows about it but us."

It was cold, so after hiding their treasure, the pair went back in the house. Alice hadn't realized what they'd done. Carol and Leland never had their strange dream again and the metal box was forgotten, never touched—until almost eighty-four years later.

METAMORPHOSE

"America's footing is gone and we are sliding precariously off our foundations. The economic disaster perpetrated by radicals against the U.S. republic was almost complete. If it wasn't for Lenard Barnes of Teletron Inc., who founded teleportation and used it to rebuild our free market, all would have been lost. We have an enormous task ahead to find our roots and grow them again, and it starts here with us."

Litton Cramer, Founder/Chief of the Network, 4/11/2055

Looking Up?

"Name?"

"Ryker Henry Cuff."

Why do all these clerks act like morons? This guy's seen me for fifteen months now and you'd think it's the first time I was here. I hope this is the last time I need to come here.

"Have you brought your papers?" In using the old-fashioned term "papers," what the clerk sought were actually Ryker's Official Documents. With that prompt, Ryker handed over the small disk he held. The clerk dropped the disk into the reader and watched the screen in front of him.

While he waited for processing, Ryker looked around. He had visited the department three times within the last year. In the corner next to the entrance, two people sat studying material. Overhead was a sign labeled, "NMA Council Referral." He noted a long line at the Credit Refund Department where people came to claim credits earned from valid referrals of anti-NMA activity. Across from the entrance he spotted a counter with a no-wait line. The clerk appeared to be doing nothing more than looking busy—so as to keep her job, he speculated. He saw a counter where his grandmother had come to apply for a special permit for her moralist stand. The sign simply stated, "Special Permits." Fifty years earlier, the department had had its own office. Next to Ryker in another line was a girl about his age applying for a job at NMA services. She stood at the recruiting counter with plenty of information and options. It was the one counter Ryker could never approach—for having been marked, he would never serve in that division.

Ryker suddenly became aware that his clerk had said something. "Huh? Excuse me. What'd you say?"

The NMA clerk looked annoyed. His weasel-like face and eyes panned to one side as he repeated himself in a high nasal voice. "Ross the scanner please."

Ryker brought the back of his left hand up to the scanner in front of the counter terminal. The station chirped three descending tones. The clerk dutifully studied the screen. His expression and tone of voice never changed. "Looks like it's your lucky day. The temporary ban on your social life privileges has been lifted. You also have a chance for a job at Communiqué Incorporated. If you wish to apply, be there at one o'clock."

Ryker was ecstatic on the inside, but on the outside he held his cool to calmly inquire, "That's really great. I've waited months just to get my privileges back and now I have a chance for a job. All in the same day! Why am I getting this chance at work already?"

The clerk narrowed his eyes lending to the weaselly appearance and shifted them to one side. His comment came in a low, irritated voice. "Probably to meet their quota of reformed Rosses." Ryker ignored the sarcasm, happy that things seemed to have turned around for him.

"Weasel-face" finished his business by returning the memory disk and giving his final information. "You need not report here again for six months unless you again jeopardize your privileges or are fortunate enough to land the job. In that event, your employer would be responsible for keeping track of your reform."

Putting the disk in his pocket, Ryker gave the man a satisfied smile. "Thanks. If I'm lucky, you won't ever see me again."

Ryker nearly floated out of the building. Walking through the doorway, he read the salutation hanging above the entrance: "Thank you for allowing the NMA Social Reform Offices to help you: January 10, 2085."

It was bitter cold outside and the snow, except on the sidewalk, was at least a foot deep. Luckily the teleport was only a block away. Ryker had too much to ponder to worry about the weather.

If there is such a thing as a God, He must've decided to give me another chance. I can't believe I have a job interview! I can't wait to tell Monica. She'll be thrilled.

The apartment had a miniature kitchen that doubled as the dining room, a bathroom, and a living room that doubled as the bedroom at night. The building had no teleport, which meant a five-block walk to get to one.

Ryker studied himself in the small bathroom mirror. He was cleaned up, clothed in his finest, and surveying his new haircut. "I hope this looks respectable enough. It's still over my ears." He combed the hair back behind his ears.

From the other side of the apartment Monica addressed him. "You look great. I don't think I did that bad a job." She walked over and brushed Ryker's hair back over his ears with her hands. He studied harder in the mirror and commanded, "Back, please." The reflection changed to show the back of his head for ten seconds and then reverted to the front view. He moved his head slightly back and forth trying to see from all available angles. "I don't know. Do you really think I look respectable enough?"

Monica turned him around, stood on her toes, and gave him a quick kiss with a smile. "It does something for me."

He returned her kiss with a peck on the forehead. "Thanks. I couldn't have gotten through this without you. These last seven months with you've been my salvation."

With an alluring smile, Monica shyly backed out of the bathroom. Ryker followed, knowing she had something to say. Without gloating she said, "I told you God would answer our prayers." She looked at the floor then half-elevated her eyes until they met his asking, "Do you think maybe you'll come back to church with me this Sunday?"

Ryker smiled. It was the trigger that allowed Monica to level her eyes completely with his and draw an appealing smile on her heart-shaped face. Ryker couldn't resist and reassured her. "Sure, it's the least I could do for all you've put up with the last few months." Monica lightly spun around on her toes and trotted back to the desk by the door.

Their discussion prompted a question Ryker had wanted to ask for some time. "Monica, are your parents still angry with me?"

She sat down at the desk to continue her work, then turned to face him with a studious look. "You know, Mom and Dad accepted our coupling as a natural extension of our rights under the law. I think it's much harder on Mogie that way. What actually hurt Dad was when you turned your back on the church."

Ryker thoughtfully gathered his winter apparel, readying to keep his appointment at Communiqué. Putting his coat on, he came to a conclusion: "You're right. I didn't mean to, but I did hurt him that way. If I get this job and start going to church again, maybe that'll patch things up for us."

Monica nodded her head to affirm the statement with a smile. Ryker leaned over and kissed her on the cheek. "Wish me luck. I'm off to a new destiny." Out the door he went. Monica turned back to the terminal and continued her work. These words appeared on the screen: "Ryker came home from the probation office this morning with great news. And the day isn't over yet! He just left for a job interview."

Ryker checked the time—for the umpteenth time in the last twenty minutes. *"Take a seat and relax," she said. She might as well have told me to chew razor blades with a smile. Stay calm, Ryker. This may be one of their elaborate tests—checking my patience and psychic stability. I'll count the bricks on the wall. That ought to keep me busy and relax my runaway emotions. 1, 2, 3, 4 . . .*

The room Ryker waited in was very elegant with a serene nature to it. He stepped off the teleport into subtle lighting, abundant plant life, and soft music. A water fountain in one corner sparkled with elaborate, colored lights and was surrounded by marble statues. When he arrived, a voice came over a speaker hidden from view. "Mr. Ryker Cuff?"

Ryker looked around the room half expecting to see someone emerge from a hidden door. When he realized it wasn't going to happen, he answered, "Huh, yes. That's me."

The voice replied, "Please make yourself comfortable. Someone will be with you in a moment."

That was almost a half-hour before the brick counting. *233, 234, 235, 236, 247, 24 . . . is it forty or thirty? Oh shoot. I don't want to start over again.*

"Mr. Cuff?"

Ryker cringed before he slowly turned to face the voice. Seeing a body out of the corner of his eye, he sprang to attention and faced the pretty young blonde. "Yes."

The blonde fabricated an alluring smile. "Please follow me."

The request was a simple task to perform. She was an attractive woman who liked men looking at her, and she made sure they would. She led Ryker through the new doorless opening in the wall that disappeared when they passed. On the other side it was a clean but empty-looking corridor. After passing two doors, the young blonde in the short, green dress stopped and motioned Ryker through an open door. The room was small and dark. Tasteful trinkets sat on antique furniture. Behind a large oak desk sat a large man, reading from an electronic tablet. Without looking up, he motioned Ryker to sit in a chair in front of the desk. Sitting, Ryker noticed the plaque on the desk advertising the personnel manager by name.

The door closed, leaving Ryker alone with J.C. Gemill. Two minutes of silence passed as Gemill studied his reading material. Ryker demonstrated his nervousness by touching the tips of his two index fingers and thumbs together while rolling them back and forth, staring through the varying hole size onto his lap.

"Ryker, are you ready to begin?"

Ryker looked up and smiled the best he could. "Oh, yes. That's fine."

No emotion graced Jerry's face. "It says here you feel you were unjustly accused of following the doctrines of the cult called Rigid Christians. Could you explain that for me?"

Ryker's mind froze. Jerry waited with a neutral expression on his large, round face. His dark, wide-set eyes gave no hint as to the purpose of his question. Ryker haltingly, but with conviction, told his story leading to the reason for his mark.

Jerry Gemill continued the interview with no comment on the explanation. "What kind of work experience do you have?"

Ryker felt much more comfortable with this question. "Before my mark, I was working for Conklin's Construction. I learned to do this kind of work at home. Dad's a farmer and as you know they do most of their own repairs and upkeep. Dad's pretty handy this way and taught me as I was growing up."

Jerry loosened a kink in his neck while pursing his lips. Another question came with no comment on the previous answer. "Have you ever done any janitorial work?"

Ryker confidently shrugged his shoulders when he answered, "Not professionally but I know I could handle it."

Jerry wrote something on his computer tablet. Ryker silently watched for what seemed like several minutes. The personnel manager put the tablet and stylus down on a shelf hidden from Ryker's view. He looked at Ryker with a smug look on his pudgy face and folded his hands on the desk. "Mr. Cuff, would you be willing to have yourself monitored by our internal security on a weekly basis until such time we deem it less frequent or not necessary at all?"

Ryker never hesitated a second. It was the reaction Jerry fished for, though Ryker never realized it. "Not at all, sir. I'd be glad to vindicate the slander on my character."

Gemill looked surprised by his quick response. He reached into his desk drawer and pulled out some papers with a card. He continued his sober, unemotional dialogue. "I've decided to give you a chance. You may report to work Monday morning at seven o'clock sharp. Before you leave, I want you to check in with Mr. Sampson across the hall. He's the counselor you'll be reporting to on a weekly basis. This key card is a clearance to use teleport B-3, which is where you'll report to work each day. The coordinates are on it. Are there any questions?"

Ryker could hardly believe his ears. He had not expected it to be so easy. He stood, faced Jerry, and stretched out his hand. "Thank you very much, sir. May I be so bold as to ask how much this job pays?"

Jerry answered with a monotone reply and without reaching for Ryker's hand. "Starting pay is three credits an hour plus regular benefits."

Ryker slowly and deliberately retracted his hand with one last question. "Where'd you say Mr. Sampson's office was?"

"Directly across the hall."

"Again, thank you Mr. Gemill. I won't let you down. I'll be a good worker."

Ryker let himself out of the office. With his back turned to the personnel manager, Gemill gave Ryker his last instructions. "When Mr. Sampson is through with you, he'll have Ms. Diller escort you back to the reception area. Have a good day, Mr. Cuff."

Without turning, Ryker replied as he shut the door, "Thank you, sir."

As promised, Ryker found another door across the hall. He knocked. A deep, mollifying voice seeped through the door. "Come in."

The office was nowhere near as elaborate as Gemill's. It had a lighter, more modern look. John Sampson stood behind his desk with a big smile on his long, hairy face and extended a friendly hand. Ryker visibly relaxed, causing John to chuckle, "Don't worry, Jerry treats everyone that way. I'm glad to meet you, Ryker. Have a seat."

Ryker sat in the chair offered and waited for John to finish shuffling papers on his desk.

John Sampson had a warm, friendly face. Ryker liked the beard and wondered what he'd look like in one as John addressed him. "Congratulations on your new job. I like to be the first to say that to people."

"Thanks. I don't think it's really sunk in yet. I don't feel hired."

"Well, you are, and I want to help you keep it that way. You'll report to me every Monday morning just before lunch at eleven o'clock. This Monday morning at seven o'clock you'll report to Ms. McBonnie who's the head custodian. I'm the one responsible for seeing that you don't revert back to your old alleged practices. I understand you've made good progress over the last fifteen months and I want to make sure we keep it that way."

Ryker nodded his head in agreement as John talked. A question came to mind as he listened. "That's fine, Mr. Sampson. May I ask if you work for the NMA?"

John leaned back in his chair and pyramided his fingers. "Good question. The answer's no. I work for Communiqué Incorporated but the NMA monitors our work and sends a person in from the government once or twice a year to audit our procedures. Fred Olmstead retired this last year and we've some new hot shot kid who's taking his place. I'm not sure how he'll operate so we'll have to keep our noses clean, at least for a while."

Without actually knowing why, Ryker heedlessly blurted out his next question. "What's his name?"

John raised his eyebrows but then began searching his desk. "I don't remember. I've the memo here somewhere. Oh, here it is. His name's Alanson Shanach."

The rest of the interview was a blur until Ryker was escorted to the lobby. The news hit him harder than anything that day. Ryker couldn't recall much of it. He had too much on his mind to concentrate.

I don't get it. It's seems I got this job because Buck wants to keep tabs on me.

Men and Women

The music was loud and motivating. The four sat at a small table in one corner of the main room of Ted's "YOUR DESIRES," one of the hot spots of Potsdam. Being a college town, it was one of the busiest times of year and the place was frantic. Ryker and Monica were celebrating Ryker's new job and reinstated social privileges. Two of Monica's friends, Annette Brown and Kevin Hamil, celebrated with them. Dinner had been almost five hours earlier; now the drinking pace had picked up.

Kevin asked Monica for a dance. Monica smiled as she accepted and followed him to the dance floor. It was a slow, close dance. Annette gave Ryker a puzzled look. But he was too busy watching the dance floor to see it.

"You look like that bothers you."

He snapped his head around to face Annette. "It doesn't . . . very much. Why do you say so?"

Annette smiled, brought her drink to her lips, and took a sip. Her dark brown hair fell short around her ears. Light brown eyes, large and almond shaped, added to her rich, tanned complexion. She had grown, fulfilling the literal expectations of her surname. She set the drink down and said, "Monica told me you'd be like this. She finds it attractive. All I see is someone who's never been able to assimilate alternative lifestyles. It shows by your jealousy. You just can't understand that clutching onto a person only makes them wiggle harder to achieve some breathing room."

Ryker thought deeply. He found it hard to spontaneously react to such a statement, so he didn't answer for several minutes. Instead he watched his girl dancing with another man. When he finally did say something, Annette found herself caught off-guard. She thought he had simply ignored the allegation.

"I don't think 'clutching' is the right verb. I care for Monica and I enjoy protecting her. I may stand between her and something I think may hurt her, but she can tell me to move if she wishes."

Annette studied Ryker for a few seconds then shrugged her shoulders looking away as she answered, "Maybe. We'll see."

The dance finished. Monica and Kevin walked back to the table just as Ryker spotted Sally. The blonde secretary from Communiqué was staring at him from the other side of the room. When she realized Ryker had noticed her, she gave him a big smile and a wink. Ryker gave a sheepish smile and a head nod as Monica sat down next to him. Kevin pulled Monica closer to whisper in her ear. He pointed to one of the rooms off the main entertainment area. Monica shook her head no. "Not this time, but thanks for the dance just the same."

Kevin was a small man but very handsome and well built. He had the looks of a movie star but lacked the talent or the wit for it. He gave Monica one of his pearly tooth grins. "Are you sure?"

Before she could respond, Ryker grabbed Kevin's arm around Monica's shoulder and threw it off. "She said no. Can't you hear?"

Monica gave Ryker a menacing stare. "I'll handle this in a *polite* manner if you don't mind."

Ryker sat numb and very still as Annette laughed robustly with her comment, "A shield cast aside to lay and watch as the arrow is easily ducked."

Monica turned to Kevin. "Yes, I'm sure." Then she spun to face Annette. "What's that supposed to mean?"

Annette relaxed, settling a bow smile on her face while cradling her drink in her hands. "Ryker can answer that better than I."

Monica turned to Ryker with a questioning glare. His simple answer was, "I was just trying to help you."

Monica answered condescendingly, "I don't need that kind of help right now. Your social graces leave much to be desired. Sometimes I think you've been too secluded from people. Regular contact might've taught you to relax in these common situations."

Ryker felt his emotions rubbed raw. He didn't mean to cause a scene and when Monica belittled his "country" upbringing it made him mad. "You don't think I know other people? You don't think I get around, huh?"

Ryker stood up from the table and walked to the other side of the room. The others watched with great interest because they couldn't guess what he might be up to. The blonde sat with two other girls who paled to her beauty. As Ryker reached her table, she looked up with a welcoming smile. He greeted her with charm. "Good evening. I couldn't help but notice you here tonight. The brightest light receives all the attention. I'm at a bit of a disadvantage though, because you know my name but I don't have the honor of knowing yours."

She had a very attractive face. Assuming doe-like innocence, she answered, "Sally Diller. I'm pleased you remembered me."

Another slow, sensual melody started up. Under the influence of liquid courage, Ryker's normal apprehension vanished and he asked, "Would you honor me with this dance?"

Without a word Sally stood, took Ryker's hand, and led him to the dance floor. She held him close. In her arms Ryker forgot his purpose for asking this strange but beautiful woman to dance in the first place. His second intoxication was barely controlled as he considered his good fortune.

The trio on the other side of the room studied the development. Ryker's spontaneous act had achieved the effect for which he aimed. Annette was the first to find her voice. "Who's that he's dancing with?"

Kevin shrugged his shoulders. "I've seen her in here before. She's always working the floor. She probably picked him up before."

Monica glared at Kevin with dagger eyes. "Ryker doesn't wait around to be picked up like some other people I know." Satisfied she had vindicated Ryker's good character, she turned back to the dance floor and spoke softly to herself. "I don't know how he'd know her. Ryker hasn't been anywhere or seen others since me, as far as I know."

Sally steered Ryker near the rooms marked, "Private, 5 credits." Sally whispered something in his ear when the music stopped. Monica watched as he looked her way. Ryker politely indicated a negative response. Sally shrugged her shoulders and walked back to her table. Ryker nearly strutted back to his companions.

A short time later, Ryker and Monica decided to go home. They had a long, heated discussion about the evening's events. In the end, Monica asked a question neither of them could answer: "How can two people guarantee they won't change their minds about who they want to live with for the rest of their lives?" Little did they know, the answer would come later.

Friday the 13th

What I wouldn't give for an old-fashioned frosty mug of ice cold beer right now. I almost think I'd kill for it.

It was a sweltering hot day. Nights were cool, but they still hovered around seventy-nine degrees. The weather was the same for over three weeks. The heat was bad enough, but the humidity made it almost unbearable. Ryker was painting the outside of the main facility at Communiqué Incorporated. He was on the shaded side of the building but the thermometer still reached ninety-four. Intently trimming white paint around a window casing, he didn't hear the approaching footsteps.

"You do that real slick."

Startled, Ryker jumped, swiping paint on the casing he had tried so hard to miss. He spoke before he turned to see who had interrupted his concentration. "D*** it!" When he realized who was visiting, Ryker was very apologetic. "Oh, excuse me, Nick. I didn't know it was you."

Nick Richards was a good three inches taller than Ryker. His large ears scarcely seemed out of place because the rest of his facial features matched so well. Nick's countenance always radiated a friendly, jovial nature. Ryker's apology was not necessary as far as Nick was concerned. The two had developed an understanding that strengthened their friendship. The thirty years between them was transparent to each. "Oh, that's OK. I shouldn't sneak up on ya like that. Ms. McBonnie wanted me to give you a message. There's a special meeting for us in Mr. Sampson's office at eleven o'clock."

It was another reason the two were so close. Nick was a marked man also. Ryker gave him a sullen look as he wiped his hands on a rag. "I wonder what this meeting's about? John didn't indicate anything wrong last Monday."

Nick shrugged. "I don't know, but don't be so pessimistic. It just might be good news."

Ryker turned to wipe paint off the window casing. While working on it, he questioned Nick about something he'd considered for months. He turned back ever so often to see Nick's reaction. "You don't have to say anything if you don't want to, Nick, but I've been pondering something about you. You're different in many ways, and yet you're supposed to be a reformed RC. Do you still believe that religious junk they use to pump into your head?"

Nick placed his large hands behind his back *(Was he trying to hide his ross?)* and paced in a small circle while thinking. He stopped to look Ryker in the eyes before answering. As he did, Nick clasped his hands in front *(Deciding there's no need for embarrassment about his mark?)* and said, "I'll tell you. Nobody's around, and I believe we're friends enough that you can be trusted. Yes, I do and always have, but I've a family to support. I remember your telling me about an uncle you had who's running from the NMA. Do you know how hard it is to feed a family when there's no job or government assistance? So I pretend, with as much conviction as I can muster, to be what I'm not."

Ryker put the rag and paintbrush down as Nick talked. He studied Nick with a sense of awe. "You're taking quite a chance telling me this. I appreciate your confidence. Thanks for telling me the truth. Your secret's safe with me, and it's nice to know I've someone to confide in if I need to."

Nick extended his left hand. Ryker had trouble assimilating the changed protocol for a handshake. He started reaching with his right hand, stopped, and haltingly gave his left. Nick smiled a big, toothy grin. "When two marked friends shake on an agreement in confidence, they use their marked hand as a symbol of the trust." When finished, Nick assumed a more serious face. "If you ever want to talk about anything, just let me know."

63

Appreciation reinforced Ryker's response. "Thanks, Nick. I'll remember that."

Nick stepped back and crossed his arms. "You'd better pick things up or you'll be late." He winked, turned, and went back inside. Ryker watched and wondered. *I always thought there was something different about him. I wonder if he has some of the same ideas Uncle Vernon has?*

After putting supplies away and cleaning up, Ryker stopped to visit Sally Diller on the way to his meeting. He paused at the doorway and slowly poked his head around the corner. With a wry smile he said, "I see you."

The blonde looked up from her work, noticed him, and gave an alluring smile. "Not as much as you'd like to, I'm sure."

Stepping the rest of the way into the office, he scanned the room. Confident they were alone, he returned the smile with a like one. "You promised it was possible one time."

Sally put her head in her hands with elbows resting on the desk. "You had your chance once. Now's not a good time."

Ryker put his hands on the desk, leaned closer, and asked, "When would be a good time?"

"I'll let you know," Sally indicated with a fake pout.

The smile evaporated from Ryker's face. "I've a meeting right now anyway."

Sally winked. "I know. I set them up. Remember?"

"You're quite a tease, aren't you?"

Sally picked her head up and moved papers on the desk. "Good-bye."

Without looking back, Ryker left. "Yeah, I'll catch ya later."

Leaving the room, Ryker noticed Nick coming down the hall. "Come on, Nick, and I'll let you walk with me."

When they had covered some distance, Nick reprimanded Ryker in a low voice. "You'd better stay away from her. She's nothing but trouble."

Ryker gave him a knowing smirk. "Trouble isn't all bad once in a while." Nick shook his head with a grim expression.

At John Sampson's office, Ryker motioned Nick on ahead. John held an unusually sober look. "Sit down, men, and relax."

As they settled into seats next to the desk, John handed a paper report to each and explained, "I thought you might be interested in the report I got from headquarters on some new procedures we're to adhere to. You don't need to read it now. Basically it says some of my duties have been transferred to the government." A cold shiver ran up Ryker's back as John continued. "Today we have the privilege of seeing our new government auditor. He wants to talk to each of you. He's in Jerry's office across the hall. You're first on his list, Nick. You may go on over."

Nick glimpsed at Ryker, and behind the desk he gave him a thumbs-up sign. He confidently stood and left the room. Ryker looked back to John. "Is it that Shanach guy?"

John seemed preoccupied and didn't give Ryker a chance to investigate. "You guessed it. Listen, I've got to go to another meeting. When Nick leaves, you can go on in. I'll leave my door open so you can see when Nick exits." John gathered some papers, locked his desk, and left Ryker alone. It was the last time Ryker was to see him.

John seemed in an awful hurry to get out of here so he wouldn't have to answer any more questions. I wonder if he knows that I know Buck? I find it amazing that Buck wants to see me after all he's done to me. I hope this won't be as unpleasant as I anticipate.

Another fifteen minutes passed as Ryker waited. When he saw Nick leaving, he was too preoccupied to look Ryker's way. Ryker sat for several seconds before gathering the resolve to meet someone he had once called friend. When he stood, there was no holding him back. Ryker had made up his mind to face the traitor. He didn't knock but opened the door, waltzed in, and sat down in the chair.

Ryker turned to face his opponent. The surprise brought a leering grin to Buck's face, but Ryker didn't see it until his old friend removed the Search Squad helmet. Besides the mocking smile, Buck couldn't help prodding his old crony with a statement. "Better close your mouth before a bug flies in and doubles your IQ." He laughed at his own witty comment.

Ryker hardly recognized his friend from months ago. Buck grew his hair shoulder length. It was as curly and wild as Buck seemed to be. His bright, blue eyes nearly snapped and sparkled with mischievous energy. If Ryker had not known him so well, he might not have recognized Buck from the man he'd last seen almost two years earlier.

Gathering his composure, Ryker addressed the man across the desk. "It looks like you've done pretty well for yourself since leaving home. Just a little over five-and-a-half years in the service and you've made it to the SS department. I'm impressed." He said it with self-confident fortitude and sincerity.

It wasn't what Buck had expected. "Thank you, but I'm not here for pleasantries. I've a job to do and part of it's to make sure this facility is doing its job with your social reform."

The comment lit a fire under Ryker's boiler, but was not noticed on the outside. He was calm and in control of himself. "The only reason I need 'reform' is because of your deceitful approach at gaining brownie points with the NMA."

Buck pounded the desk to emphasize his anger. His eyes nearly exploded with vibrant excitement. "Don't you ever accuse me of lying to get where I am today. I've proof of your decadent disregard for neutral morality."

Ryker glared at Buck with barely controlled righteous anger. "I'd like to see that proof."

Buck settled back down in his seat with a satisfied smile. "You will if I can ever bring you up on formal charges of deliberate actions to undermine the American Policies for Unbiased Ethics."

Ryker continued with the same state of mind he had moments before. "There's no way you'd ever do that. You've no substantial proof because I've never done anything like that nor do I ever plan to."

The smile grew larger. "You're right—if you've burned that book already. But if you still have it, I could fry you to the cross. It's the only thing I need to prove your misalliance."

As it all clicked together in Ryker's head, his eyes grew wide and his mouth dropped. "I get it! If you could turn in one of the only RC Bibles known to exist, you'd climb to the top so fast you'd probably be an agency first."

This recognition induced the most evil smile Ryker had ever seen on a man's face. Buck leaned forward. "That's right, buddy. As I see it, you've only three roads in life. One, if you've destroyed that book and can't prove it to me, you'll have a lifelong job of eluding my presence in your miserable life because I'll never believe you did it. Two, you can give it up now and I'll see to it that your name is reinstated to its original status with a promise to never bother you again. Three, you can fight me, make it hard for me, and waste valuable time. But when I do find it, which I promise you I will if it exists, you'll fry with the other RCs who deserve it."

Satisfied, Buck leaned back in his chair and resumed his evil smirk. "In case you don't realize it, the best road for both of us is the proverbial middle."

Ryker looked down into his lap while rolling his forefingers and thumbs together. After a few seconds without looking up, he asked, "You're the reason I have this job, aren't you?"

The smirk continued, saturated with sarcasm. "That's a good sign. If you're smart enough to figure that out, maybe you're smart enough to choose the right road in life."

Ryker's eyes never appeared so cold when he looked up. "When do you want your answer?"

Buck steeped his fingers in front. "Oh, I'm in no hurry. You think about it and let me know—soon! Or better yet, now."

Ryker moved to leave. As he opened the door, he turned to Buck one last time. "Here's your answer. I think your initials suit you perfectly." He slammed the door behind him. *I don't exactly know what I've done, but it's worth it.*

Washing up and readying to go home, Ryker heard the page. "Ryker Cuff, report to the personnel office." *Oh great. I thought maybe I had got away with telling Buck off. Must be I'm going to get my hands slapped now.*

As he walked to the front offices, he bumped into Nick. "Hey, Nick. How'd it go this morning?"

Nick gave him one of his friendly smiles. "Great. I'm getting good at this. That guy even asked me about you a little. But don't worry, I made ya look good." His friend punched him on the shoulder.

"Thanks, Nick. It looks as if I need all the help I can get. Have a nice weekend."

Reaching Jerry Gemill's office, he knocked.

"Come on in."

Jerry sat behind his desk holding his usual bland facial expression. Ryker sat down. "Ryker, I'm afraid I've some bad news. We have to lay you off for a few months. The workload has diminished these last few weeks and you're one of the last ones to be hired, so you'll be the first to go. Today's your last day until further notice."

Ryker sat benumbed in his seat and then blurted out his thoughts. "But you've hired three or four other people since me. What about them?"

The man never hesitated. "It's your job we need to cut."

Ryker tried to control himself but with little success. "This has nothing to do with the workload, does it? It's to do with the interview I had with that NMA officer this morning. Why don't you just tell me I'm fired?"

For the first time Ryker saw some emotion in Jerry's face. He looked sincere with his reply, "Now, calm down. You're not fired. All you need to do is report to the NMA Social Reform Offices for a few months and when the workload returns we'll call you back. That's unless you do something stupid between now and then." With his last sentence he gave Ryker a stern look, but then handed a small disk over to him. "You'll need this. Behave yourself, and I'll see you in a few months."

Ryker dejectedly walked to the teleport. *That son-of-a-gun Buck has a control over me I'll never shake. What should I do?*

On the Bottom Looking Up

It was supposed to be a whisper but Ryker was where he could hear it loud and clear.

"Nathan, sit still and be quiet or I'll take you outside." Nathan was a cute little red-headed eight-year-old with enough energy for five kids. His problem was, he simply had to sit next to his friend. His parents had moved them apart but it had not helped. Snickering and commotion continued while passing notes back and forth.

Young Pastor Knots made a point and leaned on the pulpit with his forearms, studying the congregation for a reaction. His curly locks of blonde hair glistened in the artificial light. After half a minute of silence he continued. "I'll say it one more time. Jesus Himself warned us about making ourselves judges. You'll find it in the Gospel chapter five, verse thirty-four. Let me read it for you: 'Do not judge or you yourself will be judged.' It's so clear. There can be no argument. We're not supposed to say whether our brother's way of life is right or wrong. Let me explain what happens whenever people appoint themselves as judges. Back in 1992 there was a man who shot and killed a doctor in his own backyard just because the doctor performed abortions. Let us look at this man who killed. He was living—"

Ryker lost focus once again. The two boys continued giggling about something. It gave him opportunity to dwell on his own situation.

I wonder what Pastor would say about Buck's control over my life? He's judged me, and it isn't fair. The only thing I've done wrong is to hang onto a treasure that now Buck wishes he'd kept for his own benefit. All I need to do is hand it over to him and my life might be different. No, I doubt it. He'd use it to prove my disloyalty to the government and then my life would really be screwed up. I don't know what to do.

Looking around the sanctuary Ryker had mixed emotions, fragmented thoughts, and unfocused purpose. Monica sat next to him. If it wasn't for her, he might have thrown in the towel a long time ago. At the same time, she complicated his life because the two of them seemed so incompatible at times. Then there were their families. Harold appeared content that Ryker was coming to church again, but it didn't seem to fulfill any needs Ryker had. Mogie sat in her usual pew taking in everything, but at many points she shook her head no to something she disagreed with. In fact, Ryker couldn't understand why anyone found interest in what the church had to offer. There was nothing here he couldn't learn out in the real world.

Nathan, the lively, little red-headed boy, was reluctantly and boisterously dragged outside for discipline. At the same time, the pastor asked the rest of the congregation to stand for a final prayer. Ryker's mind swirled with questions as he rose with everyone else. He would not hear pastor Knots' prayer because he was busy with his own.

I'm only doing this once, God. If You're real and You've any answers or plans for my life, I want a sign from You now. If I don't get a sign, it'll just prove that I was right in thinking there's nothing true about You.

Ryker listened for anything, but he heard nothing unusual. He opened his eyes to look around and saw the congregation standing with their eyes closed, shuffling around waiting for the "amen."

Just as I thought—nothing.

As Ryker lowered his head to comply with everyone else, he noticed something that would change his life. There on the pew in front of him lay a Bible. Nathan had used it as a desk for writing his notes. The boy's memo had never made it to his friend. The note lay on the book such that it obscured the words NMA-approved. The only words that could be seen were "Holy Bible" and the note, "Read Me" written in Nathan's childish handwriting.

Could it be this is my sign?

Found

Dust sparkled in beams of sunlight that drove through the thick, summer foliage. The luminous effect formed a semi-circle around Monica who sat on a rock absorbed in a book. It could have been a painting. Steam rose off the lake to her right, and water dripped from the leaves that had experienced an early morning rainstorm. Ryker occupied himself, cooking breakfast over an open fire. After a week of attempts, he was now doing it fairly well. As he straightened up to stretch his legs, he studied the lake behind Monica. A small mountain across the bay reflected in the still water like a mirror. The lake mesmerized Ryker, reflecting his thoughts of the past week.

What a sight! I wish we could've brought a 3-D camcorder. The rain all day yesterday was tough, but times like these make it worth it.

Ryker thought about the events that had led them to this morning. He and Monica were in a place where people hadn't been for many years. "Roughing it" had been given up long ago since the convenience of teleports and a philosophy of social intercourse demanded modern vices. He knew they would be safe at this spot. They could study and reflect without fear of being bothered by anyone, including the NMA. Neither told a soul where they were going or why. Ryker got the idea from reading a diary of his great-grandmother, which Mogie had let him read. In the diary, she had described details of a canoe trip that she and her husband had taken along Bog River to a bay on Lowes Lake.

It took a few weeks to work out the details of his trip because there was little to no information on traveling in the unpopulated areas of the Adirondacks. As luck would have it, Ryker stumbled upon the name James Weegar during lunch one day. His name was on an advertisement for fresh trout from spring-fed waters. The price was something he couldn't afford in a lifetime, but the name was of great interest to him. This man could show him the place he was looking for and possibly how to get there. Monica wasn't real keen on the idea from the start, but she insisted on going along. Ryker couldn't begin to talk her out of it. After the first day, when there was no turning back, she could have gleefully throttled Ryker if she hadn't thought she might need him to get back to civilization.

"What do you mean, 'Just anywhere is fine'? I'm not a raccoon. If God wanted me to just let it go anywhere, He wouldn't have me wearing clothes. I don't know about you, but I need a toilet." She discovered that she, in fact, did not need a toilet, but the decision came with great hesitation and an immense need not to embarrass herself in another way.

It was a week earlier that they had emerged from a teleport set in the woods near a ski resort. It doubled as a summer headquarters for the Environmental Forest Agency. It had a small trading post where James Weegar procured some of his supplies. He had agreed to meet Ryker and Monica if they showed up at a particular time. James drew Ryker a crude map, gave him a mini survival course, and supplied the canoe to get them where they wished to go. Then James drove them to the spot where they put it in the water. Monica found the ride a thrill in itself. She had never been in such a vehicle before.

James gave some last-minute instructions before he left them. "I'll be back here two weeks from today. I've some scouting to do below this dam and I'll be most of the day. If you're not here when I get ready to go, it's like I never met you. Understand?"

That was early in the morning. There was one carry over another · dam but the rest was all paddling. They traveled up Bog River until they hit Lowe Lake and then to the other end of the eight-mile long lake where they settled at a bay called Blue Pond. It took the rest of the day, but they managed to raise the tent just before dark.

As Ryker recalled those events, a fish jumped, rippling the water and breaking the hypnotizing effect the still water had on him. Monica finished the spell with her exciting announcement. "Ryker, look at this! We've been reading the wrong part so far. This is the first chapter of the Gospel of John. I've never read this in our church Bible. Listen as I read verses one through five and then verse fourteen. 'In the beginning was the Word, and the Word was with God, and the Word was God. He was in the beginning with God. All things came into being by Him, and apart from Him nothing came into being. In Him was life, and the life was the light of men. And the light shines in the darkness, and the darkness did not comprehend it. And the Word became flesh and dwelt among us, and we beheld His glory, glory as of the only begotten from the Father, full of grace and truth.' It sounds like this is saying Jesus is God. He's not just a good teacher like our church says."

Ryker moved the frying pan from the direct heat and trotted over to Monica. He took the Bible he'd hidden away until this trip and read where Monica pointed. He studied the whole page then scanned one page after another. He stopped when something caught his eye. He read another minute. "Monica, look at this." Ryker pointed to the words as he read, "Jesus answered and said to him, 'Truly, truly, I say to you, unless one is born again, he cannot see the kingdom of God.'" Ryker looked up and thoughtfully considered his next sentence. "You're right. I think our start with the Old Testament was a mistake. You may've discovered the place where we should be looking. I believe our answers may be here somewhere."

Monica sat up from her perch on the rock. The move captured Ryker's attention. She had gone for a swim earlier and her hair had dried with a bushy, curly texture that framed her face. It served to emphasize the smile and merriment in her bright blue eyes. She pointed behind Ryker, smiling, and reported, "That discovery will be there fresh and ready, which is more than I can say for breakfast."

Ryker spun around in time to see his frying pan being licked clean by a raccoon. "Hey! Get away from there."

Speeding into action, Ryker slipped as he scurried to chase the varmint away from their meal. He succeeded only in sitting down in a mud puddle. Monica couldn't help laughing. She tried to squelch it with both hands as Ryker gave her a disgusted look, but all it did was muffle the sound. As he sat there, the humor of it hit Ryker, and he started laughing too. "I wonder if all great revelations come with this type of appetizer?"

Monica assumed a snobbish look. "Serves you right for dragging me out here in this."

Gathering himself out of his muddy mess, Ryker reminded Monica the real way things came about. "If I remember correctly, you *insisted* on coming with me. I didn't drag you anywhere you weren't ready to run headlong into."

She sheepishly laughed at him. "OK. But seeing this was worth the inconveniences, and I'm glad I didn't miss it." She chuckled for many more minutes. Breakfast that morning consisted of something from a box.

It was a beautiful day compared to having been cooped up the previous day because of the weather. They decided to take a walk up Wolf Mountain. Packing a few supplies, the two trekked to the top of the small mount, which took them about two hours. It was time for lunch when they made their destination, so they found a nice, grassy spot overlooking the bay. The exercise had developed an appetite they had not expected, and the small lunch was devoured in short order.

With the meal gone, they sat back to enjoy the view. It was breathtaking. The experience was something Ryker and Monica would talk about often from that day forward. The sun was high but it wasn't a hot day. The breeze was a refreshing zephyr with the sweet scent of flowers, spruce, and other forest fragrances. Blue Pond was an appropriate name for the small body of water. It was sapphire blue, sparkling as the sun reflected off the ripples caused by the breezy day. The rich green color of the forest dominated the scene, but sandy beaches, gray cliffs, and bronze grasslands well broke up the monotony of it.

The sight moved Monica in a way she had never thought possible. "I'm glad I'm here to experience this. A few weeks ago I never would've believed I'd be happy in this wilderness with you. I'm not saying it's been easy, but it sure is worth it. This is absolutely beautiful. It's so much different than watching it on a view screen. I know now it needs to be experienced to be appreciated."

Ryker admired the insight and added, "There must be a God. How could such beauty and order come from nothing?" He leaned back and removed the old Bible from his backpack. "I'm going to study this some more. That gospel of John looks promising."

Monica lay back to contemplate the beauty as Ryker became intent on reading. She told him, "Go ahead. I'm just going to relax and take this all in."

She didn't realize she had dozed off to sleep. The sun had moved in the sky when she awoke. Ryker lay prone on his stomach with the book still in front of him. Involved in his reading, Ryker didn't hear Monica stretching and moving around. Monica checked her watch. She stood behind him with a confused look on her face. "Must be good. You've read for over two hours now. I've never seen you read anything that long before."

As she spoke, Ryker sat up to face her with excitement in his green eyes. "Monica! Did you know Jesus **is** God? He not only died but He rose from the dead! He's still alive today. If I read this right, He came and died for all of us who'll believe so we might join Him in heaven. There's also something or someone called the Holy Spirit that comes to help us live this life when we believe. It's amazing! God's reached down to help each one of us to find Him. Jesus is much more than a good teacher."

Monica looked slightly perplexed. "Jesus rose from the dead?"

Ryker gave an ecstatic expression. "Yes. He did many other great miracles also that are not in the church Bible. You see, sin separates us from God. Jesus will forgive us of our sins if we repent of them and don't do them anymore. It's just like Uncle Vernon tried to tell me. That's why the NMA outlawed this old Bible. The NMA allows the sins that God condemns."

The two talked for another hour. Ryker pointed out key verses in the Bible he had read earlier to prove what he was saying. They both decided it was great news, but Monica was a little hesitant to totally believe it. "It's almost too simple to believe. I wish we had a sign that this Bible is the true Word of God."

Ryker was determined to follow the tug on his heart. "Well, why don't we pray about it and ask Him to show us in some way?"

Both knelt on the grassy knoll and opened their hearts to the possibility of a personal God. They admitted their sins, the ignorance of their ways, and asked for forgiveness and a new life. It was that moment in time when each would look back and say, "That's when I became what society calls a Rigid Christian." No cult or man convinced them—only closeness to God and His Word. Each admitted the only proof they needed was what happened in their hearts, but they received their first blessing that day. Their faith doubled as they headed back to camp. Only minutes from where they had spent the afternoon was a small ledge, and in the side of that hill they found a carving in the stone:

```
J n. 3: 3   L
e           i
s           v
u           e
s  a  v  e  s
```

Algie and John Eton
5-16-1986

A NEW ROUTE

"Blaming God is like sitting in a sailboat complaining about the wind. The slow process of paddling gets you relatively nowhere. But when the wind is realized, don't fight it. Set your sail to use it."

Litton Cramer: addressing an organizational meeting of the Network, January 12, 2077

Fellowship

It was dark. The smells reminded him of a cellar he'd once explored as a child. The aroma reeked of dead mice and rotten vegetables. Water rhythmically dripped from the ceiling with an echoing sound.

Yuck! It feels like my socks are getting wet. I'll remember this the next time. The only consolation is we don't have to fight the snow outside.

Ryker held Monica's hand, leading her. His only guide was a small, old wind-up lamp his grandfather had given him. Only hours earlier Nick had given him directions and Ryker wasn't sure if his memory was correct. He kept ducking pipes and other objects. Monica and Ryker were late—something Ryker hated.

Monica tried to hold Ryker back by yanking on his arm. "Take it easy. I don't like this. The last thing I want to do is fall down in this stuff. Gross! I hate to even think what might be crawling around in this gook."

Ryker didn't appreciate the stall. "Hey! Come on. You know how I hate to be late for anything."

She stood her ground and defiantly proclaimed, "Don't worry about it. They'll start with us or without us. I certainly don't want to show up with worms crawling out of my hair." She shivered violently at her own comment.

With a little less haste the two continued their trek through the underground sewer system. Ryker's thoughts focused on being back to work at Communiqué after seven months. When Nick heard about Ryker and Monica's trip to the Adirondacks and their newfound faith, he invited the couple to his Wednesday night Bible group.

Just as Ryker wondered if he had taken a wrong turn, light appeared around one corner. The pair approached the illumination cautiously when they heard voices ahead. They came close enough to hear and understand some of the words.

"It's time. Maybe we ought to start. They may not show up." The speaker stood with his back to Ryker and Monica as they approached the cavern. In years past, the place had served as a storage area for materials and tools for maintaining the archaic disposal system. Now it was as a sanctuary for a small group of believers who wished to worship in a way that was against government policies. It seemed relatively clean, decorated with simple symbols of their faith including crude benches.

As Ryker and Monica's eyes adjusted to the light, a familiar voice greeted them.

"Ryker! I'm so glad you found us. Come on in and meet everyone. We're about to begin." Nick jumped up to greet the new arrivals, barely avoiding collision with a low-hanging pipe. He shook hands eagerly, emphasizing his joy at their presence. It was a small group of people, so Nick took time to introduce everyone.

"Ryker and Monica, this is Allen and Fern Phelix." The two were probably the oldest people in the room. Ryker guessed Allen to be about the age of Uncle Vernon. Nick continued around the room. "Here we've Betty Alvin, and next to her are Rich and Debbie Cristiano. Over on the other side are Scott Kidder, Sue and John Rubbles, and Jerry and Pat Ivies. Last, but definitely not least, is Cheryl Prince who's Dennis' wife. Dennis is our leader at these gatherings. He started this group about four years ago."

Ryker shook hands with the man whose voice he had heard a few minutes earlier. Dennis was a small person with an almost childlike appearance. A round face, topped with short, black hair, adequately displayed his friendly smile. Ryker noted that except for Monica and him, Dennis and Cheryl were the youngest ones present. *How could someone this young lead others older than himself?*

Monica had never seen so many married couples at one time outside of her church. She pointed to each of the five couples. "Are each of you married? Wow, I thought the traditional marriage idea was on the way out. Looks like I may be wrong."

Dennis gave her one of his reassuring smiles. "We hold it as one of our articles of faith for a strong family unit."

Nick decided enough time had been spent on introductions. "All right, you two, come over here and sit down next to me. Dennis likes to keep things on track. He's only being polite right now."

Everyone settled down, giving their attention. Dennis began with a prayer. It was simple but sincere and to the point. Next, there was a time of Bible study. Ryker was amazed at Dennis' and some of the others' memory of the scriptures. The only Bibles for use were a few NMA-approved versions. Some of the verses Dennis quoted were from the banned Bible, which no one had, but he effectively filled in details from memory. Rich led the group in singing four songs a cappella and from memory. It was a very worshipful time. Ryker and Monica were touched. As Dennis delivered the sermon, Ryker was again astonished at the man's memory of the scriptures and the powerful meanings he applied to everyday life.

The meeting ended at about eight-thirty. There was a time of fellowship before everyone went home. Nick approached Ryker. "How does it feel to be back to work, buddy?"

Ryker smiled from ear to ear. "I'll tell ya, when I stepped off that teleport Monday, it was like I had never left the place."

Dennis came over to say goodnight as Nick left to talk to others. Ryker never gave him a chance to say a word. "How do you remember all those scriptures?"

Dennis responded with an air of pure humility. "The Lord has gifted me with it. I read it a few times and it's right here," he pointed to his head, "for me to recall when I need it."

Ryker daunted his new friend. "Some of the verses you quoted are from the old Bible. Where'd you read them before?"

With a cocked eyebrow, he asked, "How did you know I quoted from the banned Bible?"

Without thinking, Ryker blurted, "I've read it."

The term "could've knocked him over with a feather" was never truer. After a long silence, Dennis blinked his eyes and continued further dialogue. "There're only three known copies of this book. I've the privilege to read a handwritten copy once a month at our regional office. As you probably know, any electronically developed version would be traced. We're beginning to work on a system of computers not tied into the World System, but it hasn't happened yet. Where'd you get one to read?"

For the first time, Ryker truly valued his find at the age of eleven. He never dreamed true Bibles were so scarcely available. Buck's interest in the item made a great deal more sense to him. The silence now grew to a conspicuous length. Ryker wished he'd never brought up the subject. He wasn't sure he wanted others to know of his treasure. He had to say something, and it fell out before he gave it any thought: "I have one."

As he revealed the fact, he knew it was a mistake. Dennis confirmed it by taking Ryker aside and in low tones whispered, "Don't ever say that again. Don't get me wrong. I hope it's true, but even in this kind of company, it might be your head and our chance to save another copy of the Word. We'll talk about this another time." He led Ryker back to the small crowd, speaking in normal tones, "Glad you enjoyed our gathering. We'd be happy to have you join us every week." Ryker noticed Scott Kidder watching from a distance.

Ryker played along. "Thanks. I think we just might do that." The assembly disbanded minutes later.

As they made their way home, Monica chatted about how much she enjoyed the evening, despite the location. Ryker barely acknowledged her. He had more pressing things on his mind.

Man, oh man. What kind of mess have I gotten myself into? Lord, I need Your help.

Brother Visits

He couldn't remember ever hearing that kind of racket at a door before. No one ever knocked at a residence these days. People usually just let the computer announce their arrival. The system could be programmed to recognize and announce visitors, but it had been disabled. Whoever uses the front door these days anyway? The first thing Ryker thought was that a woodpecker must have found something of interest. After a few seconds of tapping, he concluded one of his friends must have decided to do something a little out of the ordinary. As he approached the door, Ryker yelled impatiently, "Just hold on a blasted second! I'm coming."

The visitor received the desired reaction. He couldn't help laughing when he saw the look on Ryker's face. Ray hadn't seen his older brother in three years. Seeing the two standing together made it hard to believe there was four years' difference in their ages. Many times they had been mistaken for twins—fraternal twins, but twins just the same. Ray broke the spell, causing the stupefied look on his brother's face. "Happy birthday, Bro."

Ryker waved him in with a bow of his head and an extended hand to follow. As he shut the door, Ryker smiled. "Not until the day after tomorrow."

The younger brother gawked around the room, admiring his brother's living quarters. Ryker and Monica had moved into another apartment. The place made a pleasant home, and this one even had a teleport in it. It was affordable because Monica was also working. Ray was impressed, forming a seed of jealousy. He had heard his brother was doing fairly well, but things were twice as grand as he had expected. "Wow! You've a cosmic place here."

Ryker didn't respond to the statement. He was more concerned about his visitor—and more specifically, the reason for his visit. "What're you doing here? Do Mom and Dad know you're here?"

Ray turned to face his brother. Ryker felt a sense of déjà vu. Before he heard the answer, he knew it. He had been through it only a few years earlier, and it sounded like a recording of himself as Ray complained, "Mom and Dad are impossible. You know how it is. I couldn't take it anymore, so I did what you did."

Ryker walked into the kitchen to get a drink. Ray followed, still studying the apartment as the older brother did what older brothers do— lecture in the absence of their parents. "I was well over eighteen at the time. You're barely seventeen. You haven't finished school, and I doubt if you have any idea what you're going to do for a living."

Ray nonchalantly nodded his head with a "so what?" look on his face. "I thought you'd help me with that."

"It's hard enough keeping myself out of trouble and employed. What am I going to do for you?"

"I figured maybe you'd get me a job at Communiqué."

"Not without a high school diploma."

"Well, what about that construction company you first worked for?"

"You'd be better off trying there without me."

Ray began showing signs of disappointment. He turned and walked back to the living room. When things didn't go his way, he blamed everyone but himself. "I should've guessed you wouldn't give me any help."

Following his younger sibling, Ryker was about to retort the accusation when the teleport signaled. Ryker read the monitor recessed in the wall near it. "Monica's coming home from work."

The teleport glass slid into place, darkened, and the edges illuminated for a second. As the partition changed from opaque, to translucent, to transparent, the process held Ray's attention. Monica worked in an office building as a data acquisitioner and dressed accordingly. This was the first time Ray had ever laid eyes on his brother's girlfriend. Ryker smiled to himself at his sibling's dumbfounded reaction. When the glass retracted back into the wall, Ryker rescued Ray's silly response by way of an introduction. "Monica, this is my brother Ray. Ray, this is Monica Jones, the woman I'm going to marry."

Ray twirled to face Ryker. Astonishment graced his face. "Marry?! Why would you want to do that?! It's so . . . useless."

Monica walked around her future brother-in-law and gave Ryker a hug. Ryker looked at Monica, smiled, then studied Ray as he queried his brother on the subject. "Monica and I are going to send our invitations out tonight. You're invited, as well as the rest of the family and a few close friends. The ceremony will take place here in our own home. That'll be acceptable, won't it?"

Ray's expression answered his brother's question. Such a small percentage of pairs married. The percentage of married couples fell from 50 percent twenty years earlier to only 15 percent. The trend was heading downhill fast, to non-existent. Ray's surprise emulated that of most of society. So shocked, he spoke without thinking. "Buck said you're getting. . ." His voice dropped off and he lowered his eyes as he realized what he was saying and whispered, "weird."

Ryker's happy countenance changed drastically. "Where did you see Buck?"

The conversation became strange from that point on. What it boiled down to was Ray's feeble attempt to brush off any suspicions with a concocted story that seemed feasible but not probable. Finally, Ryker dropped it so as to restore a more palatable situation. "Well, whatever you say. You're welcome to stay here for a while."

Monica helped to smooth things over. "Come on, Ray. I'll show you the guest room. It's not set up for that, but I think we can work out something."

Ryker watched as Ray followed Monica down the hall from the living room.

Lord, help me with this. I haven't handled this very well. What could Buck be doing that involves my little brother?

Plans, Good and Bad

The second week in April proved a premiere for good weather to come. Ryker and Nick complained about being inside on such a nice day. They were in the boiler room. There were no boilers in the room, but the term had stuck from the previous century. There were only control panels and monitors serving the same purpose for the fusion system. The pair was alone, cleaning the area. Ryker took the opportunity to say something in private. He pulled some envelopes from his hip pocket. "Nick, I was wondering if you'd pass these out to everyone at the Bible meeting tonight. There's one there for you also."

Nick put his mop down, wiped his hands on his pant legs, and reached for the items. "Yeah, but how come you're not going to be there?"

"It's my birthday tomorrow and Monica has something special planned for me. Besides, my brother showed up last night and I don't know what we're going to do now."

"Your birthday's tomorrow? Congratulations." Nick looked at his invitation. "You and Monica are getting married? Man, you're full of surprises today. Congratulations again."

"Yes. Monica and I feel that living together is no longer an option. It's a big step, but the Bible seems to frown on our relationship the way it is. We feel we need to commit to each another the way God expects. We kind of feel guilty living together. That's why we decided to do it as soon as possible. It'll take place the last Saturday of this month."

Nick reached for a handshake with his left hand. Ryker smiled and shook it with vigorous appreciation. "Thanks, Nick. I knew you'd approve."

"We'll miss you two tonight. Who's going to perform the wedding ceremony?"

"Dennis, of course."

"That's what I thought."

Ms. McBonnie came into the room, holding the door open with her foot. She was an older woman who had worked for the company for over thirty-five years. She knew her job very well, which she learned by listening to others. She had the company's best interest in mind at all times. Everyone liked her, but she took no gruff from anyone. Ryker thought she looked like Mogie, except nine inches taller.

"OK, you guys. Is this a social event, or are you going to get any work done today?" She said it with a smile.

Nick nonchalantly put the envelopes in his shirt pocket. "No problem, Ms. McBonnie. We've got this room almost finished."

The woman shut the door behind her and looked Ryker's way. "I know I can trust you boys. I was just keying your board. I came in here to tell Ryker that Gemill wants to see you in his office."

Oh, no. Now what?

"OK, Ms. McBonnie. Thanks. I'll see you later, Nick." He left the room, and as the door closed behind him, he listened to Nick and Ms. McBonnie talking about politics.

Jerry Gemill's office door was opened. As Ryker turned the corner, he caught his breath. The first thing he noticed was the long, curly, black hair.

Buck!

To Ryker's relief, Jerry was at his desk. Buck was in uniform minus the helmet, sitting just to the left of Jerry.

"Hi, buddy."

Jerry gave Buck a puzzled look for a second. Ryker heard the sarcasm, but Jerry was only puzzled and continued by addressing his employee. "Come in and sit down, Ryker. Shut the door, please."

Ryker complied with the instructions. Jerry appeared as unpredictable as normal. "Ryker, I believe you've met agent Shanach. Because you were off work for so long last year, Mr. Shanach's here to check out our paperwork concerning your case to see if we still comply. He has the right to interview you in private to confirm our records. I'll leave you two."

As Jerry stood to go, Buck queried, "I trust you've no bugs or recording devices in this room anywhere?"

Ryker had the privilege to view a rare sight. Jerry gave Buck a blatantly disgusted look. "I assure you, sir, that you're completely alone in this room."

Buck smiled his devilish grin. "I know. I've already checked it out."

Jerry left with one short statement. "You have ten minutes."

The pair sat in a moment of silence at his departure. Buck turned his gargoyle-like grin upon his old friend. Ryker couldn't help expressively shivering on the inside. On the outside, all Buck perceived was a cool character, patiently waiting. Buck asked, "How've you been? I understand you had it kind of rough the final half of last year."

Ryker calmly responded. "I'm sure you know all about it. I won't bore you with the details."

Buck's smile changed to a questioning grin. "Yes, you're right. I know pretty much where and what you've been doing. Oh, we're not dogging you, so to speak, but from week to week I have a fair idea where you've been. I usually know what you're up to." The grin completely left, but the bright blue eyes sparkled. "All except almost three weeks last August. Where the heck were you then?"

With a knowing smirk, Ryker said, "I don't believe I need to divulge that to you. This still is a free country, you know."

Buck nonchalantly shrugged his shoulders. "True enough." The smile returned. "But remember, marked men aren't quite as free—in many ways."

Ryker was eager to get on with the purpose of the meeting. "What do you want from me now, Buck?"

The SS agent stood. Wearing his tight-fitting body suit, he was obviously fit. Buck took Jerry Gemill's seat behind the desk. This left only a few feet between them. From this vantage point Ryker could see Buck's communication implants. One small mass jutted out just below the right jaw line on the neck, and another just below the corresponding earlobe.

This was the first time Ryker had ever noticed them. The small bumps drew his attention for a moment. It brought the spontaneous question, "This room may not be bugged, but are any of your friends monitoring our conversation?"

Buck looked puzzled for a second. Then a comprehending smile developed as he responded, "Only if I wish it to be."

"Are you afraid to converse with me without someone eavesdropping?"

Buck dropped one hand to his lap area then returned it to the desktop. "A silly question, my friend," he said mordantly. "There, we're now completely alone."

Ryker assumed a bitter look. "Probably a first since I saw you at the museum," he replied cynically.

Buck chose to ignore the sarcasm. "Regulation under most situations. Now you may answer me freely. Where've you hidden that contemptible book?"

83

It was no surprise. Ryker knew the conversation was leading to this point. With that knowledge, he still hadn't developed a pat answer. The reply came from the top of his head, with no rehearsing. "In a safe place where, if anything ever happens to me, you'll never find it."

Buck's eyes stabbed like daggers. His face drew up tight and turned red at the same time. For half a second, Ryker had the comical illusion Buck's head was going to pop off his shoulders like a cork from a bottle. The fantasy evaporated quickly with the violent retort. "I'm done playing around, you ignorant fool. After today there's no more 'Mister Nice Guy' from me. If you don't cooperate right now, all hell's going to break loose on you."

Ryker leaned back in his chair as far as it would allow. His reply came with a little more apprehension than he'd wished to convey. "Is that some kind of threat?"

His old friend's face twisted and contorted to the most evil-looking smile he'd ever seen. "That's not a threat. It's not even a promise. That, you little worm, is fact!"

Three quick knocks at the door. Jerry Gemill came after his quick warning. Ryker never thought he would be glad to see Jerry, but he was wrong. "Mr. Shanach, your ten minutes are up. I trust you've found we comply with all government regulations?"

Buck's composure restored to normal the moment the knocks came. Ryker's eyes grew in astonishment at the metamorphic change. With a polite smile, Buck addressed Jerry. "No problems, Gemill. But I'd watch this one a little closer. I believe he has the capability to. . ." Buck looked at Ryker to finish his sentence, ". . . hide things from you."

Jerry held his ground. "I don't know about that, Mr. Shanach. Ryker's been an exemplary employee despite his past record."

Buck stood and faced Jerry. His expression emulated a serious businessman. "I see he's pulled the wool over your eyes. I'll be leaving now. You'll receive a copy of my report soon." Jerry caught one of Buck's amoral smiles. "It's been nice knowing you, Gemill."

Buck turned to face Ryker with the same smile. "Tell your little brother I said hello." He walked out of the room, leaving them in confused thoughts.

Jerry turned to Ryker with a puzzled look on his face. "That sounded like a threat!"

Ryker didn't reply but had plenty of questions of his own.

Oh, God. What's that guy up to now? It did sound like a threat. He seems to have my brother involved in some way. What should I do?

A week later, Ryker heard Jerry Gemill had been replaced.

Almost Married

A kaleidoscope of colors danced on the living room wall. The source of the hypnotizing display was a crystal emblem hanging in the center of a window. It was a wedding crystal portraying a bride and groom holding hands. The ornament was one of many decorations gracing Ryker's home, giving it an air of wedding festivity. Ray stood in the middle of the room with his arms folded. His mouth formed a tight line as he slowly nodded his head in a negative fashion. "You're really going through with this, aren't you?"

Ryker came out of the bathroom applying the finishing adjustments to his tie clasp. His golden brown hair, clean and shining, laid once again shoulder length. He had been growing it since landing the job at Communiqué. "Of course, we are. We weren't joking when we told you. Does my hair look all right? I had trouble getting a cow lick down in the back."

Ray never looked. "Yeah, it looks fine." The younger sibling walked away, straightening items on tables and stands. He stopped to pick up some small pieces of paper on the floor and put them in the trash disposal unit.

Ryker studied his brother with a sense of wonder. "You seem to be more nervous than I am."

Ray stopped, checking himself before any reaction. He relaxed and answered, "Who wouldn't be if one found out his brother was needlessly tying himself to one person for a lifetime."

Ryker buttoned his suit jacket but lifted his head enough to study his brother through squinted eyes of doubt. "I suppose from your point of view that'd seem to be true."

A need for further explanation bubbled out of Ray. "Ryker, I realize you see things differently than I do, but I just don't buy all this stuff you've been telling me about being born again. I mean, where's all the proof of these claims Jesus made?"

Ryker faced his brother with an exasperating look. "I told you. It's in the real Bible that existed before the NMA banned it."

The younger one proposed his challenge. "How do you know it's true? Have you read it for yourself?"

Ryker ceased from fussing. He stared at Ray, contemplating his reply. When he decided what he would say, he went back to brushing lint off his pant legs while giving his answer. "Yes, I have."

"Where? Prove it to me."

"Maybe someday. Not now."

"No one's supposed to show up for another hour or so. Why not show me now?"

Ryker walked past his brother and headed for the kitchen. "I just feel now's not the right time."

As Ryker passed him, Ray spun to face his brother's back. The contempt on his face was hidden. Ray balled both hands into fists and nearly shook with rage. He forcibly relaxed so as not to reveal his emotions. With one last indulgence of his feelings, he whispered one word to himself so Ryker couldn't hear it: "Idiot."

A few hours later the room seemed like a beehive. It was only minutes before the ceremony was to take place. The small residence seemed fairly crowded with an odd mix of people. The Bible study group was there, minus John and Sue Rubbles who were busy bringing another life into the world. Family and co-workers in the room could not figure how they fit into Ryker's and Monica's lives. Family present were Mogie, Ryker's father, mother, and the rest of his family, Monica's parents and her brother. There were a couple of people from Communiqué including Nick, who was the best man. Monica had some friends from her place of employment along with Annette who, through much persuasion, had agreed to be the maid of honor. The friendliness and willingness of the Bible study group to greet others made the rest feel a little uneasy.

Dennis cornered Ryker where he could talk privately. "I just want to remind you that this is going to be an NMA-approved ceremony. There're too many non-Christians here for us to take any chances."

Ryker gave an amicable smile and a pat on the back. "Don't worry. I understand. Monica and I can wait until this evening for the real thing when it's just the Bible study group here. We just wanted the rest of the family and our friends to see we are actually serious about this."

Dennis shifted his eyes from side to side to ensure they truly were conversing in confidence. "With all this noise, even if the place was bugged, which I doubt, it wouldn't be heard. I want to say I'm still looking forward to seeing that old Bible you've hidden. When and where would be a good place?"

Ryker looked at his watch, attempting to disguise the subject of their conversation. "I believe we should wait until my brother finds other accommodations. I'll try to set something up as soon as possible."

Dennis focused behind Ryker and still smiling, nodded his head affirmative. Nick came up from behind and grabbed Ryker's elbow.

"Come on, pal. Let's get this show on the road. I'm not about to let you get out of this now." He smiled from ear to ear.

Sensing the nearness of time, people sat in chairs packed into the small room. Dennis took his place behind the makeshift pulpit. "Everyone, please take a seat and get comfortable."

The noise slowly faded until there was only an occasional cough and the rustling of fabric against nervous, moving bodies. Ryker stood in front, facing the crowd with his hands folded. Nick stood to his left. The traditional wedding march began playing through the home sound system. From the hall walked Annette dressed in an elegant, heather blue gown with lace accents. She carried a colorful bouquet of flowers. All attention turned to her. Ray stood in the back corner of the room and saw almost nothing else for a good five minutes. If he had been where others could see him, there probably would have been some giggles at his wide-eyed gaze and gaping mouth.

Gradually, almost teasingly, Monica entered the living room with confident grace and walked to the place of joining. She was in a beautifully laced, pastel yellow wedding gown. It was a color that she and Ryker decided was more appropriate, considering their circumstances. In her arms was a bouquet of fragrant, white flowers. It symbolized how the couple wished to start their life as a man and wife. Rich, chestnut brown curls of hair framed her face and cascaded down her shoulders within inches of her slim waist. Her brilliant, blue eyes lit up her face and complemented her bow mouth, curled into a smile of complete contentment. Monica was sure of the purpose in her walk. Ryker knew in that moment that any doubts were unjustified. *I must be the luckiest man in the world. Lord, may I be worthy of this great gift.*

When Monica reached Ryker, he took her arm and all four turned to face Dennis. Dennis smiled at the crowd of people before him. "Dearly beloved, we are gathered here today to join together these two consenting adults in the government ceremony of marriage."

Dennis paused momentarily. Something sour caught in his throat. He recovered quickly and opened his mouth to continue when the teleport signal caused everyone in the room to jump. Ryker and Monica looked at each other. Monica spoke first. "I thought you locked the unit so we wouldn't be interrupted."

Ryker turned to the teleport. "I did. Someone must be overriding the controls."

Monica looked frightened. "There's only one agency that can do that."

With a bewildered look, Ryker started for the teleport. "I know. That's what's bothering me."

All eyes turned to the teleport. As the glass turned transparent, gasps were heard throughout the room. On the pad stood two NMA Search Squad agents. As Ryker made his way closer to the teleport, one of the agents began keying information into the teleport controls. The other stepped down from the pad to greet Ryker. His voice was deep with a raspy edge to it.

"Are you Ryker Cuff?"

"Yes."

The large SS agent raised his voice so all could hear him. "We have a search warrant here for the purpose of seeking contraband literature." He failed to produce any proof but continued with his booming voice. "If everyone would please stay seated and not move, no one will be hurt."

Mumbling and hysterical shrieks began, but the tall one took one of the devices off his belt and loudly announced his intentions. "I want complete silence with no moving around. If you can't or won't comply, this stunner will see to it that my wishes are carried out." Like the flip of a switch everyone became quiet as he swept the weapon menacingly.

After a minute, satisfied he had control, the tall one turned to the other SS agent. "Al, go ahead and scan the rooms. I'll watch the crowd."

Entering the last of his data, Al stepped down from the pad and took one of the devices off his belt. "OK, Devon."

Ryker snapped around to face the one named Al.

That voice!

As Al walked down the hall, a long, black, braided ponytail snaked down from the rim of his helmet. His dark suit nearly hid it.

Buck!

Ryker started out to follow Al down the hall. Devon leveled his threat at Ryker's chest. "EVERYONE is to stay right where you are." The word "everyone" boomed throughout the apartment.

Minutes seemed like hours as all held their breath. Al carefully scanned the apartment. Often he stopped to open drawers and doors or to rip open coverings to furniture. As Ryker watched, he knew without a doubt that Al was none other than Buck. While the search continued, Devon reported back to the Nest on the status of the search. Ryker paid little attention to either as he concentrated on the situation.

That Buck! What more can he do? He's beginning to scare me with his drive to eradicate all Christian influences. I'm supposed to pray for my enemies, but I find it hard to pray for him. Forgive me, Lord, but I don't know how. I wonder how he knew to show up at this time? Perfect for him. All my friends and family are here in one place, giving him the perfect opportunity to embarrass me in front of all of them. That's to say nothing about ruining one of the most important days of my life. I'm sure of one thing. He won't find what he's looking for.

Al finished and came to face Ryker. "Maybe you'd care to tell me where I'd find what you know I am looking for."

"I have no idea what you're talking about," Ryker calmly replied.

He couldn't see the devilish grin, but it came through the tone of voice and words. "My, my. Someone of your caliber shouldn't be lying like that."

Ryker involuntarily lowered his eyes. Buck laughed and then turned to the corner of the room where Ray stood. He took several steps toward Ryker's brother and stood poised facing him. Not a word was exchanged. Each knew what the other expected. Buck stood motionless in a questioning stance. Ray simply shook his head no. Buck turned once again to face Ryker. "Very well. We'll do this another way."

Buck walked to the front of the room where Monica stood. She hadn't moved from the spot where the ceremony was taking place. "Monica Jones, you're under arrest for questioning in regard to suspicions of harboring the contents of anti-American, religious literature and aiding a known RC in doing so. You'll come with me."

Ryker jumped to stop Buck. "NO!"

Devon swung his arm up into Ryker's face. He dropped to the floor with a trickle of blood running from his nose. Devon raised his voice once more. "Don't try to stop us. We wish to hurt no one but are not beyond using force if needed." A smile was conveyed through his quality of voice.

Monica covered her mouth in horror. The bouquet of flowers dropped to the floor. Buck took her arm and led her to the teleport. Ryker returned to his feet but held a hand over his nose. "You can't do this! She's done nothing wrong."

No one else in the room dared say or do anything. Stepping up onto the teleport, Buck dragged Monica with him. Devon backed up, watching the room for hostile movements, and allied with them on the pad. He keyed a switch on his belt with his free hand. "Search Squad 308 reporting the end of search sequence 51. Results negative. Transporting a suspect for questioning, code H-17. SS team 308. Destination, the Nest."

Just before the glass slid into place, Monica managed to blurt out a last request. "Ryker, if you love me, don't reveal anything that'd jeopardize our convictions." The glass was in place. Buck clamped a hand over her mouth, but too late, as the glass darkened. The trio left, to the astonishment of all.

Silence. No movement. Everyone was stunned. What just happened was unbelievable. The first one to move was Harold Jones. He came to Ryker with an overwhelmed look on his face. "What've you done to my daughter? What kind of evil have you gotten her mixed up in?"

He roughly grabbed Ryker by the shoulder, who acted like a limp sack of potatoes. Homer ran over and yanked Harold's hands off his son. "Leave him alone. Can't you see he's as stunned as the rest of us? My son and your daughter haven't done anything wrong. This is all some kind of big mix-up."

Others began to mutter and move around. Ryker brought his head up after a few seconds and saw his brother standing in the corner of the room. Ray had a wide-eyed, blank look on his face. Ryker slowly walked toward him. No words exchanged. The thoughts and questions seemed to telepathically reach each other. Tears began to run down Ray's cheeks. "Honest Ryker, it wasn't supposed to happen this way. He said there'd be a large reward in it for me if I helped him find what he's looking for. He never said anything about this." Ray's face grew whiter while he wrung his hands to hide the shaking.

When Ryker saw how scared his brother was, the murderous feeling he had held a moment before vanished. "Just get out of my sight." Ryker turned away and found a seat to settle in while he pondered the situation.

Moments later, the activity grew exponentially. Judy found a wash cloth, dampened it, and took it to Ryker. "Here, honey. Hold this on your nose. It'll help stop the bleeding."

David, Monica's brother, came over to Ryker. "Some of the guests want to leave, but the teleport's locked."

Ryker went to it, keyed in the password, and turned to face everyone. "I'm awfully sorry. Please accept my apologies." Ryker went back to his seat.

Rena Jones stationed herself at the teleport and, as gracious as possible under the circumstances, hosted the departure of guests. Sarah and Joanne busied with picking things up and putting items away.

Nick and Dennis approached Ryker. Nick extended his left hand. "Don't worry, Ryker. We'll be praying. I have a few connections in the NMA. Maybe I can get some information."

Ryker took the hand in his left one. "Thanks, Nick." Dennis clasped the left-handed handshake in his two hands. "You know how to reach me. Don't be afraid to do so."

They both left, but their reassurance had helped boost Ryker's hope.

Minutes later all had left but the two families. The reality of the past twenty minutes finally hit Ryker. He curled up on the couch and visibly held back tears. Judy, her insides torn up from watching her oldest son suffer, tried to comfort him, but Ryker kept her at arm's length. The Joneses decided to leave. Homer assured them he would keep them informed of any news. Harold said likewise, and then they left by the teleport.

Homer sat down next to his son. "We're going to go home now. I believe you need to be alone. Don't hesitate to call any time. We'll be waiting to hear from you."

Ryker looked up with red eyes to acknowledge his father. "Thanks, Dad. I will."

Homer gathered his family onto the teleport. Ray still stood in the corner. "Come on, Ray. You're going home with us. I think you've caused enough trouble here."

Ray didn't argue. With his head hanging, he took his place with the rest of the family. Homer keyed in the information, and for the first time since Ray had showed up on his doorstep, Ryker was alone.

He got down on his knees at the couch.

Dear Lord, I'm so glad that You're here. I don't know what I would do without You. I need Your guidance. Please be with Monica. Protect her. What do I do from here?

Almost as an answer, he recalled the last words Monica left him. "Ryker, if you love me, don't reveal anything that'd jeopardize our convictions."

Moving On

Nick wore a yellow wedding gown. He led Ryker through a wooded area, mumbling something about selling candles. They came to a clearing with a desk lit by a single lamppost directly behind. Nick was no longer with him, but Ray stood in front of the desk in handcuffs. A jury stood behind the lamppost. A voice came out of the darkness.

"Ladies and gentleman of the jury, what's your verdict?"

One of the ladies stood. Annette in a blue gown said, "We've found the defendant guilty of failing to recover valuable information for his country." A gavel banged as the voice proclaimed, "Twenty years' solitary confinement. Ryker, take him to his place of confinement."

Ryker found himself leading his brother up the trail on Wolf Mountain. "You'll like this. It's beautiful here."

When he turned to face his brother, Grandpa Cuff stood before him. Ryker was so glad to see him but he realized something wasn't right. It didn't make sense. One ridiculous thing happened after another. Every action led to another unrelated action. In the back of his mind, Ryker registered a fact that helped him ignore the process and just let things flow. *I'm dreaming.*

Grandpa smiled and patted Ryker on the back. "Good. You realize you're dreaming. Now pay attention."

Ryker found he was at the edge of a meadow, standing next to a grove of cedar trees. Some men were working on what looked to be the foundation of a house. Two men were laying cement blocks and two others ran supplies.

One of the men, the bigger one, stopped and faced Ryker. "Hi. Don't worry; these other guys can't see or hear you. You're here just to see me."

Ryker realized it was true. The other three kept right on working. He turned to the man. "Who are you?"

"My name is Lee Jinkens, but that doesn't matter. It's you we need to focus on." Lee was a big man—not tall but wide and squarely built. He looked like he could handle the job he was doing. Ryker found him interesting.

"What can you do for me?"

"You're in a jam, and you're wondering what to do."

"That might be true, but what can you do to help me?"

Lee moved a little closer. The other men were oblivious. Lee put his trowel down to wipe his hands on his shirt as he talked to Ryker. "You see me right now as a mason. That's true, but I'm much more than that. I'm also a Christian, and that's a bigger job than building this cellar for Algie. God's calling me to another ministry—work much different than this and, in many ways, much harder. My life's going to be altered, but what I've learned to this point is going to be my strength when I serve the Lord. I don't want my life to change, but if I'm to be obedient, it will change—and for the best."

Lee became quiet and watched Ryker, who waited for more. When it didn't come, Ryker asked, "So? What's all that mean for me?"

The large man smiled. It was a comforting smile. Ryker noticed he had one tooth missing on the bottom that showed only when he smiled that way. Lee continued, "Your life's going to change. It'll seem tough, but it's for the best. I need to tell you to be obedient to how the Lord directs you." Lee began to vanish as Ryker was whisked away, but he still heard, "Remember, be obedient."

***

With a jolt, Ryker jumped up from the couch. He looked around to discover he was in his apartment. He thought about the dream, much of which was fading from his memory. Shaking his head, he looked at his watch. It was six-thirty in the morning.

What a weird dream. I might as well get up. I have to figure out how I'm going to get Monica back.

Zombie-like, Ryker trudged from the bathroom to the kitchen. He had only managed a few hours' sleep all night. At the meal maker, Ryker keyed in some information, opened the door on the unit, and retrieved a hot cup of coffee. He took a quick sip and grimaced at the burn to his lips. Staring at the steam rising from the cup hypnotized him into a moment of thought.

MM or meal maker? What a childish name for such a sophisticated piece of equipment. I hear it had a fancy name some time ago, but it was too long and difficult for social protocol. Funny how the pendulum swings from one side to the other.

The teleport signaled. Ryker managed to slosh half his cup of coffee onto the counter, rushing to receive the information on the teleport. He pressed the controls to view the small monitor. A miniature image of Nick filled the small screen.

"Nick! What is it? Do you have some good news?"

"Great news."

"Oh please, anything. Let me hear it."

"Well, I just heard from Allen Phelix. He has more pull than I ever dreamed. It seems the SS agents made one mistake at their arrest yesterday, and now they must let Monica go home sometime this morning."

It was like the doors opening to a dungeon cell. Relief flooded Ryker's soul. "Nick, that's great. When? When will she be released?"

Nick seemed tired and out of breath, but that didn't stop him. He was as excited as Ryker. "I don't know exactly, but Ryker, listen to this. It's only temporary. I guess the plan was to get you all worked up and then arrest you also. They were going to hold both of you until they got whatever it is you're hiding from them. Must be pretty important. I never saw them after someone so diligently. Dennis wants me to tell you he has some very important information for you. He'll be coming this morning to talk to you so make sure you stay home."

Ryker smiled from ear to ear. "No problem, Nick. I'm not going anywhere until I'm holding Monica again."

Nick looked behind for a moment. Turning back, he smiled at his friend. "I have to go. Good luck and I'll try to see you later."

"Bye, Nick. I can't begin to express my appreciation for what you've done. See ya later."

The screen was dark, but Ryker's heart was as light as the mid-day sun.

Thank You, Lord. I'll never doubt you again.

The next hour-and-a-half seemed like a day-and-a-half. Waiting wasn't one of Ryker's strong points.

It might be hours before I see either Dennis or Monica. I wonder what the Lord wants me to do? I need to seek His Word, but I don't know if I dare. It did sound like the NMA couldn't hassle me for a while.

Getting up from his favorite chair, Ryker walked over to the teleport. Moving the monitor aside, a small door about a foot square became visible that most people wouldn't have noticed. He keyed a quick password on the keyboard and then slid the door open. It was empty. This type of compartment was only on the older versions. The small compartment held tools, parts, and other such material for technicians to transport from one job to another. The space had the capability to transport to a different location other than the one for which the main teleport was programmed. Years ago, it was handy. Technicians would forward supplies from one place to another ahead of work. Now the teleports were virtually maintenance-free. Newer units didn't have the small transporter units. Most people never knew of their existence.

Ryker reached inside and up into the compartment. He fished around for a second or two, grabbed something, and pulled it down and out. It was his treasure—the old Bible. He cleverly programmed the small unit to transport the contents of the upper end of the niche to a predetermined destination. If anyone ever opened the door without first entering the password, they would never know anything had been there. Not a soul, not even Monica, knew this was where Ryker had hidden his prize.

Taking the book into the kitchen, Ryker sat down at the table. He thoughtfully disguised the cover to help divert any suspicions with words "Bible Commentary" and small letters in the corner, "NMA-approved." Opening the cover, Ryker stopped. He wondered if having the book out at this time was such a good idea. Studying the inside cover, he noticed something for the first time. The inside was all black just as he knew it was, but an edge next to the inside binding made a visible line. Yes, there was something there. As he lifted at the edge he could see someone had skillfully added a pocket to the cover with some type of black material that matched the original. There were some papers inside the pocket. Ryker extracted five leafs of paper from the small, hidden area.

The handwriting on the top sheet riveted his attention. "Obedience. What is it?" As he quickly scanned the sheet, it seemed to be a handwritten outline for a sermon. Ryker studied the outline. In the corner was a small notation unrelated to the rest of the sheet.

"Algie, what do you think of this? Do you have any ideas?"

What a funny name for someone to have. First, Monica and I see it on Wolf Mountain, it was mentioned in my dream, and now here it is in my Bible!

Ryker continued reading.

95

Three points:

Obedience; Some things it's not
Judea as an example—Jeremiah 3:9&10
Jesus denounces above kind—Matthew 23:25-27

Obedience; What it is
Sacrifice versus good works—1 Samuel 15:22
How are good works and sacrifice related?—
Romans 12:1&2

Obedience; What about you?
2 Corinthians 2:9
Philippians 2:8
1 Peter 1:14
My story leading to obedience.

Lee Jinkens, March 1992

When Ryker read the bottom line, he could hardly breathe. *Lee Jinkens?! That dream was a sign! I'd better study these verses in the outline.*

Ryker grew spiritually during the next forty-five minutes. After a time of prayer and commitment, the book went back to its place.

The next few hours seemed like days until the teleport signaled. Ryker's heart leaped into his throat. As he hastened closer to the monitor for coordinates, disappointment overwhelmed him. Dennis was calling. As the glass cleared, Ryker naturally grinned at his friend. Dennis had a contagious smile. The little man stepped down and they shook hands.

Dennis could hardly contain himself. "God's really been working in this situation. Before last night, I never experienced the Network run so smoothly."

Ryker raised his eyebrows with a dubious expression. Dennis realized his confusion. "Oh, excuse me. The Network is what we Christians call our underground system of communication and transportation."

Ryker nodded with understanding and invited Dennis into the kitchen for a cup of hot chocolate. He wanted to know everything. Excitedly, Dennis explained, "Yesterday when Nick and I left, Nick contacted someone he knew named Ted Wright. Guess who he told us to reach as an underground connection?"

Ryker motioned a negative response but then blurted out what Nick had told him earlier. "Allen Phelix."

Dennis raised his eyebrows. "Right. I didn't know Allen was connected in that way. To make a very long story short, the Network discovered where Monica was. Someone in the Network who knows the laws and procedures found a loophole in the operation the SS agents used yesterday. This person appealed to a higher government official who had to listen and reluctantly agreed that the arrest was illegal. The SS team was furious when they were told they could hold Monica for only sixteen hours, and no matter what they found, she was to be released."

Ryker's question bubbled out like a glass filled too fast with soda. "When were they told that?"

Dennis smiled at Ryker's excitement. "Six-thirty last night. The Network worked pretty fast, I'd say."

Ryker didn't hear the last sentence. He was busy doing math in his head. There was a moment of silence as his lips silently moved counting to himself. His eyes brightened after calculating. "That's ten-thirty this morning. That's only a few minutes away."

Dennis smiled and said, "That's right. I'd have been here sooner, but I've been busy getting things set up for you and Monica."

Ryker was lost in thought and didn't comprehend for a moment what Dennis had said. When the statement registered, he gave Dennis a perplexed look. "What do you mean?"

Dennis re-settled in his chair. "Ryker, I didn't know an NMA agent knew you had an illegal Bible in your possession. It's a miracle you and Monica have been left alone this long."

Ryker snorted a sarcastic laugh. "Believe me, I haven't been left alone."

Dennis fatherly reprimanded Ryker. "Maybe not. But your only saving grace is that the agent who knows about it kept it a secret. He's trying to gain all the glory for such an important find."

Ryker thought solemnly for several seconds. Then, as much to himself as to his guest, he voiced his revelation. "I guess I've been lucky up to now. Lucky might not be the right word, I suppose; blessed would better describe it."

"You're right. Arrangements have been made for you and Monica to go underground."

"Underground?"

"Yes. You two are now considered enemies of the U.S. government."

"Does that mean we'll always have to run and hide, never to have a normal life again?"

"Think about it. What's normal? This is one way, or you could ditch the evidence, deny all allegations, and live a life constantly hounded by the NMA as marked radicals. They'd never leave you alone, you know."

Ryker considered the last few years. He knew his friend's statement to be true. He would be very ineffective in helping others because the government would tie his hands so effectively.

Dennis broke into Ryker's train of thought. "I've prayed about this, and it seems to me that God wants you in His underground army. Not all of His people work in that capacity, but many do. Nick is just one example."

The dream and the Bible study Ryker did earlier made more sense than ever. It was obvious that this was God's will for his life. "Thanks, Dennis. It's the right thing to do. I think God's been leading me to this point, telling me the same thing."

Dennis was aglow again. "That is great. One last thing. You only have twenty-four hours. After that, your SS friend can arrest either or both of you again if he wishes. My guess is, next time he'll have no mercy on either of you."

Ryker nodded in agreement as the teleport signaled the override signal the NMA used.

It must be they're sending Monica home!

Ryker ran to the teleport. As the glass cleared, joy filled his soul like no other time in his life. It was Monica! The glass retracted into the adjoining wall but not fast enough for Ryker. He grabbed the edge pushing it back as he clambered onto the pad to wrap his arms around the one he loved. He picked her up and twirled her around three times before setting her down. Forgetting his company, Ryker gave Monica an intense, lingering kiss.

Dennis busied himself, picking up the kitchen. After a few more moments, he purposely kicked a chair as he came into the living room area. The noise served to break the spell, and the couple stepped down into the room. "Sorry, Dennis. I forgot you were here."

Dennis shrugged his shoulders. "That's OK. I understand. Monica, it's good to see that you're all right."

Monica still wore her wedding gown, but it was all wrinkled and dirty. If she had looked in a mirror, she would have blushed at her disheveled condition. But it was the furthest thing from her mind. Dennis came to her and gave her a small hug and a handshake.

"Thanks, Dennis. You don't know how good it is to see you." She held her arm around Ryker. "If I never go back to that place, it'd be too soon. I've never been in a place so evil feeling. The Nest is a good name for it. It's like a nest of snakes."

Ryker pulled her as close as he could. "I wish they'd taken me instead, but Buck's not stupid. He knew this way would get to me quicker."

Dennis waved the couple to sit on the couch. "Relax, you two. We've much to discuss in the next few hours."

Ryker helped Monica to sit. As he did, he held her left hand. There it was plain as day—the cross encircled with the capital R. "They marked you!"

Monica smiled. "Yes, and I wear it proudly. We weren't able to marry, but we share the same mark now."

The rest of the morning was devoted to plans and praises for the way the Lord works.

***

Both families received the news that Monica had been released. The couple had time after Dennis left to clean up and change before the families arrived. Ryker's family showed up five minutes before the Joneses. Harold and Rena hugged their little girl while David patted her on the head. Rena spoke the first words to their daughter. "Oh sweetheart, it's so good to see you in such good spirits."

Monica beamed at her family. "I'm doing fine now, Mom, but I need to tell you this is the last time you may see me for some time."

Harold stepped back with a quizzical look and questioned, "What do you mean, dear? There's no reason we can't visit no matter how far away you may move."

Monica wrung her hands trying to figure out how to tell her parents the news of her predicament. Rena saw it first and seized her daughter's hand to study the mark. Rena's face dropped with surprise, but Harold's flared red with horror and amazement. "What the h— are you doing with a ross?"

Monica opened her mouth to explain, but Harold wouldn't listen. Her father shifted his focus from Monica to Ryker as he accused his near son-in-law of sedition. "I knew I shouldn't have trusted this little snake with his lies about his mark being a mistake."

Homer was about to jump in when Ryker sensed his father's reaction and brought his hand up to stop him. "Dad, you stay out of this. Monica and I'll handle this."

Harold normally was a calm person, but when something primed him to action, there was no stopping him. He looked back at his daughter after Ryker stopped his father and asked, "Just tell me one thing, young lady. Does that mark reflect what you've come to believe since living with this boy?"

Monica hesitated for a moment, stunned by her father's caustic reaction, but then replied, "Dad, it's not like that. Neither Ryker nor I believed in it before last summer. We found—"

Harold didn't let her finish. "All I want to know is if you now believe that degrading garbage of a Rigid Christian?"

"Dad, it's not garbage. It happens to be the truth."

"Are you a Rigid Christian?"

Monica looked at her father as tears welled up in her eyes. She knew how her father felt about such things, and he was a hard man to convince otherwise. The rest of the house became silent as the scene unfolded. Monica wiped her eyes, looked her father straight in the face with resolve, and answered, "Yes, Father, and I believe it to be the truth that leads to eternal life."

Harold turned and called the rest of his family. "Come on, Rena and David. We're going home. We've no daughter here."

Rena looked back and forth between her husband and daughter. "But Harold . . ." He didn't let his wife finish but kept walking to the teleport. "Don't argue with me, Rena. Come now. We've no more business here. She's made up her mind and there's no changing it now. She's brainwashed."

Rena began sobbing, ran to hug and kiss her daughter one last time, but then followed her husband back to the teleport. Ryker tried to smooth things over. "Mr. Jones, you don't need to leave. We can work something—"

He wasn't allowed to finish as Harold proclaimed, "I don't want to hear a thing YOU have to say. Your mouth is full of lies and deceit."

The Jones family stood on the teleport pad. Harold keyed in some information while Rena sobbed and David waved to his sister, mouthing the words, "I love you. Bye." The teleport reacted to commands and soon was unoccupied.

Ryker turned to Monica with sadness in his eyes. "I'm sorry, Monica. I didn't know he'd react that way."

Monica wiped her eyes and smiled as best she could. "It's OK. I figured he might be that way about it."

The rest of the afternoon, Ryker explained to his family their plans. There were more tearful eyes, but Homer and Judy promised to be open-minded about the couple's new faith and their reason for hiding.

Ray apologized for all the trouble he had caused. Ryker had an answer for him. "It's OK. God used the circumstance to put Monica and me where He wants us to serve Him. Just remember, Ray, there's much more to life than what you can seize from it." They shook hands with no more said. Not long after, Ryker and Monica were alone to get ready for their new life.

***

On the teleport sat four suitcases. It signaled for a thirty-second countdown until transportation. It was almost twelve hours earlier that Monica had come home and now they were leaving, never to return. Ryker and Monica looked around the apartment one last time, then stepped onto the pad. There was five seconds to go. They turned to face each other with a smile and held hands. The teleport worked its magic. When the glass retracted back into the wall, the only noise was the hum of the apartment. Several minutes went by. The scene didn't change. It was like a picture—until fifteen minutes later.

The teleport signaled the alarm for a password override. When it activated, two SS agents stood in combat fashion with stunners pointed. As the glass parted out of the way, one went in one direction and the other the opposite. It wasn't the same two men who had been in the apartment the day before. Both were about the same size.

When they were satisfied no one was around, the leader stopped to kick the coffee table across the room. " The little twit did it again. How is it he's always a step ahead of me? Ryker couldn't have known the twenty-four hour reprieve was just a lie, and he had only twelve hours." Whipping his helmet off in disgust, Buck turned to face the other agent. "Tell me, how could he have known?"

The other agent came closer and put his hands on his helmet. As he raised it up, he replied, "He couldn't have known. Ryker's just plain lucky. That's all there is to it. Don't worry; we'll get him yet." Scott Kidder smiled at his partner.

DEVELOPING

"Self-Righteous Morals—A belief that negates the basic rights of American citizens to conduct their affairs as society accepts, and stifles our culture's evolution toward tolerance and neutral convictions. The government will not allow any institution's rights to infringe on these human facts."

Rights for Moral Neutrality, Amendment 1

An Opportunity

Hazy, hot, damp, and sticky best described the climate. From a darkened doorway of the alley, a set of eyes slowly peered down one end and then the other of the narrow back street, glanced at a watch hidden in the shadows, and then receded. The sun was obscured at one end of the narrow lane by a dark figure that impeded the alley entrance. It was an SS agent holding a small hand stunner. Another agent entered the opposite end of the confined route. The first agent mumbled something into his communications implants and motioned the second one to wait around the corner and out of sight.

A distinctive ping sounded from the trash disposal down the alley. The inquisitive agent quickly turned in the direction of the noise. He inspected every nook and cranny as he slowly approached the unit for closer inspection. Just then, Ryker darted from the doorway clutching a bag endearingly and ran for the street.

About halfway to his goal, he heard the agent call after him. "Stop or I'll shoot!"

The loud, feminine proclamation only served to spur Ryker harder to reach the corner. Just as he rounded the bend, he heard the familiar buzz of a stunner and felt the effects as it hit his foot. With no feeling in his right leg up to his knee, Ryker stumbled into the teleport at the corner. Taking no time to glance back, he punched in his two key codes programmed only thirty minutes earlier. The glass slid into place as Ryker turned in time to see the blue beam splash across the outside surface before the partition turned black.

The teleport glass slid out of the way as Ryker hobbled out, hanging onto the unit for support and tried to rub the numbness out of his leg. Down the street, only five blocks away, he watched the two SS agents as one of them quickly keyed the control board at the teleport from which Ryker had just transported. Ryker smiled as he once more inspected his watch for the time. *Lord God, thank You. Perfect timing. Praise You for watching over me.*

As Ryker stepped back into the teleport, he could see the two agents looking at him standing in the other teleport several blocks down the street. He waved goodbye to them. Realizing they couldn't access the teleport Ryker stood in, they frantically considered their next move. They ran toward their quarry with stunners in hand. Someone activated Ryker's teleport from another location. Two blocks away, they commenced firing, but the teleport had activated. The last thing they saw was Ryker smiling and waving to them as the glass dimmed. He had slipped through their fingers.

Long, curly, black hair fanned out as one of the agents turned with excited speed to face his partner. "How'd he get around you? He's no ghost, or at least not yet."

The other agent calmly raised a small object she held in her hand. She had found it at her feet the first time she stopped to shoot at Ryker. It was a hand-made contraption with a rubber band and a trigger—a toy that many young boys made that shot paper wads.

Buck's shoulders drooped as he replied to the silent answer. "Great! Ryker fooled you with a gun I showed him how to make when we first met. I'll tell you one thing, if there's such a thing as a God, I'd have to conclude He's on the wrong side. And you were stupid enough to assist the idiot."

The two disappointed agents boarded the teleport and went back to the office to report. It would not be a pleasant task.

The corridor was narrow and dimly lit with old, incandescent light bulbs. Ryker hobbled along quickly, holding the bag to his chest. The structure through which he traveled had once served as a rich person's personal bunker against a nuclear attack. The decision was made years ago to convert it into a medical center.

As he entered the small foyer that served as the hub for other halls and passages, Ryker was greeted warmly. "Thank goodness, you're all right. What's wrong with your leg?"

The question came from a concerned but usually jovial young woman. As she hurried from behind the reception desk, the long, flowing blouse complemented her easy-going personality. Laura Shaffer was the head nurse of the facility. Ryker was impressed with her efficiency, ability, and motherly concern for others.

Ryker tried to reassure Laura before she became too carried away with concern. "I'm OK. I just got my leg stunned. The feeling's beginning to come back. How's Monica doing?"

Her eyes sparkled as she smiled. "If you don't beat all. I should chew you out for pulling such a foolish stunt, but that's hard to do with such good news." Laura reached back, pulling her shoulder-length, straw-colored hair back into a ponytail. "She and the baby are doing fine."

Ryker was shocked. "She had it already!? Can I see her? Is it a boy or a girl? Oh, man, I missed it! I thought she'd be hours yet. That was fast."

Laura openly laughed at Ryker's typical fatherly reaction. "Come with me. I'll take you to her."

As she led Ryker down one of the narrow hallways, Laura looked over her shoulder, seeking eye contact. "It's a girl, and she's healthy. We couldn't believe how quickly Monica reached full dilation. The second child usually is easier to deliver. She's been asking for you. I didn't tell her where you were. I couldn't believe it myself; say nothing about trying to explain it to her. I'll let you do that."

Laura opened a door and held a finger to her lips as she ushered Ryker into the simple, small room. Monica slept peacefully on a bantam bunk. In her arms lay a tiny bundle. As he crept closer, Ryker could see the small, red face, topped with thick, black hair combed into a single, long curl. Monica, sensing Ryker's presence, opened her eyes. A smile graced her face as she looked down into her arms. "Another girl." She looked at Ryker. "I hope you're not disappointed."

Ryker knelt at her bedside. "Not at all. I like the idea of another girl. I've gotten comfortable with having Erica around, and I don't need to worry about learning how to handle a boy. July 2, 2091, will be a day to remember." He leaned over, kissed the forehead of his newborn, and repeated the gesture for the woman who had made it possible.

A contented smile graced Monica's face, but then one of wonder as she noticed the package Ryker held. "What do you have there?"

Looking on from the doorway, Laura cringed slightly at the innocent question. She decided she had eavesdropped long enough. "I'll leave you three alone. If you need anything, Monica, just holler."

The door closed. Monica held her attention on Ryker and the package. She raised her eyebrows, prodding for an answer. No longer any pretense to hide behind, Ryker stood to veil his nervousness before answering her. "Oh, this?" He held it out in front, trying to distance himself from it. "Well, it's a small gift for Julia. That's the name we'd decided upon, right? I like the name. It's a nice, elegant name. See, it's a good thing she's a girl or we might not have a name for her. We never did agree on a boy's name."

Monica glowered at Ryker's feeble attempt to avoid the obvious. "Yes, dear, but the question is, where'd you get this gift?"

Ryker set the bag on the bed beside the child. The act had no effect on Monica's unwavering, questioning glare. Realizing there was no avoiding the inquiry, he smiled as diplomatically as possible and rationalized his actions. "This child is just as special as Erica, and she received a gift to welcome her into this world. Why shouldn't Julia be just as blessed with a special gift?"

The frown only deepened into concern. "How could you even compare the two? When Erica was born almost four years ago, things were different for us. The NMA wasn't as hot on your trail. Last time you showed yourself in public, they almost cornered you. I think it's a little thoughtless of you to put yourself in that kind of danger just for a silly little gift."

Ryker sheepishly lowered his head. He didn't try arguing with Monica's logic. "You're right. I'll try not to do it again." He lifted his head with a fragile smile and continued, "Open it. I think you'll approve."

Monica struggled to hold her stern look as she reached for the gift. "I'll forgive you this time, but I don't want to have this conversation again." Cautiously taking the bag, she peeked in. Her face softened with a small, bow smile, erasing signs of disapproval shown moments earlier. Pulling an item from the bag evoked a soft coo. "Oh, it's so adorable. Where'd you find something like this?"

She held a small, stuffed teddy bear with his closed eyes and hands folded in front. His little t-shirt read, "Prayer Bear." Pleased with her reaction, Ryker smiled. He managed to shed some of Monica's probing concerns. He fashioned a grin that reflected his pride. "A little antique shop I once visited with Mogie. I had a feeling it might have something no other place would. It turns out I was correct"

Monica fondled the bear and admired it until she remembered how her husband obtained the unique gift. Again the smile slipped from her face. "I just wish you wouldn't take these unnecessary chances."

On cue, Julia awoke, yelling at the top of her lungs. Monica slyly shifted her focus from the baby to Ryker. "See, even Julia's upset with her daddy's careless adventure."

Ryker raised his hands up in defeat. "Yes, yes. I get the message. Listen, as you take care of Julia, I've got an errand to run. I'll be back in a bit."

As he moved to the door, Monica noticed his limp. "They got closer this time, didn't they?"

Leaving the room, Ryker replied before it closed. "Don't worry. I'm not going anywhere like that again." He closed the door to hurry away before he could hear a reply.

Walking from the medical facility, Ryker entered a large cavern that served as a hub for other passages leading to numerous establishments and residences. Passing one of many alcoves, Ryker stuck his head in for a quick inspection. In the small room was a custom-made teleport that he had left only minutes earlier. The crude-looking unit held many more controls then any found in public.

Ryker smiled at the occupant and said, "Sorry I rushed off, Ryan, but my wife was in labor, or so I thought."

The man was about twelve years older than Ryker. Ryan McDougal served as one of several technicians helping to keep the community running. Ryan was probably the best they had. He was a small but powerful-looking man. His craggy face deceived many who first met him, which led them to conclude that Ryan was a sour, distant man. Ryker found the opposite to be true. When Ryan smiled, all the lines on his face smiled with him.

"Hey buddy, I understand. I'm just glad you made it back," Ryan said as he extended his right hand for a friendly handshake. His hand was wide with short, stubby fingers. Ryker had once wondered how Ryan could do such delicate work with them, but that was years ago; he no longer wondered. He knows now that they are just very deceiving.

Accepting the offered hand with zeal, Ryker praised Ryan's abilities. "It was perfect timing, Ryan. I'm so glad you stuck around and kept with the precise timing. If you hadn't, I probably would be experiencing Buck's, and who-knows-who-else's abuse right now. Thanks again."

Ryan released the handshake and also some of the smile. "I'm glad you appreciate it, but if you hadn't made it back, my butt would be in a rut for allowing you to go on an unscheduled transport."

Ryan's feeble attempt to chastise Ryker fell on deaf ears. "Yes, you're right, but you'd do it again if I asked, so thanks. I'll fill you in on the details later. I'm late for an appointment. Pat was expecting me at nine."

Ryan saluted to rush Ryker off. "Pat! You'd better move your buns. It's 9:07 right now, and Pat doesn't appreciate tardiness."

With that send-off, Ryker continued his journey.

First right then left, right, right, left, right; light, dark, dim, dark, light, very bright, dim; traveling through the underground establishment brought back memories of his early years walking the passages.

Five years ago it'd have taken me two hours to figure out where it was I'd started. Then I didn't know where I started and now I can travel these halls with my eyes closed. Life's like that sometimes. Lord, I'm beginning to understand Your ways a little better. Six years ago, if someone had told me I'd be teaching others about living a Christian life, I would've told them they'd left their keyboard out in the rain.

Ryker reached an elevator, clambered in, and hit the only button. When the contraption rattled to the top, the door opened and sunlight invaded the interior. Stepping out of what once was a closet, Ryker walked around the corner into a larger room of the log cabin. Rustic trinkets and hunting paraphernalia decorated the room. In the center, piled with papers and other office equipment, sat a desk.

Behind the desk, a distressed-looking young woman blew air through her lips while brushing back a lock of loose hair that fell in front of her lovely green eyes. The red hair stubbornly fell back in place but the lady ignored it. "It's about time you got here. I'd run out of excuses for you. He knows Monica gave birth over an hour ago so he's still been expecting you to keep this appointment. Go right in. He's waiting for you."

Ryker smiled at the woman's sudden relief at his appearance. "Thanks Barb. I owe you another one. Now relax and see to some of that paperwork."

His reward was a smile and a commanding finger pointing to Pat's office. A polite rap on the door got Ryker a simple bidding.

"Come in."

As he opened the door, sunlight almost blinded him. The room faced the morning sun, allowing it to flood the room through a large, arching window. Shadowed in the bright light were a desk and a large form that almost dwarfed the mahogany. A deep, slow voice addressed him. "Ryker, take a seat and I'll be right with you."

After the invitation, the framework rose mountainously from the desk, turned to the window, and pulled a translucent shade reducing the light by half. Ryker sat down and watched as the man resettled in his chair.

Pat Filmore was a large man. "Six-foot-seven and two hundred ninety pounds of "marshmallow" some of his closer friends would say. Marshmallow, as in gentle attitude, not physical frame. Pat could've been a wrestler or a warrior, but his heart led more to a babysitter. Because of his white hair, many people initially mistook him to be older than he was, but Ryker knew he was only seven years older than he.

Pat broke Ryker's train of thought. "I like the feel of the sun as it beats on my back. I won't let it blind you though. How come you're so late?" The question ignited a spark in Pat's lively, blue eyes.

Ryker sensed immediately that Pat knew the answer but was fishing for reality in his leaders. Ryker fell for the ploy only one time. It happened the first time the big man interviewed Ryker. With that knowledge, Ryker grinned at his friend across the desk before replying, "Well sir, I've been right where you know I've been. Already three people have chewed me out for it, but I guess I'd like your version of it."

Pat openly chuckled, reminding Ryker of Uncle Vernon years earlier. Pat's countenance took a 180-degree turn. With stern composure, he reprimanded Ryker. "You're a prize. You learn quickly. So I'm assuming my lecture for your behavior is understood without my going through the motions. Do I need say any more?"

Ryker's smile dissipated as the piercing glare of Pat's blue eyes punctuated his sincerity. After five seconds of staring to drive home the point, Pat reached for a pair of reading glasses on his desk. The smile returned upon the placement of them. The grin remained as he focused on papers in front of him. "Now, Ryker, let's get to why I set up this appointment in the first place."

Ryker soberly sat facing Pat. Without marshmallow icing, the man was extremely intimidating. Pat had forgotten Ryker's transgression and wouldn't mention it again unless Ryker brought it up.

As Pat continued, Ryker regained his previous composure. "I've been getting some good reports on you the last seven or eight months.

As a matter of fact, I placed you in for a promotion at the Upper Room Division."

Ryker simply blinked. Pat chuckled again with a big, toothy grin. "You're more fun than a room full of ferrets. You surprise so easily, and at the same time you're a surprise yourself. Yes, you've done well enough to warrant recognition."

Bewildered, Ryker's countenance slowly changed from confusion to satisfaction as he said, "Thanks for the recognition and recommendation, but I'm sure you'll be putting up with me for years to come."

Pat stood and turned to face the window. The act was amazing to watch. The man seemed to stretch up endlessly when he did it slowly. He had learned long ago that it had an effect on people, so he used it to his advantage. Turning back to face Ryker, the bright sun shadowed his face, making his smile all teeth and eyes. "That's where you're wrong, my little friend. The Upper Room would like to have you. They would appreciate an answer by the end of August. Someone seems very interested in you, and that's all I know. I guess you'll know when you get there."

Blank. No emotion or readable reaction for a good fifteen seconds. If Monica had been there, she would have nudged him to release the dumbfounded expression. The big man watched Ryker's mind work and smiled at the process. Pat stood in front of the window, shaking with held-in laughter. He was enjoying one of the few pleasures of handling such a large, underground community of believers. Seeing God at work in the young man's life thrilled Pat. It was what he lived and worked so hard for.

Ryker wasn't prepared to share Pat's enthusiasm. "I'm not sure I'm ready to go anywhere just yet."

The gentle man came around the desk to face Ryker. Pat squatted to demonstrate his intention of being on Ryker's level. Once again, the act reminded Ryker of Uncle Vernon. The gesture helped, but Ryker still needed to look up some to focus on Pat's face. Pat reminded Ryker of a large, fluffy teddy bear. "Ryker, listen. I know this is much to digest on the spot. I want you to think and pray about it for a few days until God has a chance to confirm what your response should be."

Relaxing, Ryker smiled forcibly. "Sure. That's a good idea. Thanks for understanding my hesitation and for having faith enough in me to recommend me."

Pat stood and offered his large hand for a handshake. Ryker fallowed, looking up at Pat's Adams apple, and accepted the gesture. "I'll let you know, Pat."

Leaving the office, Ryker was still in a state of shock. He knew no one who had made it to the Upper Room, say nothing of expecting to be someone.

Barb noticed the vacant look and out of curiosity questioned, "It couldn't have been that bad, could it?"

Ryker snapped out of his daze, realizing someone had spoken, and gave Barb a neutral look. "Oh, no, not at all. I just can't believe what Pat just told me. I'm too young for a commendation like that."

Barb smiled. "I think it's pretty neat. You deserve it. I've learned more from you these last two-and-a-half years than in the eight years previous." The smile softened. "I'll miss you, but you'll do even more good where you're going."

It didn't surprise Ryker that Barb knew of the conversation with her boss. She knew everything Pat had to deal with. "Thanks, Barb, but I haven't accepted the offer yet."

She managed to put the lock of hair where it belonged (it stayed this time) as her green eyes smiled at him. "You will. I remember well one of your first teachings on obedience. One thing I've learned over the last few years is that you practice what you teach."

That was the first sign Ryker considered to be direction in how he should react to Pat's news.

Infiltrated

Dastardly Doug Dillon cautiously stepped around the corner of the weather-beaten saloon. The wide rim of his black cowboy hat obscured his eyes. His right hand poised nervously within an inch of his Colt six-shooter strapped low on his right leg. Down the dusty street, women, children, and most men ran for cover in the Old West town. Tumbleweed rolled across the dirt highway. From the other end of the street, a small, white figure grew in size as he came into view. It was another cowboy dressed in white and wearing a large sheriff star. The scene quickly changed. Dastardly Doug stood on the left; Sheriff Goodman on the right. The backdrop of the old western town loomed behind them. The cowboys faced each other in a showdown. Suddenly, a three-year-old girl ran and stood in front of the sheriff, concealing a full view of him. The child impishly laughed and danced around in circles.

"Hey! I can't see. Erica, move!"

Dastardly Doug, like lightning, drew and fired upon Sheriff Goodman. The sheriff vanished.

"Just a minute! That wasn't fair. I couldn't see my man because Erica distracted me." Ryan McDougal looked comical as he swung his arms wildly in frustration. Thoughtlessly brushing hair back from his eyes causing it to stick up in places only added to the comedy. The serious look in his eyes and the relaxed line of his mouth caused Ryker to laugh robustly. "Take it easy, Ryan. Remember, it's only a game."

Reality came back to the little Irishman and so did his smile. "I think you trained her to do that. It's effective either way. You won another one."

The small home was busy. Monica came home earlier with the new addition to the family. Laura was around to help while friends came to take a peek at the newest member of the Cuff family.

Ryan had challenged Ryker to a game of "Old West Shoot-Out" on the life-size screen of the Intertell. The community used the system to communicate and view training classes, but Ryker and Ryan used it for home entertainment. Teleports usually served the same purposes, but in order to protect from any outside invasion, there were only two teleports on the premises. Technicians monitored both around the clock.

Ryan glanced around the room. "I'll come over some time when things aren't so busy and then I'll whoop ya."

"OK, but if you can't do any better than that, I'm not sure I want you handling my delicate transports."

"You'd be doing me a favor. I only get myself into trouble with you anyway."

The two friends playfully batted at one another and then went their own way to talk to others.

Laura successfully diverted most people from Monica by handling Julia and drawing a crowd away from her.

Ryker's sister, Joanne, kept her sister-in-law company. "There're more people here tonight than I expected to see. I didn't know you and Ryker had so many close friends."

Monica smiled as she set down the glass of tea. With a gleam in her eye, she gave her one word reply. "Curiosity."

Joanne scowled. The young woman had the Cuff features. She resembled her father more than either of the sons. "Haven't these people ever seen a baby before?"

Monica laughed and reached over to touch Joanne's arm. "Probably they have, but no one's talked to someone who's been asked to serve at the Upper Room." Joanne smiled, nodding her head in acknowledgment.

Monica wanted to change the subject. When the two of them got together it was customary to fill each other in on how things were going. "You've been here for a couple of weeks now. Tell me what you think of it."

Joanne set her refreshments down. "I'm getting along fine. I didn't think I'd like it very much, but I was wrong. I'm glad Mom and Dad talked me into it. I've learned so much about what it means to be a true follower of Jesus, and the lifestyle's easier than I had envisioned. It's kind of rough and crude, but it seems to bring people closer together in helping each other. Speaking of Mom and Dad, they send their love. Ever since Ryker led us to the Lord three years ago, things have really been different in that home. Sarah was already gone and Ray left shortly after that. Dad wanted me to tell Ryker he wants his home to be used for the underground system. He and Mom figure they'd be of more use like that than to come here. Did you hear about Aunt Joan? Wait until you hear this. Last January she took Cindy. . ." Monica smiled as she lifted her glass to her lips. Joanne hadn't changed much and she was enjoying the news.

Many people milled around the small, rustic but efficient apartment. None of the accommodations on the compound were very elaborate. The best equipped buildings were the medical facility and the command post where Pat Filmore worked. The command post was also the most pleasant, being the only place above ground. Most people questioned Ryker about his new job. Mainly he repeated that he hadn't yet accepted anything.

Just then, Ryker spotted someone familiar. The man had his back turned to Ryker and was filling up a small plate at the refreshments table. It was his short, dark brown crew cut, round head, and oversized ears protruding outward that captured Ryker's attention. Ryker questioned him. "Scott?" As the man turned, Ryker smiled. "Scott Kidder! What're you doing here?"

Ryker initiated a handshake. Scott beamed at the fact that Ryker had recognized him. He had a wide mouth that curled at the ends naturally. It was a little unsettling to most people because he seemed to grin with self-satisfaction. He was quirky, so his turtleneck in July passed as normal for him.

Scott handled his role as an undercover agent well. "Ryker, it's good to see you again. I just got here this morning. I heard you were having some friends over and figured you wouldn't mind if I dropped in uninvited."

Ryker answered politely, "No, not at all. I'm glad you felt you could. What brings you here?"

Scott's gray eyes were lifeless, which contrasted the energy on the rest of his features. "I was thinking of coming here for training and thought I'd stop by to check the place out. Maybe you'll see much more of me soon."

Ryker felt so off-balance, but managed not to react badly. A thought occurred to him as Scott spoke.

Funny. I never heard of someone coming to Jordan without staying. It takes long enough to get through the system just to begin a stay. I can't imagine the extended process for just a short visit. Mom and Dad went through days just to visit me last year.

Sparkling, green eyes locked onto gray, cold orbs. Scott internally fidgeted. Ryker felt it more than he could see it. "Maybe I'll see more of you, Scott. Tell me how things are going with the others from the Bible study group."

As Scott talked, Ryker led him over to a quiet corner where they could sit and visit. Scott relaxed, revealing a full-mouth smile. For twenty minutes, the two conversed about things past and present. Much of what Scott relayed was fabricated. One time during their conversation, Ryker wondered about a statement. Calmly he accepted everything at face value and cautiously gave only information not sensitive to his situation.

Scott became eager to excuse himself when Ryker seemed evasive. "Well, Ryker, it's been good to see ya after all these years. I need to get up early in the morning, so I guess I'll get going. One last thing. Did you manage to save that book and get it here?"

The thick, brown beard Ryker had grown hid well the gulp he swallowed at the question. Unruffled, he drew a frown upon his face and answered with genuine puzzlement. "What book are you talking about?"

Scott's wide mouth created a long, thin line across his face. "You know, that Bible you almost got in so much trouble over."

Pressing on with concern, Ryker punctuated each word as he responded. "Only Dennis knew anything about that. How'd you know about it?"

Cornered! Like a fly buzzing against a windowpane. Scott vocally danced around with a few incomprehensible noises until his mind worked fast enough to fabricate a reasonable response. The answer came and bought him enough time for his getaway. "I confess I overheard you and Dennis discussing it that first night you came to Bible study." With that, the conversation ended except for goodbyes.

Initially it made sense, so Ryker backed off, but a short time later he recounted the event. Scott seemed to have a lot more facts about the Bible than Ryker had shared with Dennis that night.

Scott disappeared from the compound. When Pat heard Ryker's report on the matter, he made arrangements to broadcast Scott's description and other statistics throughout the network. Scott's double agent days were over. Scott had gathered little information, and he was on the run. No one had transported out for hours, so a search party formed to canvass the surrounding wilderness. The next morning Dale Robins, the community's head security officer, found Scott's body at the bottom of a cliff about ten minutes south of the compound. Searching his clothes, they found an NMA ID badge with the name Ralph Fields. Apparently, in fear of being captured, he had run in the general direction of the nearest civilization. Not knowing exactly where he was and traveling in the dark, Scott/Ralph fell prey to his ignorance and fear and tumbled over the cliff.

A special time of praise was set aside to celebrate God's protection of the Jordan facility. That year the fourth of July was truly a day of freedom for them. Ryker, very reluctantly, let himself be recognized for his part in it. He agreed to it only when a memorial service was performed for Ralph Fields. Both events happened as planned.

The Nest

Washington NMA was quieter than usual. Three-quarters of the personnel didn't come to work. It wasn't a scheduled day off, as the day before, but had become an unwritten policy that the day after the most celebrated day of the year was for recuperating. Celebrating the birth of freedom in the USA had developed into an art of debauchery. Many people were sick or had just gotten to bed.

Buck trudged with exertion down the plush, carpeted hall. Lightning flashed through the glass outside exterior. The city skyline was momentarily illuminated. Buck covered his eyes. He was beginning to wonder why he had come to work when hardly anyone else would be around. His head throbbed, keeping rhythm with the pounding rain on the glass roof overhead.

Entering his office, he placed a briefcase on the desk and made a request. "Servant, lights 30 percent." The lights dimmed. Buck's long, black ponytail dripped with water. Thinking the cool water would help clear his head, he chose to use the corner teleport and walk into the building. His brown, yellow-trimmed jumpsuit shed water, creating a dark spot on the plush, green carpet. Another flash of lightning, followed by the clap of thunder, illuminated the window over the desk facing the hall. Buck sat down and cradled his head.

The desk also served as a communication station. A monitor and several control panels occupied half of the space. Numerous LEDs flickered with information. One rapidly blinking orange one captured Buck's attention. Lifting his head, bright blue eyes widened at the signal. He vocalized his thoughts in wonderment. "This must be a message from Ralph. It has to be important for him to burn up the power supply to his com implants."

Ralph chose to leave a short message using his implant power source to push the signal all the way back to the Nest. It was the only communication device he had. The units worked well for short-distance communications between agents, but they were also for emergency use. Surgical replacement of the power cells made this method difficult, so was done only in extreme cases.

Buck touched the control, activating the message. "Al, this is Ralph Fields. It's nine-thirty p.m., Tuesday, July fourth. I managed to infiltrate the cult's compound. It went just as we had planned months ago." His voice was labored as he continued, "I found Ryker easily enough, but I'm afraid he suspects me. I didn't get much information. Only one of the two we were hoping for. I didn't dare leave by teleport. I think they may be looking for me. I'll fill you in on what little I do know when I get back. That's why I'm leaving you this message. It may be a few days before I find a teleport. I'll tell you one thing before I sign off.

The compound is located—AAAAAAAAAAAAAAAAaaaaaaaaaaaa." The message ended with Ralph's scream as he fell off the cliff.

Buck stared at the console, waiting for Ralph to recover. Without so much as a thought of remorse for Ralph, Buck slammed both fists down upon the desk in a swearing rage. "That Ryker is the luckiest fink in the world. What can I possibly do to get a hold of that—" After several minutes of fussing and fuming over his misfortune, an evil, "Grinch-like" smile spread across his face.

A Challenge

"My goodness! What's he up to now?"

Laughter, questioning remarks, and whispers filled the room that served as a lecture hall. There were some charts and posters on the wall, thirty desks occupied by people from all walks of life, and a lectern set in front of an old white board. It was Ryker's third and final class of the week. One of his jobs was teaching adults one hour a day, three days a week. His other duties involved giving technical assistance to those who kept the Jordan facility operating. Most of his classes were filled to capacity, most likely due to the current chaos and turmoil.

With calm and deliberate action, Ryker walked to the front of the room to face his students. He spoke not a word initially as he evaluated the reaction to his entrance, then he began with a simple question: "I'm ready for class this morning. Are you?" This announcement came from a man wearing only swimming trunks. No one said anything for a good minute.

Calvin Katang grinned from ear to ear. He had seen Ryker do a few interesting things during his year at Jordan, but this surpassed them all. "I'll bite, Teach. How can you say you're ready for class when you're wearing that skimpy outfit?"

Ryker feigned a look of surprise. "I'm not ready for class? How can you tell?"

Most people knew how Ryker operated and recognized that class had begun. Helen was a grandmother, but she was also eager to learn. She often was the first to comment. She raised her hand, and Ryker nodded at her to respond. With a smirk she said, "We can tell because of what you're NOT wearing."

Once things began, there was much interaction between the leader and the students. "What does Helen mean by that? What am I missing?"

"Pants." Laughter filled the room. More answers followed.

"Shirt."

"Shoes."

"Depending on who you may be meeting, you might want to wear a tie."

"In the winter, you'd need a coat, gloves, and a hat."

Some strange ideas came his way, so Ryker acted to put the people back on track. "How about spiritually? What do I need to wear?" It became quiet as people thought. This was going somewhere, and they wanted to make the connection.

Everett Myron sat to the back of the room, calmly waiting for answers. Everett had attended classes for years. The man was tall but thin, with short, light brown hair and hazel eyes. Many years earlier, a stunner shot, taken point blank to his neck, had disabled him. The SS agent responsible lost his job, but Everett paid by requiring a cane to get around. Told he would never walk again, he had made it a point to prove them wrong. Ryker learned early that Everett could answer tough questions when no one else had a clue. The reserved man graciously gave others the first opportunity, but when they couldn't deliver, he would effectively prompt them with a simple answer or question.

Ryker rewarded Everett with a nod to go ahead. "Does it say something somewhere in the New Testament about wearing the armor of God?"

Ryker smiled as others' faces lit up or hands were raised. "Good question, Everett. How about it, Mary Ellen? You look like you have an idea."

The women dropped her hand, but kept her wide smile. "I think it's in Paul's letter to the Ephesians. God doesn't ask us to fight His battles without offering us the tools, or in this case, the clothes to wear."

Ryker casually affirmed the answer. "Very good. You're right. Normally I wouldn't dream of going anywhere in public dressed like this. But did you know many Christians walk into the world every day and forget to put on the armor of God before they go? This morning we're going to look at the sixth chapter of Ephesians to determine what spiritual clothes we should wear. Christians are more foolish going without this armor than I am this morning without my clothes. Let's take a moment for prayer, and then we'll begin."

As the morning progressed, Ryker put on an article of clothing to correspond to each piece of armor mentioned in the Bible passage. Lively discussion surrounded the meanings Paul had outlined, and before they were ready, time was up.

Ryker drew things to a conclusion. He stood before the class, straightened his clothes, and tucked in loose ends. "Now I'm ready for class. Would you agree this is better than when I came in earlier?"

There were some smart remarks, but all agreed to the point. "Good. Now go and don't forget—" Ryker scanned the room encouraging a response. Helen took up the challenge. ". . . to put on the armor of God."

Ryker smiled and pointed to the door. "Correct. We're funny-looking, ineffective, and powerless Christians without it. You may leave, but go prepared."

Hubbub dominated the room. People gathered papers and handwritten notebooks of the Bible. As students filed out of the room, Joanne approached her brother. "Do you always do something this wild?"

Ryker wondered if she felt embarrassed. He smiled and consoled her, "Don't worry, Sis. That's the most eccentric thing I've tried—so far. I like getting attention and involvement on the subject as soon as possible."

Joanne smiled, holding her papers to her chest. "You certainly got their attention this morning. I believe no one else but you could have gotten away with that." Then she asked, "What time would you like me to show up tonight? Erica must be excited."

Ryker collected his materials as he replied, "About five o' clock is when we plan on eating. It's hard to believe she's four years old already. Erica just can't wait for the party tonight. She asked if you'd be there. So you'd better show up."

The two stepped out in the hall and parted ways. "I'll be there. See ya later."

Ryker watched for a few seconds as she walked away, then he left to help Ryan McDougal.

The noise coming from Ryker's and Monica's apartment suggested a festive family gathering. The cake, with candles blown out, sat waiting for Monica to cut. The birthday girl was compelled to convey her wishes. "I want a corner piece. I want a corner piece. I want a corner piece . . ."

The four-year-old was wearing a pointed, cone-shaped birthday hat. Next to her were three other children sporting different colored hats. Two were older boys, ages seven and nine. Another girl, age three, crowded between them.

Erica's brilliant, blue eyes danced with excitement. She turned her attention to her father. "Daddy, I want a corner piece." Talking to Nancy, Ryan's wife, Erica's plea garnered his attention. "Yes, sweetheart, you can have a corner piece."

Erica beamed, bouncing up and down in her seat. It was a small party with only two other couples and Joanne. Lee and Kathy Pike were the other couple present. Lee was one of the community's security personnel. The evening was going well until the Intertell signaled. Ryker nonchalantly attended to it while the others watched the birthday girl open her gifts.

Contentment with the evening's activities evaporated when Ryker saw Pat looking at him nervously. "Hi, Ryker. I'm sorry to interrupt your family festivities, but I've some important information. Along with it, I'm looking for some direction on how to handle it. It's my understanding that you have Ryan McDougal and Lee Pike there with you. Could the three of you meet Dale Robins and me in my office in . . . say, about ten minutes?"

Ryker stood staring at the Intertell, digesting Pat's inflections and question. He answered only as he could. "Sure thing, Pat." He looked at his watch. "We'll see ya about six-thirty."

Pat smiled and settled back into his chair, relaxing. "Thanks. See ya then." The screen went black.

Noticing how quiet it was, Ryker turned to see all the adults looking at him. "I guess you all heard that. We'd better go see what Pat has in store for us."

Monica watched with concern as the three men left. The other women returned to their previous conversations and attended to the birthday girl.

No one tended the outer office after regular hours, so Ryan, Ryker, and Lee knew to walk straight into Pat's office. The trio greeted Pat as he directed them to sit at the conference table. Seated already were Dale Robins and another man. The stranger was a little guy with short, black, curly hair peppered with white, a sure sign of his age. His large, steel-gray eyes grabbed attention as did a gracious smile on his dark brown skin.

Pat joined everyone by sitting at the head of the table next to the stranger. The two men made an interesting pair, to say the least. One was tall; the other, short. One was black; the other, white. One was young; the other, a man of experience and age. Pat wasted no time introducing everyone. Calling the name of each of his men, he finished by politely acknowledging the guest. "I'm proud to introduce each of you to Ted Burnap. Ted's been with the Network almost since its inception." Pat continued with more of Ted's credentials but Ryker's memory kept him from listening.

Ted Burnap? I've heard that name somewhere. It seems I've read it before. I don't think I've ever seen the man, but that name sure sounds familiar.

Ted thanked Pat for his generous introduction then continued with further explanation. "I'm an undercover Christian for the Network. I know there are some who have a problem with that concept, but I've done nothing but good for our cause. My title to the rest of the world is an NMA Statistics Officer. As you might imagine, that's a handy place to be for gathering important information."

Ryker snapped to attention picking his head up several inches. "That's it!"

Everyone looked at him. He settled back in his chair sheepishly and explained, "I know where I've seen your name before, Ted. You've an office on Elm Street back in Potsdam, New York."

Ted smiled at Ryker's slight moment of embarrassment. His large, white teeth gleamed, enhancing his friendly expression. "That happens to be where I first came across your name, Ryker." Ted looked to others as he spoke. "Agent Fields had come into my office to report a find. My ears picked up when he mentioned an original Bible that Ryker owns." Ted turned to face Ryker directly. "I've kept tabs on you ever since."

It was quiet for a moment. Ryker pondered how people had been interwoven in his life throughout his adult years. Noticing the silence, he looked around to see all eyes on him. "Hey, lighten up. I don't know what's going on."

Pat piped in to give Ryker a hand. "That's correct, but it does involve Ryker, in a way. Ted came here for our help." His concern was evident as Pat focused on Ryker. "I'm sorry to report that all the members of your former Bible study group have been arrested. They were taken directly from their meeting last Wednesday evening."

Lee's sense of investigation prompted him to respond. "How'd they know where to find them?"

Dale Robins scowled. His long face contributed to the unbecoming appearance. His short, dark hair and dark eyes added to the deception. "Remember Scott Kidder—or Ralph Fields—whatever his name is? He was part of that group. The NMA knew exactly where to find them . . ." A stern look washed across Dale's face as he continued, ". . . anytime they wanted to."

Ryker stared off into the distance with a glassy-eyed expression. His mouth formed a long, thin line while he slightly nodded an acknowledgment to the statement.

Ryan pushed his chair back on two legs as he leaned against a wall. His arms were crossed, indicating his mental posture. "That's too bad for those people, but what're we going to do about it?"

What happened next gave Ted Burnap his first sign of hope in return for the risk of coming to Jordan. Ryker, with very little forethought, reacted to the question calmly and with resolve: "We'll go get them out."

The chair slammed forward on all four legs. Ryan scowled, as Lee cocked an eyebrow and allowed the corner of his mouth to follow it. Dale retorted, "You have to be nuts! Few Christians who have been in that place have ever walked out freely. Most times, they're never seen again!"

Pat raised his hand to stop any other outbursts. "I believe we ought to take time out to pray about this."

No one argued. Pat started by focusing on God's ability and promise to help them choose the right course of action. After everyone had prayed, the team then focused on tackling the challenge before them.

Ted wanted everyone to understand why he was there. "I apologize for bringing this problem before you. But after reaching the Network and explaining the arrest of the small group of believers, things became kind of strange. They told me there was nothing they could do, that all their available people were tied up on special assignments, and there was no legal recourse to be taken. Legally, the NMA can do just about anything to stop the criminal act of Ryker's friends. Instead of leaving me with no recourse, my contact told me to try getting hold of you, Ryker. That's why I'm here."

The silence became deafening. After a minute, Ryker let his feeling be made known. "I know these people are virtually unknown to you, but I know they're unique. If it weren't for this group of believers, I wouldn't be here today. I can't help but feel a strong need to help my friends. Monica's told me how they treat Christians in that place. I can't stand the thought of just sitting back, waiting, and doing nothing. But I do understand if you others don't want to get involved."

When no one else spoke up, Lee decided to comment. "I don't know about the rest of you guys, but I don't have any qualms about doing something. I just haven't the slightest idea what."

Ryan nodded affirmative to the statement. Dale followed suit while Ted simply held his hands up in the air, palms up at shoulder height. "I just brought the problem. Excuse me for not having a plan."

Pat glanced at the clock on the wall above Ryan's head. "We'll think of something. We're going to have some more help any minute now." No one questioned him. It wouldn't have done any good, because Pat was known to let his plans unfold on their own.

After a short time, a very basic plan began to develop. During a disagreement, the office door opened. Faces turned to observe who had interrupted. Everett Myron came in with the help of his cane. Pat stood up, drew another chair to the table, and told Everett to have a seat.

Ryker smiled at Pat. "If this is our extra help, I'm excited." He turned to face Everett. "Another new gadget, Everett?"

Pat intercepted the question and reprimanded Ryker with a smile. "Hang on, Ryker. We'll get to it in a moment." Next, he introduced Everett to Ted and briefly explained what had taken place so far. "I was thinking, Ev, that your latest project might prove to be of interest to this group. That's why I called you up. Would you mind telling us what you've been working on?"

As a man of solitude, Everett was slightly nervous in the setting. When he began, his eyes half closed, giving him a sleepy look. In forming his sentences, his eyes would first droop and then open wider as he continued. "Well, it's nothing special. A project I'd begun years ago came to my attention last month when I was cleaning out my desk. Back when I was an electronic engineer for Teletron Incorporated, I worked on a personnel-tracking device. Teletron had a contract with the NMA to come up with an implant for all U.S. citizens that'd be used to track anyone called up on a computer. The NMA wanted the ability to pinpoint any one person they wished, any time they wished it. The total plan never culminated for two reasons: (1) There were still some legal issues that needed to be worked out; and (2) I was the sole engineer on the project, with total information on the design. And before I'd completed it, I had my crippling encounter with an SS agent. I disappeared after my recovery. That's when I came here. They're still looking for me."

Everyone leaned forward, waiting for Everett to continue. When it seemed he might not, Ted prodded him. "Have you developed this tracking device?"

The eyelids drooped just before Everett answered, "Not according to the original plan. With my new devices I can track anyone, up to six people at a time, anywhere in the United States. On a terminal, numbered blue lights on an overlay of a map can be followed. Without a detailed map of the area, you've no real information. But what I've learned to do is to have the signal change when someone's standing on a teleport pad. The point on the screen will change to red and a short report on the teleport reads out below it. The information includes the teleport code number so you can activate it."

Ryker was all smiles, but before he could jubilantly proclaim the value of Everett's invention, Ryan quizzed him. "Have you tested this thing to make sure it works?"

Everett's eyes drooped as he answered, "Yes, I've done preliminary testing, and it seems to work just fine. I've yet given it a good field test though."

Ryker got the opportunity to say his piece. "I think this is an answer to our prayers. All we need to do is figure a way to lead our people to a teleport, and Ryan can zap us home."

There was silence for another minute except the noise of chairs as people fidgeted in them. Pat then summed up the discussion to that point. As the next few hours passed, consensus was reached among the group to devise a plan to free the Christians who were taken the previous Wednesday night.

Worried

"I don't like it."

She sashayed away from the kitchen table, rocking a fussy Julia in her arms. Monica had refused to discuss the subject when Ryker came home late the night before and announced what he was going to do. He had diplomatically brought the subject up again at the breakfast table. Ryker watched Monica move to the sink with the pretense of work to ignore him.

As he contemplated his dilemma, Ryker focused heavily on a picture in the living room. He jumped when Monica suddenly appeared in front of him. Her blue eyes danced with emotion. She had tried to bottle it up, but the effervescence of anxiety finally won out. "You aren't some superman, you know. You're not going to fix the whole world by yourself."

"Of course not. I have Ryan, Lee, and Dale to help me."

She recoiled momentarily, then suddenly returned. "See! All you can do is joke about it."

"I'm not joking around. It's just that I don't know what to tell you. Do you want me to leave all our old friends in the hands of the NMA?"

"No. But must you go? Are there not others who can do better what you're attempting to do?"

"Probably. There may be many but I was one of the ones asked. I believe it's something God wants me to do."

It was out now, and both had an opportunity to say what was on their hearts. With frustration alleviated somewhat, the two calmly discussed their options and prayed together about the outcome. Monica reluctantly gave her blessing and didn't mention her concerns again.

The Nest Visited

It was a beautiful, sunny, midsummer morning. There was very little activity in the main lobby of the huge government complex. The burnished sunlight flooded the large area, making all the glass and chrome sparkle in contrast to the rich, dark woods of the desk and other furniture. Pictures and plaques hung all around the room. Scattered about were several live plants. The ceiling was high—at least two stories, if not more. Hanging high over the large reception counter was the emblem picturing the organization's purpose. Depicted was a morning sun in the background, rising over a cross lying on the ground. The cross lay broken on the earth, with grass and vines growing around it. Audaciously sitting on the cross, taking up most of the image was the ornate letters, NMA.

From the lobby's main teleport walked two figures, both dressed in uniforms of high-ranking government officials. Black jumpsuits with red trim and a tan hat of the same colors augmented Lee's and Dale's disciplined approach. As they reached the desk, Dale searched his pocket for a disk. "Good morning. I'm Ambrose Brundge, Chief Administrator for the Miami facility, and this is my assistant, John Knickerbocker. We've special orders to transport some of your RCs to our facility in Florida. It seems someone has special requirements for them." Dale smiled with the last sentence, giving an impression of pleasure in his task. Finally, he managed to produce the disk.

The woman at the counter remained stoic. A colorful, periwinkle badge on the left shoulder of her dark blue outfit indicated that she was the shift's chief of security. The name read Brenda Holding. She was a large woman, but not fat. Rather, she seemed very powerful-looking. Her short, blonde hair barely covered her ears. The dark blue eyes looked down at the disk Dale elevated to her attention. Calmly pinching the information, she dropped it into the reader in front of her. Reflected light from the monitor flashed repeatedly across Brenda's face as she studied the information.

Waiting was too much for Lee. He took a moment to look around. As he turned his back to the woman, he scanned the large foyer noticing no one else in the place. He closed his eyes and mouthed a quick prayer. He snapped back to attention and faced the desk when Brenda addressed them. "Everything seems to be in order. It's a little unusual, though, that I wasn't informed of your visit ahead of time."

Dale didn't hesitate to react to the statement. "It's a procedure not used very often. Transfer sequence fifty-three might be familiar to you. Whoever's waiting for these people didn't want to take a chance of many people knowing the details."

Satisfied, Brenda returned the disk to Dale, then gave some instructions. "You'll find your people at Base Levels Two and Three. You may take all but Nick Richards. He's not available at this time. Bring the prisoners back here for transportation. There'll be two SS agents to greet you at Level One. One of them will escort you to the next levels. Enter the door on my left at the end of the counter."

She touched a sensor on the desk releasing the door to partly open. With a small bow of the head, Dale smiled and thanked Brenda. Lee headed for the door when Dale made one more inquire of the security officer. "Is this where the cells are—on Levels Two and Three?" He pointed to a map on the wall to Brenda's right. As she politely went over the directions again, Dale purposely sounded confused. He didn't want to appear as if he had already planned out the visit.

Lee trotted over to the door leading outside and opened it. An SS agent quickly walked in and headed for the opened security door. Behind him, Lee stopped in the doorway to hold it open while waiting for Dale. Seconds later, Dale thanked Brenda and joined Lee as they entered together.

The three figures found themselves in a small room, facing three elevator doors. The first was labeled "Base Levels"; the second, "Upper Levels"; and the third, "Executive." Two of the doors had red lights over them. Only the Base levels had a green light. The SS agent reached over and touched the sensor, releasing the elevator door. It was empty until the trio stepped in.

The ride down was brief, but long enough for a quick sigh of relief. Lee couldn't suppress his pretense any longer. "So far, so good. Everett's forged passes worked for us, but when we pull off this next part, I'll begin to believe we might make it."

The SS agent shook his head affirmative. Dale brought their focus back on track. "It's now or never. You two get ready. Ryker, I hope this works out as you planned."

Reaching the first level, the elevator stopped and opened. The light was dim, almost unnatural. It took a moment to get used to. Stepping out of the elevator helped. As promised, two SS agents stood waiting about twenty feet away, facing the three arrivals. One of them raised a finger and pointed it at Ryker. "Who're you? Brenda said nothing about an SS agent escorting you."

Ryker nonchalantly pulled the stunner off his belt and raised it at the pair. "They call me the sandman. Good night, folks." A micron of a second later, the agents were out of commission. They had hardly hit the floor when Dale and Lee ran over, grabbed the two men, and dragged them into the elevator. Ryker snatched the two stunners and the pass cards from their belts. He then keyed the controls at the door to let it close. Taking one of the small cards, he slid it into a slot. A red light lit over the elevator door. "There. It'll be a while before they find those guys. We'd better get moving."

The hall was lined with doors along both sides. About two hundred feet to the other end was another elevator door with a red light. The three intruders confidently walked for the elevator. Halfway there, they noticed a lounge area on their right. Across from it was a control room with a teleport. This was where the two SS agents worked, and the lounge across the hall was for their pleasure. Lee spoke his thoughts out loud. "I bet all these levels are laid out the same. We'll have to remember this. I guess our intel seems pretty good. Someone at the main office knows their stuff."

Agreeing with him, they all moved for the elevator. Reaching their destination, Ryker took one of the cards and slid it into the slot. As the light indicated go, Dale touched the sensor for the door. They all stepped in, and the door closed. Lee and Ryker both leaned against a wall as Dale faced them. Ryker took his helmet off for eye contact as he spoke. "We're lucky all our people are on two floors. That means we'll go with plan B."

He handed Lee and Dale each one of the stunners confiscated; and to Dale, the other pass card. "You two take Level Two. I'll get off at Level Three. Dale, what cells was that Brenda woman showing you?"

Dale's face reflected the emotion of the other two. His eyes danced with excitement as lines elsewhere developed with the tension of self-control. He was puzzled. "On Level Three were two cells next to each other, just about halfway down the hall. I'd say they were on our left next to the control room. I'm not sure. It didn't look right. Lee and I'll get the three cells on Level Two. They're on the other end, but we'll be OK because we're expected. You be careful, Ryker."

With a nod, Ryker had one last idea before they parted. "A quick prayer and we're off." He bowed his head. The other two followed his lead. "Dear Lord, I ask for Your protection and guidance. Thank You for supplying both. In Jesus' name, Amen."

Ryker's helmet went back on as Dale turned and touched the sensor for the second level. As the elevator made its descent, Lee said what they were all thinking. "Any minute now, they'll discover they've been penetrated. I pray that prayer works."

Dale and Lee

Level Two appeared tantamount to Level One. The Network duo walked casually toward the center of the hall. As they passed each cell door, Lee, under his breath, counted, "2B-18 and 19, 2B-17 and 16, . . . "

Walking closer to the control room, an SS agent burst into the hall. "You must be Mr. Brundge and Mr. Knickerbocker." The female agent nervously reached for her weapon. "Where's your SS escort?"

As planned, Dale managed to halt the agent's first reaction by informing her, "One of them became violently sick just as we got here. He's having a heart attack or something. His buddy rushed him to the teleport and told us to come right down here to see you. He said one of you should watch his post."

The nervous hand relaxed as the other agent popped his helmeted head out. "What's going on, Gloria?"

Gloria stepped around the two men and over her shoulder informed her partner of the situation. "I'm going to watch station one, Burt. There seems to be a medical emergency there. You help these people with the prisoners."

The male SS agent watched for a moment and then turned to Lee and Dale. "Come on. We'll gather 'em up and wait until someone comes to escort you to the top."

Burt led the two guests to the cell labeled "2B-5." Taking a glove off, he laid his palm on the sensor next to the door. The door slid open. "Come out here and stand in the hall."

Hair disheveled and clothing rumpled, John and Sue Rubbles hesitantly walked out. From the next door came Allen and Fern Phelix and Betty Alvin in about the same condition as the first couple. Across the hall, Burt opened the last door to release Jerry and Pat Ives from their confines.

Burt indicated, "We'll wait in the control room. Mr. Brundge and Mr. Knickerbocker, would you please lead the way while I watch these follow you." Walking back, Burt replaced his glove.

Dale and Lee moved into the control room, followed by a sundry crowd. The seven prisoners cautiously evaluated the situation. Burt settled in a chair where he could watch everyone. Focusing on the RCs, one could hear the smile in his voice. "I don't know what Florida wants with you people, but I bet it'll be interesting. I hear they do some pretty cruel things to RCs down there. I heard tell once that—"

Lee studied his surroundings while ignoring Burt's cruel story. There was the teleport. It seemed almost too easy. All they needed to do was step up on it and Ryan would probably transport them home.

As Lee and Dale readied themselves for their next move, a siren wailed in the hall. Burt jumped to his feet. In reflex, Dale looked to the doorway and drew his stunner from his pocket.

The SS agent had time enough to say one thing. "Something's wrong. Someone's infiltrated the Base levels." He focused back on the group and knew before he saw the stunner he was in trouble. Dale was smiling. "That's correct, my friend. They'll tell you all about it later." He shot, and Burt fell to the floor.

All seven of the prisoners turned to face Lee and Dale. Jerry voiced the wonder of the others. "Who are you guys?"

Lee took no time for introductions. "Hurry! Everyone onto the teleport."

Without questions, all did as they were told. Dale, the last one on, reached into his pocket. His confidence increased when he felt that the device Everett had given him was secure. He took it out and kissed it. "You'd better work."

Jordan Control

The control room was small, so Pat made most wait outside for results. He ran his fingers through his white hair and asked Ryan, "I'm beginning to get a little worried. Nothing yet, Ryan?"

Every few seconds the little man touched another button and studied the monitor. Without looking up he answered, "Not yet. I know it's a little past our scheduled time, but everything should be all right for another few minutes. I still have three blue signals. One seems to be below the other two. They must be going with plan B. I hope Ryker remembers he only has three charges on that stunner we gave him."

Everett hobbled over to stand behind Ryan. Talking to himself, he gave a voice to the fear everyone had. "I sure hope my trackers work." Ryan and Pat silently registered the comment.

Seconds later everyone jumped at Ryan's proclamation: "YES! I have two red signals. Look Everett, the teleport code reads out."

Ryan wasted no time keying in the information and then tapped the button for transportation. The glass slid into place and darkened. As the reverse action occurred, shouts of joy rose up from the control room and hall. Lee and Dale rushed their people from the crowded teleport. The room was abuzz with congratulations and other praises. Ryan busily ignored the excitement, awaiting another red light. Pat preoccupied himself, maintaining order. "OK, people, everyone out of here. We need the room, and it's too early for a party. The whole team's not home."

Things returned to quiet and concentration. Pat and Everett looked over Ryan's shoulder trying to view the blue signal. Two minutes seemed like two hours. Monica stood in the doorway of the control room. She leaned against the casing with her head bowed. The only thing she could do was pray. Ryan's comment caused her to look up.

"What the devil? See that? It turned red and then blue again. What's going on? Oh, there it is. It's red again." Automatically Ryan punched keys and activated the teleport. "We got them!"

Without realizing it, everyone in the room grinned at the darkened glass anticipating another happy event. Bow mouths straightened into lines of concern as the glass cleared. Four grim looking people stood on the pad. Pat haltingly greeted his guests. "Good . . . good to see you made it, but where's Ryker?"

Dennis stepped down to face the large man. "He jumped off to stop some SS agents from coming into the control room. He threw me this thing and told me to stay put." Dennis held the tracking device up to show Pat.

Monica held her hand over her mouth to squelch the gasp. Cheryl Prince and Debbie Cristiano both ran to help her. Rich looked back and forth between the men in the room with a quizzical look and asked, "What should we do? Can you send someone back to get Ryker?"

Ryan looked to Pat. Time passed at a snail's pace as Pat made the toughest choice of his life. "No, we can't. It'd be suicide, and they'd know how to find us. Ryker's on his own. We'd better pray for him."

All was silent in the hall. Five men gathered together, lifting prayers for Ryker as two women consoled Monica, sitting on the floor sobbing.

Left Behind

Reaching his level when the elevator door opened, Ryker knew he had problems. Straight in front was a wall. Stepping out, he looked right then left. It seemed he was halfway in a hall similar to the one he left a minute earlier. *Great! Where's the control room?*

Knowing there was no time to waste, Ryker turned right and slowly moved on. The cell doors were marked as he had seen above. On his right was B3-16 and across the hall from it was the lounge. *OK, if the lounge is here, where's the control room? Maybe it's on the same side of the hall only on the other side of the elevator.*

Turning to investigate, he saw an SS agent come out the doorway he was about to head into. The agent asked, "Where's Mr. Brundge and Mr. Knickerbocker?"

Ryker's reaction came naturally. "They'll be right here. I guess there's some confusion regarding the identification of one of the prisoners. While they called to straighten it out, I was asked to check and see if these people are ready and check their identification."

The dark agent turned to face the control room. "Come on in and we'll check out the names again." He disappeared through the doorway.

Oh, I hope he doesn't call anybody. Ryker hurried to catch up. Entering the control room, he noticed only one agent keying information on a panel. "Where's your partner?"

Without looking up, the agent answered, "She was called to the top. I guess there's a problem with one of the elevators. I see you're not use to Level Three. I always went the wrong way at first also. I was told when they dug these tunnels they ran into something they had to go around. This is the only level laid out this way and it messes everyone up at first."

Great! Time's running short. It won't be long before they discover why that elevator won't work.

Ryker felt the need to hasten the agent along. "Got that information yet?"

Pointing to the monitor, he said, "Rich and Debra Cristiano in B3-13 and Dennis and Cheryl Prince in B3-11. Are those the names?"

Moving back out into the hall to hurry things along, Ryker answered, "Yes, that's correct. Maybe I can take them up to the officers above."

Shrugging his shoulders the SS agent followed Ryker out into the hall. "I don't see why we can't at least get them out here and ready."

Down a few doors the NMA agent stopped, took his glove off, and palmed the door lock to cell number B3-13. The door slid opened. Sitting in a bare room except for double bunks, a crude toilet, and a single faucet sink, sat Dennis and Cheryl staring back at the intruders. The facility agent rudely called to them. "Come out here. You're moving on to a better place." He laughed with knowledge of the prisoners' fate.

Reluctantly, the couple joined the agents out in the hall. Moving to the next door the same procedure occurred for Rich and Debbie. Standing in the hall, all but one agent jumped when a siren went off. The less nervous NMA agent pulled his stunner and looked to the elevator. "Someone's infiltrated the Base levels."

Ryker also grabbed his stunner. But to the surprise of the two couples, his target was the other SS agent. The agent was on the floor before he could turn back around. Allowing no time to waste, Ryker urged his friends, "Quick, to the control room!"

Rich and Cheryl led the way, running. Both recognized the voice and knew they needed to move fast. Entering the control room, Ryker took off his helmet. "Hurry, onto the teleport. We're going home."

Stunned but happy, the couples boarded the pad with Ryker. He reached into his pocket and held the tracker device as a lifeline. At the same moment, Ryker heard the elevator door open in the hall. On the third level, that was too close for the time needed. It was then that Ryker remembered his stunner was only good for three shots and he'd just used his last one. He had regrettably given the others to his partners without thinking.

Whoever that is will be here in seconds. They could stop this transmission before it's finished!

With a quick decision, Ryker jumped off the teleport and went to greet the unwanted guest. After three steps, he remembered the tracking device. Taking it from his pocket, he tossed it to Dennis. "Hang on to that and STAY PUT!"

Ryker turned in time to face an SS agent coming through the doorway. He tackled the agent, knocking him to the floor, which dislodged the stunner from his hand. While the two wrestled on the floor, the teleport activated to the surprise of the four standing on it. Seconds later, Ryker heard the elevator again. The last thing he

133

remembered was being thrown against the wall—and then the numbing effect of a stunner. Everything went black.

Captured

While Ryker was unconscious, they dressed him in a simple, gray jumpsuit. On his windowless cell bunk, he sat in serious meditation. He was giving much thought to things he had learned of the Lord so far in his life.

The door to cell B15-4 opened. Standing before Ryker, a large SS agent issued a booming command: "Follow me."

Walking out, Ryker noticed another agent waiting to bring up the rear. The elevator was nearby and the three boarded, ascending to ground level. Upon exiting, Ryker recognized the place from the day before. In front of them was the door that led to the main lobby. Natural sunlight was difficult to assimilate at first as Ryker walked into the elaborate foyer. He followed the SS agent around the desk to stand in front of a twin door. Behind the desk sat a very large black man with a potbelly. When the big SS agent showed his pass to the guard, he touched a sensor that released the door.

The other side of the access was much different from the one leading to the elevators. The city skyline dominated the main view through the glass, which served as the outside walls and roofs encircling the ground floor hallway. The trek proved interesting compared to the dim cell. Outside on the left, a sign to the government facility loomed in front of the city backdrop. On the right, offices with active people attending to business added to the hustle and bustle of the city. Reaching a particular office, the SS agent stopped and touched a pad on the door. After a few moments, it opened and the agent signaled Ryker to enter.

The interior was very pleasant. A plush carpet accented the elaborate room decorated in pleasing greens. On a small couch sat an SS agent minus his helmet. Black, curly hair cascaded past Buck's shoulders. Ryker never noticed until that moment how much his old friend resembled a Native American. The smile quickly dispelled the illusion. "Ryker, old buddy, close the door and have a seat."

Buck pointed to a matching, stuffed chair across from him. Ryker settled into it but somehow couldn't get comfortable as he asked, "I suppose this visit isn't going to be all pleasure."

The smile on Buck's face evaporated, replaced with a poker face. "Of course not. You managed to deprive me of one of my biggest arrests to date. I admit it was done to fish you out, but I did expect to have ALL of you to report. I'm impressed by your jailbreak. That's never happened in this facility before. It leaves a very dark spot on my reputation. My only chance to erase it is to bring you and that book before my superiors."

"You have me, but you'll never see that Bible."

"Not good enough, I'm afraid."

"If I thought you'd read it, I might let you see it, but I don't believe that's your intention."

"The only god in this world is the one you make."

"You may believe that, but the one you make can't replace the one and only true God."

Buck laughed. "If your God is so great, why are you in this predicament?"

Ryker grinned and settled back in his seat, relaxed with discussing a subject dear to his heart. "The rain will fall on the just and the unjust. God may very well save me from this predicament, or He may use it in some other way. But whatever He chooses, I know the Redeemer of my soul. And when I die, I'll go to be with my Lord forever."

Complete incomprehension shrouded Buck's face. Saying nothing for a minute, he studied the words he had just heard. He came to a quick conclusion. "You're nuts! See what that blasted book's done to you? This country's just beginning to eradicate the frenzy of moralizers it fell prey to hundreds of years ago, and we don't need people like you dragging us back into it."

Ryker said nothing, but waited penitently. Buck stood and walked to the window facing the hall. Sunlight flooded in and covered him in an eerie, filtered light. The desk in front of him blinked with many different colored lights. After some thought, Buck spoke without turning around. "You'll never see daylight again until you give to me the book in question."

Ryker stood to face the back of his childhood friend. For the first time in a long time, he felt only pity for him. Slowly and very calmly, Ryker responded, "Then I may never see daylight again. But let me tell you, heaven will not deprive me of the Son-light, spelled S-o-n."

Staying firm in his stance, Buck touched a button in front of him. The door opened and the large SS agent came in to retrieve Ryker. Minutes later, he was back in his cell.

When he was alone, Al S. Shanach once again sat down on the couch. "Servant, playback the last conversation with prisoner B15-4."

Listening to a recording of minutes earlier, Buck pyramided his fingers in thought. When it was through, he stood. "Servant, save conversation with prisoner B15-4 under file name of 'Fool.'"

Buck left his office for other pressing business.

Caged Witness

People have gone through much more than a few months of solitary confinement. Ryker spent enough time in cell B15-4 to comprehend the dreadfulness that multiplied days could bring. The difference for Ryker, compared to some, was his relationship with Jesus. He focused on using it for real soul searching. He'd gone through many emotional mood swings, which tested his faith. The last few days were ones Ryker would remember as the most peaceful he'd ever experienced as a Christian. He had come to a place where he'd emptied himself completely of his own needs and filled himself with full rest in God. Had Buck known the struggle in Ryker's heart earlier, he would have moved much sooner to do what was planned for this day.

The intrusion of Buck into B15-4 raised little notice to Ryker, but he reluctantly acknowledged his foe with simple eye contact. "Ryker, old buddy, how'd you like to come out and play for a while?" Buck stood in the doorway with his hands behind his back.

Ryker thought Buck seemed different and then realized he was— for two reasons. First, Buck wore a colorful brown-and-gold jumpsuit. Ryker had never seen him in anything but black until now. Ryker commented on the second reason. "The mustache is cute. Couldn't grow a beard, huh?"

Buck's congenial smile dissipated, replaced with a dark frown. "You're in no position to make those kinds of remarks."

Ryker stood. His hair was long and unruly. The beard looked like a rat's nest. "I'm sorry. You're right. I've no right to insult you that way."

Buck showed surprise at Ryker's reply. The frown softened as he instructed Ryker to follow him. Another SS agent stood in the hall to follow the two. Buck allowed Ryker to walk to his right. "Are you ready to tell me where to find that book?" A single shake of the head from right to left was the only response. "I thought not. I've a surprise for you today. I'm in hopes it'll help convince you otherwise." The comment preceded the now familiar, evil smile.

The elevator traveled one floor to Level Sixteen. Stepping out, Ryker realized this was not like the other levels. It was smaller and well lit. Control panels with blinking colored lights peppered the short hallway. The left wall consisted of glass ramparts. Divided into several rooms, each held a clear view and was designated by a plaque hung overhead. Slowly walking to one end, Ryker observed that each room housed a large, bright, steel cross in the center. Ryker questioned his sanity, wondering if he was hallucinating. He shook his head but the scene persisted.

A small crowd of people stood looking in on one of the small rooms. Above it the sign indicated it was the "Hasselman Chamber." Sitting at the control panel, a technician programmed the unit. Behind him stood a decorated high official with lots of silver, gold, and ribbons hanging from his dark blue, tailored outfit. His nametag at the top of all the metal read, "NMA Councilor Alfred D. Hyman." There were also a doctor and a nurse. Buck was the SS agent present who completed the group of officials required for the event.

When Ryker walked near enough to see into the small room, he gasped and spread himself up against the glass.

"NICK!"

Upon the silver cross hung Nick Richards. He looked thin and very fatigued. Wires hooked to the straps held him to the cross. Nick looked up at the commotion. Nick smiled when he recognized Ryker. Nick spoke in muted tones, but reading his lips, Ryker was able to make out Nick's wishes. "Don't give in, Ryker. I'm only going home."

Buck pulled Ryker back away from the glass wall. "I thought maybe this demonstration would enlighten you to just how serious your crime is."

The proceedings began when Alfred spoke. "Nicholas G. Richards, the government has found you guilty of deliberately undermining the neutral morals this country has learned to hold as the rights of every person. You've worked with others and yourself to promote the false idea that there's a right and wrong for every situation. In doing so, you've greatly interfered with the freedom of other citizens.

Do you, Nicholas Richards, still hold to the belief that there is a right and a wrong to moral issues dealing with life?"

From the cross, Nick raised his head to look his accuser in the eyes and plainly answered, "Yes."

Alfred asked one more question. "Nicholas Richards, how do you plead to these charges, guilty or not guilty?"

Nick held his gaze upon the man. "Guilty."

Alfred turned to Buck. "Who charges this man with the crime for which he's been found guilty, and who will witness his punishment?"

Buck stood at attention and replied, "I, Search Squad Agent Alanson S. Shanach, witness the accurate person and the proceedings of this execution."

Alfred turned to the man at the control panel, waiting for the signal. Alfred gave a simple nod of his head. The technician turned keyed switches and poised his hand over a large, red button. Buck looked to the cross and proclaimed ceremonially, "May the USA benefit from the act of this government action. Proceed."

Looking boldly at his accusers, Nick smiled as the hand pressed the button. His smile instantly changed to contorted agony. Spasms riddled every muscle in Nick's body. In five seconds, it was done. As his head relaxed against his right shoulder, there was a smile on his face. The doctor turned to the nurse when he saw it. "It amazes me how many times that happens with these people."

Buck had observed the same many times before, but this was the first time since Ryker's visit to his office months earlier. For a few brief seconds, he wondered, but then mentally shook it off and turned to Ryker.

Eyes closed and head slightly bowed, Ryker prayed silently. Tears rolled down his cheeks. Again, Buck frowned at Ryker's reaction. He roughly clamped Ryker's arm and spun him around. "Come on. Back to your cell for some real reflection."

As they made their way to the elevator, Buck continued his reprimand. "What just happened to Richards could easily happen to you. But that wouldn't help me any, would it? No, that's too good for you." A cruel smile engulfed Buck's face. "You do have family and friends though, and I'm sure you wouldn't want anything to happen to them. All I request is one little item. Think about it."

They reached the elevator, entered it, and left Level Sixteen. A pair of eyes from the first room watched as they departed. He held a mop, standing in the shadow of the large cross.

138

Free

Though he hadn't endured years in solitary confinement as others had, Ryker did get a taste of what it could do to a man. One month had passed since Nick's death, and Ryker's only visitor had been Buck, who'd checked about a week-and-a-half earlier to see if Ryker had changed his mind. The conversation had lasted about half a minute, then Ryker was left alone again.

The door slid open. Ryker didn't react to it at first. He figured it was nothing but trouble. Being left alone was better than what he dreamed might happen. When he turned from his bunk to look up, he thought he had looked into a mirror. Ray looked down at his brother with concern on his face. "Ryker, come on. We haven't much time."

The brother forced a small satchel into Ryker's hand and pulled him to his feet. To help simulate day and night for the employees, the hall's ambiance mimicked midnight, which gave Ryker his only hint of the time. Ray led Ryker to the control room. Once there, he began keying in information to the teleport controls. Moving around helped Ryker revive. Questions began coming to mind. "Where're the SS agents?"

"I sent them on a wild goose chase."

"How'd you get in here?"

"I work here."

Ray led his brother to the teleport while giving him some quick instructions. "I've programmed this to deposit you on the corner of Maple and Sisson Streets in Potsdam. They'll know immediately where to go for you so I've arranged another teleport on the corner of Sisson and Elm to transport you to another destination. It'll activate at 11:55. Make sure you're in it. I believe you'll recognize where you are. There's some food, medical supplies, a watch with the correct time, and other things in the bag."

Dumbfounded, Ryker hardly knew what to say. "How about you? Are you going to be all right?"

Ray stepped back to the controls, looked at his brother, and smiled. "I'll be fine." He snapped his head around the door. "I believe I hear the elevator working. Remember, you haven't much time. They'll know you're gone in about twenty minutes. That's only a guess on my part. They may be quicker. Good luck."

As the glass slid into place, Ryker felt compelled to say, "Thanks, Brother. I do love you."

139

Seconds later, he was free—but not safe.

***

Many times Buck had spent late nights and weekends planning or doing whatever was possible to get ahead in his business. It happened to be one of those times when Ryker managed to break out. It was 11:45, and he was just getting ready to go home when Base Level Fifteen reported to him by intercom.

"Mr. Shanach! Cell B15-4 is vacant. Did you have him moved?"

Buck faced the source and replied, "No. How can he be gone?"

Another voice came over the intercom. "Teleport fifteen was activated about seven minutes ago. We've the coordinates. Do you wish to pursue him, sir?"

Buck rolled his eyes. "Of course, you idiot. Give me a moment and I'll be right there."

As he reached for his helmet, a thought came to him. Over the door hung one of his antique guns. It was a 7mm night rifle of the old Iraq Civil War of 2018. Smiling, he took it down and checked to see that the clip was full. Running down the hall with gun and helmet in hand, Buck spoke to no one in particular. "You might out-distance my stunner, but this reaches much further. You haven't a chance, Cuff."

***

Ryker took time to scan the sack to see what items his brother had left for him, including a heated jacket and hat. He was now halfway to the other teleport. *You gave this some thought, Brother. There're quite a few goodies I'll be able to use. Thank You, Lord, for guiding him.*

The old familiar setting helped Ryker to gain confidence. It was quiet, and the moon hung low in the skyline. Ryker was out of sight of the teleport he had departed when he heard it activate. The inconspicuous buzz was common to him.

Oh, no! They've found out already that I'm missing. I've about three minutes before my next teleport and they could easily reach it before then.

The teleport he needed was in sight on the other end of the block. Knowing he needed to lure the agents away from it, he ran for the dark alley on his left. The move put him in sight of the teleport he'd come from. Before he darted into the dark maw, he stalled to view the agent (only one?). The person had a rifle slung over his shoulder and was only a block-and-a-half away.

That must be Buck! He loves those old antique guns. But why's he alone?

The alley was very dark. Tripping and stumbling along, Ryker knew his foe wasn't far behind. Almost to the other end, Ryker heard Buck behind him. "Give up. You haven't got a chance."

When Buck realized his prey wasn't about to stop, he pulled the rifle to his shoulder. The scope was specially designed for nighttime maneuvers. Through it Buck could see Ryker as clearly as if it were daytime. As he put the cross hairs on him, Ryker darted around the corner. In frustration, Buck shot at the space his foe had been a second earlier. He thought it might scare Ryker enough to give up. It wasn't to be.

As Ryker dashed around the corner, he heard the bullet whiz by him. *Dear Jesus, help me. Just get me to that teleport.*

The run to the other end of the block was harder than Ryker had anticipated. The street, well lit, gave the SS agent ample opportunity. Buck had one good chance to shoot, but something inside wouldn't let him. He whispered his feelings to himself. "This is a night gun. I'll wait to use it in the dark alley to his right. I know that's where the jerk's headed." Just as he said it, Ryker virtually lunged into the passage. Buck ran for all he was worth.

Blindly racing on, Ryker was fortunate enough to avoid obstacles and made good time. He stopped fifteen feet short of the end. A six-foot fence blocked the alley. *The teleport is around the corner on the other side of this fence. Lord, if I'm to make it, You have to give me the strength.*

Laughter echoed throughout the narrow street. Buck knelt down on one knee and watched Ryker through the night scope while hollering down the alley at him. "You've no place to go, buddy. Give up now, or I'll have to wound you. I won't let you die, but it won't be any fun either."

Without further hesitation, Ryker sprang to the wall and jumped. As he was in the air, he felt a searing pain in his right leg, then heard a resounding crack in his ears. He found himself scrambling to the teleport on his left. Only seconds after he stood in it, the control panel came alive and the glass partition moved into place. He relaxed for the first time since leaving cell B15-4.

Buck climbed over the fence in time to see the teleport partition slide back into the opened position. He ran to the controls only to discover no information to retrieve. The helmet slammed to the sidewalk as he fell to his knees and screamed his bitter rage. Aiming the rifle up into the night sky he emptied the clip in frustration. It was symbolic of all his aims in life up to that point. He sat there for a long time boiling, and then simmering about his failure in dealings with Ryker. The same question kept coming back. Why?

Wounded

Sunlight flickered through branches swaying in a breeze. The light flashed upon Ryker's face. He squeezed his eyelids tighter together, trying to reject the light. Sounds of water lapping at the river bank lulled him into ignoring the light. Ryker wrapped himself tighter in the heated blanket that Ray provided. Slowly awakening, the certainty of his location eluded him. Lying in the comfort of the heated mantle Ryker reflected on events the night before.

When the teleport opened, Ryker recognized he was looking at a childhood memory. It was a place his mother and father visited a few times a year for farm supplies not usually found in the big city. The teleport was outside the Colton General Supplies Depot, which sat on the very edge of the town. It was the closest community to the Cuff homestead and was still eight miles away. The small town of less than a thousand served as a resort area for retirees and well-to-do families. The scenic town was situated along the Racquet River.

In realizing where he was, Ryker's first priority was to find a place to hide before anyone saw him. He had a fair idea of the direction his parents' place lay. Ray, Sarah, and he had walked it once just for the fun of it. He gathered his satchel and began walking in that direction. At such a late hour, no one was in sight. His leg slowed his progress but about fifteen minutes away he found a nice spot along the river hidden from any view. It was there he tended to his leg. The bullet had passed through the fleshy part just below the knee. Luckily, the bullet hit no bones or major arteries. The projectile must have been an armor-piercing type. There was a small hole where it entered and another where it exited. There was a relatively minimal amount of bleeding. At the time it didn't bother Ryker much. He quickly bandaged it, got comfortable, and fell asleep.

When Ryker partly awoke, because the sun wouldn't relent, the pain in his leg finished the job. Unwrapping himself from the blanket and attempting to stand he stumbled, grimacing at the pain. It seemed much worse than the night before. Inspecting the bandage he knew it needed changing. For the next half hour Ryker tended to his leg, his stomach, and then he spent time in prayer before his next move.

The morning warmed up quickly into a nice Indian summer day. That was the good news. The bad news was his leg made his progress slower and slower. It was several hours later and he still had miles to go. Had the leg rested, its healing would have been much swifter, but the constant moving was causing it to bleed again. Putting down his make-shift crutch, Ryker sat on a rock to replace his bandage once more.

He traveled an old path through the wooded hills—many old meadows and brush-infested, peppered areas reclaimed by nature. Years earlier the path was a road for the wheeled vehicles that traveled it. After his repair job, Ryker sat up to look around. Most of the leaves had fallen but there was still enough color on the hills for him to imagine the beauty a few weeks earlier.

God paints beautiful pictures. I was really very lucky to have grown up on a farm.

It was then that Ryker noticed the old farmstead on the next hill about two miles away. It was enough to spur him on. The leg was of almost no use to him, but he knew he was going to make it one way or another.

A few more hours passed and the leg was bleeding again. Ryker merely dragged it along, determined to finish his trek. Exhaustion set in as he pushed himself on to make it to the top of the foothill. Along the crest of the knoll was one of his father's meadows. It had a breath-taking view that Ryker had enjoyed as a young boy. He was in no shape to admire it now and struggled to keep his wits about him. The home was in sight but he wasn't sure if he could make it. Ryker concentrated, deciding whether to keep going or drop where he was to rest.

As providence would have it, Homer was in his field taking advantage of the weather to finish repairing the electronic fences. Movement caught his attention. Stopping to take a closer look, he saw Ryker resting on his crutch. Homer slowly walked to investigate who might be on his land. Near enough to see it was his son, Homer ran to greet him. "Ryker! Is that you? My boy, what're you doing here?"

Barely able to comprehend someone yelling, Ryker looked up to see his father running toward him. He smiled at the sight. "I made it."

As Homer reached him, Ryker collapsed into his arms, gave a sigh, and relaxed into unconsciousness.

The Dream

Babbling water gurgled along the little narrow creek. The stream traveled through a forest of spruce and hemlock trees. It was one of Ryker's favorite childhood memories. Stealthily he moved along the water's edge and dropped a baited hook into a swirling pool next to a large rock.

He heard a voice. Ryker looked up to view a green-covered meadow where a young boy played with his dog. The boy was wearing a shepherd's outfit. Intrigued, Ryker walked toward the boy who quickly ran over the hill. Jogging to catch up with him, Ryker found himself at the cave Buck and he discovered years ago.

This is a juncture in my life that everything seems to point to.

Someone yelled, breaking Ryker's concentration. It was the boy again but this time he was older, donned with animal skins and leather sandals. Another boy hollered to him. "David, come back here. You're foolish to go up against such a large man."

David stood his ground. "I've no choice. No one else will do it."

A rifle cracked. Ryker involuntarily ducked and turned to see the source. Buck stood laughing manically with his gun aimed at Ryker. Running as fast as he could Ryker seemed to be on a treadmill going nowhere. Suddenly, in front of him loomed the large NMA sign he first saw at the government agency. Jumping over it gave great pain in his leg. As he landed on the other side, David the shepherd yelled, "How dare you insult the name of the Living God!"

Ryker watched David twirl a sling at his opponent. Following the path of the intended target Ryker flinched at the sight. A twelve-foot-tall Buck laughed as he raised his rifle to shoot him. He wore his black SS agent outfit minus the helmet.

As Buck squeezed the trigger, Ryker stopped him. "Alanson! Buck, old buddy, are you looking for this?" Ryker held up an old, tattered, black Bible and waved it at Buck. He slowly turned to face Ryker and in the process lost his smile; it was replaced with a frightened look. "Give that to me." Buck dropped to the ground with a thud. David's sling found its mark.

Ryker turned and leisurely ambled away. He walked and walked and walked. Other odd events happened around him but his focus was on the castle ahead of him. When he reached it, David came out dressed in kingly clothes, wearing a crown. "You've come a long ways. What brings you here?"

"I don't know."

David robotically continued. "Being the king's not easy. I've made some mistakes but people need me. God has been gracious to help me through it."

Ryker replied, "I wouldn't want to be a king. I don't think I could handle it."

"Neither did I but God asked me."

A voice from far away called. "David, come here. I need you."

David turned and headed to the castle.

Confused, Ryker turned to go and discovered he was standing in his father's meadow but not alone. "Grandpa? What're you doing here?"

The man looked somewhat like his son Homer but smaller. The nose was larger and fit well on his face. His large smile was very inviting. "I thought you might need a hand."

Ryker relaxed in the presence of a mentor. "I'm so confused, Grandpa. What am I supposed to do?"

"Follow David's example. You've been doing well so far."

"But David's a king and I'm not."

"David wasn't, but now he is. You aren't, but you may be. Follow your heart. If it's His," he pointed to the sky, "then it's God's voice to your soul."

Ryker turned to study the apple tree and familiar view, then looked to the sky before turning back to reply. But Grandpa was gone. Still confused and tired, Ryker sat under the apple tree to rest and pray.

"Ry y y y y y y y y ker."

"Ryker, wake up. Son, wake up, please."

The dream faded as he opened his eyes. Ryker smiled at his mother looking down at him. She grinned with concern. "How're you feeling now that you've slept awhile?"

Ryker sat up. He had forgotten his leg until then, and grimaced through it. "I feel much better, Mom. It's good to see you. How're you and Dad doing?"

Judy stood to open the curtains in Ryker's old room. "Your father and I are doing fine. Much better seeing you're safe again."

Ryker closed his eyes and thought for a moment. *If it hadn't been for Ray, I wouldn't be here. I hope he's OK. If not, I sure pray he knows the Lord.*

145

Homer entered the room when he heard voices. "It's good to see you're feeling better. Doc Austin says you're going to be fine in no time."

A sudden thought caused Ryker to attempt leaving the bed, until Homer stopped him. "Dad, I don't want anyone to know I'm here."

Homer and Judy sat on the edge of the bed. Judy touched his arm. "It's OK, dear. Doc Austin is one of us. He belongs to our study group."

Another thought flashed before his mother hardly finished. "Oh my goodness! I need to get out of here. Buck'll look for me here."

Homer hushed him before Ryker got carried away. "No problem. He's already been here. Busted in on us early this morning about six o'clock. He searched everywhere and everything. He even went to that old cave you guys use to play in. Before he left he gave you a compliment. Said you were too smart to come here. Doc thought you would be safe here after that."

Ryker relaxed against the headboard of the bed, smiled about Buck's comment, and said, "I fooled him, didn't I?"

After a moment of silence, Ryker started again. "I'm so glad to see you two are learning about the Lord. He's so good to us. Dad? Why didn't you know about the Lord before? Grandpa and Uncle Vern seemed to know so much about it."

Homer drew a deep breath before he answered. "Well, it's like this. I had too many friends who helped me ignore any teaching about it. Besides, Dad had so little knowledge about it himself. In his heart he knew, but he had no real way to convey it to me." Homer's eyes glazed over in deep thought. "I remember only one thing tangible. It was what finally did my father in. He died because of it, giving me an excuse to totally reject his ideals. It was a painting he had and often used to show me God's love. I don't know how he got a hold of it, but he kept it away from the NMA." A calming silence prevailed for several minutes as Homer thought. He patted Ryker on his good leg. "Tell me what you think you're going to do from here?"

Ryker wasn't ready for the question. Staring off through the window he reflected for a minute. "I don't really know."

Onward

"This is really unnecessary. I've only done what anyone else would do and besides, I had a lot of help." Ryker was back at the Jordan facility. They had decorated one of the small halls in his honor. Everyone was there to celebrate. Laura Shaffer wheeled him down in an old wheel chair for the surprise party. She felt it was her job to make sure he didn't do something to injure the leg again. The only one closer to him was Monica. It would be a long time before Ryker got very far away again.

The evening went well. It was a wonderful opportunity for Ryker to talk with old friends from his Bible study group and catch up on the news he missed while gone. He learned there was almost a constant concert of prayer lifted up for him while he was incarcerated. He had the opportunity to see John and Sue Rubbles' little daughter. They were very thankful the child was with friends when they were captured.

After most everyone left for the evening, Ryan, Lee, Dale, Pat, and Everett spent some special time with Ryker discussing how things went that memorable day. The women talked nearby, privately congratulating Monica who had a permanent glow about her.

Pat finally had an opportunity to say something many others were thinking. "You seem different. I'm not saying it's bad, but you're a different person in some way. I have to ask, what're your plans for the future?"

To gain a moment of reflection, Ryker sat up in his chair to position his leg for more comfort. Laura saw him and ran over to assist but Ryker waved her back. He smiled at her and told her he was fine. Turning back to Pat he answered. "God's made it very apparent to me what He wishes. I haven't got the slightest idea what it entails, but it looks like I'm going to serve at the Upper Room."

THE SEARCH REALIZED

"This new ethical bill of rights will soon be realized as every American's true freedom. Neutral morals means what it says."

James Teamont: First Chairman under the New American Democratic Party (NADP) 10/9/2026—Sponsor of the NMA Bill

Buck's Second Chance

Outside the large, glass wall a wind blew debris around in tiny tornado-like swirls. Gray-and-white cumulus clouds obscured the sunlight. The teleport activated and an SS agent stepped out into the lobby of the Washington NMA building. Walking slowly to the door leading to his office, Buck took his helmet off. When he reached the counter area, the woman behind the desk stopped him.

"Mr. Shanach, there's a message for you." The woman was average looking with short, curly, brown hair. Her periwinkle badge matched the color of her eyes.

Buck halted, whispered something obscure under his breath, and turned to the security officer. "Thanks, Margaret. Which terminal?"

Margaret pointed to the one on the opposite end of the long counter. Setting his helmet on the desk, Buck keyed the terminal keyboard and waited. A moment later an attractive woman with long, black hair graced the monitor screen. When Buck recognized her, he involuntarily stood at attention. "Ms. Pringle, what can I do for you?"

Her red lips parted, revealing pearly white teeth. "Al, Mr. Hawkins would like to see you right away."

With professional decorum, Buck tilted his head in acknowledgment. "By all means. I'll be there momentarily."

The screen went blank, followed by Buck's face. He turned to Margaret. "Mr. Hawkins wants to see me."

The petite woman smiled as she reached under the counter and touched a sensor. "I heard. Go ahead. You're all set."

The door opposite from the one Buck normally traveled through opened. He took the released route and found himself facing three elevator doors. Taking the pass card from his belt he slid it into the slot causing a green light to glow over the door marked "Executive." He touched the sensor allowing the door to open, and once inside he activated the only button available. A minute later he was at the top floor of the building.

Elegant and exquisite were two adjectives used often to describe the top floor. Buck found himself deposited in a wide hallway. Small trees planted in large, ornate pots lined both sides. Muted daylight flooded in from the glass roof. Situated between the trees, lampposts lit the area when natural illumination wasn't available. Buck briskly walked halfway down the hall carrying his helmet under his arm. He stopped in front of a door on his left. It was one of five along the huge hall. Taking his right glove off, he placed his palm on a plate next to the door. Two seconds later, the door opened.

The room looked much like a very fancy family room. The only thing taking away from the illusion was a desk near a door opposite the one entered. Behind the desk sat the dark-haired woman seen minutes earlier. She gave Buck one of her bewitching smiles. "Hello Al. Have a seat. Mr. Hawkins will be with you as soon as possible."

The smile evaporated when she realized Buck wasn't in a mood to flirt, as was his usual reaction. Instead, she watched as he sat down in a plush chair away from her. Angel Pringle blinked her eyes, shrugged her shoulders, and went back to reading the terminal in front of her.

Time ticked off ten of its tedious minutes before the door behind Angel opened. An Asian woman of striking beauty waltzed into the outer office. She looked over her shoulder as she pulled on a thin, white glove. "Thank you, Sly. I'll see to it that the president sees it just that way. I'll be talking to you later. Bye."

Without looking around, she trotted to the other door and departed. Angel glanced over at Buck with a smile. "You may go right on in, Al."

Buck stood, walked over to the desk, and smiled. "May I leave this here?"

He set his helmet on the corner of the desk. Angel slid her eyes up to meet his. "You know you can—anytime."

Buck wiped his face clean of any positive reaction. "I know." He turned and entered Mr. Hawkins' office.

The office was magnificent. It was very large with rich, wood paneling covering three walls. Expensive paintings elegantly peppered the wood with enough taste to satisfy any connoisseur of art. All fixtures sparkled of gold and silver. The whole outside wall was glass, revealing a breathtaking panoramic view of the city skyline. It was Buck's ambition to achieve a position granting him the same privileges this office afforded.

To one side in a corner between one paneled wall and the outside glass wall was an immense wooden desk. Behind it sat the man who controlled many of the actions of the NMA. Sly Hawkins was not very impressive removed from his work setting. The job alone is what gave the man any real character. He was of average size with short, mousy hair that was as unimpressive as his dull, brown eyes. His position in society pumped power through his voice, which was his only redeeming quality. When Sly Hawkins spoke with his rich, deep voice, people and careers bowed to his command.

With great purpose, Buck walked over to the desk and stood at attention. Sly looked up and leaned back into his soft, leather chair. He fashioned a smile. "Have a seat, Al, and relax." Buck sat in one of two chairs and focused on the desktop of his boss. Sly cracked his knuckles before he began. For those who knew the man and his idiosyncrasies, the sign was ominous. "Al, tell me how you've been feeling these last few months."

Inside Buck squirmed, but on the outside he managed a relaxed facade. Sly knew the difference and mentally noted the control as Buck said, "Well sir, I feel as good as ever. I don't believe you'll find any negative reports on my physical or mental abilities."

The boss balled his fists up and held them together under his chin. The act underlined his professional smile. "Relax, Al. I'm not questioning your loyalty or intentions toward the organization. But it's been brought to my attention that you've had some minor setbacks in your endeavors the last nine or ten months." He folded his hands together on the desk and continued, "Our records show that you've never taken a vacation. That *does* show your dedication. But I'm concerned maybe you need some rest and time for reflection. You're one of our most promising agents and I'd hate to see you blow your career by neglecting to take care of yourself. Remember, you're one of the elite now."

Something on the inside lit his eyes up to their usual vigor as Buck lifted them to Sly. "Devon Damon's worked here for sixteen years and has never taken a vacation; he's only one of many. Why do you feel I need one?"

A stone cold look replaced Sly's smile, matching his eyes. Slowly, he stood and put his hands behind his back. He turned to a portrait hanging behind his desk. "I'm sure you're familiar with the late Dr. Eli Grossman. Back in 2024 Eli managed to pass the United States' first nonpartisan New America Bill of Rights through the legal system. It was the basis for the neutral morals we live by today. Let me quote one of Dr. Grossman's five basic rights for those who embrace neutral morals. This is number four. 'The creative leaders and managers of society's new and fair morals deserve and require times to fully take advantage of this society's best. This has a two-fold purpose. First, minds that mold and direct the course of this society, work best when they relax and meditate upon the common good. Second, one must experience the thing one intends on maintaining or bettering.' The man knew what he was talking about."

Sly turned to face Buck. "The work horses of this organization can labor well without this time, but we who're the molders and watch dogs of it, according to Dr. Grossman, need to take advantage of our rights. Tell me Al, are you happy being a work horse or are you ready to move onward and upward?"

Confusion dominated Buck's mind for the moment. He wasn't sure if he was insulted or being prodded into working smarter. He concluded it was both. He chose a reaction that diplomatically handled his situation. The actor smiled with some embarrassment. "Thank you, sir, for correcting my attitude. I wasn't aware I may be jeopardizing my career. I appreciate your confidence in me enough to set me straight."

Sitting back into his chair, Sly picked up a rubber band and played with it while he smiled at his subordinate. "Smart move, Al. My bet was you'd see it my way. Consider yourself on vacation for the next four weeks. We'll pay you for it this time with the assumption it will help you get back on track. If I need to suggest another vacation sometime in the near future, you may not be so lucky. When you come back to work, report to the Albany department in New York. That's not a demotion— at least at this time it's not. It'll put you a little closer to your roots, which may help you. And to augment that recovery you'll have an apprentice under your wing, which will help your focus. I believe all of this will assist you back on your feet. Any questions, Al?"

A clever artist can paint personality on a stone. Buck painted his face with a docile smile and bowed his head in a submissive attitude. "Very gracious of you, sir, to pay that much attention to my career. I do not plan on disappointing you."

Sly placed the rubber band back on his desk to finish his mentoring. "You've only one life to live and someone of your potential deserves all the opportunity to make the best of it."

The fake facade slipped. Buck's concentration shifted to another avenue, one he'd no intentions of purposely courting. Before he had realized, the thought surfaced as a vocal response. "Do we really have only one life?" Inside, Buck cringed at his mistake. Before his boss had a chance to dwell on the question, Buck quickly recovered. The lapsed smile regained its previous mask. "What I mean, sir, is that we can make one or two mistakes and still have a chance. Isn't that correct?"

Sly Hawkins was a man who discerned the intentions and attitudes of people well. The gift put him where he was in the organization. There were moments he was unsure. When that happened, he diplomatically skirted the issue but noted it mentally for future reference. "Many times that statement is true. Your situation is a case in point. I'm sure you'll handle it wisely. I'm glad we had this little talk. Now go enjoy yourself for a few weeks and sometime before the end of the year, I'll be getting together with you again."

To indicate the interview was through Sly turned to his terminal to key information into the system. Buck stood and briskly walked out of the office. Passing by Angel's desk, Buck scooped up his helmet and kept moving. Angel followed him with her eyes for a moment. "See you later, Al. Have a good day." She might as well have talked to her monitor. It would have responded quicker.

Out in the hall Buck calmly walked to the elevator. Someone exited and headed his way. Buck didn't want to draw any attention by reacting to his feelings at the moment. Once in the elevator alone, he vented his emotions. Slamming his helmet against the wall twice he stood still with fire in his eyes. "What in hell possessed me to ask such a stupid question?"

The elevator silently made its way to the bottom as Buck gazed off into the distance. His face went white, and his lower lip quivered slightly. It wasn't an audible voice but it seemed as if Ryker spoke to him.

"Wrong question." *What in heaven?* "That's where you'll find your answer."

The New Church

The auditorium was full with standing room only. A quiet murmur floated about the room as a man came to the front center of the stage. Behind him three others prepared by adjusting their instruments. His friend and co-writer, Carol, had dark hair and olive eyes that sparkled, accenting the dimples on each cheek. The bass guitar hanging from her shoulder was nothing more than a narrow board with four strings. Center stage, Mike adjusted his guitar and looked out at the crowd.

The volume in the room descended as Mike looked out over the assembly with light blue eyes that danced with excitement under long, dark lashes. His hair was styled short in the front revealing his receding hairline, but the back was tied into a short ponytail.

Mike's earring shimmered in the lights as he spoke. "I'm honored to be here tonight." He turned to indicate his fellow musicians then turned back to the crowd. "Collectively we are known as Dove and we feel it a privilege to bring you an art that was almost lost to us. Gospel music used to be a vital part of the Christian life and it's our wish to re-institute its influence. We hope you enjoy it, but pray it'll touch your life in a tangible way. Our speaker is an expert on God's Word and how it relates to what happened to our nation's foundation. We are going to learn tonight how the political progressive Bush and Obama administrations at the turn of the century contributed to a major move to collapse our economic structure. The purpose was to change our nation to something other than the republic it was intended. If it hadn't of been for the power discovery that led to teleportation technology by the public sector, big government may have totally succeeded. We have an opportunity to reverse and re-found our nation, but there is a lot of work to get there. This song reflects a nation under God and could replace the anthem we lost long ago. Carol and I are proud to claim it as such for now."

Dove sang and received loud affirmation to their ministry. The sermon, given by Barry Button, was unique and powerful. The whole evening focused on what a Christian, the church, and an American should be. There was laughter, deep thought, and tears before Barry finished. The altar filled with people seeking the voice of God and committing their hearts and minds to the will of God. It was proof of the activity and power of the new underground church. The evening was one not to be forgotten.

It was the first revival meeting Ryker or Monica had ever attended. Recently, teams had resurrected the concept and began working the mechanics out. The couple was lucky enough to attend one of the first events.

The Big Apple

The teleport glass door slid opened revealing a sight Ryker had never seen before. The city was still called the Big Apple even though there were seventeen cities more magnificent. The old metropolis was still very impressive. Ryker craned his head back to stare up at the heights the buildings reached.

"Don't do that. You'll draw attention to yourself as a tourist." Mike Grotto tapped Ryker on the back of the head to help dispel the look on his face. He laughed at his friend. "Someone could quickly tell you're a farm boy."

Carol Philips switched shoulders with the bag she carried. When she smiled, both dimples appeared as periods to accent the exclamations of her dark green eyes. "It's really cosmic, Mike. I know someone who's never seen a big city except through the windows of the NMA."

Ryker gained his composure enough to smile at both of them. "OK, OK. I get the point. Let's get moving."

Mike took the lead as the three walked down the busy avenue. Ryker, as casual and inconspicuous as possible, soaked in the sights. He observed flashing signs, a melting pot of races jostling around each other, transparent enclosed travel carts using the streets, and teleports on almost every corner. Most teleports were for inter-city travel. Entering the city by one of the long, distant teleports one could travel by inter-city teleports or the bubble carts. The traveling bubbles parked next to the curb until someone stepped into it. Then it would pull out into the travel lane and move along double a walking pace until the occupant touched the sensor, which reversed the procedure.

I can't believe the number of people walking around at one time. I think this is the most people I've seen outside at once.

About eight blocks from their arrival point Mike halted in front of a small shop. "Here we are, Ryker. Remember to let Carol and I handle this. The chief wanted you tagging along only for the experience."

Mike would have explained further except for the commotion a block down from them. All three turned to watch the turmoil. Two SS

155

agents corralled a small group of people together. They emerged from an old subway entrance. One of the men broke free and ran toward the trio. An agent aimed his stunner and discharged upon the man. He collapsed to the sidewalk with a grunt only twenty feet from Mike, Ryker, and Carol.

The shot was low and only paralyzed the man from the waist down. Lying there with his eyes closed Ryker heard the man pray, "Dear Jesus it's up to you now."

Finished with the quick appeal, he lifted his head to focus on the three before him. His eyes locked on Ryker with a surprised expression of recognition. In a low tone he talked to Ryker. "Take this and see to it the Network gets it." As an SS agent ran up behind the man, he slipped a small disc into a crack in the sidewalk.

No sooner had he finished when the agent reached him and stood over top. Ryker put his hands in his pockets. He almost forgot his ross until the agent was close. The person in black fingered a button on his belt. "This one isn't going anywhere, Derek. You take the others on ahead and I'll follow with this dim wit."

Then the helmeted agent turned to focus on the small crowd gathered, which included the trio. "What're you starring at? It's only an RC." In a gloating tone he continued, "There won't be as many a few months from now. There's a nationwide sweep to collect the ones we've knowledge about. These fools gathered together to pray about obstructing the very thing we succeeded in doing." His voice changed again to a stern, professional tone. "Now get! Go about your business before I run you in for obstructing the law."

Before the Upper Room group reacted, the natives disappeared. The SS agent questioned them. "What's the matter? Is this one of your friends?"

Mike answered quickly, "We don't know him. We're just headed into this shop. We're already where we were going." As the agent reached over to pick the man up, the three walked into the store.

The last one to enter was Ryker. As he came through the door, a terminal on the counter beeped three descending tones. Mike and Carol hardly notice it but Ryker froze in his tracks. The shop was empty until a man came out from the back room. A look of horror covered his face. His teeth protruded slightly below his upper lip. His thin face matched the frame it sat upon. Nervousness radiated from his vibrating, dark eyes behind the gold-framed glasses.

Mike noticed the distress. "Larry! What's wrong?"

Larry glanced at Ryker. "Is he with you?"

When excited, Carol's eyes became big and round. She looked extremely excited. "Ya Larry. He's new to our division and we're showing him some of the ropes."

The thin man trotted over to the terminal. "Does he have a ross?"

Immediately, Ryker knew why he was on alert when he heard the tones. "Yes I do but I've never heard it scanned anywhere except at the NMA Social Reform Offices."

Larry keyed the terminal board. "They began installing these new units about a month ago in all the shops and offices. The NMA has developed this scanning ability and installed them in doorways to signal any predetermined codes they have on record." He looked up at Ryker. "You must be one of the ones they're looking for." Larry shifted his focus to Mike and Carol. "We've only a few minutes until a Search Squad will be here to investigate."

No one moved. Minds raced to analyze the new information. Mike reacted first. "We've got to hide Ryker where a scanner can't pick him up."

Larry's eyes lit up at the statement. He bent down under the counter and began pulling boxes out from underneath. "Over here. I've a special compartment to protect sensitive discs and other material from scanner waves. I hope you can fit." Larry, Mike, and Carol tucked Ryker into the small compartment and shut the door. He barely fit in the tiny cubical.

The other two visitors quickly busied themselves with the music paraphernalia the store sold as two hurried SS agents ran through the door. One, with a stunner in one hand and a scanner in the other, began searching the shop. The other agent headed for Larry. "Where is he? Our scanners picked up the ross code for a Ryker H. Cuff." He turned to Mike before Larry could respond. "Are you him?"

With no need to fake his nervousness Mike reacted normally. "No sir, I'm not. I've my ID right here." He reached for his shirt pocket when the agent stopped him.

"Never mind. You don't even have a ross. Fred, do you detect anything unusual?" Fred came back to his partner. "Sorry Bruce. I don't read a thing out of the ordinary."

Bruce turned to Larry." What's going on here? Your door scanner signaled us."

157

Larry fidgeted and fumbled at the keyboard. "I'm sorry gentlemen but I think I accidentally did something to trigger the thing. I know I'm not suppose to play with the code but I was curious as to how it's programmed, and I must've keyed something in wrong."

Bruce shoved his way behind the counter and rudely knocked Larry out of the way. He stabbed the keys in high speed. "You're right. You're not to play around with the program but I don't understand how you could have triggered it with the correct code for an RC."

The agent played several minutes at the terminal. In frustration, he slapped the side of the monitor. "All right, but don't fool around with it again. I'm going to send an expert over to look at it. This software is fairly new and a bug may have gotten by us. Come on, Fred. I want to talk to Irene about this." They left as quickly as they came.

A silent half a minute went by to make sure they were truly gone. Then all three rushed to the counter compartment. Ryker came out hopping and hobbling around. "Oooooooo. I've a charley horse in my leg."

Carol visibly relaxed by sitting down on a stool. "You're lucky that's all you have. Goodness, I can't believe this last fifteen minutes. I've seen as many SS agents today as I've seen in the last three years all together. Being your friend could be detrimental to my health. They told me you've had many experiences with SS agents. Hate to give it up, huh? I think I'll leave you home next time."

The way she rambled on was comical. Mike began laughing. After some reflection, Carol joined him as the others followed. When the jocularity slowed, Mike made an introduction. "Larry Farrell, as you might have guessed, this is Ryker Cuff. It's hard to believe the only thing we came here for was to get a few supplies for the band."

Reaching for a handshake Larry smiled. "I have to say I'll not be quick to forget this introduction." He turned to Mike with a much more sober look. "If I knew you were bringing someone, I'd have warned you. They've just put this new system in as I've said and I found out a little while ago they're making arrests of those they've scouted out."

Carol said what the three others were thinking. "We'd better get what we came for and get back before we get caught. Sorry Larry, no lengthy discourses today."

Something occurred to Ryker the others hadn't thought of. "How am I to get out of here? I can't go through the door. I don't think Larry'd be able to explain it another time."

Carol rolled her eyes up in her head as Mike slumped in his seat. A quick answer came from Larry. "I've a back door but that's been rigged also. Why doesn't Ryker leave through my office window in the back room?"

Mike straightened back up. "Good idea, Larry."

Ryker readily concurred, "That's a fine idea. I think I'll go now and meet you guys out front. I'm kind of nervous about getting too close to those things," he said, pointing at doorway.

After showing Ryker to his office, Larry went back and helped Mike and Carol find what they were looking for. Ryker made his way around the back and found an alley that took him to the street. In all the excitement everyone had forgotten the disc the man had left in the sidewalk earlier. Ryker remembered when he reached the spot. Many people milled about. Not wanting to draw any attention to his actions, Ryker reached into his pocket, pulled out his wallet and with an accidental look to it, dropped a card on the sidewalk. When he picked it up, he reached for the disc in the crack and managed to pinch it with his second try. He put the disc in his wallet with the card and returned it to his pocket.

Minutes later, Mike and Carol came out saying goodbye to their friend. The trio nonchalantly walked back to the teleport. On the way they initiated a casual conversation. Carol began hoping it would help calm her. "I have to say, Ryker, when you take a girl out it certainly isn't boring."

Ryker grinned at the playful comment. "I must remind you that you're the one taking *me* out. I can't help it if I'm so well loved."

Mike interjected with a mock snooty attitude. "We have to love you—you're a brother." He laughed at his remark and then remembered something. "This Friday you have your conference with the chief, right?"

After a sigh, Ryker answered, "Yes. I'm a little anxious about it. I'm not sure where I'm going to fit in. I don't have the education, training, or talents the rest of you people have. I don't know what I'm doing here."

They'd made it to the long-distance teleport. A wait was needed because of a line, longer than Ryker had seen before.

Eventually the trio had their turn and transported to an obscure teleport in a small village. They walked across the town and waited for a short time at another teleport. Checking his watch, Mike led as the others climbed on. A technician at the Upper Room activated the machine—the first of four scheduled tries, fifteen minutes apart—making any other attempts unnecessary.

The Upper Room facility was architecturally similar to the Jordan. It was larger with several disguised buildings above ground. The facility directed all activities throughout the Network.

Ryker didn't have his own office to check into but there was the library. The difference this library had over others was much of the reading material. It contained all the usual materials and much more not found anywhere else in the USA. Most of America's founding history was erased in favor the "modern" structure supporting neutral morals. The Network providentially worked to save key information that would eventually be used to help re-found the nation, if and when that time came.

During regular hours the library was very busy. This late in the afternoon most people had gone home so there were only a few people browsing around. Ryker found a computer terminal in a place of solitude and fished out the disc he'd picked up earlier. Dropping it into the reader he patiently waited for it to process. The file turned out to be a video recording. Filling the monitor stood the man who had left the disc. Ryker remembered him being tall and slender. The oval face looked a little different than Ryker remembered; and then he realized it was because the man was smiling. Thinning, dirty blonde hair complimented his light hazel eyes.

The video clip started. "Hello, I'm Dick Steel. I don't know who'll get this but I trust the Lord it'll be in the hands of the right people. I know I shouldn't have a recording like this but in this case it's only information they already know. My prayer is someone high up in the Network will get it."

So far, Dick, your prayers have been answered. The Lord definitely handled this operation for you.

Closing his eyes for a moment and gathering his thoughts, Dick continued, "I've a friend who's connected with the NMA. I'm going to call him Jim to protect his name. Jim has managed to convey some rather disturbing news. It seems the NMA is stepping up its crack down on Christians. This friend told me that somehow some RCs had managed to infiltrate a government facility and freed a number of Christians scheduled for appropriate punishment." Dick shrugged his shoulders with widened eyes for the next statement. "Whatever that means."

Relaxing once again he continued, "The NMA is afraid we're getting too organized and sophisticated to ignore much longer. They believe one of the RCs who escaped had help from the inside. Jim says they're upset with that news because it was thought to be impossible. Someone high up is getting extremely nervous. I learned they've decided to crack down both internally and externally.

"Here's the good news." Dick smiled at his opportunity to disclose it. "I've a list from Jim of all the small groups of Christians the NMA is aware of. I'm sure it's not all the ones out there, but it does seem like quite a few. I'm leaving this list with you so those on it can be contacted and warned. Some may need to go underground. I hope this has made it into the right hands. Here's the list."

The screen began scrolling a roster of places and key people. Under each register of names were listed individuals belonging to a group. As Ryker watched, he was amazed at the length of the index. After a few minutes, he estimated there were thousands of Christians in danger. He didn't finish watching the roll. Instead, Ryker took the disc and gave it to another of his new friends. He knew Cindy Tanner had direct connections to the chief.

As luck would have it, Cindy was still in her office. Ryker knocked on the doorjamb. The woman looked up with a smile. Her heart-shaped face was enunciated by the short, blonde hair, which barely covered her ears. Her smile revealed two front teeth that helped form the u-shaped, petite smile. The color of her eyes supported the old phrase, "blue-eyed blonde." When Cindy saw Ryker's serious countenance her smile dissipated. "Ryker, what's the problem. Can I help?"

Ryker came into the office and forced a small smile. "I'm sorry. I didn't mean to look so contrite. I was just deep in thought." He took time to explain the disc, how he came to possess it, and briefly explained the information on it.

The two talked about the information for several minutes. Cindy finished up. "This is really great, Ryker. Thanks for bringing it directly to me. I know you've an appointment with the chief this Friday and could've waited to give this to him personally. But every minute counts so I'll take it directly to him now. Good work."

That night, the Network began operations saving many Christians from the hands of the NMA.

Meeting the Chief

His destination was a complete surprise to Ryker. He assumed the chief would have had an office in one of the above-ground buildings. Shawn Martin, one of the chief's aides, took Ryker deep into the lower levels where the hallway became constricting. Shawn popped into a small but pleasantly accommodating room. At a small desk sat an efficient, energetic-acting, petite lady. She was typing and talking on the Intertell at the same time.

Shawn whispered to Ryker, "This is Joyce Hughes." When she gave them the "just a minute" sign with a finger, Shawn politely indicated that Ryker have a seat. He then retreated to the hall. Ryker settled into the wooden chair and watched the act at the desk.

A signal demanded Joyce's attention. Still typing with one hand, saying goodbye to someone on the Intertell ,and touching a sensor to quiet the indication, she smiled the whole time. Joyce turned that smile to Ryker when she was through. He guessed her to be about his mother's age. Dark brown hair curled around her thin neck and floated above her blue eyes.

Joyce's voice had a lilt to it, which worked well to communicate hospitality. "That's the chief. He's ready to receive you, Ryker. I'm glad to meet you. Maybe next time we'll have a chance to visit. Go right through that door," she said, indicating a closed door in front of her. Ryker smiled politely, thanked Joyce, and told her he was looking forward to their visit.

Wonderment was the rule for the day. The other side of the door proved interesting. It opened into a small cavern. There were lights, bookshelves, and other office furniture, but it resided in a natural cave. Walking in Ryker found a desk with a high-backed chair turned away, hiding the view of the occupant. Standing at the front of the desk Ryker put his hands behind his back and cleared his throat. When the chair slowly swiveled around, Ryker's hands dropped to his side and his mouth nearly followed suit. Sitting there, grinning from ear to ear, was Vernon Cuff.

"Uncle Vern! I don't believe it! I thought I'd never see you again!"

Vernon stood up chuckling at his grandnephew and reached for a handshake. Ryker's stunned look reminded Vernon of a scene from years earlier. "How's my wise but not so little owl been doing?"

Ryker couldn't find his voice. With a dazed look, he studied the man with disbelief. Vernon hadn't changed much. He looked older with more gray hair and a few wrinkles, but there was no mistaking it was

Uncle Vern. A large grin grew on Ryker's face as he came around the desk and gave his great-uncle a warm hug.

Vernon returned the gesture with emotion that surfaced as tears that rolled down his cheeks to disappear into his beard. "My boy, my boy. I've been praying for your father, his family, and for you specifically for years. The Lord made known to me those many years ago that somehow I was going to see you again. I confess I thought maybe after this life, but when I received word you were at the Jordan facility my heart jumped for joy. I was in hopes the Lord would lead you here."

The small cave comfortably housed a petite couch, a few chairs, and a coffee table in one corner. Vernon led Ryker over to the area so they could relax. The younger shook his head at the older. "I just can't believe it. How long've you been here, Uncle Vern?"

Vernon patted Ryker's knee. "Just call me, Vern. You're old enough and have been through enough; we're equal in that respect." He took the same hand and began pulling at his beard while he looked off in thought. "Let me see. Well, you can figure out how many years it's been. We were headed here when Rose and I visited you."

Ryker screwed his face up in a moment of calculation. "That's only two months from being fifteen years. Have you been the chief all that time?"

Vern's eyes laughed as he mouthed an O. "Goodness no. Only since August of eighty-five. We had a good leader then. Litton Cramer pulled this organization together from the ground up back in the fifties. This office is where it all started. Everything else grew from here. No, I took over by default when Litton died. He was sixty-three when the NMA executed him. It was going to be his last field mission but the job was successful just the same."

Vernon paused deep in thought and then shook himself out of it. "But that's another story for another time. We're here to talk about you." It was quiet for a minute until Vernon started chuckling. "For a young man who's been through so much you don't seem very anxious to talk about it." The chuckles stopped and Vernon simply smiled. "That's a good sign. You've allowed the Lord to keep you humble."

Ryker returned the smile and lowered his head slightly. "Maybe, but it's more likely I'm nervous as to where this is leading. What do you know about me?"

Vernon sat sideways on the couch and placed his elbow upon the back of it to rest his head against his fist. "I know enough to tell you your grandfather would've been extremely proud of you. It's not that you've forced or forged your way to this point in your life, but rather God's decided to use you and you've been sensitive enough to allow Him to. There're many Christians who never learn that. I know about your Bible and what it's almost cost you. I heard about your work at the Jordan, the friends you helped rescue from the NMA, and about your incarceration at the NMA. It doesn't end there. Just a few days ago God used you to save the fate of literally thousands of Christians in this country."

Standing, Ryker thoughtfully walked around the room. After a few minutes, he turned to his uncle. "That's right; but in all of those cases I didn't act alone. I can give you numerous names of people who helped me in every one of those situations. Without anyone of them, I wouldn't have been successful or for that matter even be involved."

Vernon rose from the couch and joined Ryker. He put his arm around his nephew's shoulder. "Exactly, son. You're well aware of the team effort. You know the workings of the NMA and those of a true Christian. People respect you and look up to you without feeling any need to treat you better than them. The church is just beginning to make a comeback and organize. It's going to take people like you to make sure it happens as it should. Someone who's young enough to stay and work with all the new aspects of its growth is going to be vital. I'm not going to be around long enough to do all that."

Vernon positioned himself to face Ryker. Without the smile, his face took on a very serious look. "What I'm asking is if you'll work with me until such time as God takes me home. Then I'll have someone in position to take over where Litton and I left off."

The dream Ryker had at his parents' house recovering from his wound flooded back to him. He had tried to forget it but now it wouldn't let him. "I haven't really a choice. I must accept because God's told me I'd be in this position."

Vernon smiled and pounded Ryker on the shoulder twice. "Yes, I know. He's told me you would be here."

The two spent hours discussing whatever came to mind.

Later that evening, Ryker's small apartment was full of Cuffs. He'd invited Vern and Rose for a meal and to visit his family. Monica and Rose hit it off well. Rose won Monica's heart because of some of the boyhood stories she could tell about Ryker. Monica enjoyed it immensely and picked on her husband. Erica bounced around from person to person as she learned which ones would grant her their attention. It wasn't long before she learned Aunt Rose was a vast wealth of love and care. Monica spent much of her time trying to keep Julia from climbing everything in sight. She had turned into a little monkey in that respect. Monica and Rose enjoyed each other in the kitchen while they entertained the girls at the same time.

The men settled down in the living room. Some questions came to Ryker's mind during the day so he asked one. "Vern, what's the ultimate purpose of the Network?"

Vernon lit up. "Good question. Litton started it to have a system of communication between the small bands of believers scattered across the country. He was extremely surprised to learn there were so many out there. Litton estimated at one time that almost 10 percent of the population consisted of real Christians."

The wheels of Ryker's mind turned. "Mr. Cramer did a good job. What I was wondering is what's the direction since you've been in charge?"

Crossing his arms, Vernon eyed Ryker's profile. "Is it that obvious?"

The young man smiled at the reaction. "Sort of. For several years now, there's been a focus on teaching Christians and training them to reach others with the Gospel. You're seeking to evangelize aren't you?"

Hands rose up and dropped onto his lap in a sign of defeat. "That's right. If we're ever to get back our country as it was when our founding fathers formed it, we need our roots back. That means the people need to know God."

Heredity could be seen at work. Ryker slouched down on the couch, put his legs out in front of him, and crossed his arms. "Seems like an impossible task. There're so many out there who want nothing to believe except that there's no God or He's dead or that there's someone or something other than Jesus and God. Those SS agents are nothing less than demons from hell." Ryker lowered his voice and turned his eyes away from his uncle. "Why would God want one of them anyway?"

Vernon understood the young man's prejudice after all that the NMA put him through. But Vern needed his new recruit to understand that perspective was destructive. "Remember what second Peter chapter three, verse nine says. I'll paraphrase and amplify it. 'God wishes no one to perish, die in their sin, or go to hell, but wishes everyone, no matter who they are or what they've done, to come to repentance, not just say they are sorry they got caught but sorry enough to turn completely

165

around and not do it again so they may have eternal life and live forever in heaven.'"

Relinquishing focus from his lap Ryker looked to Vernon. "I know but God's not going to force anyone to that place. It's our choice and the way things are now the choice is either against Him or to ignore Him, which is the same thing. It seems impossible when it comes to the NMA."

Vernon's face reflected the compassion in his voice. "It would be but you're leaving out one important element of the whole thing. The Holy Spirit goes before us and prepares the way. Just think back to your own beginning. Could you sense God drawing you?"

Ryker took a moment to think about it. "Yes, but I had a family with some sense of God. I also had God's full Word to read and study. How could anyone sense God without that?"

When it came to the things of God, Vernon seldom hesitated. "Romans chapter one tells us the wonders of this world are enough to indicate there's a God, so all of us are without excuse. Yes, you had more than most but sometimes all that's needed is the Holy Spirit. Did you know your good friend, Mike Grotto, was an SS agent at one time?" Ryker sat up on the couch with eyes wide open.

Vernon chuckled. "Yes he was. He was one of the most sadistic agents they had. As a maverick in his own organization, they punished him for his actions. It seems he put a stunner to an RC's neck and shot him just to see what it'd do. Almost killed the guy I guess. You see what God's grace has done for Mike? It wasn't long after that Mike felt a need to find someone who could help answer some of his questions. He found one of his reformed RCs who helped direct him to a group."

Sitting back into his seat, Ryker had only one comment. "Wow. I would've never guessed it." He pondered how ironic his friendships had been as the women and children joined them in the living room. Rose asked Ryker a question as she settled down. "Well, Ryker, are you finding out what you've gotten yourself into by teaming up with this old coot?" She indicated to her husband with a smile.

Ryker laughed at the rascality and played at the same game. "If I'm ever to become an 'old coot' I've much to learn, I can tell you that."

Julia waddled over to her father and Ryker picked her up to love her. The older man watched the act with interest and said, "There's one other thing I wanted to cover this evening. Rose and I've talked about it and we thought it'd be important for you and Monica to take a vacation before you begin this ministry that'll take much of your time. Our thought was maybe we'd watch the girls for you while the two of you take time to be together alone for a few days."

Monica shrugged her shoulders with a neutral expression. "Gee, I don't know. I haven't even thought about time without the girls. I think I would enjoy it but I might just worry about them."

Looking at his wife, Ryker thought while he spoke. "That sounds very nice. Erica and Julia might enjoy some time with Uncle Vern and Aunt Rose. I'm sure they'd be spoiled and we'd have quite a time straightening them out again." He smiled at the last sentence and then turned to Monica. "You know, Monica, I can think of a place I'd like to visit again. How about you?"

A puzzled look started the metaphoric change as Monica comprehended where Ryker alluded to. A large smile confirmed her agreement.

The Search Realized

A line of diamond reflections rippled across the blue water along a small wake, capturing the sunlight. Monica broke through the surface of the blue rippling water. Her laughter reflected off the water. "You said the last one in was a rotten egg."

Ryker stood on the bank looking down at his wife with a glint in his eye and a smile upon his lips. "Yes I did, but I thought you'd put a swimming suit on first."

Water rolled off Monica's hair as she walked out of the water and up to the bank. The curls in her dark, thick hair relented little to the weight of the water. Her clothing clung to her body. To be a step ahead of her husband she jumped into the water—clothes, shoes, and all. She smiled at her spouse. "Let that be a lesson to you. Never put yourself in a position to be what you don't want to become."

She walked up to Ryker and stood toe to toe with him. Ryker looked slightly down at her to return a remark. "Very profound but you're the one wet, not me."

Before he realized her motive, Monica wrapped her arms around Ryker and held him close. "Hey! Let go of me! Aaaaaaaaaaaa, get away!" It was too late. He was wet also. He couldn't get away and they both ended up on the ground. Giving up the fight they lay there laughing.

It was a beautiful day. The couple camped in the wilderness for almost a week. The next morning they planned on heading home. Laying on the ground soaking up the view, Monica studied Wolf Mountain and asked, "Can we go up there once more before we return? The other day was nice but it was cloudy and cool. Today would be more like it was that day."

Ryker lazily followed her gaze and smiled. "Yes. I'd like that." He turned over on one elbow, rested his head on his hand, and with his other hand used a finger to touch Monica's nose. "It might be a good idea if you put something dry on."

She jumped up. "I'll be ready in a minute. You get a bag together and maybe we'll have our meal up there."

She left before Ryker could reply. He turned the corners of his mouth downwards then said to himself, "I don't think that was a question." He stood and did as he was told.

***

It was all they had expected. The day paralleled the one when they asked Jesus to be their Lord. Sitting on the grassy knoll they talked about their life so far. The natural outcome was to talk about the future.

"Monica? What'd ya think of me taking on this new responsibility?"

Monica looked out over the bay toward their camp. "I'm a little scared but I know it's something you must do. I'm proud of you." She turned back to face Ryker and gave him a wink and a smile.

He grinned back. "You're no more scared than I am. I've prayed, hoping this is where God would have me. It seems to be the right but the task is so large. Uncle Vern and I were talking the other night. One of our biggest obstacles is the NMA organization. If only we could penetrate it somehow with the Gospel message. It might be a way to reach the rest of the country." He looked off into the panoramic view. "I don't know if it could ever happen. I wish God would show me how to begin."

Monica lovingly held Ryker's arm and rested her head upon his shoulder. They sat that way for fifteen minutes, talking about simpler things of life. At one point, Ryker felt something and turned to look over Monica's head. He froze at the sight. Standing about hundred feet away a person watched them. When the fact clicked, Ryker jumped to his feet.

Monica looked puzzled until she saw he was looking at someone. Standing with him, Monica held his arm again. "Who's that?"

Ryker didn't answer. As the man walked toward them, Ryker knew who it was. The long, black hair was unmistakable.

Dear Jesus, help me to know what I should do.

Ryker no sooner thought his prayer when a reply flooded his being. It wasn't an audible voice, but he knew what it meant.

It's OK, my son. This is of Me, and I will guide you through it.

Monica felt Ryker relax, which helped her do the same.

Buck walked to within a few yards of the couple. He was dressed in his SS suit minus the helmet, which he held under one arm. His long, dark hair of curls moved in the breeze. "Nice spot. A long ways from home though."

Ryker stood his ground with no fear. "What can I do for you?"

Buck cocked one eyebrow. "Don't worry. I realize you haven't got that book with you." He smiled. "I've been around for two days now."

It made Monica shiver. Ryker questioned his old friend with a bit of sarcasm. "That's comforting. Tell me; how'd you know where to find me?"

Buck allowed most of his smile to slip away. "Luck mostly. I was as surprised to find you here, almost as much as you are to see me now. I had some help though." Turning to one side Buck spoke to the bushes just to his left. "Come on out—Jim Dandy." Out through the brush walked another man dressed in black, holding his helmet. It was Ray. "Meet my new apprentice partner."

Ray stood next to Buck. "Hello, Brother. Its' real good to see you enjoying life."

Emotions tore at Ryker's heart. He didn't know how to react. The battle showed on his face making Ray laugh. "Quite a surprise, isn't it? I remember you telling me about this place. I wasn't sure if I'd find it though. Imagine my surprise when Buck and I discovered you were here."

A strong gust of wind blew Buck's hair around his face. He brushed it back with his hand. "I asked Ray if maybe he could find you. He wasn't too sure at first until he found out what I wanted."

Ryker's head spun with the event. His mind lagged processing several thoughts at once. "Why'd you call Ray, Jim Dandy?"

A slight smile appeared. "He uses that name when he's doing undercover work."

169

Ryker turned his head to his brother. "Whose side are you on?"

In a moment of reflection, Ray scanned the view. As he looked to the sky he answered. "I don't know." He turned back and smiled. "I've decided to keep my mind opened for now."

Ryker locked his stare back at Buck. "I'm almost afraid to ask what you want."

Glaring at Ryker for several seconds Buck answered, "Let's just say I've considered this place neutral ground." He sheepishly grinned at the last statement. "No pun intended."

On the small mountain top, four figures stood with the backdrop of a lake shimmering in the breeze. The wind played at their hair as silence prevailed for another minute.

Buck continued, "I started out with a promising career ahead of me. I'm being given a second chance, but I've been questioning why it should even be necessary. Every time we've bumped heads I've lost. You're no one special. You've never had any formal education or any kind of special training. But you seem to have something and I'm a little interested as to what it may be. What's this religious stuff you hold on to?"

For the first time, Ryker smiled. "I don't believe in religion." The look on Buck's face caused Ryker to grin and continue, "Religion is man reaching for God. I'm a Christian. Christianity is when God reaches down and touches me."

Buck's perplexed look prevailed. "What's the difference?"

Rolling his eyes to heaven, Ryker looked for some direction. It came to him and he looked back to Buck. "What's your job?"

"To seek out people like you who undermine our social structure."

"Why do you have to go looking for them?"

"They're not about to come to me."

"Why?"

"If they had any brains, they'd be scared to." The senior SS agent didn't move or say a word. He chose not to admit he felt trapped.

Ryker saw his dilemma and continued with compassion that came from the Lord. "Don't you see, Buck? God's been searching for you because you refuse to seek Him. He loves you that much. Once He has your attention, like He does now, He'll not force you but give Him the chance and He'll answer your questions."

Looking down and crossing his arms, Ray stepped to one side about ten feet away. After a moment, he looked out over the bay and stood there until Buck finished.

Buck shifted his weight to one leg and crossed his arms. "Interesting concept—God searching for me. Tell me, buddy, what if it's all a bad joke and there is no God?"

Arm in arm Ryker and Monica stood facing the SS agent. Ryker took a moment to look down at Monica and smile. He lifted that smile to his friend. "I don't think much of gambling but let's look at this from your point of view. If there's no God or heaven, I don't regret my life. I'm happier living by the principals of Christianity than I ever could without them. If I'm wrong, then when I die I lose nothing, but have gained a fruitful and fulfilling life here. If there is a God, then when I die I win everything. Now, I don't know what kind of life you're having but I can guess. God's Word says without Him we're nothing. So, if you're right and there is no God, you win nothing. But if you're wrong and there is a God, you lose everything by not accepting Him. Jesus said that no one can come to the Father except through Him. You tell me which one is the best bet."

A picture froze in time. The only sounds were the breeze blowing through the trees and a hawk that chose that moment to screech his amen. It was more than Buck could handle. He had no argument to counter and was smart enough not to make something up. The wind blew hair around his stone-cold face. After a minute, he decided to move and faced his apprentice. "Come on, Ray, we're going." He turned to Ryker and Monica. "I want you to know I consider this place neutral ground, but I'm not guaranteeing anything once you're away from here."

He turned and walked away. Ray trotted to catch up then turned to look over a shoulder at his brother. He gave Ryker a small smile, turned, and walked out of sight with Buck.

Five minutes passed. The couple turned into each other's arms and embraced. Over the shimmering blue bay the hawk flew high. Ryker watched for a moment. "I learned one thing today. God will never stop His search."

PART TWO

I will search for the lost and bring back the strays.
I will bind up the injured and strengthen the weak,
but the sleek and the strong I will destroy.
I will shepherd the flock with justice.

EZEKIEL 34:16

I am the good shepherd;
the good shepherd lays down His life for the sheep.
I am the good shepherd,
and I know My own and My own know Me,
My sheep hear My voice, and I know them,
and they follow Me;

JOHN 10:11, 14, 27

LOOKING BACK

Buck was never as nervous in Sly Hawkins' presence. It was six years since he had anything to do with Ryker Cuff after the mountain visit. That fact was the catalyst that resulted in his career taking off like an unburdened helium balloon. But now the SS agent felt the old emotions associated with the failures to those former times. Ryker Cuff returned to haunt him and he again faced those helpless feelings of ambiguity. Alanson S. Shanach was about to see who he was through the perception of someone other than himself. Someone he had questioned Ryker about before.

His eyes were the same vibrant blue but the face was softer looking under the short-cut, black hair. Buck sat in a darkened location, lit only with a crude candle found with some other primitive accommodations in the small cave. As the flame flickered subtly, the light revealed several scars on the weathered face and hands. Fingers trembled slightly as Buck reached for the . . .

Buck stopped mid stream of his faltering action. He thought about the events leading to this time and this situation. The last year rolled back in his memory.

MAJOR JUNCTION

"This is a major junction in U.S. history. The laws have finally recognized the progressive advancement of the American social structure. The Christian view, as the right wing defines it, is not the only voice or measure of the people's rights under a free society."

Glenda Seymore—N.O.W. delegate speaking to the taskforce developing the revised standards for the United States new bill of rights. 5/20/2022

April

Time passed quickly and effectively for Buck after he decided to ignore his old opponent. These five years seemed like a blink. The smile on his face, as he surveyed his Albany office one last time, was the first real one he produced from genuine pleasure in a long time. Black, curly hair cascaded past his shoulders framing the vibrant blue eyes and wide smile.

"You're going to miss it aren't you?"

With his back to her, Buck almost laughed. Stifling the desire to guffaw in her face, he turned a smile to the questioner. "You miss-judge me. I'm only relishing the fact that it'll be the last time I'll ever see this hell hole again."

No insult taken, April quickly replied by returning his smirk with a like one. April Goulay was a pretty woman, not an overpowering beauty but a second look proved very pleasant. Her gray-green eyes were a little too close together, though the small, pouting mouth offset the obvious fact of it. April flung a length of her light brown hair back over her shoulders. "Can't really blame me. How can anyone know what a tin man's thinking? A mind without a heart is like a book in the dark. You've heard it's pretty good but you can't read it for yourself."

Buck gallantly closed his eyes and gave a slight nod of his head. "Point well taken. Excuse my sarcasm." He wore his brown-and-yellow trimmed office outfit. The Search Squad agent closed the door, gently held the woman's arm in his, and escorted her down the hall. "You must excuse my causticity, for I sometimes lack the immediacy of my situation. The last thing I wish to do is earn your dissatisfaction in me. You've been an excellent apprentice and partner since Ray left me two months ago."

Walking out of the building Buck told April of his past concerning Ryker Cuff and his brother Ray. Somewhat out of character for this man, April listened intently to the whole story as Buck relayed it to her. It was a warm, breezy early summer morning. The street was busy with others walking to work or a similar errand. Passing the sign to the building the pair walked leisurely northbound to a teleport at the next corner. The twosome ignored the emblem, but visitors read it for its historic reminder. The sign was large and quit graphic: "Albany NMA. Where your rights to neutral morals began. The home of Dr. Eli Grossman—father of the new United States."

Someone exited the teleport as Buck and April arrived. With a puzzled look upon her face, April turned to follow the man with her eyes. "I've seen that guy somewhere. Do you know who he is?"

Buck casually glanced in the correct direction, shrugged his shoulders, and shook his head no. He took up the conversation without interruption and continued recounting his story as the teleport whisked the couple away to another section of town.

Entering the building, which Buck and April had just departed, the man April considered turned to examine his trod. He pondered upon the couple who teleported away. A gentle wind fluttered his long, scraggly, rust-colored hair. Dark brooding eyes under a single long eyebrow stared distantly in solitude. The untidy beard resembled a cat-torn ball of yarn, but it was his thought process that would interest someone watching. No one else saw it. No one else knew about it, but forgotten thoughts flashed through the hazy mind. Once he remembered a thought, he became more aware of who he once was. He smiled realizing the recollection stayed with him. After some hesitation, he turned back and walked lamely into the Albany NMA building.

At the main reception desk, the man cradled his notebooks. Across the top of one of them, scribbled in hurried handwriting, was the name Hank Bronson. The head security officer waited patiently behind the counter for the newcomer to state his business. Finally, out of impatience, the beautiful dark-haired woman prodded the man for information. "State your name and your business please."

Staring at the name at the top of his papers, Hank purposely hid the contents from view and blankly responded. "My name is . . ." Many seconds passed before fingers impatiently tapped at the counter top. Like cold water thrown in his face, the man's eyes opened wide with sudden recollection. "VanTimons. Craig VanTimons is my name." Relaxing, Hank/Craig continued, "All my friends call me Red. I use to have bright orange-red hair."

Tina Getling keyed the information on the terminal then replied, "I've no appointment scheduled for a VanTimons. What can I do for you Mr. VanTimons?"

Craig slowly became more alert, realizing who he was and acted with that personality. He beamed for the first time. "Just call me Red. I'm looking for a certain SS agent named Alanson Shanach."

The Amazon young woman didn't hesitate. The dark red lips parted into a smile at the mention of Buck's name. "You just missed him. He's been transferred to the Washington DC office. Al's left for the day and won't be back here. You'll have catch him at home or wait to see him in Washington next Monday."

The eyebrow made a V as Red frowned at the information. Seconds passed before a slight smile symbolized the inward thought process. With a glint in his dark eyes, Red gathered his material and turned to leave as he responded, "No problem. I'll call on my old friend another time. Thanks just the same."

Red walked out the building ignoring the question posed to him by the security officer. "Would you like me to forward a message to Mr. Shanach's Washington office?"

The wretched man, looking younger by the minute, briskly walked out onto the street with no hint of a limp. Tina shook her head, mumbled something about bad hearing, and went about her duties.

Holly

The bird feeder bounced swinging in a stiff breeze tethered to a branch outside his window. The scene changed slightly with rhythmic beats of the sunlight affected by fast-moving clouds, varying the light intensity. Unfocused eyes stared at the image through the dusty window. Other thoughts obscured the picture. Ryker had more important items to consider. A decision had to be made and made soon.

The years matured Ryker's appearance. His beard had developed into a rich, thick bubble that hid his weak chin. The once long hair was thinner, especially at the crown, and cut short above the ears. He studied a computer terminal carrying the message he read minutes earlier.

To: Ryker
From: Vernon

I know you're not going to enjoy this, but Calvin is bringing a guest in at two o'clock this afternoon. I'm leaving this issue up to you to handle. I think it's about time I gave you the responsibilities as long as you're accountable for the outcome. I know we have talked about this and are not in total agreement. You do what you feel is correct. I will back it up 100 percent no matter what your final decision is. May God be with you.

The clock on the wall read 1:56 p.m. A voice floated over his terminal that shook Ryker from his deep contemplation. He pushed his wire-frame glasses back up on the bridge of his nose as he turned to listen. "Mr. Cuff, Calvin Katang is here with a Holly Tarbell and says he's an appointment with you. Should I send them in?" The image on the screen revealed a pleasant-looking dark woman with braided hair done up in rings and beads. The large smile added depth to her dark eyes.

"Yes, Kimberly. That'll be fine, but send Calvin in first please."

Calvin Katang closed the door behind him. He and Ryker were comparable in general physical stature, but it was the extent of their similarities. Calvin's shoulders were wider and his waist thinner. He had a thick head of hair, wavy and much darker than his superior. Long eyelashes shadowed the deep blue eyes, which smiled even when the rest of the face didn't. Calvin's chiseled chin was bare except for the dimple in the center of it. The man was a few years younger than the Network Chief. Ryker figured Calvin would be an asset to the underground operations of the Network when he first met him eight years earlier.

Calvin's voice was low and soft when he wasn't anxious. "I've Holly in Kim's room next door. Is there something I can do for you?"

A moment of silence seemed liked minutes. One of Ryker's many character oddities included his patience during conversations. Until experienced a few times, Ryker seemed to be dazed. His friends knew he chose his vocal delivery with much deliberation. Seldom misunderstood, he infrequently had to repeat himself. His people learned to appreciate the virtue. "Maybe you can, Cal. Have a seat for a minute."

The chamber was small with a single window just behind Ryker's desk. The only other furniture in the pale blue room was a file cabinet, a small table, and two other chairs besides the one Calvin settled into.

Softly pulling at the hairs on his chin Ryker said, "I value your opinion. I'm not saying I'll be swayed by it but I'd like your insight to this situation. It'll help me gage the validity of my decision and understand the outcome no matter what happens."

Calvin blankly stared for a moment before allowing a smile to deepen the dimple on his chin. "Pretty easy for me to express. I'm not going to be held accountable. I was thinking about this though and I remember a passage in the gospel of John about the woman caught in the act of adultery and brought to Jesus. He forgave her and told her not to do it again. But the interesting part of the story is that Jesus asked her accusers to throw the first stone if they'd never sinned. They were honest enough to leave. Relative to our brothers and sisters we'd better be cautious about what we accuse them of."

Ryker leaned back in his chair and calmly tapped his fingertips together. With a smile he commented. "OK. Thanks, Calvin. Send Holly in and I'll see you later."

Calvin left and moments later sat a petite woman about six years Ryker's junior. She was nervous and showed it by nibbling at her lower lip. Long, golden brown hair shimmered past her shoulders and disappeared somewhere around her waist. Large, taupe-colored eyes evaded direct contact with Ryker's.

Ryker attempted to ease Holly's apprehension. "I believe you don't need to worry. This could've never gone this far if others in the Network hadn't thought you a good risk. The only real service in this interview is to satisfy my own curiosity. Why don't we start by having you tell me why you'd like to seek permanent refuge from the government?"

Large nervous eyes looked up. The lower lip was released with a voice as small as the woman-child. Holly haltingly began. "I'd . . . I'd like to thank you first for . . . giving me this opportunity. Loren said you'd understand."

Puzzled at the statement Ryker asked, "Loren?"

"Loren Richards. He's Nick Richards' son. I met him at one of my first Christian gatherings. He is a great speaker. Later I moved to his area and started attending his services."

"Nick Richards' son?" Ryker looked distant for a moment until Holly continued.

"I know Nick was a good friend of yours. Loren said after you witnessed his father's martyrdom it started a new revival in the church. It was half expected what happened to Christians at the NMA but now that we know for sure, it's given a new urgency to combat it."

A time of silence prevailed while Ryker reflected upon his old friend. "Nick would be glad to know his life's made a difference."

Holly's nervous habit returned in the absence of other dialogue. Sensing her anxiety, Ryker continued his interview with a soft, understanding tone. "How long've you been a Christian?"

Holly's large, roaming eyes locked onto Ryker's with conviction. "It's been over a year now. As a matter of fact," she squinted in calculation and continued, "it was April 5, 2096. That makes it almost a year."

A large smile and slight nodding of his head kept Holly from being nervous. Not wishing his guest to see any negative expressions with his next question, Ryker slowly rose and faced his window, relaxing. After some thought to the delivery, he nonchalantly proceeded. "What did Ray do when he found out you'd become a Christian?"

Added to the other nervous reaction, Holly began wringing her hands in her lap. "That's one thing that really made me scared. He hardly reacted to it. I couldn't tell what his thoughts were. I could've related to a violent outburst, seeing as he'd just learned his best informant may have ruined years of work. But he didn't do anything." She whispered the next sentence with her head down. "I decided to hide and haven't seen him since."

Ryker turned to face the woman and sat back down at his desk. "I realize this is somewhat hard for you but I need to ask. How close were you and Ray?"

Pushing back a lock of hair fallen into her face Holly looked up. Ryker noticed her eyes shimmering as she said, "We'd lived together for almost three years. I've known him for about twice that long. He told me about you and Monica and how you two got married. I had many questions about it. Once, half in jest, I asked him if we could do the same." The eyes no longer contained her emotions as a tear tracked down along her cheek. "He shocked me by saying he'd have to think about it. I believe he meant it even though the subject was never brought up again."

Offering her a tissue, Ryker continued the interview. "Thanks for your honesty but that does leave doubts about your motives for going underground. How am I to be guaranteed your alliances are truly to our causes and won't be swayed back to Ray?" The question carried little empathy and a stern tone to the seriousness of the concern.

Holly recognized the pivotal point and dried her eyes. Gathering her courage she confidently replied, "I understand the concern. I'm probably responsible for more arrest of religious cult members, as the NMA calls them, than most. Al and Ray taught me well how to act and gain confidence of underground Christians. It earned Al a promotion to a higher position at the Washington office, more prestigious than before. I'm not the same person I was. I got close enough to you people that I've learned what you really believe. I've met Jesus for myself and accepted Him."

They sat staring at one another in silence. Ryker determined he needed to test the knowledge and conviction of Holly's testimony. Leaning forward with his hands folded upon his desk he cross-examined her. "Let's say you were to die in the next few minutes. For the sake of argument, pretend you found yourself at the gate to heaven. There's a gatekeeper there. Before he'll allow you in, you need to answer one question correctly. He simply asks why he should allow you into heaven. What would your answer be?"

She vacillated for a moment. Holly turned her attention to a picture on the other side of the room but focused back to Ryker for her answer. "Because Jesus died for my sins. I could've done nothing to deserve heaven. If I've done any good, it's because of what Jesus has done for me. I could not earn any favors or rights to be there."

Conversation halted for half a minute. Holly became nervous and started chewing her lip while wringing her hands. Ryker noticed her sudden uneasiness and gave the small woman a smile. "That's fine. You gave a good answer, one that reveals what you've learned about your faith. Do you have any questions for me?"

A thin hand reached up and again moved a lock of hair away from a golden brown eye. "Just one. Do you think you can ever come to trust me? I've done so much to hurt the Christian cause in the past."

Ryker rose from his desk and came around to face Holly. She stood when he did so. The look of fear in her eyes made Ryker empathize with her. "A good friend reminded me of something this afternoon. If Jesus has forgiven you, and you desire to serve Him, who am I to stand in the way? I've no real choice but to trust you will be nothing except a great blessing to this organization. I concur with our Lord. Your transgressions have been forgiven. Be at peace and serve well; sin no more."

Holly could not help hugging Ryker in great relief as her eyes finally flooded all her emotions. "Thank you so much for allowing me this opportunity to right all my wrongs. I know it'll please God and I want to do it. Thank you again from the bottom of my heart."

A few minutes later, Ryker sat alone in his office. He was glad and still apprehensive at the same time. He meditated upon the event.

Lord, I sense this is right but I can't help feeling concerned. Have I allowed Your will or have I let the devil himself into Your sanctuary?

Red

Craig VanTimons felt like a brand-new man. The chances were one in a million and he was one of the rare ones to come out of a mind alteration. Craig felt strange but empowered to realize Hank Bronson was the only programming he had endured. Ecstasy filled him to remember so much and more as time passed.

As he often did, Red spoke to his parrot, "Well Casey, I'm going to need to re-train you. I'm not who you think I am."

The bird responded, "Hank's home. Hank's home."

Red gave him a large, amiable smile. "See what I mean, buddy. You don't even know who I am. Red's home. Red's home."

Hank's meager accommodations were appalling. Casey's cage, which hung from a metal stand, was safe from the mess. The floor was so filthy it could be mistaken for a dirt floor. A table and chair sat centered in the room with counter space taking up two of the walls. One door served as the main entrance and another led to a dingy bedroom. The adjoining roomette had a bed; one broken dresser with a plain, cracked mirror above it; and another door that led to the bathroom. The small, closet-sized bathroom housed only a toilet and a small sink. The apartment never did nor could it ever house a teleport.

Laying his material on the table Red sat in the lone chair. Brushing dried food, papers and other debris off he made room to look at the notebooks. The wild-looking man touched the name at the top of the first notebook with hesitancy. A minute passed before he spoke to his bird. "You know something, Casey? Hank Bronson wasn't much of a man. He barely lived from day to day. Craig is nothing like him. I remember back on the farm when Dad and I talked about a career. Dad talked of pursuing some kind of medical program. Mom and Dad were so proud of me and my ambitions for life."

With a faraway look, Red's eyes glistened with the recollection. Very softly and to himself the lonely man whispered. "Mom and Dad? Where are you? What happened to you?"

Hours passed as Red contemplated the memories flooding back to his original conscience. Tracks lined his face to his chin, which was hidden by the beard. A smile settled upon his appearance. He got up from the table and routinely grabbed the birdseed next to the cage and spilled some to his pet. In his excitement, the bird became vocal. "Hank's home. Hank's home. Life's fine. Life's fine. Shut up. Shut up."

Red laughed at the old reality of his very recent past. "My fine, feathered friend you've much more to learn. I haven't had much to say these last few years but that's going to change."

The smile faded with a blank look of deep thought. Red absently talked to the parrot. "I don't know how I ever got the idea to look for Buck. I didn't know who he was, but the name Alanson Shanach kept pounding at my vacant like mind. As luck would have it, I saw him today as I blindly looked for him. I didn't know it was him until he was gone but as the reality of it sunk in, my mind nearly exploded with memories."

Casey jabbered some more meaningless phrases as Red came to a conclusive thought to all he remembered. *Buck, old buddy, we will meet again. You're going to pay for what you maliciously did to me.*

Kayla

Wind whistled past her smiling expression. Long, white-blonde hair trailed straight back from the short, oval face with rosy cheeks and light blue eyes. Except for her eyes, which at the moment danced with excitement, Kayla Keating resembled an albino. She screamed as the roller coaster made its final decent and stopped.

"Wheeee! That felt real. Can you believe how that felt, Jesse?" The young woman turned to the person sitting beside her with the question. He was as pale looking as Kayla—an unnatural shade for him. Jesse Bronchetti was close to twice the size of his friend. His short, dark hair laid helter skelter and his deep-set eyes closed as he gulped, "Too real for me. I've got to get out of here and get some air."

As the ride ended, the lights came on. The couple sat in a special seat facing a 180-degree dome screen. A door opened on one side and Jesse hurried to exit as the chair released him. Kayla wasn't far behind with a tooth-producing grin on her cheerful face. Passing through the lobby quickly, Jesse made it outside and took a deep breath. The steady breeze washed away the queasy feeling.

Kayla laughed robustly rushing through the door. "I can't believe that bothered you that much. If the Rapture is anything like that, you're in big trouble."

Jesse smiled for the first time. From his bent-over position he peered at Kayla with raised eyes. They were a deep brown, which complemented his tanned complexion. "I think you're enjoying my discomfort more than that detestable ride."

Kayla chortled again. "You never went anywhere! It's all a mind trip. I love it! Finally I've found something I can do that you've a hard time with."

The big man straightened and allowed his chest to level with Kayla's smile. A breeze picked up the ends of her long, straight, blonde hair and tossed it about. "We'd better get going, Jesse. They're expecting us at one o'clock."

Laughing and joking, the pair walked to the corner teleport.

***

The SS agent waited patiently on the corner across from the entrance to the Washington DC NMA building. He was careful to position himself so he wasn't conspicuous to those leaving the building. A stiff breeze tumbled paper debris across the walkway as the sun moved behind a cloud. Several people exited the edifice and walked to various establishments for lunch. The agent pulled back into a corner as he noticed a distinguished gentleman leaving. Jim was graying slightly at the temples but the honey-colored hair hid it well. He wore a white suite trimmed with red. As he traveled down the sidewalk the SS agent followed.

Several blocks further Jim came to an obscure teleport used little by the aristocrats of the area. For many years, he had used it to meet his mistress. Jim cared little if others knew but she would rather some didn't know of their relationship. As he entered the teleport, the large SS agent roughly slammed him in and took over the controls. After allowing the glass panel to shut, he halted the process and removed an access panel. He worked on a few components. Jim Rice shook his head to clear it and stood to see the agent adjusting the controls. His blue eyes widened in disbelief and pounded on the glass from inside. The effect was futile on the agent as he typed commands to continue the teleport operation. Hollering and hammering continued as the glass darkened. A brief segment of a scream died with the flash behind the opaque partition, and then silence.

The agent reversed the work he did to the unit as the glass lightened and slid back in the open position. A mangled mass of human flesh and cloth lay where the man stood. Jim Rice, the head of the NMA, was dead. The investigation would prove a freak teleport transmission was the cause. It was the first one in twenty years. Devon Damon finished covering his tracks and went to report on his progress.

***

Twenty minutes later, Kayla and Jesse sat in a more regimented setting. The room was dim, exuding a musty smell. The little group of four sat around a square, wooden table. A single light source in the ceiling made shadows dance low upon the walls as the foursome moved around. The Bethany facility was very small but played a major role in the Network's operations. Kayla and Jesse listened as John Ball and Felicia Rederman quibbled about the situation that brought them together.

Felicia was adamant. "You can't do that! What if no one had given Saul of Tarsus a chance?" The tight line formed by her mouth underscored the intensity in her bright blue eyes. The sphere of red, curly hair bounced as she snapped her head to a stop when she finished.

The older, balding man folded his arms in front defensively. John resembled a Buddha statue as he did it.

Kayla intervened. "I don't believe John meant it that way, Felicia. He's only trying to point out that there's a real danger to the Network if this man isn't closely monitored, even IF he's allowed in."

The squatty little man moved none, except his jowls, as he responded. "That's right. I don't want us going into this thing without understanding all the consequences it entails, both good and bad."

187

The redhead relaxed in her seat. "Sorry I misunderstood you, John. I'm ready to vote."

Jesse frowned before proposing his question. "Am I to understand that he'd be limited to the core group only? Then there'd be special sessions before he'd have an opportunity to visit the rest of the group?"

John sat straight up to punctuate his quick retort. "Only if this group comes to a consensus after the interview."

Felicia rolled her eyes. "Yes, exactly. You're both right."

Silence pressed Kayla to move things along. "I think we all agree. Bring the visitor in."

Felicia left the room and was absent long enough for John to vent some of his frustration. "That woman's just a little too liberal in my way of thinking. I believe everyone should have a chance, but this one's a BIG chance as far as I'm concerned. I wish Lois could've been here. She could've helped balance out priorities here."

Kayla beamed one of her appealing smiles. "Don't worry, John. Just allow the Spirit to guide us and we can't go wrong. Let's hear this man out and then we'll have information for a more intelligent decision."

As she came through the door, Felicia stood aside and introduced her guest. He had a long, sandy blonde ponytail and a dark brown beard. Glasses perked upon his nose enlarged his blue eyes. "Everyone, this is Ray Cuff."

CHANGING TIMES

"Things are changing and I don't like the direction they're taking. I believe what is happening at the Albany office is our best line of attack to remedying this."

Sly Hawkins, special meeting with the USA President, 1/14/2096

Buck

"Freedom, an unalienable right. Choice, to be protected above all. To die for either, an honor to treasure." The words voiced in unison reverberated throughout the large room. The monotone chant was spoken with concise syllabication and conviction. The chamber, fabulously adorned with great arts, sparkling fixtures, and rich woods swallowed the echo as a baron plucking fortunes from a foe. Deafening silence lingered, stiffly mimicking the people in the room at attention.

When the three figures at the front of the auditorium sat down, a wave of black and brown settled in their seats, much like "follow the leader." At center stage, two figures were contrasted in color to the rest in the room and each other. Sly Hawkins nearly shone in his white-with-red-trim suit. He decreed respect and military protocol throughout the organization. Sitting next to him, Alanson Shanach puffed up like a pancake on a hot griddle. Finally, after years of hard work and disappointments, he was on track to goals envisioned originally. Buck wore the prized colors of deep blue with crimson trim. He could hardly contain his professional demeanor. Behind and to their left, April sat in her yellow-trimmed, brown jumpsuit waiting patiently.

Sly lightly ran a hand over his thin, mousy hair before beginning. In a deep, melodious tone he started the meeting. "Thank you for being here this morning. As you're all aware—I know because gossip travels through this place faster than a teleport transmission—some changes start this morning. I've moved from second in command to first, taking the late Jim Rice's place. It's a pleasure for me to officially introduce you to my replacement, the man you'll all be reporting to. Many of you recognize Al from when he worked here before. His record is one of unequaled achievements for someone his age. He burst into the government a promising supervisor. Unfathomable circumstances almost ruined his career, but this man is a prime example of what relentless work and dedication will do if turned upon the virtues this agency offers. It's with great pleasure I give the floor to one I hope you can emulate your career after, Alanson S. Shanach."

The pancake had a little too much baking powder and resembled something closer to a big biscuit. Buck couldn't contain his pride and self-worth. Long, black, curly hair shimmered in the lights, encircling the beaming face. He stood, raised arms to silence the applause, but the act resembled an embrace. A long, thin smile underlined his bright blue eyes. Placing his hands behind him Buck patiently waited for the noise level to subside.

To avoid an awkward moment, Buck addressed the crowd. "Thank you. It's my intention the respect you show will not be in vain. I'll earn it next time. My goal's to take the mightiest division of the NMA raised by Sly Hawkins," Buck turned, saluted his superior, and returned, "and continue molding it into the strongest, meanest, most determined adversary for freedom and rights this nation embraces. We'll not fail because this, without a doubt, is the best prepared group of SS agents in the nation."

Like a rooster, Buck strutted back and forth, satisfied for the applause and enjoying the accolade. When the moment arrived, he painted on a serious expression. "I know what it's like out there. Things are much different than eight or ten years ago. We've an underground movement, which has escalated in intensity with a purpose to destroy the freedoms our new founding fathers struggled to achieve. I have plans that when instituted will greatly hinder that movement. The procedures work. I know they work because I've used them successfully for several years now. I want you to take these ideas and with my guidance, use them on a larger scale to achieve the ultimate goal of eradicating the RC movement in our great nation."

Buck sat down. After the applause calmed down, Sly took the floor. "That's why I've commissioned Al to take my place. I've witnessed the results of his operation and I'm confident what he says will come to pass. So prepare yourself to work. Al's going to have a special meeting this morning with your supervisors and then they will inform you of our new strategy. The dawn of a new age is upon us. Stand and let us prepare for the revival of modern American ethics."

Everyone complied and rose. In unison, they finished the meeting with the ceremonial salutation. "Together we stand, together we crush. Forward until Rigid Christians are hushed."

The volume of murmuring increased as everyone left. The excitement carried over into the halls. Sly and Buck shook hands and exchanged a few words before departing for their offices.

April followed her partner out the door. "Tell me, Al, why didn't you inform me of your popularity here? I'm almost jealous."

Buck turned one of his amoral smiles to her as they strolled down the hall from the auditorium. "You're always popular when you're engaging. Let that be a lesson to you. Always look like you're winning, even if you're losing."

He turned, entered an elevator, and left April nodding her head in deep thought.

Revenge Planned

Casey didn't like it. He squawked and fluttered about under the dark, covered cage. Moving anywhere made him unsettled. Carrying Casey, Red didn't relate to his pet's sentiment. People who had any contact with Hank Bronson wouldn't have recognized him. He was clean cut, wearing new cloths, and his hair was much shorter. A handle bar mustache was the only facial hair the elated man kept. He set the cage down in one corner of the room and took the cover off. "Now quit your chattering. You'll like your new home. See Casey, you even have a view now."

A picture window allowed a vista of Washington DC. At the large window the redhead put his hands in his pockets and stared out over the city. He dyed his hair to its natural red-orange color, which was more familiar to him. It lay neatly on the collar of his flowered shirt. Several minutes went by as Red thought deeply about his plans.

Casey settled down and fell back into old habits. "Hank's home. Hank's home." Red turned his dark blue eyes to his feathered friend. The eyes seemed lighter than many days before, which only added to his new brighter countenance. "It didn't take you long to learn where home is.

Now, why can't you learn my real name?" The question came with a smile on his face.

A signal caused Red to lose the grin and turn to the teleport in the room. The glass wall of the unit slid into place and became opaque for a visual conference. Above the screen on the ceiling a small, blue light blinked ambiguously, indicating a scrambled and private visual transmission. It put Red on guard.

The person on the large screen probably was a male but one couldn't really tell. The voice was just as cryptic. "Mr. Craig VanTimons, 'We know the judgment of God rightly falls upon those who practice such things.' Do you understand?"

Red's eyebrows V-ed as he reached in his shirt pocket for a scrap of paper. He read his short response. "Romans two, verse two." He couldn't help his query about the strange reply. "What's Romans—a piece of poetry?"

The indefinite figure hardly moved when he spoke. "For now that's no concern of yours. You've contacted a unique organization devoted to black market NMA information. How'd you know to contact us? We've no privileges listed for a VanTimons."

Putting the scrap of paper back in his pocket, Red turned and walked back to Casey before turning again to answer. "My mother told me how to get help if I ever needed it, but to never use it unless it was an emergency."

There was a moment of silence until the person realized Red wasn't offering any more information. "Who's your mother?"

Looking at his bird, the redhead simply riposted, "Casey—Margie Casey."

The figure turned sideways looking to someone, nodded his head in a simple affirmative response, and returned to face the teleport. "Welcome Mr. VanTimons. How might we help you?"

Red braced himself erect and blinked before continuing. "That easy? I half expected to be ignored; thought I might be arrested or worst, society would never hear from me again. Now as simple as that you're going to allow me a request?"

"Margie would've made sure you were a good risk before ever divulging any information about us."

"I'm her son. That doesn't necessarily mean I have her convictions."

"She knew you were safe or you wouldn't be talking to us now."

If ever Craig VanTimons had a doubt of his mother's love for him, it vanished. He continued with a hint of pride in his voice. "All she ever told me was to get a hold of John, uh, this certain person, whom I've never met until yesterday. No one ever squeezed that information out of me." He paused in deep thought, proud about keeping that information from Buck before snapping out of his trance to continue. "I need to know all the personal information I can get on an Alanson Samuel Shanach of the Washington DC NMA."

The vague image typed the information on a keyboard. Studying the information before him on the screen, invisible to Red, seemed funny enough to get a simple chuckle from Red. The negotiator's frown was indistinguishable, but it came through the oracular voice. "This might be a tough one. Since he's moved from Albany, his security level's raised several notches. We'll have to get back to you sometime later. This will also require some substantial information from you in return. Do you have any?"

Red thought about things he'd learned while Buck was holding him before his mind alteration. "Ya. I believe I've much you'll be very interested in. Just get back to me as soon as you can."

A simple OK was the unknown person's elementary reply before the teleport went black, and the glass partition cleared and retracted back into the wall. Sitting at the table under the picture window, Red carefully thought about his next move.

"Well Casey, things are working out better than I thought. I presume we're going to succeed." A wide smile grew on Red's face as he studied his panorama of the city.

Romance

Night was like black velvet, studded with sparkling diamonds all draped across the heavens, blanketing any hint of daytime. Hanging low in the sky a thin crescent moon slightly rippled reflected off the slow-moving waters of the Potomac River. The city skyline was a dark silhouette under the pale moonlight. Two figures stood close, studying the caliginous view from a small, barge-type boat riding in the middle of the river. Contrasting against the night, the pale moonlight caused a florescent glow to Kayla's hair. It was free flowing and shimmered in the delicate breeze. Ray's long, dusty-colored hair was tied up in a ponytail. His full chestnut beard contrasted against his hair.

Their backs were to the shadowed orb to study the night. Several minutes went by before she saw it. A faint amber color of light rippled up and away from the city. Ray quickly leaned to Kayla, pointing out the phenomena. "See! You have to be patient or you'll miss it. A moonless night is best time to view it."

With excitement Kayla expressed, "I wouldn't have believed it if I hadn't seen it for myself. I never knew you could see one. I wonder why I never heard of it before."

Ray turned to face her. He was soft and persuasive as he spoke, "There're many things I'd like to tell you when I get the opportunity." He gently moved a lock of the silky hair back from Kayla's face with the back of his fingers, and looked deep into her eyes.

Kayla lost herself momentarily to the inviting blue eyes framed with the smiling face. In that moment, something happened she never experienced before. A longing to indulge in the attraction strongly felt was only averted because a quiet intuition that told her to pray. Closing her eyes she silently asked for strength and guidance before turning her head to face the city skyline once more. "You probably will. Maybe sometime you'll be able to."

Ray was disappointed but concealed the truth. Instead, he turned to study the view with Kayla and said, "Ya. I'd like that. Maybe sometime soon we could share many things."

Endeavoring to keep her balance, Kayla brought things back to a more comfortable atmosphere. "It's interesting the things we don't ever question. I never thought about looking for a teleport transmission. It has to be oodles of energy to see one like that."

Placing his hands behind his back, Ray began slightly rolling back and forth from the balls of his feet to his heels. He had assumed a college professor's role. "It's usually not visible to the naked eye but very large transports take so much power that some of the energy falls into the visible light spectrum. That was probably a large equipment transport or many people using a mass teleport going to the same place."

"Does it always look the same?"

"No. It can be different colors or several colors. Some are so visible you can almost make out what's being transported. Conditions have to be right for that and it's rare enough to see one at all."

194

"Well, thanks for showing me. I have to admit when you first mentioned it, I thought you were pulling my leg."

Moonlight made Ray's eyes shimmer when he turned a serious face to Kayla. "I'd never do anything to make you look foolish, Kayla. I need your confidence in me for two reasons now."

She could feel her heart pounding in the silence that followed. Not daring to look Ray full in the face, she turned half way to him to respond. Her mouth was the only visible moving part of her silhouette. "I hope my trust in you is validated soon but that's all up to you. So far you've nothing to fear. Tomorrow Felicia is suppose to . . ." She stopped realizing she was about to divulge more than she should.

As she lowered her head in thought, Ray leaned over and kissed her on the cheek. Stunned, Kayla lightly wiped her cheek with the back of her hand before she turned away and walked to the other side of the barge. "We should probably get back. If anyone ever finds out we were out here alone, I'd be in big trouble."

Ray's eyes traced each step she took. "I should apologize for that kiss, but it wouldn't be the truth. You're right. We'd better get going. And Kayla—thanks for your sensitive response. It won't happen again."

Every fiber of her being wanted to yell it was OK but she controlled the urge. The only encouragement she gave was a platonic smile. "Don't worry about it. I'm glad you understand."

As Ray turned and took the uncomplicated controls to the water hovercraft, he smiled an indistinguishable smile.

Ryker

Terror violently projected from Monica's usually demurer face. Her eyes—round blue orbs swimming on a sweat-drenched façade— were riveted on danger. The long, curly, chestnut hair was tangled and matted to her head. She sat on a crude wooden bench screaming a silent outcry in horror. Her phobia was in complete control of all her reasoning as a snake crawled across her shoulder. The room was full of them and all headed for her. The chamber was a dark, smelly hole with bars blocking the only opening in the cell. Sitting on a small stool outside of the barrier Buck smiled his most amoral smile, feeding another large, black snake through the bars. As the serpent slowly made its way to the intended victim, Buck threw his head back in a melodious depraved laugh.

It was a shock, a jolt that caused the outcry and sudden reaction to set up in bed. Ryker quickly touched the sensor causing the lights in his room to come to life. Shading her eyes from the glare, Monica groggily queried him. "What's the matter? Are you all right?"

Running his hand over his face and his hair, Ryker reached for his glasses on the nightstand. "Ya. I'm OK. Probably something I ate."

Placing glasses on his face he looked to his wife to make sure she was safe and then smiled. She knew then. "You had that nightmare again didn't you?"

Ryker stood deliberately to his feet and began to dress himself. "It's been a while since the last time. I thought I'd beaten it. Don't worry about it. It's just a stupid dream."

Monica settled back down in bed. "Why won't you tell me what it's about?"

His T-shirt popped over his head, dragging his glasses off his face. He replaced them before pulling the garment the rest of the way on. "It's just a stupid dream. You don't worry about it."

She rolled over to get better eye contact. "I know all about your dreams. That's what's troubling me. They have a tendency of relating to some future event."

Ryker sat on the edge of the bed to put his shoes on. "You forget I dream all the time and 99.9 percent of them are just ridiculous apparitions."

She knew it wasn't worth talking about any further and turned back over to sleep. "Kind of early to get up. That means something."

As he left the room, Ryker turned the lights off. "All it means is that I wouldn't get back to sleep and I've things to do."

As he left the small apartment, Ryker covered his eyes momentarily against the lighting of the underground facility until they became acclimated. It was six o'clock in the morning and no one else seemed up as Ryker made his way to the office.

I wish I hadn't had that weird dream. It's not some kind of message is it, Lord? Today's a special day and that's the first time in quite awhile I've had that nightmare. Lord, I ask for Your guidance and wisdom today.

The office was about ten minutes from his apartment and Ryker continued his internal monologue until about halfway there. A light burning in the auditorium stopped him. Curiosity took over as Ryker temporarily forgot his original destination. Stealthily, he walked into the large room and listened intently. Mike Grotto strummed lightly on an old guitar and softly sang a slow song. He stopped abruptly and placed his head on the guitar in thought.

Ryker walked within a few feet of the stage without being noticed. After a moment, he softly clapped his hands reverently. Mike smiled with his whole face. The blue eyes sparkled under the long lashes. He sat on a stool with a stand in front of him. "I didn't know I had an audience. Woke up a while ago with this song bouncing around in my head and I needed to get it out. It's not coming easily but it's beginning to form."

Walking up to the stage, Ryker placed his arms on it and looked up at his friend. "Sounded great to me. What little I heard had much truth in it and I like the melody."

The princely man leaned over, put his guitar on a rest, and focused attentively on his friend. "Fairly early for you to be around. Maybe one of us is supposed to help the other work something out?"

The lips widened between Ryker's beard and mustache revealing his pearly front teeth. Then he made his way to the stairs leading up on the stage and confronted Mike with his thoughts. "I was speculating on the same detail. We've helped each other before, so perhaps it's time again."

Mike brought his legs up and arranged them on the highest rung of the stool placing his elbows upon his knees. The posture reminded Ryker of a childhood image seen in a book his mother read to him often. All Mike needed was a derby hat with a four-leaf clover stuck in the brim and he could've been a leprechaun. The elf said, "Well Ryker, I'll tell you this. I've just about finished this song so I don't see how you could help me."

Ryker pulled up another stool and leaned back against it with his arms folded. "I have hardly started my 'song' and there're many verses unfinished."

Two lights softly glowed in the auditorium—the entrance light and the spotlight Mike worked under. Someone looking on might believe a play was in process. After a moment of consideration, Ryker said, "At one time you were a staunch Search Squad agent. What's it that drives, motivates a person to gleefully hinder the Christian values you now hold dear?"

With a little thought, Mike answered, "What is it that drives you to operate under the Christian modus operandi?"

"I now know there is purpose in life beyond myself that's nobler than any aspirations I could come up with. But if one doesn't believe that, what would motivate them to trust in the opposite so strongly?"

"What motivated you before you were a Christian?"

Ryker's green eyes narrowed into slits as he concentrated on the question. Uncrossing his arms to gain balance he changed his position to sit upon the stool before replying, "There was a time when I was very apathetic about life. It's easier to take what comes at you and accept it as long as you feel it's more convenient than taking any kind of charge. That way, you can always blame somebody or something else for the outcome. In thinking this way, a person's at the whims of the emotions and philosophies he is surrounded by or working under. It doesn't matter so you go with the flow. Later, I became more aware of myself and felt a need to feed or satisfy the desire to be whatever I might be if I tried. That meant taking a risk of failing but when there was success, man that did something to the old ego. I wanted to do it again and again so I might feel really important."

When half a minute went by in silence, Mike stepped down from his stool and began writing in his notebook as he responded to his friend. "There! You answered your own question and I have a finish to my song."

Ryker continued, talking more to himself than anyone else, "Amazing. Had the answer to my problem the whole time and didn't realize it until now." Ryker also stepped down from his stool and looked over Mike's shoulder and continued, "There're basically two types of people we're endeavoring to reach for Christ, and each case needs to be handled entirely different. Thanks for the talk, Mike. It helped immensely."

The songwriter/security chief finished writing, turned to his friend, and put a large hand on Ryker's shoulder. "Praise the Lord, buddy. It's neat how He uses us to help one another. We both received what we needed this morning."

After Ryker patted Mike's shoulder in response, he turned to leave, stopped in mid action, and turned back. "You know, Mike; I'm going to let you in on a little secret. I wasn't sure how I was going to respond to a situation I need to address today; but after this, I now anticipate what I should do. Uncle Vernon and I developed this vague idea about placing an evangelist-type person in the NMA organization. We need someone who knows the workings of the NMA but who they wouldn't expect. We thought of you but realize you're too well known to them. They'd love it if you walked right into their hands. After this morning though, I realize who'd be a good person for the job. Again, thanks."

Something back stage fell with a resounding crash and caused both men to turn toward the noise. A moment later, Calvin Katang came forward with a sheepish smile on his face. "I thought I heard you in here somewhere as I walked by. Monica said she thought you were headed for your office. When I didn't find you I thought I'd meet you on the way. Would've walked right by and missed you if I hadn't heard you. It's dark back there. I almost broke my neck."

The man was rambling and the other two knew it. Ryker smiled with amusement as he informed his assistant with a chuckling tone, "First embarrassing thing I've ever seen you do. You don't wear it very dignified."

With a neutral expression, Calvin moved quickly to change the subject. "Something came up over night and it needs your immediate attention."

Ryker gave Mike a hurried adieu as Calvin and he made their way through the halls, up the secret elevator, and to the office. As they finished their destination, Ryker asked what was so important. "Never had you look for me this time of day before. What could be so weighty?"

Calvin was silent until the two went through Kim's office, into Ryker's office, and closed the door. Calvin tended to be serious but Ryker could tell this was beyond his usual sobriety. "We found out one of the Network's satellite groups is screening a potential candidate for underground protection."

The report seemed unexciting enough to Ryker. He waited for more electrifying news but was rewarded with nothing else. He took his seat behind the desk and motioned Calvin to sit. "I don't see anything earthshaking about that. We do it often. There must be more."

There was and Calvin had a tough time with the information. "Obviously, you're right. It may've never reached our attention because it's so common, but this one's a little different for a couple of reasons. One, it happens to be an SS agent."

That garnered Ryker's interest. "Great. I'm sure the people involved will make sure the person's not a threat to our security before he's able to get too deep into the organization. I still don't understand why the focus came this far up in the Network."

Calvin silently gathered his thoughts before continuing. "It probably wouldn't have except the name happened to be recognized.

199

That alone is interesting because few people know the names of the top people in the Network."

After a moment, the statement sank in to make Ryker ask, "Is it someone who has something to do with one of our people?"

The answer was short and to the point but the implications took longer to digest. "It's your brother."

Languidly, Ryker focused his attention back to the room after minutes of deep thought. Calvin patiently waited for further instructions. It wasn't what he expected. "Thanks, Cal. I'll talk to you later. Right now I've some things I need to do." Ryker turned to his keyboard and began typing. Calvin took the cue and left.

Hours passed as Ryker unconscientiously performed menial office tasks. His mind raced too fast to accomplish thought-provoking assignments. Kim came in once to ask for directions but realized she was wasting her time. At about nine o'clock, Ryker made a trek to his uncle's office down in the bowels of the complex. Joyce greeted him with her usual congenial manner, but knew this wasn't a regular visit for the younger chief. "Vernon just wandered in a minute ago. I'll let him know you're here."

Half a minute later Ryker walked into the cavern as his uncle pawed through the books at his private library behind the sitting area. "Come in and have a seat, Ryker. I was just looking for information I remembered reading years ago. For some strange reason, I've been thinking of a particular story about a man and his grandson who betrayed the grandfather. The grandfather ends up dying but there's this line of thought or rational I wanted to read again. The man took his grandson in who just left a crime boss."

Vernon's age was showing more as Ryker took over the everyday tasks of the operation. It was as if he allowed himself the privilege to do so. When he heard nothing from his nephew, he turned with a curious look as to why the silence prevailed. Ryker waited for Vernon to face him. "This is the most uncanny day I've ever experienced. Believe it or not, I've come to talk about such a thing."

Unruffled, Vernon smiled and motioned for his nephew to have a seat as he made his way to his favorite chair and sat in front of Ryker. "I'm not surprised. I can't think of another good reason why I was obsessed with that old story."

Relaxing for the first time in hours, Ryker slowly informed Vernon what had happened so far that day. The older man wisely took a dispassionate reaction to the events as he heard them. "Ray, huh? How's that make you feel?"

Ryker sat forward and rested his arms on his legs looking ready to jump to his feet. "I don't really know. Happy maybe that he's come to understand Jesus and has a meaning for his life. Disappointed he didn't let me in on it. Worried it might be his crafty way of getting to the Network to destroy it. Concerned that Buck might be using him as a pawn in all this no matter what Ray's true alliances might be."

Nodding his head slightly, Vernon applied a thin-lipped grimace. "You've thought about this already I see. The timing is interesting is it not? It's almost like the devil's made his move before we've completed our plans."

Ryker threw himself back into the couch. "Ya and I thought I might've come up with a final candidate—until now."

Vernon pulled at his brown and gray-peppered beard and motioned Ryker to explain himself with a circular gesture using two of his right fingers. The young man went into more detail of the discussion he had with Mike Grotto and then continued. "So I thought of your grandson, Mark. He's young enough to start in the NMA academy but very mature in the Lord for his age."

Vernon was much quieter than Ryker anticipated. After a minute, Vernon struggled to his feet and made it back to the books behind him, searching again for his text. The reaction puzzled Ryker. "Did I say something wrong?"

Gathering his thoughts Vernon turned with a smile and assured his disciple. "No, not at all. You might have a very good idea. There's an irony here you couldn't possibly conceive at this time. Someday you'll probably understand but for now, let's look at this option."

Ryker considered querying his granduncle for further explanation but thought better of it. Instead, he expounded on his idea. "Well, Mark's extremely knowledgeable on Christian issues; he has an indeterminate but pleasant personality, and has never been in contact with the NMA. There's a risk—a big risk—and for that reason I hesitate to mention someone so close to you."

His mouth a thin line, Vernon contemplated the suggestion with his head slightly down as he walked around his chair. Ryker watched him for several minutes until the elderly gentleman stopped and gave him a large grin. "I believe you're on the right track. Run with it. You have my blessing. I've one concern right at this minute and that's how many people know about our plan and the names it involves."

Standing to his feet Ryker made his way to his mentor and stood face to face with him. "Don't worry, Vern, no one knows of this plan but you and I. Mike Grotto is in on the basic plan and I've no concern with that. For one thing, no names were mentioned until now. Also Mike will be a good resource for Mark when it comes to understanding the SS agent. We'll want to bring him in on the planning. Besides the three of us, not a soul even perceives of this operation."

The senior man relaxed with a smile and put a hand on Ryker's shoulder. "Good! Your first move will be to go visit Mark. I'll be glad to see him when the time comes."

Mark

The ceiling was high. Athletic equipment and other gym paraphernalia lay scattered about the large room. At one end of the domain a small group of people watched a demonstration. The instructor was a large man with white hair. Ryker recognized him from the other end of the field house. Pat Filmore was a head taller than anyone else in the room. As Ryker made his way across the huge area, he watched with interest. Pat seemed ready to pounce on a young woman about half his size. When he moved to grab his frail-looking prey, there were a few quick but simple moves by the woman. Pat lie on his back looking up at his student. Surprised, the young lady squealed as she covered her mouth with her hands.

With a smile, Pat jumped to his feet to assure her he was fine and finished explaining what took place as he put an arm around the woman. "So don't let the size or ferocity of your attacker frighten you into immobility. Use their energy against them just as Ally so well showed us. See you next week at the same time."

Everyone swarmed around Ally, chattering about the demonstration. It was then Pat noticed his visitor. With a large, white-enhanced grin he waited until Ryker was almost to him. "I didn't expect you this early. How've things been for my little buddy since he's moved up in the world?"

Grabbing the large hand extended to him, the ex-Jordanite shook his head with a smile of his own. "Sometimes I think about cursing you out for putting me in this position. But I know that would only amuse you, so I resist. Time has passed so fast it hardly seems I left. It's good to see you, Pat. How've things been here?"

Ignoring the last question Pat motioned Ryker to follow him as he made his way to the hallway. They were alone in the small, dim hall as Pat leisurely led them to the shower room. "I know you're not here to see me so I won't ask many questions. What can I do for you?"

Being so much shorter, Ryker craned his head back slightly to garner eye contact with his friend. "I need to see one of your people and there's a good chance he'll be going back with me."

The pair reached the door to the locker room when Pat stopped. One of his bushy, gray eyebrows cocked up. "Must be a secret operation if you won't even let me in on it. So this is why you wouldn't tell me the reason you were coming." Replacing the quizzical expression with his more familiar smile Pat continued, "That leaves me with the only other question I'll ask. Who do you need to see?"

Ryker leaned against the door casing, blocking the entrance. Not that the move could've stopped the large man but Ryker foreshadowed his perceived reaction to the request. With a half grin he stated the name, "Mark Jacobson."

Rolling his eyes back in his head, Pat brought them back into focus with a mocking grin on his lips. "I should've known. I was lucky enough to get someone in here to replace you and you want him. Can't I keep any of the good ones?" Ryker shifted his position and took on a puppy dog expression. It made Pat laugh openly and then say, "Don't give me that look. You go ahead and talk to Mark. Just remember, I want to see you later so we can talk over the old times."

"I wouldn't think of leaving without seeing you and the others for a good visit."

"Good. I'll see you later then."

"Where will I find Mark?"

Pat opened his eyes wide and leaned close to Ryker. "Where would *you* be right now?"

Ryker moved down the hall and then turned back to Pat. "That's another question! You weren't to ask any more. Thanks again. See you later." He took off before his former boss could respond.

Knowing he had some time before Mark would be available, Ryker stopped along the way to talk to old friends. The first one he came across was Laura Shaffer, who insisted on examining his leg before she would allow him to leave.

His trek took him past Everett Myron who was busy working on improving the communications system within the Network. Ryker wanted to see Everett for a special reason and the conversation came around to it after a few minutes. "Yes, I've made many new friends. You'd be interested in one of them. His name's Mike Grotto."

Everett blinked once slowly and commented in disbelief. "The same Mike—the SS agent Mike who crippled me?"

Ryker smiled from ear to ear. "The very one and the same."

Given a moment to get over the initial shock, Everett gave a big grin. "Well, praise the Lord! I've prayed for him but I never guessed it'd do any good."

Ryker figured it was time when Mark could receive him. Walking into his old classroom brought back many memories, but he had little time to reflect. His attention was drawn to a strange sight. The room was full of students—most were on their hands and knees! People of all types and ages groveled around the floor looking for something.

Ryker arrived just in time for Mark to finish his class for the day saying, "It's hard to find something valuable especially when you're looking in the wrong place."

All heads turned to Mark with varying degrees of amusement. With mumbling and questioning, people began returning to their seats leaving the person at the head of the room smiling. Ryker had never met Mark but couldn't help thinking he looked familiar. Though they were related Ryker knew little, only that Mark had been adopted. The younger man's smile was wide and opened slightly showing pearly white teeth. He was an average built man with a thin mustache. Dark brown curly hair encircled his head covering his ears and framing the heart-shaped face, which housed bright deep blue eyes. Mark looked young for his age. A piece of scripture came to Ryker as the picture penetrated his cognizance. He thought of Jesus as a young boy sitting with the teachers of the law and astounding them with his command of scripture.

Mark's characteristic voice broke the spell that Ryker had momentarily fallen into. Speaking to his class his voice was warm and amiable. It reminded Ryker of an old friend. "See how easily we fall prey to the trap. I simply indicated that something very small, easily dropped and of great value, was placed somewhere not readily noticeable. If you could've found it within thirty seconds it'd have been yours. Time's up and not one of you is even close."

One of the women spoke up. "It's probably disguised as something we wouldn't recognize as valuable."

Energetically Mark took two steps forward and accented his next four words with his fist and a smile. "Just like the Pharisees. Remember we discussed how they misunderstood Jesus. If we're not careful, we'll think just as them." Standing still with his hands behind his back the teacher slowly rolled his bright blue eyes up toward the ceiling. After a moment, all eyes followed suit and discovered the treasure. Taped to the ceiling was a beautiful diamond engagement ring.

The room became noisy with differing reactions as Mark dismissed the class above the noise. "Thank you all for your participation. See ya Friday."

One student was a person Ryker recognized and the two talked for a moment while the rest filed out of the room. It wasn't long and Ryker was alone with Mark. The younger reached his hand out. "You must be Ryker Cuff. Pat called ahead a while ago and told me you'd be around to see me. I must tell you I consider this a great honor. I've heard much about you and had my hands full trying to fill your shoes."

Ryker took the hand and hung onto it for his first sentence. "I'm impressed with your technique. Reminds me of something I might do."

It was obvious the statement pleased Mark. "Thanks! I learned it from you. I've studied your back lesson plans and liked your approach so I copied some of it."

Motioned by Mark to do so the two sat down. They got acquainted with small talk before Ryker launched into the purpose for the visit. After explaining the plan he and Vernon had for reaching the NMA for Christ, Mark became quiet. Ryker patiently waited for his new confidant to digest the information. In the silence, Mark slowly stood and stepped up on the desk. Bewilderment turned to comprehension as Ryker watched Mark take the diamond ring from the ceiling and sat back down. "I believe you and Grandpa have a viable idea and I hesitate for one reason only." He held up the engagement ring. "I had plans on using this."

Ryker didn't say a word but wisely waited for Mark to think through all the implications. Another minute passed. Ryker was just about to tell Mark he could wait for an answer until the next day when Mark abruptly put the ring in his pocket. "This can wait. I know I should do this plan of yours. God's been dealing with me in this area for some time. You're just an answer to my prayers about it."

Calmly, Ryker pulled at his beard. "Are you sure? I can give you until tomorrow to think about it."

Abruptly Mark stood with the same determination that came through his voice. "No, I don't need any more time. I want to do this."

Slightly lowering his head, Mark reached into his pocket and fondled the ring. Standing to face his new team member, Ryker smiled scantily and reached to touch the young man's shoulder. "Some young lady's going to be disappointed. What's her name?"

Lifting his head level Mark looked through Ryker and uttered quietly. "I haven't officially asked her yet. Her name's Kayla Keating."

Ryker held to his smile and gave an honest response. "Pretty name. Just remember when you see her again not to mention anything about this operation. I know that'll be difficult but when we put this plan in motion, you might not see her for some time."

Mark was adamant about following through with his decision and the two discussed more details about the operation.

The Past Visits Again

It was pitch black and silent, until a crack, accompanied by a thin thread of light in the wall, expanded far enough to allow a shadow to slip in. Once again, blackness drew back over the evading light by the closing door. Seconds later, a small spot light scanned the room, at first very quickly, but then as the layout of the area became familiar, it stopped to investigate items. The walls were made of rock or at least most of them. An old, wooden desk with a high-back chair sat directly behind. The light and one hand under its illumination began slowly sweeping the top of the desk. The items that seemed to attract investigation were papers and books. They were separately studied before moving on. Each desk drawer was taken into account and meticulously searched.

Like a beacon, the miniature spotlight began exploring other parts of the den. There was a couch, a couple of chairs, coffee table, pictures on the wall . . . THERE! A whole wall of books! Illumination anchored upon the find and seemingly dragged the source behind it to within reaching distance. Once again the delicate hand fingered the titles exposed on the binding of each book and tediously worked its way down the length of shelves. Halfway through the inventory all motion came to a stop. The spotlight brightened and narrowed as it focused on a black binding with raised gold-flecked letter—Holy Bible. The well-used tattered old book shook slightly under a hand of anticipation.

Over to the couch and onto the coffee table floated the Bible under the light, resembling an old ghost movie. With the book settled on the table, the hand carefully but anxiously opened the cover. A white page glowed under the light as the words stood out: **Happy birthday to Algie Eton from your loving wife Alice and daughter Carol, April 11, 1981.** Dainty fingers reverently caressed the letters before carefully turning the page back to the black inside cover. Next to the inside edge a finger mindfully lifted the edge and dragged out pieces of paper hiding behind the cleverly designed pocket. Each item received a thoughtful examination. There were notes for a sermon, a couple of colorful pamphlets, and finally, the item longed for.

The small, yellowed envelope with its torn flap and canceled stamp were an oddity for this point in time. Inside was a small card folded once with a picture of a loon on the front. When opened to the handwritten message, a piece of green paper fell out. Setting aside the green paper the note was read first.

Dear Algie:

I can hardly wait until two weeks when we marry. I long to be with you but I must confess, I'm also apprehensive. The promise we're to make to one another will be a solemn pledge before God. He expects us to always be true to each other. I feel it will be so easy right now, but I've seen so many others spilt and hurt one another that I know there will be times of struggle. To get us through that I wanted something to remind us of how we started. Enclosed you'll find half of a dollar bill. I have the other portion. When put together I've made a special message for us to have. I'll show you Friday night when we meet. Keep it close to your heart until then.

With all my Love, Alice Tarbell

The green slip of paper became the object of scrutiny. It was an old United States one dollar bill torn in half. It appeared to be the right half. The dissected face of a man was to the left with the word "GTON" underneath him. Partial and full words were on the top and bottom: SERVE NOTE, above TES OF AMERICA on the top and OLLAR at the bottom. The number "1" was ornately printed on the right, twice, top and bottom. In the center of everything was a serial number above a seal with ONE written on it. Examining it close under the light, the hand slowly turned it over to study the back. At first, it was a disappointment until the finger lightly touched writing near the torn edge side. Again the note contained the number "1" twice, but this time with the word "one" on top of them. An interesting picture of a pyramid with an eye above it dominated this side. There were more words with half words on the top and bottom: THE UNITED STA at the top and ONE D on the bottom. Found in the center of the torn side was Alice's handwriting. Above the large O half N and before smaller words IN GOD, sat the simple handwritten word "If" in black ink. "If" IN GOD . . . what could the other half say?

Putting the torn bill and note back in the envelope, the hand reached back behind the light and tucked the treasure away before replacing the other papers in the book and closing the Bible. Back to the bookshelf the volume returned to its proper place minus the newfound treasure. In the process of bending over, a lamp was bumped, which caused it to automatically come on. The cavern flooded with light revealing Vernon's office. Long, light brown hair flew as Holly spun around and screeched at the lamp in fear. Covering her mouth with her hand she closed her eyes and breathed a sigh of relief. Thinking she had been discovered she relaxed having only scared herself. Touching the lamp to shut it off, Holly Tarbell used her flashlight and quietly retreated back out of the room leaving it the way she entered.

School Begins

"This is without a doubt the most dangerous weapon of the enemy you'll encounter!"

He wildly waved an old, soft-covered book over his balding head. Sweat ran down the shiny crown to disappear in the band of gray hair that encircled his head above his large ears. Paul Egger was a riveting orator because of his energy, his odd appearance, and his knowledge of the subject. As grandfatherly as any man could look, Paul was deceiving in many ways. He was a large man with an egg-shaped torso that made him hike his pants up over his waist, exposing most of his socks. Suspenders served this problem well, so he wore them consistently. In secret, people nicknamed him Humpty Dumpy. Large jowls shook with each vocal delivery, which was clear but raspy because of an injury to his throat. Paul's eyes were dark and set deep under large, bushy eyebrows. A smile looked very out of place on Paul.

Sunlight flooded the room from large panes of glass serving as the outside wall. The brightness enhanced Paul's imposing appearance. Standing long enough to punctuate his statement, he lowered the book to the podium and continued. "Yes, it's the most lethal but you'll never see them carrying one. We know of two they might have in this form. They usually sustain it in their heads. They've poisoned thousands of minds with only a couple of these menacing brainwashing words of insular trash."

Silence oozed with anticipation and suspense. It was the exact effect Paul drove for. He calmly picked the book back up and carried it around with him as he strolled around the room to continue his lecture.

"No one will be allowed to read this one. Some of you may've seen or maybe even read one of the NMA-approved versions but they're developed to appease the immature appetite of a certain lower intellectual void some people have. These government Bibles satisfy the basic need to fulfill a religious compulsion for some, without any of the harmful brainwashing elements. But this," he held the book up once more before he proceeded, "defies all natural logic and intelligence common to man. It's full of fantasies and unrealistic goals for anyone to reach ,say nothing of the need to try."

Across the assembly room NMA personnel sat mesmerized by the first lecture most ever heard concerning the scriptures they've worked so hard to combat. Having made his way back to the lectern, Paul toggled a switch that caused the outside glass wall to turn opaque and display a prerecorded photoplay, which he narrated to. Many disturbing scenes of people within the RC cult were depicted: sacrificing something (was it a child?); bowing down to a cross with a tortured bleeding man upon it and gathering the blood, which dripped from his bare feet; people living in filthy, crowded, underground caverns with no modern convenience; the beating of children who'd done some wrong in the eyes of their father; and many other atrocities that drew groans from the class.

Facing his students once more, Paul propped the book up in front of the podium so all could view it. On the dirty, white leather in big gold letters—faded from the years—were the words Holy Bible. He motioned to the windows, which had returned to view the outside. "This pictures what some of the beliefs this book invokes upon these Rigid Christians. They honestly believe their leader, Jesus, will give them immortality if they follow His absurd teachings. It's all learned from this book, which was banned from the USA almost seventy years ago. This is the only copy the government has or will even allow. I'll share with you some portions of its detestable writings, but never write down or copy any direct quotes. I trained for years before undertaking a full study of its contents. The untrained mind can easily be subdued by it without proper understandings of the religious hocus pocus."

April Goulay raised her hand. Paul looked down upon her like peering over glasses that he never wore. "I'll entertain questions at specified times but seeing as how I wasn't given opportunity to explain that yet, I'll allow you this one now."

Sheepishly, April stated the question gritting her teeth afterwards. "Is it true that some of our own SS agents have fallen prey to this cult and have become Rigid Christians?"

Paul pursed his lips, smacking them once before his reply. "It's true we've lost a few to the enemy but none have ever been heard from again. I feel they've been sacrificed for some kind of atonement, and we'll never hear from them again. I'll believe otherwise when I can talk to one."

Like a commercial, Paul decided to explain what the class objectives were before he went any further. "You should be a proud bunch. You're the first, in a series of classes, to be trained for the new Cobra operation. This is an informational session designed to educate all NMA personnel on the basics. Some of you may go on to be special agents with detailed training on how to infiltrate the cult and win their confidence. Once we have enough of you in every level of their organization the fatal blow will be incurred, which will destroy or permanently cripple this radical group. The details of that will be withheld from all but me, Al Shanach, Sly Hawkins, and those special agents."

Most in the room muttered simple acknowledgments or head nods—even Mark Jacobson.

LIFE CONTINUES

"Time is a great modifier of moral compost. With time and within insipid meekness, rich soils of liberality are formed."

Dr. Eli Grossman, July 14, 2019 speaking on his vision for the tenets of the NMA.

Home

Looking through the large window, at a great distance, he could see the lights of Washington DC. Large, white pines obscured much of the view down Turk Mountain. An obscure view of Crimora Lake surrounded with several lights of smaller residences outlined the water's perimeter. Just outside the window a large elaborate gazebo held a bench swing suspended from the ceiling. A large, fluffy, gray cat with one leg dangling slept peacefully. Buck drew drapes across the windowpane.

Soft lighting gave a relaxed atmosphere as Buck made his way back to the sitting area. He carried two glasses, one in each hand. Soothing music played low in the background. "This MM works better than any other I've ever had. Wait until you taste these daiquiris."

The new director of the Washington NMA wore a black silk lounging outfit. Plush cream-colored carpet temporarily exhibited Buck's trail across the large room. Exquisite opulent furnishings artistically sat around. April lounged upon a velvety brown couch attired in a matching outfit. She smiled at Buck as he handed her one of the drinks. "You do have a beautiful place here, Al. Why'd you choose a location so far away from the city? It's so lonely once you step outside of here."

Settling on the couch against the opposite arm Buck smirked as he lowered the glass from his lips. His hair was in a long braid, giving all facile expressions principal attention. "Interesting that you'd ask." He lost himself for half a minute with a faraway look. "I had an opportunity to see some very provocative country in pursue of an RC one time. I was rather drawn to the ruggedness and beauty of it. Since that time I've enjoyed the solitude of that kind of environment. I took advantage of needing new accommodations and had this place built above a small resort area. I don't expect anything to happen to the teleport system, but if something does, there's civilization only two-and-a-half miles down the mountain."

Setting her drink down, April gave Buck a sly look. "You're a fascinating man, Al Shanach. Most times I don't quite know how to take you."

Buck put his glass next to hers and rested his arm up on the back of the couch. He assumed his neutral appearance. "I need to be that way. I learned long ago that it makes an excellent cover." He softened his demeanor with an inviting grin. "I really like you, April. I'll tell you what. I believe we're going to make a great team. You're intelligent, ambitious, and my kind of girl. I'm going to entrust you with something special. My closest friends call me Buck. I'd like it if you'd feel free to use that name."

An amused expression wiped across April's face. "Buck? Where'd you get a nickname like that?"

In the quiet, a meowing was heard over the serene music. Buck gingerly stood up and went to the front door to let his cat in. "Come on in, Mr. Tubbs. You be a good boy and leave the pretty lady and me alone."

The fluffy ball of gray rubbed up against Buck's legs while purring loudly. Picking the cat up, Buck took it in the kitchen to show his pet there was new food for him.

Shortly he came back to the couch and began the conversation where they left off. "I'll tell you why. My stepfather always called me that when I was young. He would tell me I was his brave little Indian."

April studied the man a little closer with a smile. She reached over and gently traced Buck's face with her fingers. "It suits you well. I like the name. It's almost natural for you."

He took the hand and kissed two fingers once before letting them go. "It's just for you to appreciate. There're only a few other people who know of it and none of them we work with. It's my gift to you. May we work that close together. A true team."

April picked her glass up from the table. "Shall we toast to our new relationship?"

It was done.

The next morning, April came to the kitchen area wearing a heavy blue terrycloth bathrobe and a white towel wrapped around her head. Buck sipped a cup of coffee reading news on a terminal set in the middle of the table. April peered out from underneath the wrap. "I still enjoy washing my hair the old-fashioned way. That electronic thing just doesn't feel the same as water and shampoo." She began vigorously rubbing her hair under the towel.

Sunlight shone through high windows on the east side of the room. The kitchen area was white with black-and-gold trim fixtures giving it a bright cheerful look. Letting the towel hang around her neck April went to the MM and touched a few of the sensors invoking a slight hum to the machinery. She brought her foaming cup of cappuccino over to the table and sat with Buck, who had yet to look up. She brought the steaming cup to her lips and blew softly. "Buck, are you listening? Must be interesting information you're perusing. I'm not sure you can hear me now."

Buck wore his long, black hair loose. Looking up he brushed some back from his amused expression. "You needn't worry. I wouldn't miss anything you had to say. It's just I was reading this morning's early news to find Ray Cuff has made the information highway gossip columns. Somehow the knowledge leaked out that Jim Dandy hasn't reported to the agency in awhile, so now the media has speculated about another SS agent defection to the RCs."

April finished patting her hair, leaving it all curly and wild as she engagingly replied. "I never met the guy but does that information worry you?"

Eyes smiled as Buck touched the sensor to retract the monitor back into the table. "No. My guess is the reporters have it all wrong. Ray's a conniving ambitious fellow. The only reason we couldn't get along was because we're too much alike. He thought I was hogging all the credit for our successful campaign against RCs. I bet he's just ventured out on his own to make a name for himself. I'd be surprised if he didn't succeed. I'm ready for that though. If anyone ever finds out that he is related to the Network Cuffs, he'll be all done."

"Were you being a little devious with Ray?"

"I'm not sure devious is the right way to put it."

"Let me ask it this way then. Did Ray play a large part in your promotion?"

The smiling eyes finally affected the rest of Buck's facial expression. His large, devilish grin closely resembled his professional amoral smile, but the added amusement of it made it endearing. "My my, but you've caught on quick. If I deny it, you know I'd be lying but if I answer in the positive, you've made me answer your first question, which makes me out to be slightly dishonest. So I'll not incriminate myself. I believe you already know the answer." He took a large gulp of his coffee, draining the cup.

Anyone could see April was proud of herself. She relished the compliment while watching Buck put his cup in the MM dispenser. April felt confident starting another topic. "How're things going with the Cobra project?"

Leaning against the counter, Buck shook hair out of his face and folded his arms. "A little slower than I'd like but maybe that's good. The professor is being cautious and complete in his lectures. What do you think of him?"

April finished her drink and put it in the dispenser also, then faced Buck. "He's fascinating. Some of the things those people believe is almost incomprehensible. I'll tell you though. It'll be much easier knowing how to act around RCs after this. It's the little things we've been doing wrong all these years that have given us away."

"Yup. Ray was right about that one. Ryker was a real help also. The sucker told me something to get me asking questions. I finally found professor Egger who could answer them for me. That's when the whole idea gelled together and we put this plan together. It worked well in the Albany area."

"How many have you caught?"

"We've pretty well crippled a growing community at Albany."

"Just crippled it?"

"Yes. The ringleader, a Loren Richards, was lucky enough to disappear. When I thought we were going to nail him, Ray went a little berserk and things got screwed up. But the operation still worked well enough to get me recognition."

April wrapped her arm around Buck's. "Don't worry; I won't go berserk on you, at least not in that way. We'll succeed in a big way this time."

Buck leaned close and kissed her on the forehead. "You bet we will. That's why you're in this special training. I'm making you my lead underground undercover agent. I want you to pay close attention because I'm sending you in right at the throat."

She looked pleasantly surprised. "I thought professor Egger had already made his decision. He seems really impressed with Mark Jacobson."

"He can use Mark somewhere but I've decided you're the one for the actual kill."

"Thanks—Buck." April used his nickname as a password to his soul. "With your help and wisdom, I know we'll have our day."

The two embraced as someone watched. In one of the pines outside, a redhead sat perched behind some boughs holding small binoculars to his eyes. Red softly chuckled to himself. "This is going to almost be too easy."

Concerns

Ketchup sat precariously close to his elbow as Jesse cupped his chin in his hand. He waited for a response from his cohort. They sat in a small booth with high-back, red benches. The burgundy curtains were drawn back, allowing the sun to pour in. Kayla starred at her drink mindlessly stirring the ice cubes around with a straw. It was a small diner they often used to get lunch. The decor was of the late twentieth century with a realistic-looking grill and other cooking equipment, including all the utensils of the era. The food was good but it was still made in the conventional meal maker.

A short, chubby, elderly lady came to the table dressed in a red outfit laced with white. She poised herself at the table with a stylus and E-pad. "Are you ready to order?" Her large smile ended with two deep dimples.

Kayla looked up, shook herself from deep thought, and said, "Umm, yes, Judy. I'll have the special with no onions."

Judy looked to Jesse with the identical plastic smile. "Give me the same, Judy, only with onions and I'll just have water to drink. Thank you." As the waitress walked away, he replaced his head in his hand and smiled at Kayla with his deep brown eyes.

She frowned at him. "I don't know! Why're you bugging me about it?"

Jesse sat back with large eyes. "My, my. Must've hit a nerve. I'll leave you alone. I just thought you might want to talk to your best friend about it."

Replacing a lock of her fine hair behind an ear, Kayla apologized with a grim expression. "I know. I didn't mean to snap. It's just that I'm a little confused. I'm not sure I want to talk about it right now."

Jesse never let much bother him. He winked at his crony and reached over to pat her hand. "No problem, but remember; I care and I only want to help. We've been friends for almost four years now. This is the first time one of us didn't feel like verbalizing a dilemma he had."

Judy approached with plates of food and efficiently set them down. "Is there anything else I can get you?"

Both replied in the negative, allowing Judy to go about other business. Kayla poked at her food with a fork for a minute and then looked up. She glanced around to make sure they were truly alone. "I've asked about this but God's been silent. Why don't I sense any direction from Him?"

As was common practice when in a public establishment, the rest of the conversation was based on the subject of God, but listening ears couldn't distinguish it from any other normal discussion. Jesse finished chewing his food and took a drink. "Are you looking for an answer or a conformation?"

"What do you mean by that?"

"My father told me once that we could look right by a diamond gem if we were intent on finding a piece of flint."

"Are you trying to tell me that Dad may have given me what I want but I'm not seeing it?"

Leaning forward anticipating a reply, Kayla waited patiently as Jesse took one more bite of food. When it was gone, he allowed the fork to droop in his fingers causing it to point at her. "Not what you want but what you need."

The rest of the lunch was eaten in silence. When she was done, Kayla wadded her napkin up and threw it on the half-full plate. Resting her chin on clasped hands she smiled at Jesse. "I believe I understand what you're trying to tell me. I'll give it some thought. Thanks."

Jessie grinned and pantomimed taking a hat off in salute. "Always at your service. I know you'd do the same for me."

Judy stopped between them once more. "How about dessert today?"

Both declined as Kayla gave Judy her ID disc. They talked about trivial details on the day's agenda in the waitress' absence. When Judy returned with the ID disc, they thanked her and left. Judy watched them go, then reached behind the fake flowers against the wall and retrieved a very small recording device to place in her pocket.

A Stunning Day

Mud. That's all it was. A soupy brown mess with twigs, grass, stones, and other natural ingredients giving it a realistic texture. Julia carried it with pride in her delicate little hands over to her mother who lounged under a tree reading a book. The eight-year-old was tiny for her age, resembling a little cherub smiling from ear to ear. Her halo of nut-brown curly hair encircled the happy face like a picture frame.

"See, Mom. I made this for you!"

Engrossed in her book, Monica looked up in time to see the prized accomplishment twist and spill its contents all over her legs. Erica covered her mouth and giggled with loud restraint, attempting to hide behind her sister. She was twice as tall as her little sister, leaving much to conceal.

Monica scrambled quickly to get away but only floundered in the lounge chair like a fish out of water. With intelligible words associated with surprise, she helplessly watched as her littlest one finished the job by completely dropping the rest of the creation in horror of her mistake.

Julia's eyes enlarged two fold as she uttered a low, simple sound through her now mud-smeared face. "Oh, oh." There she was. Large blue eyes matching the O-shaped mouth of shock. A half a minute past before Monica gathered her composure and began to laugh. "That surprised you as much as it did me, didn't it, Julia?" Relieved her mother was only amused at her mistake, Julia smiled a sheepish grin through the mess on her face.

It was a beautiful day outside. The sun was high and a refreshing breeze kept the small, black flies at bay. It was the kind of day that made the locus sing their high, eerie-sounding song, reminding everyone of the dry, hot weather. Underneath the shade of a large maple tree, Julia wriggled under her mother's attempt to clean her up. She heard the intimidating sound of the insect. The bright blue eyes rolled from side to side in search of the source. "What's that?"

Erica, even at eleven years old, eased over closer to her mother at the sound. Monica's hair was done up in a long, single braid, which Erica found comforting to grab, waiting for her mother's response to Julia's question.

Smiling, Mother reassured her children. "To tell you the truth, I was a little apprehensive the first time I heard one years ago. Your father laughed at me and tried to tell me it was a squirrel playing a tiny flute."

Erica let go of her mother's hair and grinned. "That silly daddy."

Julia wasn't inclined to catch on to the joke as quick. The blue eyes grew large once more. "Squirrels can play the flute?" It was a perfect opportunity for a quick lesson and Monica took advantage of it to educate her two girls. Minutes later the youngsters were back to playing as Monica cleaned and adjusted her recliner once more to settle down and read.

Content with the situation, the pair played happily for some time while nature became objects of their imagination. Deep in the woods the family hid from most of society's technology. Not very far away, nestled under several large trees, was a large, old single-story building. A simple small bird feeder hung from one of the branches in front of a window. Ryker allowed his girls the privilege of playing outside once in a while on certain occasions. This day was one of the better because the chances of discovery were small. Society was making preparations for the Fourth of July the next day. It was a birthday wish easily fulfilled for Julia. Occasionally, Ryker looked from his window to watch his family enjoying themselves.

Lord, if only it was more natural for us to experience the joy of this simple life more readily. Thank You for the opportunities provided, but I pray it'd be a regular privilege.

Ryker's face vanished from the window as he went back to work on an important plan to help fulfill his prayer.

In their game, Erica and Julia ran around the rock making funny noises, when Julia stopped cold stiff in her tracks. Erica watched with curiosity as the younger one reached down and picked something up. The eleven-year-old screamed when she realized what Julia was holding. It was a small grass snake about a foot long, wiggling and wrapping its self around Julia's wrist.

Monica heard the screech and looked up with horror. She scrambled to her feet. "Julia! Drop that thing right now!"

The child did as she was told but still intrigued began studiously following the squirming creature as it made its way to taller grass. Snakes were something Monica could not tolerate. She frantically tried to coach Julia away from the reptile while making her way closer. Julia was engrossed in the antics of the snake and stayed on its trail. Erica waited to follow her mother in the pursuit. Before Monica reached her, Julia followed the snake into the bushes.

Frenzied upon losing sight of her youngest child, Monica began yelling at her to stop and come to her. Julia was gone out of sight. The mother began running at full speed while yelling the child's name at the top of her lungs. Erica, frightened because of the fear her mother showed, stopped to watch with hands over her mouth. Before Monica made it to the spot where the shrubs swallowed Julia, the brush began moving again. Walking slowly backwards Julia stared into the dense foliage as she emerged from the undergrowth. She pointed at her retreat gibbering something, but Monica was so relieved to see Julia safe she merely picked her up and held her close.

Monica felt so foolish being hysterical about the simple episode that Erica had to repeat for her mother what Julia said. "She's saying someone is asleep in there."

By this time, Ryker made it to the scene alerted by all the bellowing. Holding Julia, Monica took Erica's hand and began backing up. "Ryker, Julia says there's someone in there."

He stepped in front of them all. "Get back to the building. Now!"

The three hastened to comply while Ryker peered into the brush. He was ready for the worst and nearly jumped out of his skin when he saw the black NMA outfit. He might have reacted differently but the person was face down and not moving. Checking for signs of life he shook the person by the arm. When he received no response, he grabbed a tight hold and dragged the body out into the open. After turning the person over, Ryker sat back and waited for a reaction. Not a muscle moved.

From a distance, Monica and the girls looked on. "Ryker, is it an SS agent?"

He was quiet for a few moments thinking. There was the black, tight-fitting body suit with the yellow-and-red emblem on the shoulder: "NMA SS." The head was enveloped with the slick, black helmet. A blue band of light glowed where the eyes were. "Yes it is. You take the children into the compound and send security out here. I don't know if he's alive or not. Better send the doctor also." Monica took the girls inside and quickly followed orders.

Ryker cautiously checked for any obvious injuries. Having the opportunity, he removed the stunner and other instruments from the belt and tucked them in his pockets. In the process, he laid his head on the chest to determine if the person was alive. He discovered that he was a she and she was breathing. Ryker carefully took the helmet off. He also realized in doing so he had eliminated the agent's ability to communicate long distance, both vocal and visual. If there was another agent nearby, they could still converse short distance through the communication implants. Long, tawny hair fell from underneath the removed shielding. Feeling for a pulse in the neck, Ryker found the implants.

Those will have to be disabled before someone tracks her here if they haven't done so already. Lord, I'm relying on You to be in this situation. I ask for wisdom and knowledge on what I should be doing.

Hearing footsteps behind him, Ryker turned to see Mike Grotto, Calvin Katang, and Dr. Linda Paquin running up to him. Mike reached down and touched a sensor on the agent's belt. "There! That'll disable the implants. I see you've taken the interface instruments."

Linda went to work on the patient as the men stood back and gave her room. Ryker held the helmet. "I wonder who we have and what she's doing way out here?"

Mike took the head gear from Ryker and peered inside. Touching a small sensor he studied a second before shrugging his shoulders. "April Goulay. I've never heard of her."

Calvin watched the whole event unfold with distress on his face but never said a word. The doctor looked up. Short, black hair curled around her ears. The eyes of azure held great concern. "She's been stunned—hard. May've been out for twelve hours or more. We'd better get her inside where I can monitor her."

Her light blue eyes of concern locked on to Ryker's green ones in a questioning fashion. Moments of silence passed as the warm breeze played at everyone's hair and clothes. They waited for Ryker's decision knowing it would come after some thought. It began with a slight nodding of the head. "Let's carry her in. I want her in a special room. I don't want anyone else seeing her and you let me know when she becomes conscious."

The SS agent was taken into the heart of the Network organization. It was the first time ever without intense screening.

A Diller

Blue with crimson trim wore well on Buck. Several people came to attention as he strolled into the main lobby of the Washington NMA. The centuries would mentally roll back if one envisioned the man wearing a broad-brimmed hat with a large feather drooping from it. The long curls of hair to the middle of his back could easily remind one of The Three Musketeers, if the imaginary hat was added. In his presence, no such thought crossed anyone's mind. Buck was very diplomatic about his new powers but subtly encouraged fear to the contrary. He had become an artist at the mind control technique developed earlier in his career.

With a military stance, the chief of security stiffly acknowledged his superior. "Morning, sir. Is there something I might do for you?"

Enjoying himself, Buck gave one of his evil grins. "Relax, Mr. Evans. I'm only going to visit my old office if you'll let me through please."

Bob Evans reached under the counter and touched the sensor releasing the door as he questioned Buck. "Should I call ahead, sir, and inform Sally of your visit?"

Walking to the door Buck looked back over his shoulder and replied, "That won't be necessary. Thank you for asking."

The tone of voice and menacing stare was understood as Bob watched Buck disappear through the door. No one was to know Buck's intentions unless he deemed it necessary.

The slightly arching glass-walled hallway brought old memories as he meandered to his old office. When he palmed the sensor on the door, it released. The simple act painted another wide grin upon his face. There was no door to this complex he couldn't enter whenever he wished. His former office had scarcely changed. There were different items decorating the desk and cabinets, but all the original basic furnishings were still there. The office was empty of personnel. Thinking he was alone, Buck began fingering buttons on the communication control panel. After a couple of beeps from the unit, he stopped in mid search at the voice.

"Hello? If someone's there, I'll be out in a minute."

He smiled and responded in a very low voice to himself. "OOPS. Forgot about the restroom."

Buck decided to sit in one of the plush chairs and wait. He received the reaction he wished when the occupant came out. As the door softly shut behind her, Sally Diller stiffened to attention at the sight of her superior. Buck chuckled, "Please relax. This is more of a social call than anything."

The young woman looked as she did years earlier when she was an uncover agent working at Communiqué Incorporated. Her blonde hair was cut in the common military style for new recruits—short and trimmed revealing the ears. The tight-fitting, brown-and-yellow jumpsuit revealed Sally's physical fitness.

Sally seemed not to have heard Buck's comment, so he tried again. He indicated to the couch across from him. "Have a seat."

Something seemed to click inside the woman and she relaxed with a smile, while sitting as directed. After the initial shock, Sally began the conversation. "It's been some time since I've had the pleasure of your company. Now that I have the opportunity, I'd like to personally thank you for the promotion from that dreaded Tucson facility. I never was keen on that much hot weather."

To keep the conversation informal, Buck word played with her. "Not your kind of heat, I'm sure."

Being her forte, Sally picked up on the volley and played it. Crossing her legs, she smiled sweetly with her reply. "Yea. Too dry. I like things a little more—steamy."

Enough was said to establish a comfortable coalition between the two. Buck plunged into the reason for his sojourn. "Well, in that case how would you like to be my temporary assistant? My other is going to be busy for an undetermined amount of time and I thought you might prove to be a very good replacement until her return."

Sally held her expression controlled, but the time of silence before her reply gave away the true concern behind the mask. She wondered if Al knew she was the one who managed to make sure he received the information he needed for his operation. Did April know about her past? Dark green eyes shimmered in the moments of deep thought. Her plump, red lips parted as she began to say something, but stopped with a slight frown growing on her face.

Buck saw her dilemma and came to her rescue. He sat at the edge of the chair. "Now, I've an idea why you're hesitating but don't worry about that. I've had time to think about what happened between us and I realize I might've over reacted. I don't admit this often but I was wrong, and I want to put that behind us as if it never happened."

The plastic expression dissolved as the woman stood and thoughtfully walked over to her desk. Her high cheeks rose higher and depressions formed as she pursed her lips. It attracted Buck to the point he almost missed what Sally was doing as she fondled an item from her desk. When Buck noticed what she was doing, he cocked an eyebrow. "My, my. You still have that thing?"

Sally brought the item up, aimed it at Buck, and pulled the trigger. It hit, producing a dull snap. After a moment, he lifted a smile as she lightly wet her lips and said, "Yes, I still have it. I use it to remind me that all mistakes have consequences—even if they're not deserved."

Buck walked over and took the homemade contraption from Sally and examined it. "You're right. I was a little hard on you but I think we both learned and grew from the experience. I was just so angry because Ryker managed to slip through my fingers once more, all because of a stupid little thing I myself taught him to make when we were kids." He held the elementary gun up between them. "This silly paper wad shooter signified the simplicity of Ryker's dumb luck, and I took it out on you for falling for it. It was wrong. Deep down I knew it could've been me but I denied that and took it out on you. I am sorry."

After a moment, Sally's neutral expression softened as a smile graced her lips. "Thank you. I needed to hear that from you."

Taking the toy gun from Buck, she placed it back on her desk before swaying back to the couch and sitting down. He turned to watch and waited with arms folded for her to answer his first question. Sally knew he was waiting for it. She crossed her legs, put an arm up along the back of the couch, and sweetly smiled. "I'll take you up on that offer. Do you want me working from this office or would you prefer I come upstairs with you?"

Delighted, Buck reached back for the door before giving his answer. "Upstairs. I'll see you after the holiday." Not waiting for any other comment, he slipped from his old office and was gone.

Sweetness changed to evil rapture as Sally stood moments after Buck left. She went to her desk, retrieved the simple project Ryker made years earlier, and softly spoke to it so that other ears wouldn't hear. "This is working out better than I thought." She laughed to herself gleefully.

Upon reaching his office, Buck discovered he had a visitor. Angel greeted her boss with a large smile. "Mr. Shanach, you're supposed to call Mr. Hawkins as soon as you're available. Also, as you can see, SS agent Damon is here to see you."

Buck nodded to Devon and turned to Angel. "Thanks. Please place a call to Sly for me."

The door closed behind him as he entered his office. Angel feigned placing a call for Buck. The deception was always unnoticed by anyone in the office. Her boss had coached Angel on how to make someone wait until he deemed an audience necessary. Buck made Devon linger another fifteen minutes. Except for the scar across his nose and left cheek, he was a handsome blue-eyed, muscular man. His short, black hair was as dark as his SS outfit. The wait made no difference to Devon Damon. He was a well-programmed SS agent and one of the best. Buck's tactic served no purpose except for the practice it allowed Angel in her deception.

When Devon was received, he stood at attention and announced, "Search Squad Agent Devon Damon reporting status on special assignment Sleeping Cobra."

Buck glowed with pride from the reverence Devon showed him. "At ease, Devon. I hope all went well?"

The SS agent relaxed, swinging his hands behind his back and supplied Buck with a respectful neutral expression. "Just as planned, sir. We met with our underground contact at the predetermined location." Devon smiled with his next comment. "April was very surprised when I produced my weapon to stun her. It was only then she realized how we were going to get her inside the Network. The mole made sure she'd be found." The neutral face returned. "I assure you, sir, that she is fine. The mole has informed me April's inside and healthy. It'll be a few days before she fully recovers."

Sitting back in his chair, Buck pyramided his fingers and grimly smirked. "I hope she understands it was the only way. That kind of a stun can leave someone pretty sick for a few days. I'm glad she's doing well." He focused his attention back to Devon. "Thank you, Devon. That's a job well done and I'll see that it's added to your record."

Buck went to work at his computer terminal. Devon took the cue and left without another word.

Making Friends

She was next in line and getting restless. The NMA Social Reform Office was busy. Kayla had her arms crossed, tapping her toe lightly. Finally, the tall, thin Asian woman in front of her finished her business and stepped out of the way. The young woman behind the counter might be considered very pretty but for the leathery face developed with her continuous caustic expression. "Your name please."

Despite her internal impatience, Kayla fashioned a courteous facade and politely responded. "Kayla A. Keating." She went on to spell her first name because so many asked.

Leather face lived up to her appearance. "Data disc please." Kayla smiled as she handed it to the sour-faced woman.

The office was busy because it was the day before a holiday and it would be closed the next day. People who normally reported on Fridays were coming a day early to fulfill their obligation. The agent behind the desk squinted at the terminal screen, then turned her dark brown eyes and prune-like expression to Kayla. "Would you ross the scanner please."

With a relaxed expression, Kayla turned her left hand to the small screen in front of her and let the eye read her ross tattoo. The machinery signaled a three note descending tone. The large hair bun on leather face's head bounced as she turned to retrieve an item behind her, then snapped back to face Kayla. "I have a report here that you were heard spreading radical Christian propaganda with an unnamed man in a public place."

Kayla's blue eyes widened with comprehended implications of the accusation. "But I've no idea what you might be referring to."

For the first time, the sour woman behind the desk smiled. It made her face crack with lines hardly used under the unusual expression. She dropped a disc into the reader and allowed Kayla to listen to the proof. It was Kayla's voice. "I've asked about this but God's been silent. Why don't I sense any direction from Him?" She recognized it as the conversation she and Jesse had at the restaurant. They had been going there so long they had quit scanning for bugs. Now her carelessness had gotten her into deep trouble concerning her probation status.

Nothing was said for several seconds. Kayla didn't have a good response and was ready to admit to the crime when someone behind her spoke. "If that's all you have, I believe there's been a big misunderstanding."

225

White-blonde hair slid across Kayla's right shoulder as she slowly turned to see who her "knight in shining armor" was. He was tall, so she looked upwards as he came into view. The redhead ignored Kayla and continued with a deep voice as he focused on leather face. "I'm a good friend of Kayla's. Her reference to God in that conversation was none other than her father. I believe it'd be evident if you played the rest of the conversation. Her father isn't a very pleasant man and she uses the title sarcastically. She meant nothing else by it at all." Red looked down at Kayla with a warm smile. "Isn't that right, Kayla?"

Still looking at Red, Kayla played along. "You surprised me. I didn't realize you were behind me." She returned to the NMA agent. "I call my father that often. I'm sorry if it confused you."

The woman behind the desk looked back and forth between Red and Kayla. She was computing what she should do next. It was up to her if this referral was going any further. Her gaze stopped upon Red. "You're Hank Bronson aren't you?"

With a small grin, Red nodded affirmative. "That is right, Gail." He had been going to this office for years and knew Gail behind the desk fairly well.

Gail turned to Kayla again. "Why're you using this office instead of your own home one?"

A nonchalant expression and shoulder shrug accompanied Kayla's answer. "I was visiting friends for the holiday."

Gail punched at the keyboard and looked back to Kayla as she handed the disc back to her. "OK. I'll accept that. But I've recorded the 'misunderstanding' about the event. If it later turns out to be the opposite of what you reported . . ." She let the sentence hang, punctuated with her normal countenance.

Kayla smiled and thanked her. Putting the disc in a pocket, she turned to Red. "I'll wait for you outside, Hank."

It was a beautiful, warm, summer morning as Kayla stepped outside. Letting out a big sigh of relief she sat on a bench outside the building and lifted a silent prayer of thanksgiving. She couldn't wait to personally thank her new friend. It wasn't long before Red came out of the building and noticed Kayla waiting for him. "I thought you'd be long gone by now."

Her round little face glowed with a smile but her first comment was a question. "How'd you know if that woman listened to the rest of the conversation that I would've referred to God as Dad?"

Red shrugged his shoulders. "I didn't for sure, but my mother worked with an underground operation and she talked cryptically like that at times."

Kayla asked Red to walk with her as she made her way to the teleport. No one was on the street at the time. Kayla answered Red's first statement. "I couldn't just take off like that Hank. You saved me a lot of grief back there."

"My name's Craig VanTimons. My friends call me Red. Why don't you call me Red?"

"I thought your name was Hank Bronson?"

"So did I for a long time. That's who the NMA say I am. But I have learned otherwise recently."

The pair stopped in front of a small park only a block away from the office. Kayla screwed her face in a puzzled look, but then her eyes grew large with comprehension. "You've been through a mind alteration haven't you?"

His mouth was a thin line, as Red simply signaled yes. Kayla hung to her surprised expression. "But that's supposed to be irreversible!"

"I know."

"You remember your life from before?"

"I believe all of it, just like it'd never been obscured."

Kayla looked around, concerned. The park was empty of people. "You want to sit down so we can talk about this? I have a friend who no longer knows who she is, nor remembers me."

They sat down on a bench in the middle of the park. A burden slowly lifted from Red as they shared. He had talked to no one about his situation and things poured out in relief as he expressed himself. The two talked for hours about all of their problems and other experiences.

Loren

USA PARTY DAY. The signs hung anywhere. Crowds milled in and out of shops as people shouted over loud music and did numbers of lewd things with complete abandonment. The weather was an exceptional day. A gentle breeze carried away smoke or other side effects of the firecrackers and fireworks. Hollywood Falls wasn't a big town, but it was as festive as any large city. Nestled in the Adirondack Mountains of New York, it had become one of the places to go on the Fourth of July.

The town specialized in celebrating all manumissions of America's modern freedom.

For the last few years, it also drew another small group of people. Loren Richards was busy looking for someone on the street. His search kept him oblivious to the drinking, drug use, and sexual activities played out before him. A little smaller than average, Loren stood on his toes at times trying to peer over crowds of people. The man would have never been mistaken for his father. His ears were small, surrounded by thick, blonde, curly hair. The round face contained only two small characteristics linking him to his father. The eyes and how his chin squared off were Loren's only resemblance to Nick. In his late forties, Loren came late in life to understanding his father's faith. Now his evangelic activities grew exponentially, fueled by knowledge of his father's demise. As providence would have it, wisdom came just as timely, keeping him from the clutches of the Neutral Morals Agency.

Someone stopped him by grabbing his elbow. "Here, comrade, take this. You'll find paradise in no time." The young woman was beautiful in spite of the gaudy makeup and clothes. She handed Loren several small blue pills with a wild, inviting look in her eyes.

Loren smiled politely and took the items. "Thanks. Could you tell me what paradise is to you?"

Dark blue eye shadow narrowed as the woman frowned in confusion. "Paradise? Well, it's feeling good forever. Having a great time with no problems." The quizzical painted face changed little in anticipation of an unknown response. She was rewarded for her intuitive insight.

The blonde man smiled deeper. "You plan on living forever?"

Releasing the hold on his elbow, she assumed a neutral expression. "I'm living for now, which is better than any wishful fantasy of the hereafter."

"Do you use a teleport?"

"That's a stupid question. I couldn't get anywhere without one."

"Do you know how it works?"

"Ya! You climb aboard, punch in the address you want to go to, and let it happen."

"That's right . . . what's your name?"

"Melinda."

"You know how to operate one, Melinda, but how does it work?"

"How should I know?"

"You don't know how a teleport works but you use one. Correct?"

Melinda took a step back away from Loren. "So what?"

No one paid attention to the couple among all the other confusion. Loren felt comfortable with his new acquaintance. "There're many things in life we don't understand but we rely on them just the same. We can't see the wind, but we can feel it if we expose ourselves to it. You'll live forever . . . somewhere. The choice is yours but you won't have that choice if you don't allow yourself to be exposed to the possibility of that reality."

Melinda stood silently and starred at him. Loren patiently waited until she reacted. After half a minute she responded. "Have you already taken some kind of weird drug or what?"

Without a thought, Loren turned and threw the pills Melinda gave him into a nearby disposal unit and then said, "The real mind trip is exploring the possibilities of heaven. You might come to a different conclusion, but don't take anyone's word for it. You've learned to trust a teleport and use it every day. Not because you know how it works but you've tried it and experienced it for yourself."

In the distance, firecrackers went off followed by hooting and hollering. Finally, Melinda began to move but stopped. "Where'd you learn all this stuff?"

Smiling once more Loren stepped toward her. "If you'd really like to learn more, there'll be a special meeting tonight. All you've to do is show up at the entrance to Heaven's Haven on River Street at nine o'clock. I'll show you where we can go and talk freely about any of these things."

The brunette made a neutral shrug with her shoulders. "Maybe. Right now I've got other plans." She was gone, lost to the throng of people.

Loren closed his eyes and breathed a quick silent prayer. Moving down the street, he went back to his search. He hadn't gone much further when he discovered the object of his quest. She stood in front of small restaurant with a colorful sign: "America, Century 2000." When he was in ear shot, Loren called out. "Holly! It's so good to see you again."

He gave Holly Tarbell a hug, who returned the affection. "I'm glad you found me, Loren. Is everything all set for this year?"

The little man wrapped his arm around Holly's as the couple continued down the street. "Yes. I wouldn't be surprised if we had a better turn out than last year. It works out so well because this is one of the few times the NMA is off duty. It seems nice not to be looking over our shoulders all the time."

Holly listened intently with a smile as Loren prattled on about his successful operation. Reaching the teleport he stopped momentarily to allow his mind to shift gears. Climbing aboard the transportation unit he queried Holly as she keyed in the coordinates. "How're things going for you? Were you successful?"

The glass partition slid into place just as she replied. "I have it."

Enraptured delight washed across his face as the screen turned black for transportation.

Family Time

Monica popped another wintergreen candy in her mouth and sucked at it with counterfeit ecstasy. Looking on at the game played out, Ryker smiled at his wife. "I know. You like those pink candies. I just haven't figured out why you think they're so great."

Giggling at her wit, Monica playfully explained. "As you know, wintergreen is good for an upset stomach. I can eat these until I'm sick and then take one more for the cure."

Laughing at his spouse's logic, Ryker stopped and continued with a more serious tone. "That's pretty clever but you know something . . . that's just about the way American society treats life."

They sat in their living room playing a board game at a card table with their girls. Julia made up the rules as they went, which made for an interesting one-sided game. It was Julia's turn to pick what they would do on family night. It took a little while for Monica to convince Erica it was OK this time. It was the family camaraderie that made the apartment a comfortable home. It proved to be a relaxing time enjoyed by the Cuff family at least once a week.

Laughing, joking, and playing around dominated the evening, but once in a while Ryker and Monica conversed on more mature subjects.

"How's that April woman doing?"

"Oh, she came out of the stun-coma just fine. We haven't had much chance to talk to her yet. She's really pretty sick. The only thing she has mumbled so far is, 'I'm going to kill him!' It sounds like she knew who stunned her."

"What're you going to do with her when she's better?"

"I don't know. Several options have been suggested, but I'm counting on the Lord's direction. It's too soon to make any rash decisions.

I want to talk to and study her for a time before any directions are pursued. Uncle Vernon has an idea, but he hasn't discussed it with me yet."

Erica began laughing at her little sister. "Ha, ha! I beat you and it was with your own rules."

Mother and father watched with interest, wondering how the younger one was going to handle this situation. Julia studied the board with a frown. Then she smiled with great inspiration. "No you don't. The one closest to the start when someone finishes is the winner. That seems to be me!"

Erica dropped her mouth open and stared in disbelief before complaining. "Mom! That's not fair. I won, didn't I?"

The parents smiled and then Ryker helped his eldest daughter understand. "Well, sweetheart, that's often how the outside world plays the game of life. It's pretty tough when there's no set of rules or standards, huh?"

The Way

People came and went both ways upon the busy pedestrian walkway. The time was 9:25 at night, but all the lights veiled the reality of it. Loud laughter emitted from the opening door of the nightclub, Heaven's Haven. The exiting patrons shouldered past Mark Jacobson and his companion. The two leaned up against a corner teleport waiting. Both were dressed in civilian garb. Mark seemed quite relaxed compared to his partner. He smiled at her and tried to relax her. "Don't worry, Candy. We're not expected to know anything about Christian protocol here. You don't need to remember your homework yet."

Candy was a very attractive black woman several inches taller than Mark. Her long face enhanced her large, white smile with grace as she responded, "You're right. It's just that getting so close to RCs is very foreign to me. If my father ever finds out, he'll skin me alive. It wouldn't matter to him if it was for an undercover operation or not."

The couple was early for their appointed meeting and spent the duration in natural conversation while watching the multitudes mill about. Candy's light blue eyes danced as she studied every detail. It was a new habit developed through her training. Reaching up to scratch beneath her ear, she turned her attention to Mark. "I feel naked without my comms. It's funny how fast you can get use to having something like that. I feel crippled in some way."

Mark smiled and gently touched her arm. "Don't worry. We have each other and we won't be that far apart tonight. We can't chance them discovering those devices on us."

Mark would have continued but he noticed someone of interest coming their way. Loren stopped next to them and scanned the area. He smiled politely at Mark. "So, you've decided to check us out, huh?"

Mark played his part well. Acting slightly hesitant, he smirked, but didn't look Loren straight in the eye. "Yea. I told my friend here about it and she'd be interested in hearing what you have to say also."

Loren carefully sized up Candy and then motioned both of them to step up on the teleport. He climbed in behind them and scrutinized his watch. "We've a little less than a minute. We're using this method to protect anyone being followed."

Loren had time for an introduction, with an alias, before the teleport stripped them away.

It was a whole different world they had come to. The destination was the home of someone who seemed pretty well to do. A technician stood at the teleport controls as the trio stepped off the pad into a lavish living room. A buffet table graced one end of the large room with several people mingling about it. The ceiling was high, making room for many pieces of artwork to grace the walls. Scattered about sat several statues proficiently placed with the skill apt only to a professional. There was a hodge podge of people giving a contrary effect to the aristocratic setting. A few looked as though they belonged, but most were definitely out of place.

Loren quickly directed the new arrivals to the buffet table and excused himself. Mark and Candy studied the room, talking quietly as they mingled about the food. There were about fifty people to their estimation. The menagerie was of varying sizes, colors, and mannerisms. Mark's heart jumped up to his throat when he saw who he thought was Ryker. Candy had to shake him from his stupor, which wouldn't help much except Mark noticed Ray's long pony tail.

"I thought I saw someone I knew, but he just looks like him." He forced a smile to assure his partner that all was fine. Mark remembered Ryker had a brother whom he had never met. The forced smile relaxed as he turned to Candy. "I know the guy's brother. I heard they looked much alike, but I didn't realize it was so exact."

The person of their discussion realized he was being observed. Ray came over to the NMA undercover agents and introduced himself. Mark was careful not to give his last name in the event Ray might recognize the name. "I'm Mark and this is Candy Dixon."

The charmer smiled handsomely with his reply. Candy was amused by Ray's charm as he kissed her hand at Mark's introductions. "A delicious name. It suits you to a tee." After a moment for the effect to take hold, Ray took another look at Mark. In concentration, the smile slid from his face. "Do I know you?"

Eyebrows rose as Mark shook his head. His curly hair swayed slightly with the move. "No, I don't believe I've ever met you."

Ray may have pursued the subject but Loren called for attention from the front of the room. He stood upon a raised platform behind a makeshift podium. "Welcome, everyone, and thank you for coming. This may be the most important night of your life. You're here because of an interest you developed talking to me or one of my colleagues on the street. I know one of your concerns is being discovered investigating a philosophy, which has been outlawed. Let me assure you that safety is of the utmost importance. This place is secret, not to be revealed to anyone. You'll be taken back to where you were first picked up and cannot be traced back to here. None of you have ever been here before and probably will never visit again, no matter what you may do with the knowledge you garner tonight. Now if you'll all step back and take a place next to the walls somewhere I'll see to it that seating arrangements are prepared."

With differing responses of curiosity, everyone headed for a wall. Mark and Candy stood next to Melinda Carter, who Loren had met earlier. They all watched in fascination while plush theater seats materialized in the center of the room.

"Please, everyone make yourselves comfortable," Loren said, smiling patiently while murmuring filled the room and all found a seat.

Mark and Candy sat between Melinda and another young man with rusty-colored hair. Mark leaned over to Candy. "Pretty impressive the way they provided the seating."

Before she could respond Loren began. "Is the seating comfortable?"

He waited for a few reactions and then continued. "Close your eyes and relax. Think about your body fitting into your seat and how well it serves its purpose. Feels good after a long day doesn't it? Now meditate upon this thought. These seats came from nothing. They developed on their own out of nothing. A moment ago there was a void and now seats are here for us to enjoy and use. Wonderful isn't it?"

Silence for a half a minute prevailed as one by one people began opening their eyes. They looked at one another with questioning frowns and then back to Loren as someone asked the question on everyone's mind.

"You mean like the MM machines? A raw material is supplied and a molecular re-establisher produces the desired product through advanced technologies. Right?"

The little blonde man stood with a serious studious expression and further explained as if he couldn't believe the people didn't understand. "No. That's not what I mean at all. It just happened. At first, there was nothing here, and now we have these nice, comfortable seats."

People began whispering to one another, "What's this guy saying?" "This is really weird!" "I thought this was going to be enlightening, but maybe we've wasted our time."

With the noise level escalating, the man with the rusty-colored hair raised his voice over the crowd with a statement, which again stilled the place with anticipation to Loren's reaction. "That's the most ignorant thing anyone can believe. Do you think we're idiots or something? Everyone understands teleportation is a wonderful invention, but it works because we've been smart enough to use our energy and resources to our advantage. These chairs are stored in another room, possibly a floor above or below this one and transported here. The floor is obviously a translator pad. It's nothing mystical or magical, just good creative ingenuity on your part."

Loren held his neutral expression. "Are you saying this just couldn't have happened on its own, no matter how long we gave the conditions a chance to work on their own?"

The young man nodded his head. "Of course not. A cake doesn't simply appear. It needs to be made."

Loren couldn't have been happier at the way things were going. His new facial expression gave immediate truth to that. "Everyone agree with that?"

The room bussed with varying replies, all agreeing in some form or fashion.

Loren continued, "Good then. At least we all agree there must be a God of some kind. You agree this world was created. It couldn't have developed on its own. And you came to that conclusion when you weren't allowed to draw upon your pre-conceived programmed schooling. Logic dictates the world has a design that demands the conclusion to a Creator. A cake needs to be made to exist. Our world, especially one as intricate as this one, had to be developed. There's a Creator. We haven't touched upon the scriptures as yet, but in Romans chapter one, Paul qualifies the truth of this logic. Now that I have proposed this fact, can we all come to a consensus on this point before we move on?"

It took more discussion and questions, but in short time everyone agreed to the point, at least for the time being, and Loren continued. "OK. You might go home and later refute this premise for the sake of ignoring all other truths presented here tonight. But if you do, it'll be against all intelligent and logical thinking. If it's the truth you've come to find, this is the first. All the other premises rest upon it. Let us continue with further defining the Creator as a personal God. Bear with me as I continue to use logic and other evidences to define this fact. We'll explore how we, the created, and all true scripture testifies to a holy and righteous God, Who seeks all people to come and receive Him. Also, that we all are created for immortality, either to heaven or to hell as our choice. We'll not answer all questions here tonight. Time itself dictates the truth to that. But if you'll listen for a short time, I'll at least educate you enough that you might have the right questions to ask."

Stillness permeated the room. Loren had their attention and took full advantage to teach the main doctrines and foundation of the Christian faith. The RC leader talked for well over an hour without any interruptions as he led everyone through the fundamentals. He was careful to point out there were many elements that could not be proven, but taken by faith led to a personal understanding of God's work of grace through Jesus Christ. When looked at with common scientific methods and logical philosophies, Christianity made more sense and fulfilled greater purpose than any other ideas. Mark was impressed with Loren's presentation. Loren left little room for a logical rejection of Christianity and knew many people present would further investigate the presentation. Mark realized his job to accept the lecture was going to be a very believable act to pull off.

Completing his homily, Loren gave the floor back to the people. He told them he and others would make themselves available for the next hour for those who had questions to ask or would like to accept Jesus now. As he finished his last instructions, he noticed Holly hiding herself, trying to get his attention. "So if you must leave now, John at the teleport will send you back to where we picked you up. Please feel free to stay around and talk if you wish. Thank you for your hospitable attention."

Finished, he left the room to meet up with Holly as the gathering came alive with many conversations. She didn't take long, informing Loren why she wasn't out with everyone else. "Ray's out there! I don't want him to find me so I'm afraid you'll have to do it without me."

After a minute, Loren smiled. "Great! Don't worry; we can handle it without you. Just point out who he is."

Many people left. Others gathered into one of four groups discussing different aspects of what they'd learned. In one of the groups were Ray, Mark, Candy, Melinda, the boy with rust-colored hair, and Jesse Bronchetti.

Jesse finished his introduction and answered the first question. "I wish my partner could've been here tonight. She could answer that better than me. She seems to have a sharper comprehension of the forgiveness of God. I was brought up by Christian parents and have always known God's grace. I never indulged in many of the sins people partake of today, but I learned that I too needed to be forgiven because we've all sinned and fallen short of the glory of God. To God, one sin is no worse than another. My partner's even been forgiven of murder. She has a heightened sense of forgiveness probably because we tend to rank sin; that's something God doesn't do."

Mark watched Loren walk over and take Ray aside before involving himself with his group once again.

Loren wandered over to the buffet table with Ray and made introductions, careful not to use a last name. He prattled some trivial dialogue before plunging into his intentional query. "Would your great-great grandfather have been Algie Eton?"

Ray picked up a morsel of food, popped it into his mouth, and chewed for a moment before replying, "Yes, I believe that was his name." Ray smiled with an insightful grin with his next statement. "And his wife's name was Alice, maiden name Tarbell."

Loren was taken back with the answer to a question he hadn't even determined to ask. Dumbfounded, he stood still while Ray picked up some more food and ate it. Ray held his smile. "I have to be going. Maybe we can talk again another time."

Reclaiming his composure, Loren politely said he'd enjoy the opportunity and walked Ray to the teleport. Part way there Felicia Rederman clamped onto Ray. Her red hair was done up in high fashion and decorated with a diamond tiara. Wearing a sequenced green evening gown, she was one of the few who looked to belong in the lavish setting. "There you are. If I didn't know better, I'd thought you were trying to avoid me."

Loren had a hard time hiding another surprise. "Felicia? You know this person?"

Her long face ended with a ball-tip chin, which served as an exclamation point to her light blue eyes of pride. "Yes. I'm sponsoring Ray as a candidate to the Network."

Loren held his plaster smile and nodded a quaint, positive response. "Well, he's in good hands. That's for sure. Nice meeting you, Ray. Maybe another time we'll have an opportunity to continue our conversation."

Loren politely turned and tended to his other guests as Ray and Felicia took leave.

Later that evening, Holly and Loren sat alone carefully tallying the names collected. They sat in a small, but pleasantly furnished room with a round, oak table. The single light source set of subdued intensity. Holly finished the last entry in a ledger.

"There. That's three people who asked Jesus into their hearts tonight and twenty-nine who still have an interest. That's twice as good as last year, Loren." Her fine, brown hair lay straight, touching the ends of her wide smile as it trailed down past her shoulders.

Loren was too preoccupied in thought to notice. He looked past the woman. "Ray bothers me. I don't trust him. Felicia's never been wrong yet, but . . ." He snapped his attention to Holly with a sudden thought. "He anticipated my interest in his great-great grandmother. It's as if he knows."

Holly's pleasant smile melted from her face as Loren informed her of his feelings. She seemed concerned. "Ray knows of my investigation. I told him all of what I'd discovered and suspected before we split. I wonder if he came here tonight hoping to find me?"

The leader stood and paced the floor a few times before speaking. "Possibly, but it probably was just one of several reasons. If he truly has seen the light, it'll be of no great concern to us. It's hard to believe he'd fool Felicia, but if he has . . ."

The two simply looked at one another. No more words were needed.

NOT AS THEY SEEM

"I'm a conscientious objector to the way the United States is handling religious rights. I want to live and be a part of a country that allows me my religious freedoms."

Jesse Eton—Application form applying for Canadian citizenship, 07/31/2020

The Reservation

Everything seemed as it was two hundred years earlier. Making a living came through hard work and good planning. The men were out in their boats trying to catch as many fish as the great St. Lawrence River would relent. The work was fun when it wasn't work. Today was a serious day with little festivity involved. Mary was glad the men were out on the river and not around. Her visitor might have been an embarrassment if her husband had been there. The garden was doing very well that year and she relaxed for a minute from toiling in it when she noticed him coming toward her.

For Mark, it seemed like a picture from a history book. Mary's long, black braid and dark, wrinkled, sanguine complexion could be enough to convince him of her heritage without the traditional clothing. The last day of August was always very unpredictable this far north. After such an extended period of hot weather, the breeze coming off the river seemed very chilling. He pulled his thin, colorful windbreaker around as he stopped in front of Mary. "Would you tell me where I might find Mary Tarbell?"

Small wrinkles developed around Mary's dark eyes as she studied the man before her. "May I ask who's inquiring?"

Looking out across the rippling water he studied a small boat in contemplation before returning his reply to Mary. "My name's Mark Jacobson."

Mary stood still for many moments before her unrelenting eyes softened under the developing smile. She took several steps and threw herself around Mark who reacted with surprise. Realizing Mark was at a loss to her direct response, the older woman stepped back but held her smile. "I'm Mary Tarbell."

It was Mark's turn to respond spontaneously. Mary stood almost a head shorter than him. He slowly reached over and gently touched her cheek. "Mom?"

With a smile revealing several teeth missing, Mary took Mark's hand and kissed it. "Yes, son."

Mark took her in his arms and softly talked over her head. "I didn't think I'd find you this easy. I'm so glad to finally see you." They stood for several minutes before Mary finally invited him into the house.

The home was a simple, wood-frame structure over 150 years old. Many artifacts testified to the occupant's Indian heritage. Mark studied many of them while Mary started water boiling for tea. The Akwesasne Mohawk reservation was one of the few in the whole country that voluntarily decided to keep its roots in spite of the new NMA regulations. Income from the casino was no longer allowed. Electric power from the nearby dam carried all its power to large cities south. The electric plant was one of only two such hydroelectric plants left in the country. These ran only for the museums, which kept them going. Fusion power was much cheaper and efficient to make. Gas from the Iroquois pipeline was the only resource allowed by the government. The executive branch decided long ago that if the Native Americans wanted to live their religious heritage, they would have to fend for themselves. Natural gas was the only compromise achieved by their ancestors.

Mary placed the cup of tea down in front of her son and sat across from him. The cuckoo clock on the wall ticked loudly in the following silence. The scene could've been a Norman Rockwell painting. The kitchen was small with light-colored, blue-flowered wallpaper peeling in one corner. Antique appliances covered one wall, including the gas stove and refrigerator. Counters and cabinets took up most of the other two walls. At one time, the woodwork was a nice white, but had yellowed. The warped wooden table they sat at contained a vase with one dusty silk daisy, an opened book with a frayed cover, and a plate of cookies that Mary had set down moments before. The woman wore a long skirt with dark but colorful patterns and a thin shawl over her shoulders. Mark was an anachronism for the time displayed.

A smile slowly developed on Mary's face. "Why've you come to see me? How'd you know I'm your mother?"

The young man wrapped his hands around the hot, steaming cup and starred at the vapor rising up from it. "Mom and Dad—I mean, my stepparents—thought it best to tell me the truth right from the beginning." He looked into Mary's eyes. He sensed a calming effect from the rich, dark brown orbs giving him the good judgment to be honest. "They're the best. I lack for nothing and they'll always be Mom and Dad to me, but they told me about you. I was nearby so I thought I'd visit."

Mary reached over and put a hand on one of his. It was rough and callused from hard work but gentle with much feeling. "It's so good to know how one of my sons has done. I think of you often. You said you were nearby. What're you doing?"

Something said caught Mark's attention but he ignored it and stumbled through answering the question. "Umm . . . aahh . . . I was on an assignment at Massena and had some free time. My parents told me you're from this reservation. It took a little longer to get here than I thought. There isn't a teleport within miles of here. I'd made up my mind I wasn't going to spend a lot of time searching. The Lord led me right to you when I got here. Must be I was suppose to find you."

Mary lifted her cup to her lips. "What do you do?"

Mark planned for the question. He prayed about it and came to the conclusion to tell her the truth. "I'm a Rigid Christian and work underground in supporting that effort." Not knowing what to expect, Mark intently watched her countenance.

Graced with wrinkles, Mary's face still showed the beauty she had with youth. He observed it soften into a relaxed smile with her answer. "Good. They're fine people who've helped us many times. This is good to know of you. I am proud."

Satisfied, he brought his cup to his relieved expression and nodded a thank you. "Somehow I knew you'd approve."

They talked for another half-hour on various subjects before Mary gave Mark another opportunity to inquire on one of Mary's earlier statements. She told her feelings about giving Mark up for adoption. "You were the hardest one for me to give up . . ." She hung her head without finishing.

Mark felt her distress in revealing something she had not intended. He slid their empty cups aside and held her hands. "Mother—I'm not the only one you gave up for adoption, am I?"

Mary looked up and studied her son's face for a moment, then stood and faced the door. She looked out across the wide meadow watching the sun glint off the few boats out on the river. She didn't turn around and spoke as if to the men fishing. "You, I gave up out of necessity. I was twenty-six. You were my fifth child and the first after the oldest to live through delivery. I was so excited but knew I couldn't take care of you. Don had just died from a hunting accident, and there was no one to take care of me. The best thing I could do was give you to someone who'd provide for you. A friend told me about the Rigid Christians and gave me a name to contact. I gave you to a nice family and they did well by you."

Mark sat back in his chair and folded his arms. He didn't want to rush Mary into something he could see was uncomfortable. Another minute passed before she turned from the door. Folding her hands, Mary looked boldly at Mark. Her voice was soft with a childlike quality. "I was fifteen when some SS agents came looking for a runaway RC. I didn't even know then what an RC was. I was alone in the house because my dad was busy running an errand. Mother had died several years earlier. One of the agents stayed and told the other he'd catch up with him. He raped me. I learned a little later that day my father had drown. The SS agents found the RC they were looking for in my father's boat. He was trying to smuggle the person across the river into Canada. At that time, Canada protected Christians. I think the SS agents drown my father for his actions, though it was never reported that way."

Stunned, Mark stared blankly at his mother with wide eyes as she continued. She couldn't stop once she started. "I was alone and pregnant. I couldn't wait to give up my first son. He reminded me of all the grief I had to bare. I was only sixteen when he was born. The elders of the tribe found him a home. Some know what's come of him, but I care not to. Maybe I should, but I can't make myself and have resolved to leave it that way."

The clock tic tocked nine more times. Mark stood to face his mother. "I have one brother. Are there any others?"

She slowly moved her head from side to side with a thin-lined mouth. After a moment she smiled. "Glen has been good to me. He's a good man who's brought me back to my Indian heritage after Don died, but we were unable to have any children."

Mary sat down again. "I gave each of you a family heirloom to have and pass on. The first one was kind of a silly little thing, but yours

I knew I wasn't going to have anyone else to pass it on to, so I gave it to you."

She searched Mark's face for a hint of comprehension. A large smile rewarded Mary as Mark said, "I have it. As a matter of fact, there's a girl I already have plans to give it to. Thanks, Mother. It means more than ever now."

Another hour passed in conversation and sharing before Mark had to leave. Upon his parting, Mary asked that he consider never visiting again. Her husband knew nothing of her children and she preferred to keep things that way. Mark reluctantly agreed. With a tear in his eye, he said goodbye to his real mother. Mary went back to her garden as she sobbed with a smile on her face, praising God.

Found Out

Air screamed past his ears so fast he couldn't hear Sally's terrified screech. Her blue eyes were in owl mode. Wind tore at her hair and cloths in all fury trying to separate from her. Frantically she reached out for Buck as they free fell to earth from two thousand feet. She couldn't get his attention. Black hair whipped two feet up from Buck's head. He had a smile as wide as his features would allow. He was enjoying himself, laughing with complete abandonment. Sudden contact with the ground was only seconds away when Sally closed her eyes. Instantly, the sensation vanished. Buck reached down to help his assistance up from the floor. His laughter slowed to a chuckle as he helped Sally down from the teleport-like unit.

Still holding onto Buck for support, Sally announced her feelings on the experience. "I never want to do that again!"

Catching his breath once and arranging his hair, Buck grinned at the pretty woman. "I told you it's a real rush. I couldn't come here without doing that once more."

Sally struggled to gather her composure with little success. "That wasn't assimilation, was it?"

Buck took Sally's arm and led her out of the park they visited. After a minute, he answered her. "No. It's a special teleport system that takes you to two thousand feet and lets you go. The system's set up to re-transport you to the start just before you hit the ground. Scary as all hell, isn't it?" He looked at her with one of his evil grins.

Sally didn't see the humor in it. "Don't ever do anything like that again unless you tell me what you're up to." She quickly walked ahead of Buck and led the way to their destination. He watched for half a second, shrugged his shoulders, and with a nonchalant expression tried to catch up.

It was a day off and Buck invited Sally to accompany him to the Albany NMA. His errand was to pick up some personal possessions left behind and he thought Sally would enjoy the time with him. Her reaction to the skydive ride slightly puzzled him. April had rather enjoyed it when he took her. The ride was seven blocks from the office.

Sally had just begun to get over the experience when they arrived at the building. "Maybe I should go home when you finish your business here."

Buck stopped midway up the stairs to the old building and looked to her. "Look, I'm sorry. I made a mistake. I shouldn't have done that to you. I didn't know you were frightened of heights. I'll never do anything like that to you again."

Sally had never seen him so serious. For the first time since the adventure, she smiled. It was rather sheepish but a smile just the same. "OK."

Buck reached up and straightened some of the short, blonde hair. "Good. Now let's get this over with. Then I'll show you some more of Albany before we leave. No more surprises like that."

The pair trotted up the rest of the stairs and entered the large front doors. Inside the main lobby a security desk took up most of the room. As luck would have it, Tina Getling was the officer on duty. She smiled after looking up to see who came in. "Well, look who's here. How've you been, Al? What brings you to these parts?"

Buck refrained from flirting with one of his old flames. He didn't want to upset Sally again so soon. "I'm doing just great, Tina. I'd like you to meet my temporary assistant, Sally Diller."

Tina caught the subtle warning in his tone and behaved herself. "Glad to meet you, Sally."

They talked for a few more minutes before Buck stated his business. "I left some personal notes in the vault. I've come to sign them out. It'll only take a few minute and we'll be out of your hair."

Tina reached under the desk to touch a sensor releasing the door to the elevator. "Help yourself."

The pair made it to the unlocked door when Tina called to Buck, "Oh, did that VanTimons guy ever get a hold of you, Al?"

Reaching for the door he stopped in mid-action. In the two half seconds it took, Buck's eyes grew twofold before he caught himself and regained his composure. He managed to paint a puzzled expression as he turned to Tina. "Who?"

The security officer continued. "I can't remember his first name. Seems like it was Greg or something like that, but I remember the last name was VanTimons. How could anyone forget a funny name like that? He came here the day you left. I didn't think you'd know him. He was real scruffy looking but he asked for you and said he was a friend."

Buck was extremely careful to keep a neutral countenance. "Are you sure he didn't say his name was Hank Bronson?"

Tina frowned deeply at the statement. "No. He never said anything like that."

Being the artist he was, Buck continued with a blank look. "You're right. I never heard of the man. Probably some nut who thought I might get him a job or something. Thanks anyway, Tina."

He continued his trek to the vault. Sally paused and looked back and forth between Buck and Tina before she followed. She carefully weighed the conversation and tucked it away in her mind.

Sunday

Dove finished the special music for the morning and was rewarded with applause and amens. Many wiped their eyes dry. Carol, Steve, and Debra walked away from the stage as Mike came forward to introduce the speaker of the morning. "That song came with heart-wrenching reality from Carol. She had an experience early this summer showing the heart of Jesus. Her prayer's that you could grasp the same reality without the heartache she went through." He turned to watch Carol as she made her way to a seat in the front. "Thank you, Carol." She smiled and sat down.

Mike continued. "Now for a message from one of our new preachers. Please welcome, Gabriel Sanders." Mike made way for the speaker and sat down front with his family while the applause subsided.

Gabriel Sanders was young. He was an excellent preacher and held everyone's attention—not bad for his first public address to so many people. The Upper Room auditorium could hold three hundred easily. Gathered on one side, a few rows back, sat April Goulay with Ryker and his family. It was her first church service and she took it all in like a sponge. The sermon couldn't have been a better one for April. It was very basic and to the point about salvation through Jesus Christ. At the end of the service, Gabriel gave the opportunity for those who wished to come forward. He explained he would lead them through a prayer of salvation but expected others to rededicate their lives to Jesus. April was one of seventeen to accept the altar call. Ryker watched the event with much scrutiny.

Dear God, please grant me discernment. April seems sincere, but I want to be completely sure. I still don't have a good feeling about the way she came to us. In Jesus' name, I ask for Your guidance.

While April was up front, Monica asked Ryker if he'd allow the woman to come home for dinner. Ryker consented and asked April when she came back.

"Yes, I'd enjoy that very much."

Mike approached his friend as Ryker made the invitation. He pulled Ryker aside with a worried look upon his face. "Would you like me to have one of my people come along to help keep an eye on her."

The man was doing his job and Ryker knew it. "Thanks for the offer but I don't believe it'll be a problem. Maybe if she has a chance to relax she might make a slip. I'd like to give her that opportunity if it's going to happen." Mike gave an understanding nod and excused himself.

***

The afternoon went well even though April began it slightly embarrassed. Monica came from the kitchen after the meal carrying a cake with twelve lit candles. They sang the birthday song as Monica set the cake down in front of Erica. April protested. "If I'd have known you were celebrating a birthday, I'd have declined this opportunity."

Monica turned her attention to April. "Don't be foolish. You're more than welcomed or I wouldn't have asked you."

April might have rebutted but Julia got her attention with a strange request directed at her sister. "Do it, Erica. Do it. Come on, Erica, do it."

The tall, thin girl smiled a forced grin at her sister. "I'm too old for that now. You ought to be the one carrying on."

Julia didn't hesitate. "OK, I will. I want a corner piece. I want a corner piece. I want a corner piece." Monica vividly explained Erica's fourth birthday party.

April enjoyed the family camaraderie. The girls busied themselves with the opened birthday gifts, laughing and sharing their games. Monica took care of the dishes after convincing April she didn't need to help.

Ryker took advantage of the opportunity while they were alone in the living room. "Tell me, April, how're you fairing with Calvin and the doctor? Linda tells me you're glad you took the chance you did in trying to find some real Christians who could help you defect. Is that true?"

April's hair was done up in a single, bushy ponytail. It bounced with her reply. "Oh yes. I never dreamed it'd be this good. The government has filled our minds so full of lies about you people—well, it's hard to comprehend the good I see happening here. I'm happy I chanced it."

Moments of tense silence followed. Ryker weighed his next question. April seemed as patient and relaxed as a young boy sitting under a shade tree fishing, watching his bobber.

After this morning, I should take April's story into consideration again. Lord, I give these next few minutes to you. Show me in some way this woman's heart. In Your Name I ask it, amen.

With a quick prayer, Ryker forged forward. "Linda tells me you've officially announced your rejection of NMA policies and want to come here to serve the Network. Tell me once more how you came to us."

Meticulously a smile developed on April's face as she leaned back in her soft, easy chair. Monica finished in the kitchen and upon eavesdropping on the conversation, excused herself to be with her girls as she walked through the room. April's hazel green eyes followed Ryker's wife out of the room. "Monica's pretty intuitive, isn't she?"

Ryker adjusted his position to stretch his legs and then looked to April with a half grin. "Giving that observation I'd say you recognize that quality because it's one of yours."

"It was something I had to learn fast around Buck." The smile dropped off her face and then reappeared again, equal to the click of a camera. April thought the faux pas wouldn't be noticeable, but she hastened to cover her mistake just in case. "In order to be a good partner to someone, it helps to be on the same wavelength."

The ploy had no obvious effect on Ryker but April's statement and reaction didn't get by him.

Buck? Why'd she wish she hadn't mentioned that name?

Ryker didn't wish to give her any time to skirt the issue. He came back with a question before April could continue. "Do you know Mr. Shanach personally?"

Wrinkles developed between April's close set eyes. "Is that Mr. Shanach's first name? No. I was referring to different person I worked with."

Pushing to keep the momentum, Ryker quickly came back with another question. "What's his last name?"

She smiled sheepishly and tried to recover but it wasn't smooth enough. "Oh, umm, uh, Washburn. He was my first instructor after basic training."

Ryker innocently nodded and smiled. "My mistake. I know you said it was a Devon who left you to die. I thought maybe you misspoke yourself."

April continued with her story on how she came to them. It was as smooth and as well articulated as the other times she informed them. When finished, April made her appeal once more. "I've learned so much from Calvin and Dr. Paquin these seven weeks that I'd really like to be considered for further instruction through your regular training process. Calvin planned to present the idea to you tomorrow. I didn't mean to beat him to it, but I did have this opportunity to talk to you myself. Thank you for this morning. I'll never forget it."

Checking his watch Ryker stood. "I'm glad you found it so enlightening. I'll give some serious thought to your request. Maybe you'll have more opportunities. Linda will be here in a minute to take you back to your room. Maybe you'd like to say goodbye to the rest of my family before she and Calvin get here."

April stood with him. "Yes, I would. Thanks for listening."

As the guest concluded her time, Linda and Calvin showed up. One of the rules was April could not be alone with any single person at a time. Linda had an infectious smile, which caused others to take to her quickly. "Hi, April. I trust you found these folks interesting to say the least, but it's time to go back to your room. Maybe it won't be long and you can have a little more freedom around here."

With goodbyes submitted, Calvin and Linda escorted April to her room. The space accommodated all necessary items the woman needed but was secured so she couldn't wander around the complex. The trio talked for a minute in April's room before Calvin and Linda excused themselves. Paper and pen were available for April's convenience. She sat down and wrote a quick note at the desk provided.

> I am sorry to report that I may have made a major slip. I don't know for sure, but I thought you should be aware of the only thing that has gone wrong so far.

The letter went into details on the visit she and Ryker had earlier. When she finished, she sealed it in a special envelope. Fourteen minutes later a knock came to April's door—three quick ones, then two more followed by a pause with one more tap. The woman smiled, walked over to the door, and slipped her letter under it. With a sigh of relief, she leaned against the door and listened as the person walked away with her note.

Trouble Begins

Massena was a large booming town 150 years earlier. Now it was a simple tourist attraction. As part of the Seaway Trail, it was home to the museum, which took care of its three major attractions. They included the hydroelectric plant, one of the few bridges spanning the St. Lawrence River and a working lock that could move large ships up and down the differing levels of the river. A couple of the old ships were docked for tours and sometimes used for demonstrations. During the summer, expeditions were offered, which took people up and down the river's sights from Niagara Falls to end at Massena. Special teleports were setup to take folks from one site to another. On September 1, business was beginning to slow down for the year, but the weather wasn't helping either. A cloud cast day sent rain drizzling down.

Raging waters boiled at the bottom of the long dam as raindrops fell and lost their individuality to the moving waters of the great river. Patiently waiting inside the glass-walled observatory, Mark and Candy took in the sight. The pair was dressed in civilian clothes, blending in as regular tourists. It was early and no one else was in the large room at the moment. Mark was very quiet, deep in thought, while he looked beyond the spectacle before him.

Candy noticed Mark's distant veneer and tried to bring him back. "I finished taking the tour that we started Saturday. What'd you do with your day off yesterday?"

Mark snapped out of his trance and turned a smile to his partner. "Oh, I visited a relative who lives down the river a ways. I hadn't seen them in quite a while."

Candy might have pursued the discussion but a group of people came in. Scattered around the room were many exhibits to examine. Written history on the Seaway project and the operation of a hydroelectric generator helped the visitors understand the models observed. The noise level increased as more people came in and chattered to one another. Mark checked his watch. "It's almost nine o'clock. We'd better get into position."

On one side of the large observatory sat a door to a small auditorium. At specified times, a presentation would give in-depth information on the dam and its operation. The sign read: "Next Presentation at 10:00." When they entered the darkened room, two people sat in the back next to the door. Mark and Candy took seats about halfway to the front. The room was very dim with dark red velvety curtains hanging all around.

The undercover agents whispered to one another. "Mark, are you sure Paul meant this room?"

"Yes. He said to be here by nine fifteen. Remember we're here for the interview."

"I wonder what that's supposed to mean?"

"I don't know but he said we'd figure it out. If the person doesn't introduce himself as Paul Tarsus, we're to leave like we just realized we're in the wrong place."

Candy questioned, "And if he does introduce himself correctly, he's going to ask if there're any questions. We're to raise our hands. Right?"

More people came in, one sitting down next to Mark and Candy. Silently, Mark shook his head affirmative to the last question. At nine fifteen, a man and woman came into the auditorium, closed the door behind them, and locked it. The man made his way to the front and stood. "Greetings to each of you. Before I continue, if anyone's here for the presentation and not the job interview, you should leave now. The Seaway presentation is at ten o'clock."

In the room of a little over twenty people, five stood to excuse themselves. One elderly couple became very vocal as they left. The woman used her purse on the man. "I told you it wasn't until ten o'clock, you nit wit, but no, you couldn't believe me. I wish you'd quit embarrassing me at these things."

The woman at the back politely allowed the five out and shut the door again with an amused smile on her face.

Paul was tall and thin. Wavy, brown hair piled on one side added to the imbalanced appearance of his large, bulb nose. He interlaced his fingers and smiled widely at the group gathered. "Welcome to the Massena Seaway Historic Museum. My name's Paul Tarsus. At the door is Helen Campbell. We'll be selecting one of you today as this building's Sanitary Engineer. Are there any questions before we begin?"

About half raised their hand. Paul took a moment to count those. "OK, keep your hands up. Those of you who don't have your hands up go with Helen and she'll begin with some forms for you to fill out. The rest of you stay here."

People made their way to the door as Helen held it opened again. When they left, Paul took notice of one woman who stayed but hadn't raised her hand. "Excuse me, but I noticed you did not have a question before. Have you changed your mind?"

Slightly startled for being noticed and questioned directly the woman hesitated. "Ah, umm—yes. I thought of something afterwards."

Paul was very congenial and smooth but pressed the lady further. "Good. We'll begin with you. What's your question?"

It was pitifully obvious she was at a loss for words. After a half a minute, she blurted out the first thing that came to mind. "Is this a permanent or temporary job?"

The tall man used his professional etiquette and skillfully directed his next statement with grace. "That depends upon you. It's determined by your answers in the interview."

Paul took a step back and triggered an intercom on the wall. "I've one more for you." Paul directed the woman. "If you'd follow Helen, she'll get you started on the interview process."

As neat as that, Paul had who he wanted in the auditorium. When silence prevailed again, he began with the purpose for the gathering. "This leaves us with the eight I was expecting. I truly would like to welcome each one of you. My real name's Anthony Glassine. This is the new group, which I would like to lead into a closer Christian walk. Before

251

we're through this morning, I'll let you know where our meeting place will be. I doubt if you know each other, even though we're all from the same area. My prayer's that we'd grow strong and effectively lead others to the truth of the gospel message. For the next few minutes, why don't we just mingle, introduce ourselves, and then I'll reveal our meeting place for next Wednesday."

Mark and Candy stood to do as directed. Mark's heart jumped to his throat when he turned to find someone to greet. In the back of the room, Kayla stood talking to a tall, red-headed man. Mark spun around to face the front again with a horrified look on his face. Candy studied him with a frown. "What's the matter?"

He didn't say a word. Anthony came forward, introduced himself, and waited for returned acknowledgment. Mark couldn't react fast enough because of the shock, so Candy did the job. Mark managed a weak smile when she was through, but he said nothing to the tall man. Candy quickly covered for him. "He's real shy. When Mark gets to know you better, he'll open up." Candy's pretty smile and calm explanation diverted Anthony's attention and he excused himself to visit others.

Knowing his cover was blown, Mark quickly thought about repairing the damage before it happened. He had to be very careful what he said. Kayla didn't know he was undercover with the NMA and Candy didn't know he was an RC. He had about five seconds to formulate his statement to Candy. "I know one of the girls in the back. She hasn't seen me in a while. I'd rather not see her."

Mark needed to smile. The tall, redhead introduced himself. "Hi. I'm Craig VanTimons. My friends call me Red. Why don't we consider ourselves friends?"

Mark gallantly made his introduction. Flippantly he informed Red that until he knew him better, he'd call him by his nickname. While they all chuckled over the reply, Mark glanced around Red to see Kayla coming their way. When Red moved to greet Candy, it put Mark in full view of his girlfriend. Kayla's expression metamorphosed from neutral, to surprise, and settled on joy. "Mark! Oh my goodness, I don't believe it!"

Mark hurried to get to her before she said much more. So enthralled, Kayla talked over Mark's attempts to hush her. "What're you doing here? I didn't think I'd see you for—maybe a couple of years. I thought you were on some mission to . . ."

Mark didn't give her a chance to finish. To quiet her, he took Kayla in his arms and gave her a long, lingering kiss. The couple had everyone's attention until the length of their embrace caused modesty in the people to return to their conversations.

Looking up, Mark noticed Red and Candy staring at them. Frantically trying to think of something so he could talk to Kayla for a few seconds, Mark smiled at the two. Red rescued the younger man from his dilemma by taking Candy aside in conversation. Mark turned to Kayla to explain but she beat him to it. Evaluating what had taken place in the last few minutes drew a grimaced comment. "I shouldn't have said anything should I?"

Mark forced a smile. "It's OK. Just play it cool until we've a chance to be alone."

Red's short-lived tactic ended as Candy led him to the couple. The ebony-skinned beauty smiled a sarcastic grin. "How long've you two known each other?"

Lying was not Mark's forte. His upbringing made the mechanics of it unnatural. It showed in his delivery. "Ahh . . . well . . . for about . . . I don't know . . . a year or so maybe." The four stood looking back and forth between each other.

Candy would've probed further except Anthony didn't allow the chance. "All right everybody have a seat again and I'll finish up here. We've only a few minutes and we'll need to be out of here and I want to make sure we all know where we're going from here."

Mark and Kayla walked past Red and Candy to sit. Red made room but Candy defiantly stood where she was to make the couple skirt her while she glared at them. As he passed her, Mark whispered to Candy, "I'll explain after this. Come on and sit down."

She did as Mark directed but behind the other three. She wanted to be where she could watch them all. Anthony took about five more minutes to explain some procedures and divulge some key information. Satisfied with how things went, Anthony excused everybody and went to the door to see each one out.

Back in the observatory, the small crowd of people began to scatter and mingle with the rest of the tourists. Kayla introduced her new friend to Mark before the three noticed Candy was nowhere in sight. Anxiously Mark began scanning the area. "Where'd Candy go? Have you guys seen her?"

The three searched the ins and outs of the immediate area. Just as Mark was going to suggest some drastic measures, Candy came to them from the outside corridor. She nonchalantly queried Mark. "Shouldn't we be going, partner? There're some other things we need to do."

Without meaning to, Mark caustically addressed her. "Where'd you go?"

Candy rolled her head back and frown at him. "Can't a girl go to the bathroom without getting her head bit off?"

Abashed, Mark recovered from his great concern. He placed a relaxed smile as he said, "Sorry. I must be more nervous than I thought. You're right. We've gotta to go."

He turned to Red, said goodbye, and then lingered his gaze upon Kayla before saying the same. The undercover agents walked together out of the room.

Leaving the building with Red, Kayla tried to explain about her and Mark. She stopped when she noticed a small commotion ahead of them on the wet sidewalk. Two SS agents, followed by Candy, were herding Mark into a teleport unit. All she could make out was Candy hollering over Mark's protests. "I don't want to hear it now, but you've a lot of explaining to do back at the office."

Kayla started to run for Mark when Red stopped her. She tried to resist but Red simply shook his head at her. She knew he was right and turned her back to the teleport as it whisked her love away. Red stepped in front of her. "I know it's hard to think right now, but shouldn't we see about talking to Anthony before he goes? He's going to need to change his plans now before anyone else is arrested."

Kayla looked up at Red with huge tears in her eyes and solemnly shook her head yes. The new group of believers was saved from being found out, but Kayla couldn't rejoice with them.

***

Not politely, the door was smashed in. Thundering in stormed an SS agent with stunner in hand. He was alone, something that was never to be. Quickly he made his way through the tiny, dingy three-room apartment. After a minute, he determined the place was empty. There wasn't much to look at but he wasn't going to leave anything to chance. Holstering his weapon, the agent searched for any kind of clue. Hank Bronson's place seemed abandoned and for quite some time. When the preliminary investigation was complete, Buck took his helmet off and placed it on the little rickety table. The skin between his dancing blue eyes wrinkled in absent-minded frustration.

Inquisitive fingers and eyes carefully combed every drawer, cabinet, and other places that might house some information on the occupant's activities. Buck felt fear and he didn't like it. Craig VanTimons could ruin his whole career. Thoughts of regrets washed over his consciousness as he searched. He wished he had permanently neutralized Red, but who'd have guessed he might come out of a mind alteration. The process was fool proof even though it was illegal.

In frustration, Buck picked up a glass sitting next to the single bunk and verbalized his thought process. "The problem is Craig's no fool. I thought I'd taken care of you VanTimons."

In a rage, he threw the glass at the cracked mirror and finished the process with a resounding crash. Deep in contemplation, Buck stood clenching and unclenching his hands. He looked at the destruction for a long time before he noticed it. The small card had been stuck in the frame of the mirror and now lay with the shards of glass on the top of the dresser. Coming back to reality, the dark blue eyes focus upon the item. Almost racing to it Buck picked it up and read it. An evil smile graced his lips as he chuckled at his good fortune. It was an address card to an apartment in Washington DC, dated only a few weeks earlier. Nimbly he placed the card in a pouch at his belt and picked up his helmet to leave. Buck thought maybe his luck was holding out after all. As he went through the demolished door, he placed his helmet over his vivacious face.

All Have Sinned

Bethany was small, but a strategic facility for the Network. It was the closest to Washington DC, which also made it the hardest to keep a secret. Only those who were well proven, extremely hard working, and excellent students of the Word could serve. When not confined to his room, Ray had two people with him at all times. He still had no idea of the facility's location. When teleporting to and from the place his escort would place e-blinders on him. These devices electronically blinded and deafened him so he couldn't determine the teleport codes.

While wearing a self-satisfied smile, Ray compiled his notes when the knock came to his door. He scurried to shut his computer down and place the information disk in his pocket. The computer was for personal use only, with no possible way to be networked. He called when he was though. "Come in."

Surprise and then euphoria evolved upon his face when he saw his visitor and she was by herself! He stood to greet her. "Kayla! Come on in. Have a seat. It's been awhile since I've seen you."

He directed her to a couch away from his desk. The room was small and comfortable with almost everything anyone needed. It smelled of sweet incense, which Ray was burning. Settling next to Kayla on the couch, half of his elated expression faded. "What's the problem? You look extremely sober."

Kayla's eyes were puffy and red. The usually straight, silky hair was askew and tangled in places. "Remember once, quite a while ago now, I told you I had a boyfriend?"

Ray's hair was down and neatly lying on his shoulders. Concern developed within its framework. "Yes. You wouldn't talk to me about him."

Her large eyes shimmered as Kayla related the recent story of her beau. Quietness blanketed the scene when she finished. After a minute, Ray stood and walked over to his desk but turned suddenly upon Kayla. "Why're you telling me this? What could I possibly do?"

Adjusting her sitting position to face him squarely, Kayla explained, "I know where you've come from. You still have connections fairly high up in the NMA. I thought maybe you'd pull a few strings and see about getting Mark freed. Or something that might at least help him. Red said he had a few contacts but I'm not sure there's much he could do. Jesse's on vacation visiting his family. I'll admit you're not my first choice, but you're one of my best ones."

Ray leaned up against his desk, cupped an elbow in his hand, and lightly tapped his lips with a finger. He thought some time in that position and then smiled. Returning to the couch he sat down to face Kayla again. "It might be pretty dangerous for me to allow my name to come up anywhere at the NMA after all this time. That's not to say if I was careful I couldn't be effective. I'm just not sure it'd be a wise thing for me to do right now. I'm assuming you've told no one that you were going to ask me this; otherwise, someone else would be here with you. I need to ask—what's in it for me? Obviously, not to be found out assisting you is in my best interest for getting into Network service. If the NMA gets me—well, you can only guess what'd happen to me then."

Kayla looked down into her lap. Moments went by with screaming silence. Then Kayla stood to leave. "I'm sorry. You're right; I haven't given this much thought I guess."

Ray quickly but gently seized her arm before Kayla could go anywhere. Looking up at her he allowed raw emotion for Kayla to sculpt his countenance and butter his words. "I didn't say I wouldn't. As a matter of fact, I don't think I could NOT help you. Maybe I'm simply looking for something from you that I know you've reserved for another. That's very selfish of me and I apologize."

Kayla had buried it, denied it existed, but at that moment felt it flood her being as Ray gazed upon her. It wasn't reason or wisdom. Neither was it comfort or gain. The time of closeness threatened to surface as physical attraction mixed with intrigue and excitement that had been buried for weeks. She no longer had the strength or will to suppress it. Collapsing upon the couch, the young lady buried her face in Ray's chest and sobbed uncontrollably. Softly he ran his fingers through Kayla's hair as he lightly held her and patted the back of her head. "There, there. It's all right. I'll see what might be done for your friend."

Gently Ray lifted her face from his chest and looked deeply into her eyes. Behind the shimmering pools he could see there was no longer any resistance. Softly he leaned over and kissed her. Kayla remembers the rest of the afternoon with nothing but regret.

Information

Felix Benjamin eyed Sally with some reservation for her directions. He was a big man and could look very intimidating when need be. "In Mr. Shanach's office you say?"

With a stern expression, Sally stopped short on her trek to the administration offices to the top floor. Facing the main counter of the Washington NMA she looked the shift security officer in the eyes. Felix saw the anger behind Sally's dark blue ones. "Yes, that's correct. Don't play ignorant with me. I know Al's made it known I'm his assistant until further notice." The stern expression softened into a self-satisfied look with her next comment. "Or maybe you're not playing. I'm sure Al wouldn't like it if he found that to be true."

Felix immediately assumed a professional demeanor. He reached under the counter for the correct sensor as he made his comment. "No problem, Ms. Diller."

The young woman swaggered to the newly released door at the other end of the long counter. "Thank you, Mr. Benjamin. Make sure my visitor has instructions to Al's office."

As Sally left, Felix sarcastically saluted her. He made some entries at the terminal and then relaxed behind the counter with the cup of coffee that Sally interrupted. A few signals on the main console demanded his attention for the next twenty minutes. Felix had relaxed again when a red light blinked, accompanied with a quiet two-tone pitch. The lobby teleport activated after Felix checked the incoming information and allowed the transmission.

When the glass partition cleared and retracted back out of the way, Holly stepped down. She wore an attractive blue dress. Her long, front bangs were pulled back and tied in a tail behind the rest of her long hair. At the counter she reported, "My name is Holly Tarbell. I've an appointment with Sally Diller."

Felix gave Holly directions to Buck's office. When she left, he called ahead to inform Angel that Sally's appointment was on her way.

Holly scanned the upper floor of the NMA building with awe. It was an elegance she only recently began to appreciate. Angel cordially invited Holly to have a seat. She had five minutes to gawk around the room before Sally called her in.

After offering Holly a seat, Sally picked up a piece of pastry and nibbled on it. The women were different in many ways. Sally was very mod with her slick yellow-and-brown body suit, short, cropped, blonde hair and assured confidence. Holly looked old fashioned with long, brown, straight hair, a flowery blue dress, and she was nibbling on her lip. Giving her a moment to stew, Sally finally queried the visitor. "You indicated this was rather important, Ms. Tarbell. I know you wanted to talk to Mr. Shanach yourself, but he's rather busy right now. Maybe, if you can convince me that what you have merits it, I might see if he could privilege you with an audience." The pastry went to Sally's smiling red lips as she waited for the response.

Holly looked to her lap for a few seconds and then forced a smile for Sally. "I do appreciate that, Ms. Diller, but what I have is of a personal nature. Not being able to reveal much of it to you, I hope the subject matter is enough to convince you."

Popping the last of the sweet into her mouth, Sally stood and looked out the window over the city. She turned with her hands behind her back and addressed Holly. "I know you said Al knew you, but he's not the same person you knew back then. He has larger responsibilities and little time for trivial personal details on office time. I'm afraid if you can't convince me in another few minutes that I'm not wasting time, you'll be out of here." She finished up with a smirk on her face.

Holly began biting her lip again as she stared into her lap. Gathering her thoughts she looked up at the items on the desk. Holly didn't know she was in Buck's office but suspected it when she saw the frame. Housed in a small silver frame was half-of-a-century-old dollar bill. Only the front side showed, hiding any writing on the backside. The object transfixed Holly. She had only hoped to get confirmation that Buck had it, but never dreamed of seeing it for herself.

Sally said something. Holly caught Sally repeating it but still didn't register what she said. Sally sat down and looked her visitor in the face. "Are you all right, Ms. Tarbell?"

Holly detached herself from her thoughts and sketched a smile. "I'm sorry. It's just I've heard of the ancient currency but I've never seen one. I thought the old money was outlawed because of what it said on it. I was told they were all destroyed."

Puzzled, Sally looked to see what Holly was talking about. When she noticed the framed bill she smiled. "Oh that? I guess it's something sentimental. Al's allowed to keep it because it's not the whole thing. The quote that caused the controversy isn't entirely on it."

Holly was able to gather her thoughts. She accomplished what she hoped in finding out. It came so easy she totally relaxed. Sally noticed it as Holly explained, "I'm sorry to distract you, Ms. Diller. What I've to relay to Mr. Shanach has to do with his heritage. It may have a great impact on his career. That's all I can say but if you would tell him, I believe he might want to hear about it."

The young blonde woman leaned back in her chair and steeple her fingers. "That's it? You can't tell me anymore?"

With a little smile, Holly shook her head no. "I'm afraid not but Al will understand. Just tell him."

Not knowing what else to do with her visitor, Sally professionally excused Holly with the promise she would relay the message.

Half an hour later, Sally was still in Buck's office working when he came in. He changed into his office uniform and did his hair up in a long, single ponytail. His smile told Sally things had gone well. He told her, "Angel said you were in here. Don't get too comfortable. I plan on sticking around for quite awhile."

Inwardly Sally gave a sigh of relief. She could see Buck was in a good mood. She hastened to relinquish his chair. "I'm sorry. I thought you said you'd be gone all day."

Buck studied the card he found at Red's old place and placed it on the desk. Continuing his smile he took his seat saying, "Don't sweat it. I thought I'd be longer. Things turned out better than I expected."

Sally took a relaxed stance at the front of the desk. "You had someone asking for an audience on a personal nature. I handled it for you. She said you might be interested in the information."

Buck studied the address on the card he brought with him. Sally noticed the interest as he queried her. "Did the lady give a name?"

"Holly Tarbell."

Momentarily forgetting the information, Buck set the card back down on the desk. It was the first time Sally saw surprise on the man's face. "Holly Tarbell? She's Ray Cuff's girlfriend. They disappeared about the same time. What's she up to now?"

Sally innocently responded. "Said it had something to do with your heritage."

A moment of horror washed across his eyes before Buck managed to control it. He stood and faced the Washington DC view to reflect. Sally took advantage of Buck's preoccupation and turned the card on the desk to read it. She put it to memory in case it was something of value. The woman had just enough time to digest the bit of information when Buck turned back to face her. "What'd she say about my heritage?"

Sally gave a lopsided smile with one cocked eyebrow. "Nothing. She wouldn't tell me." She registered his relief. Few people would have observed the minute change.

Buck smiled and said, "Thanks, Sally. That'll be all."

She gave a complimentary nod for a salute and left the man to his business.

The Innocent Suffer

VanTimons was a name known for having lots of luck—most of it bad. Red thought upon this while going to his apartment. Maybe things would be different now that he was a Christian. He had finished a special meeting with his new Bible group and thought he might take care of some of his old life. There were the notes he had on Buck he wanted to get rid of. Red didn't want anyone to find the plans he had written down to get revenge on his old childhood friend. The Lord had taken the vindictive nature from him as he learned more about the Jesus who Kayla had introduced him to. Red decided it was time to bury the past and his heart was light with the thoughts of it. As he entered a corner teleport, he smiled with his newfound plans to abandon his revenge.

The common tingling sensation of the teleport faded as Red waited for the glass partition to clear and move. The smile he teleported with vanished as his senses evaluated his apartment. The mess indicated a complete search. Almost everything seemed destroyed, which indicated something more than a regular search. Before he did anything else, Red called the police. He would have used the small monitor but its condition reflected the destruction. The controls to the teleport still worked so he used the large screen of the teleport itself.

An officer showed in seconds. "Precinct 34, Officer Calihand speaking. How may I help you?" Calihand was a crusty-looking older man. He had been through these things a million times and he handled it as such. Red's excitement fazed him little. "My apartment's been broken into and torn apart!"

"Calm down. Give me your name, citizen ID number, and address."

"Craig . . ." That name didn't exist. Red started again. "I'm sorry. My name's Hank Bronson; ID number 54758411; Essex complex, Decatur Street, apartment 38."

The square face of Calihand remained neutral as he punched the information on the keyboard. In less than a half a minute, the old veteran assumed an amused expression. "Interesting. You have a real break-in. There's no reported NMA activity at that address. It seems someone managed to decode your teleport and get in. We haven't had one of these in years." Gathering his composure Calihand resumed a more professional countenance. "Please stay right where you are, Mr. Bronson. I'll send someone over to investigate." The teleport went dark, cleared, and then retracted back into the wall.

Red knew it was going to be a few minutes before anyone arrived so he began looking around. It seemed not a drawer or cupboard survived. Smashed glass, broken furniture, and torn upholstery detailed every room of the small apartment. Then Red remembered his notes! He re-examined the room with a horrified expression. He turned over the smashed coffee table to expose the pocket under the top he'd made to hold his secrets. Everything was gone! Stunned, he didn't know what to do. As he stared out his picture window in thought, another sight made his heart jump. Casey's cage was in place but the door was open.

Making his way to the bird's corner, Red couldn't contain his apprehensions. "Oh, Casey. I hope they didn't let you go, or worse, take you with them."

He relaxed slightly when he was close enough to see the bird was in his cage . . . but . . . he was lying down! Tears burst from his eyes when Red saw Casey's neck was at an odd angle. Carefully, the man reached past a note stuck to the side of the cage and picked his pet up. Casey's neck had been broken. The reality of the situation hit Red as he wailed out loud and lovingly, put the bird to his lips, and kissed it. The only friend he had for years was dead. Grief gripped the big man's heart as he sagged into the only piece of furniture left in one piece—a dining room chair. Red held Casey and bawled for a good minute.

Wiping his eyes, Red remembered the note hanging on the cage. He reached up and took it. The message was short and to the point.

> Well old buddy, I'm on to you now. I'd better not see you try and fulfill these plans. Forget you ever had them or your neck might end up like the bird's. By the way, if the police get any information on this, you and your friends will regret it.

No signature, but Red knew. The teleport signaled for him to receive someone. He put the bird back in his cage and went to the unit. The police had shown up. After he punched the code in to allow them entrance, Red calmly crumpled the note and placed it in his pocket. Later, after they finished their investigation he destroyed it without saying a word to the police about it.

When Good is Bad

Golden rays of sun weaved through the thick forest foliage. It felt like summer but looked like September. The air had an autumn smell as Loren inhaled a large sample of it and exhaled with loud pleasure. "Aaah. I love this time of year."

It was mid morning as he walked back to camp with Holly. They were following an old trail through the woods, walking hand in hand. The age difference between the two was fairly obvious but it wasn't that to come between them. Holly looked to Loren as they leisurely walked along. "This is a beautiful place to hold these special services, Loren. You seem to have so many nice places to bring people on these ministries. Where do you find all these locations?" The little man was quiet for an interesting length of time.

They came to a small clearing, which gave way to many larger older trees. Maples dominated the area with some large yellow birch, beech and American elm. The trees formed a canopy for a grand, red, two-story building. At one time, it was a camp on a twenty-thousand-acre lot. A sign found in the attic of the structure years earlier read: "The Ponderosa" and was hung over the main entrance. Assuming it was the original name for the park, the new owners kept it for their retreat. The building looked in fine shape for its age. The retreat remained deep in the wilderness, well hidden from the government.

The pair looked across the distance of the pond and watched people eating breakfast on the deck or walking around. The perm in Loren's hair had relaxed to lie in its normal wavy short lengths. His round face mellowed as he concluded his reply to Holly's question. "Simple really. I own them."

The young woman would have been no more surprised if the earth had swallowed her. Her face went through many expressions before it rested upon blank surprise. "You own them? This and that mansion near Hollywood Falls? How can that be? You didn't inherit that kind of money did you?"

Loren's face showed he enjoyed the moment. Only a few people had the privilege to know what he decided to reveal to Holly. "No, I didn't get it from family. Dad left us with nothing and Mom earns everything she needs to live on. I've managed to appropriate what is needed to run my ministry."

Someone hollered to Loren from the deck. He told Loren to come in with large sweeping arm movements. "I've got some news for you," floated across the water to them. Many people watched the man. Loren turned to Holly. "Come on. It's back to work we go."

He was in no hurry and as they meandered back. Loren continued their conversation. "The work I've established has done more for the gospel of Christ than any one thing in recent history. The more I have to work with the more I can do."

"I realize that, Loren, but who pays for all this?"

"They do." He pointed to the people, indicating every Christian in general. "And businesses."

"What business would support a radical group such as Rigid Christians?"

"You'd be very surprised." He quickly scanned the area to determine they were still alone. "Even the NMA."

Holly's surprise stopped her dead in her tracks. Loren smiled at her. "Don't look at me that way. It's true. You got to know how to play them."

A quick breeze came up and blew some of Holly's hair into her face. If anything, she looked more puzzled when she replaced it behind her ear. "This isn't making any sense to me. I've no idea what you could be alluding to."

Loren gently grabbed Holly's arm and continued their trek. "I'll explain more later. Right now I'd better see what I'm needed for."

In less than a half a minute, the couple was at the deck. There to greet them was Calvin Katang. "Hi Loren. Holly." After the happy greeting, Calvin turned to Loren while losing his cheerful expression. "I need to talk to you. Is there a place where we can converse in private?"

Calm and collective as usual, Loren held his air of gaiety and slapped Calvin on the back. "Cheer up, friend. I'd be more than happy to talk to an old crony. I haven't seen you in quite some time. How've you been doing?"

Loren's attitude spurred Calvin to return to his previous expression. He smiled. "I'm doing great. Been real busy these last few months. A lot's been happening."

The little man turned to Holly. "I'll be only a little while. I'll catch up with you later. OK?"

Holly grinned in return. "That's fine. I'm anxious to continue our conversation."

Nodding yes to Holly, Loren and Calvin retreated into the house. In one of the upstairs attic rooms, Loren had set up an office. There was a small bay window in the end overlooking the pond. In front of it sat two plush chairs and a coffee table to relax at. Loren led Calvin to the area and offered him a seat. "I hope nothing's wrong, Calvin. I wasn't expecting you."

Calvin's voice was deep and soft spoken. The developing furrows between his eyes were almost as deep as the dimple on his chin. "Things are getting pretty complicated. I'm having second thoughts about all this. Many times it seems right, but . . ." He couldn't find the words to express himself.

Loren leaned on his knees with his elbows, using his hands as he spoke. "Listen Calvin, you've got to remember all the good we're doing. Look at the people we've reached for the Lord. They may've never heard the good news, if we didn't have the resources we have now. There's no other way to get the things we need to operate. The Network can't supply the means. They barely manage to keep themselves operating. All we're doing is getting back from the enemy what they've stole from us."

Calvin relaxed in his seat, slouching down slightly. "You're right in a way, but—but then I've heard it preached, and the Bible supports it, that the ends don't justify the means."

With a thin-lined mouth, Loren stood and walked to the window. Looking down he saw Pete Pope leading a class on discipleship. It was such a nice day Pete decided to hold it on the deck. Loren called Calvin over to the window. "See this. These people are learning what it means to be a servant of the Lord. Most of these people wouldn't have been here if they hadn't had the invitation in July. July wouldn't have happened if we didn't have the technology to keep them safe and secure to pursue an interest in Christianity. You go down there and tell those people they should be headed for hell because the means we used in setting up this system are wrong. What would they tell you?"

"I hope they could see that God can use any situation for His purpose—even ones out of His will."

"God's will is that none should parish, but all would come to repentance and be saved."

"I know what you're saying, Loren, but if Jesus is our prime example of how we should walk this Christian walk, then let me ask you this. Would Jesus have traded information with the Roman government and the Sanhedrin, pitting them one against the other, while He used the money to buy His way off from the cross?"

"It's not the same thing and you know it."

"Why isn't it?"

"I know Jesus wouldn't want to 'buy' His way out of the Father's plan for the salvation of the world, but He wouldn't be against using tax money that the people worked hard for."

"Would Jesus have used Judas' twenty pieces of silver?"

Loren looked slightly up at Calvin with a determined frown on his boxy face. The two stood still at the window starring one another down. Loren was resolute but Calvin still vacillated upon the moral dilemma he saw. The more he talked himself through it, the more convinced he was that Loren was wrong.

Debate was something Loren was very good at. Over and over again the little man was able to convince people in strategic places of the overall good he was doing for the Network. No one could argue with his results but few knew of the tactics used. Loren had been careful to include only those he could convince in the rationale of his thinking. He hadn't counted on Calvin's defection. Nor had Loren conceived of the effect constant variations in biblical interpretation could have on someone. He truly believed in his worldview with its lofty goals. Good goals, yes, but he missed the fact of Jesus' concern with the process as much as the outcome.

The pair glared at one another. Calvin wasn't sure if he'd reached Loren with logic that would cause him to think or if the man was just so angry he was choosing his words with reprisal. After another minute, Loren brushed the bangs back from his face and turned to look out the window again before speaking. "I see they've managed to brainwash you with that legalistic bent the 'church' is so famous for. It doesn't matter that more people are touched for Jesus at one time than ever before."

Sadness came to Calvin's eyes as he turned to face Loren's back and softly spoke. "Why do you try so hard? Why do you need to reach so many with your own efforts?"

Slowly Loren turned his head to meet Calvin's eyes. "The answer to that is so obvious I don't understand why you even ask. Because people need to know the salvation God has planned for them."

The younger man's face softened with the insight that came to him. "There's truth in that but is it just a pretense you hide behind?

266

Could it be that for everyone who comes to know Jesus through your ministry it validates your father's martyrdom that much more?"

Loren's mouth thinned as his face hardened under the convicting words of his subordinate. Calvin managed to give Loren something to reflect upon that he had been hiding from himself. He had a choice to make—whether to accept the criticism or rationalize it away. In the seconds that passed, the blonde man took a third option, which was to ignore the possibilities until another time when he could meditate on it. Loren relaxed into a neutral posture. "Thank you, Calvin, for your respect in bringing this to me before you made any rash decisions. I release you of our business arrangement. I'd appreciate it if you'd keep things to yourself, at least for a while, until I decide how I'm going to continue. I wouldn't want to force you to operate against your newfound moral convictions."

With a developing smile, the cleft of Calvin's chin intensified. "Thank you, Loren. Please think about these things. You've done much good, but what might it cost us if all Christians took your—our example and operated the same way? Who could we trust?"

Loren smiled for the first time since his accomplice's report. "You may have a point and I'll give it some thought. Consider yourself relieved from my services. The information you supplied me with was extremely helpful but I'll find another way."

Calvin's smile slipped. Loren seemed to have considered the options already and decided to simply continue without him. Before anymore could be said on the subject, Loren cordially ushered Calvin out of the office. Calvin left the compound with dubious feelings to the success of his mission.

It might have been wrong. She felt guilty about it but Holly was in the next room listening to everything that transpired between Calvin and Loren. While Loren sat in his office to reorganize his thoughts, priorities, and ministry, Holly gave consideration to what she had been doing for Loren. Suddenly she began rifling through her small hand purse. From a pocket within, she drew out the half a dollar bill she had taken from Vernon Cuff's office. She was supposed to use it to blackmail Alanson Shanach. After listening to Calvin talk to her teacher, she was having second thoughts, which re-enforced earlier convictions about Loren's tactics. The rationale she'd been using no longer seemed to hold water. Holly meditated on these things. A prayer later, Loren had lost another collaborator—but he knew of it too late.

When Bad is Good

Jamming his thumb upon the throttle, the snowcruiser operator raced across the white snow dunes skipping from one crest to another. Snow lightly fell as the eerie daylight fought to exist through the cloud cover rapidly moving in. Puffs of snow billowed out from under the jets of the hovercraft. The machine looked some like a snowmobile of the previous century but without the track. Skis still served to ride on the snow for control but a smooth jet system propelled and suspended the rest of the vehicle. The operator had an NMA helmet but a set of heavy, red, winter coveralls obscured the rest of the black suit. A small, dark-colored building popped into view as the snowcruiser topped a hill. Slowing down, the small vehicle squatted closer to the ground. The building was a small above-ground parking garage. As the vehicle neared, a door in the center opened allowing entrance. A simple sign hung on the wall above the door: "Byrd Penitentiary."

Once inside, the small vehicle settled to the floor next to several other machines like it. The NMA recruit dismounted the cruiser and walked to the back of the building. One person manned a facility door. She sat poised at a desk closely watching the new arrival. The small desk held an arsenal of electronic communications and defense mechanisms. Velma Black's training in every operation of the post allowed her to react in a split second and have a small army at her command. The visitor made his way to Velma. The SS agent pulled a glove off as he approached the desk. Velma, at thirty years old and physically fit, attracted many men. Her auburn hair was long enough to cover her ears and framed her oval face. The eyes were a steel blue and drew one's attention immediately. The professional woman held her smiles for after work. She seldom used her social countenance on company time.

The NMA agent stopped in front of the desk, which triggered Velma to query him. "Are you agent 5261 who called ahead a half an hour ago?"

With a simple nod yes, the helmeted figure handed over a disk. Velma installed the information as she directed the man before her. "You may take off your winter gear and leave it here. Also, if you'd please hand over your helmet, stunner, and scanner, I'll see to their security."

While the agent complied, Velma read the information from the disk. Taking his helmet off, Ray listened to Velma continue the short instructions. "Mr. Dandy, you'll be escorted the entire time of your inspection. A special recorder and disk will be supplied to you for your convenience. After the disk has been evaluated, you'll be allowed to take it with you."

For the first time, Velma had the opportunity to view her visitor. She took a moment to study him. Ray held an inviting, friendly smile. He had trimmed his beard into a simple goatee and styled his fine, sandy-colored hair short in the front but layered long in the back. Complying with Velma's requests he bared the interface equipment on the desk. "Very efficient procedure so far, but what if I've concealed something on me?"

She was attractive and had heard it many times but Velma couldn't to be swayed by anyone's charms or other distracting actions. "You're being scanned as we speak. I'm aware of your complaints and the small recording device you have in your right front shirt pocket. If you'd please hand that over also, I'd appreciate it."

Cocking an eyebrow in surprise, Ray's smile changed to one of amusement. "Oh, that. I forgot I even had it. It's my niece's. She wanted me to record my day's activities for a school project."

He gave it over to the security officer while she scrutinized it. "I'm afraid you'll have to use the one provided and then be careful what you report."

Ray relaxed, understanding he wasn't going to get anywhere with this one except further into the facility. He decided to save his energies for the latter and handed over the small recorder he had hoped to use. Velma finished entering information and taking care of equipment before returning her attention to Ray. "You're all set. If you'd please enter the elevator behind me, I'll see to your entry to level one."

Without a smile, the cerulean eyes drilled into a man's subconscious and demanded reverence. Ray complied with a sense of respect. As he made his way to the door, he saw it release with a touch to a sensor from Velma's desk. Entering the small area was a surprise to first-time visitors. The other three walls were of glass. Outside Ray could see another small building about a hundred yards away. Snow began to come down with greater fury, obscuring the view. The door clicked shut behind him. Snow dunes disappeared giving way to solid dark rock as Ray descended with dizzying speed downward. He didn't know the exact speed, but it was fast and the duration was long enough to put him hundreds of feet down into the earth. His stomach settled back to normal as the elevator slowed before it stopped.

When the door slid back out of the way, Ray could see a well-lit large room. A small group of carmine color clad men and women faced him. Standing in front of them stood the man in charge. He wore a cobalt outfit with colorful, ornate trim. Smiling, the man stepped forward and introduced himself. "Welcome. I'm Sherman Bagnick, warden of the Byrd Federal Penitentiary. I'm sure you'll find our facility more than up to government requirements."

The dark-skinned man smiled wide but thin, not revealing any teeth. He wasted no time and performed his duty so others could take over. "We don't usually have political prisoners so I hope you'll excuse our pace in presenting what may be required. It's been some time since we had an NMA inspection and we wish to be thorough."

Reaching for the warden's hand at the introduction, Ray noticed other guards flanking his far right and left. Stepping into the room he noted they had stun rifles, which they lowered as the warden made it obvious he had no concerns. Sherman's smile deepened as he discerned Ray's observation. "You'll soon see security is of the utmost importance here. No one's ever successfully escaped from here in our fifty-eight-year history."

Ray gathered his professional composure. No smiling for this man. Ray realized he needed to keep as much respect for his position as possible. "Thank you, Mr. Bagnick. I expected nothing else."

Sherman's smile relaxed. "Good. Sonya Hamilton will be your escort. It looks like you'll have more time than you wished. A storm is rolling in and it may be hours before you'll be able to sled back to Main Point."

At the mention of her name, a young woman stepped forward and stood beside Sherman. Ray hadn't noticed her until she moved. The words "Plain Jane" came to mind as he looked upon her. She was tall, almost even with Sherman, and only an inch shorter than Ray. Her short hair was so black it resisted any sheen under the high lights. Sonya's triangle-shaped face looked chiseled with its high cheekbones. It was then that Ray noticed her eyes. They were large, round, deep, dark pools, which seemed to reflect all the light her hair absorbed. She was a stocky woman, not fat or over weight, but very capable looking. Ray thought to himself, *She would have made a good pioneer woman.*

Sherman finished his expected appearance by turning things over to the woman. "Sonya can answer any questions you have but if you need it, I'll make myself available."

The warden excused himself. Ray watched as all but Sonya retreated with the man. Two followed him through a hall at the end of the large room, while the other two took posts at the other corners of the room. Ray shifted his face to Sonya. "Hi Sonya. My name is . . ."

She wouldn't allow him to finish. Her voice had a sweet, low quality to it, which betrayed the stoic words delivered. "I know. James Dandy, NMA Search Squad agent 5261; Special Services department. I assume it's because you're in special services that no record of your activities has been registered for the past four months."

Ray grinned slightly for the first time since arriving below. "I'm impressed. You've done your homework and your assumption is correct. My assignment's the closest to here so I was elected to perform this bureaucratic function. I'll try to make it as pleasant as possible for both of us."

She smiled. The small act was her winning feature and made Ray think she wasn't so plain after all. "Very good. I was in hopes this would be easy for both of us, Mr. Dandy. You lead me to believe my wishes may come true."

She turned and led Ray down the hall Sherman went through a minute before. The corridor was wide with many doors lining both sides. She led them to the third door on the left and entered. The desk dominated the room and was the only impersonal item present. Sonya spent much time here and made it as comfortable as possible. As she sat behind the desk, she indicated for Ray to sit in a large comfortable-looking, high-back leather chair opposite from her. The desk had piles of neatly stacked papers set along in an orderly manner.

Interlacing her fingers at the desk, Sonya addressed Ray. "Where would you like to begin, Mr. Dandy?"

In the privacy of her office, Ray allowed one of his endearing smiles. "Please call me Ray. It's my middle name, well, actually Raymond but that is too stoic. My friends call me Ray. Mr. Dandy is my father's name."

Sonya allowed one of her smiles to emerge. Ray thought the young woman should practice it often, because it endeared her so. As if reading his mind, Sonya commented on the matter. "My friends call me Sunny. It's a nickname they gave me because I've such a hard time keeping the straight-laced looks this place demands. Please call me Sunny, only not in front of Mr. Bagnick. He thinks the name's irreverent."

Ray reached his hand out for an informal handshake. "You have a deal, Sunny. I like the name. It fits you."

271

Hurdle one was passed. Ray made a friend who he might need later. The next few hours the couple went through the piles of reports on Sonya's desk. It became a lighthearted affair, which both enjoyed in spite of the momentous task. Ray knew the procedures for an NMA inspection and was careful to attend to all necessary details. During one of the studies he came across Mark Jacobson's name. "So this is the guy who's the reason I need to be here."

Sonya applied a puzzled look. "Yes it is. I don't really understand because we seldom deal with these kinds of people. As you know, everyone else we have here is of grave danger to society—murderers, terrorists, and such as that. This guy doesn't seem to fit the mold we've cast. Why a little RC undercover agent, who seems to be nobody, would warrant such attention is beyond me. Why send this person to the North Pole for security reasons? What harm is he going to do?"

While she expounded, Ray noticed the pin holding Sonya's badge to her shirt. It was the symbol of the fish. He'd been with the Christians long enough to know it was one of the signs they used for their faith. Careful not to gawk at it to draw attention, he looked back to her eyes. "Well, I can't reveal that to you but I can see it's illogical to you. Let me guess, your zodiac sign is Pisces."

The inviting smile with captivating indigo eyes appeared. "No, I'm not. I don't believe in that mumbo jumbo anyway."

Ray found himself strangely drawn to this 'Plain Jane.' He was so lost in her eyes he almost missed her answer. But it did prompt an inquiry. "What *do* you believe?"

Her eyes gave away the fact the question surprised her. Sonya contemplated the query then moved her hand to touch her pin. Just as quickly, she moved her hand back to the desk. She figured out what Ray was alluding to. A more plastic smile replaced the earlier ones. "Maybe we should get back to the work at hand. Whatever I might believe matters little to your audit."

Ray hadn't counted on the woman understanding the question, but since she had he took it a step further. This might be his only chance for a successful finish to his mission. Friendly concern exuded from him. "Don't let this outfit concern you. I just came from a Network facility. My purpose is to find out what I can about Mark and how we might help him." Sincerity dripped from his words.

Sonya felt a need to determine if it was an act. The situation demanded caution and thought on her part. A minute went by in silence.

Finally, she had an idea. Sonya reverted to her professional mode. "Are you a Rigid Christian?"

The way she said it led Ray to believe he may have mistaken Sonya's religious affiliation. It was his turn to stall as he thought about his response. One thing he learned from his stay with the Bethany facility was they believed honesty is always the best policy. He decided to give it a try. "No I'm not, but I am looking into it. The NMA doesn't even know of my plans. My original purpose was to infiltrate the Network, but I am having second thoughts about my allegiances. I was going to try and make a name for myself by single-handedly undermining the Network. I believe I could have succeeded, except for Mark's fiancée. She managed to show me the love that motivates Christians. It's for her that I'm here. I'm ashamed to admit the lengths I made her go. I wished now that I hadn't asked it of her."

Sonya discerned Ray honesty. Running a hand over her short, black hair she leaned back in her chair. Sonya made a decision. "No sense in going over all this paper work then. What can I do to help?"

Ray gave a relieved smile. "I need to know as much as possible about this facility and how it operates. I'm taking the information back with me." He locked eyes with his new friend. His next statement developed into an unspoken question. "If we decide to do something about breaking Mark out, I could use some inside help."

Large, dark eyes blinked twice before a grin developed with Sonya's reply. "OK. You're entitled to a tour of the facility. Why don't we do that? Before we go—how'd you manage to get this assignment?"

A smirk spread across his face. "I didn't. The real NMA agent is scheduled to be here in ten days. When he shows up, my days as an SS agent are through."

Sonya gave a grim look. "That doesn't leave us much time. We'd better get moving." Ray reached over the desk for a handshake. "Thanks, Sunny."

An unexplainable bond developed between the two as Sonya led Ray around the compound. It puzzled and bewildered him. Only women of obvious beauty attracted him until now. Not that Sonya was ugly but her beauty wasn't instantly apparent. He saw it as they got to know one another. Ryker's brother, for the first time, saw a person inside the skin and he liked what he discovered. Ray had opportunity to meet several other people and became amused at the difference personalities Sonya portrayed in their presence. With a few she smiled, but with most, she was very professional.

The last place Sonya showed was the holding area. The couple made it to the farthest side of the underground building and found themselves facing a teleport unit. With a puzzled expression, Ray queried her on it. "I thought there were no teleports here for security reasons. Why couldn't I have zapped myself here rather than take that long snowcruiser ride?"

He enjoyed her smile before Sunny answered him. "This is a special unit. It only transports a very short distance. Five hundred feet below us are the holding cells for prisoners. There's no other entrance in or out of it. These will teleport us there and back here again but nowhere else."

Ray shook his head up and down with a frown on his lips. "Clever."

Stepping into the unit activated the door to slide in place. Sonya keyed a lengthy series of numbers and letters. Ray commented, "A security code I presume."

"Yes. It changes every week. If you enter the wrong code an alarm sounds, you're trapped, and in about twenty seconds there're ten guards here to secure the area."

"Wouldn't want to make a mistake would you?"

Sonya smiled with a twinkle in her eye. "The first time you get a warning; the second time, a week off without pay. There is no fourth time." The teleport activated.

Ray held the contemplative frown when the glass cleared for his first view of the holding area. Before him was a wide, long, well-lit hall. Down the middle every fifty feet was an island of counters shaped in squares. The pattern went on until it was out of sight. Two guards dressed in emerald jumpsuits occupied each set of counters. Ray saw a few of these people on the level above but here there seemed to be a sea of them. They wore matching helmets with clear face shield. Each had a weapon and a scanner on his belt. The weapon didn't represent a regular stunner. It appeared much more menacing.

While the glass partition retracted, one of the guards stepped forward. Sonya pulled a card from her belt and handed it to him. Taking it, he placed it in the scanner taken from his waist. He studied the output. "Ms. Hamilton, you've fifteen minutes to show SS agent Dandy whatever he needs. Please be back here by then."

It didn't take long for Ray to learn while he was here Sunny would not smile her captivating expression. Staying a step ahead, Sonya led Ray to the third counter down the hall. In passing he could see cells on both sides about twenty feet apart. Protected portals eliminated the need for a door. Old-fashioned bars set in front of a shimmering force field gave double protection. Around the edges of the doorway a band of green light encircled it: the source of the force field. One cell held one occupant. The people all looked so different Ray couldn't help wondering why each was there. The island counter stations had scores of controls at the guard's disposal. The seats set back to back so each had a side of the hall he was responsible for. Sonya stopped between the counter and one of the cell doors on their right. She stood facing the cell entrance stiffly without saying a word.

Turning his face from Sonya, Ray looked to see why they had stopped. As with all the prisoners, Mark's head was shaven. Even the women were not exempt from the policy. Mark Jacobson sat up from his bunk to see who was at his cell. Their eyes locked as Mark remembered Ray from Loren's gathering in July. It was a moment before Ray considered what he came to do. His SS agent instincts returned. "Are you Mark Jacobson, defector and saboteur of American freedoms?"

Mark didn't know what to say or do with Ray. He took a neutral position. "Maybe." Ray glanced to Sonya for direction. She accommodated by turning her attention to Mark. "Place your hand on the scan plate please."

Mark knew what she wanted. Standing from his bunk, he walked to the entrance and placed his palm on a glass plate next to the force field. A visual display set close to Mark's door on the outside wall came alive. Ray and Sonya watched as a picture of Mark and a dossier displayed. Mark, having no record, left little for anyone to read. The bottom line stated his crime, which was the only one for him. The young man went back to his bunk. The only other items in the cell were a toilet (no privacy here), sink, and a table with chair for eating at. The MM unit was on the wall behind but only the guards could activate it when it was time.

Ray's escort moved and he migrated to catch up with her. Sonya stepped to the island behind them and began an explanation while she pointed out items. "As you can see, we've an alarm for just about everything that could trigger an escape situation. At least one man is in this watch station at all times but he is never alone for longer than five minutes. Do you need to see anything else, Mr. Cuff?"

275

To Ray it wasn't the same woman he grew to know on the first level. She was very careful about her job and revealing her political preferences. "No thank you. Everything seems to be more than adequate."

With a slight nod, Sonya led the way back to the teleport. The guard who greeted them waited. Sonya handed him her card once more and again he slid it into his scanner, punched a few buttons, and returned it. Stepping into the teleport activated the door and it closed. While Sonya keyed in the information Ray noticed a cover panel to the unit on the back wall. In seconds, they were back on the first level. Sonya reverted back to the person Ray had grown to like. He was glad to see her smile as they made their way back to her office.

Sonya spoke first. "That's an experience all should have, don't you think?"

They were at her door as Ray replied, "Only once."

The pair sat in their respective places. Folding her hands upon the desk, Sonya turned her large dark eyes to Ray. "So, now what do we do?"

Ray reached across the desk and held her hands in his. "I don't know, Sunny. All I can say is that if your assistance is needed it'll be before ten days from now."

A short time later, Sonya and Ray returned to the main lobby only to have Sherman informed them that the storm was going to delay Ray's trip back to Main Point for several hours. "Sorry, Mr. Dandy, but that's the way it is up here. I hope it's no big inconvenience."

Before her boss could say anything more, Sonya made a suggestion. "Maybe Mr. Dandy would like to have me buy him dinner. It's past my quitting time and I was going to find something to eat before I went home."

Sherman raised an eyebrow to his visitor in a questioning manner. Ray shrugged his shoulders with a slight smile on his face. "Sounds fine with me. I accept the invitation."

An elevator took the pair to a level below them. It was a small, underground town. Shops and small business wove in amongst the apartments that housed the people who worked at the government complex. Ray and Sonya had a leisurely dinner in one of the small restaurants. In a short time, they found they were very compatible. Ray gave his new partner some scenarios she might expect in the event the Network attempted to rescue Mark. Ray felt it was too soon when Velma signaled that weather conditions cleared so he could leave. Surprising himself, he leaned over and kissed Sonya before he left. He rushed off before he made a bigger fool of himself.

TOUCHWOOD

"Back in 2020 when the NMA, known as something else at the time, began my father called it the touchwood. I asked him what that was and he told me it referred to cannons back in the old wars. The touchwood was used to light the powder and set the weapon a blaze."

Sly Hawkins: Email to Al Shanach dated 8/3/2091

What To Do?

Limitations were a frustration for Ryker. It seemed no matter what he and Vernon came up with there was an obstacle in the way. Ryker pounded his fist on Vernon's desk a second time within the last five minutes. "This information Kayla Keating supplied is as frustrating as eating imaginary ice cream in the middle of July. Sounds good, ought to be good, but something's missing."

The scowl on Ryker's face caused Vernon to laugh. It was the first time since he had found out about his grandson. Sitting in his high-back chair the older man stifled a laugh to Ryker's statement with a couple of snickers. Ryker tuned the expression on his uncle. Vernon relinquished most of his jocularity momentarily. "I'm sorry. I know it's not funny but you have a way of making a point that really comes in by the back door."

The pair finished the day by discussing the information Ryker received from the Bethany compound about Mark. "Uncle Vern, it's just that . . . well, it seems so impossible. I know we need to get some of our best people on this problem and maybe that'll help, but it looks like a major problem. Who got all this information anyway?" It was a rhetorical question for which Ryker didn't expect an answer. He was deep in thought and initially missed the answer.

"Your brother Ray."

It took a few seconds for the comment to sink in. "Yea . . . what's that? Ray! Ray got this information? Who authorized him to work in that capacity?"

Vernon leaned back in his chair and laced his fingers upon his lap. "No one. Kayla asked him and he did it. The young lady told me because she realized it was wrong. She's handed in her resignation. It's there on my desk. I thought I'd let you handle it."

Taking his glasses off Ryker leaned back in his chair and wiped his face with his hand. "Boy! When it rains, it pours." He replaced the spectacles. "What else could possibly happen today?"

It was a question he wished he had never asked. The words had no sooner left his mouth when they heard a commotion in Joyce's office. Calvin's muffled yell sounded through the closed door. "It can't wait!"

The door banged against the wall as Calvin pounded through it. He had a wild look in his eyes and sweat poured from his forehead. "I'm sorry. I'm so sorry. I didn't expect this to happen."

Vernon stood at his desk. "Calm down, man. Come on in and tell us what has you so riled up."

Calvin held a piece of paper wadded up in his fist. His face contorted with the emotional pain he faced. Tears began to trickle from his eyes as he staggered in and plunked down in a chair beside Ryker.

Ryker turned in his chair to face his assistant. "Calvin, what has you so upset?"

The younger man had trouble controlling himself. After a moment, he managed four words. "I looked. She's gone." Calvin's body racked with sobs.

Ryker looked to Vernon who settled into his chair once again. Vernon lightly shrugged his shoulders with a puzzled looked but then his face brightened with a revelation. "April? Is April gone?"

Calvin's body shook with sobs as he wobbled his head no and then yes. Finally, he resumed some control and explained. "Yes she's gone. I helped her escape."

With that statement, both men tried to query him at the same time with the same question. Ryker pointed to Vernon indicating for him to ask. "Why would you let April escape?"

A big, sobbing sigh escaped Calvin as he sat straighter in his seat. Wiping his eyes with the back of his hand, he began telling how he helped Loren; how he used important information gathered from his position and gave it to Loren to use. The NMA and other agencies received information for money or other assets that Loren used in his ministry. He finished up by telling how he'd gone to Loren and told him he no longer felt it was right.

Calvin explained his decision to quit what he was doing for Loren. "I was the one who managed to get April in here. I knew she was a spy so I thought I could tell her when she needed to go and control the situation. I talked it over with her and we decided the best thing for both of us was to have her escape. I fixed it so her room was unlocked and the teleport would be unmanned. I programmed it so she couldn't get any information back from the unit." He started sobbing again losing all control. "But I didn't . . . know she . . ." Calvin couldn't continue.

Ryker reached over and gently held Calvin's shoulder and shook it carefully. "Calvin, calm down. I wish you would have come to me before but maybe the best thing for us is that the woman is gone, if she's a spy."

With his head down and a hand over his eyes, Calvin handed Ryker the paper he held in the other hand. With a puzzled expression, Ryker straightened out the wad and began to read. Horror washed over his face as he threw the slip on Vernon's desk and dashed out of the office. Vernon sat there and watched the whole thing in complete amazement. "What the . . ." He snagged the note and read it.

To Ryker Cuff:

It's the only way now. I have your oldest daughter. Don't do anything rash, and I'll get a hold of you. Maybe we can work out some kind of deal. April.

Bethany Plans

Jesse stood trying to bring order back to the gathering. "Calm down for just a minute will you?" Within seconds, the conference room stilled to a point Jesse could continue. "OK. I think we've a plan here that could work. Now let's carefully and orderly discuss who should be the ones to carry it out. No more hollering and screaming, please." He looked directly at Felicia Rederman and John Ball.

Others present included Kayla Keating, Ray Cuff, Mike Grotto from the Upper Room, Everett Myron from the Jordan facility, Red

VanTimons and Bethany's Chief of Security, Lois Green. Mike and Everett had an opportunity to meet again. This time it was as Christian brothers. The pair had a time of tearful repentance and healing before the meeting and became close friends.

The underground room was one of the nicer ones Bethany had. The long, wood table they sat at was mahogany. The chairs were high-back swivels and contoured to fit. There were some ancient paintings on the wall. One was the one Henry Cuff had saved.

Jesse continued after his reprimand to Felicia and John. As he talked, he looked from person to person settling on no one in particular. "Now, we agree that four will be enough to carry off this rescue if it happens at all. Right?" Heads nodded and simple affirmations were spoken before Jesse continued. "I suggest each who has something to say be given the opportunity. Lois, why don't you facilitate that for us? You're the senior security officer responsible for the outcome."

Jesse sat down looking to Lois. She was the senior officer because she had been on the job longer, but she was a few years younger than Mike. Lois was more attractive than average. A tall woman, she carried well her fit body with poise. The oval face hollowed slightly at the cheeks giving her broad mouth an appealing characteristic. She had a soft, sonorous voice and her lips seemed to move in a way that molded each word as she produced it. Her eyes were dark, almond-shaped orbs, with long, thick lashes. Her ocher hair held highlights of blonde and covered her ears to her neck. Lois had intrigued more than one man, but her career was her only suitor at the time.

Lois sat at one end of the lengthy table and all heads turned her way. Unlike many people, she relaxed with the attention and smiled invitingly. With her easygoing delivery her mouth sculptured words with "ah" and "oh" in them. "Thanks, Jesse. I would like to start with Mike and get his perspective on our pool of personnel."

She turned to Mike as she spoke. He smiled and explained his views. "I'm not sure who should go but I think we can narrow it down a bit." Mike glanced at each as he spoke of them. "Kayla's too close to this. She's very capable but we'll need clear thinking and no distractions beyond our goal. Sorry Kayla, but I believe you know what I mean."

The young blonde began to protest but thought better of it. Given half a minute to think about it she grimly nodded her head in agreement without saying a word. Tears developed in her eyes as she lowered her head and sat back in her chair.

Mike turned to face another way. "Everett's done his part all ready and we may need him back here if things require some adjustments." The Upper Room security chief smiled deeply with newfound respect for the man he almost killed.

Everett dipped his eyes at Mike. "Yes and if we had to run for it, I'd hate to show the rest of you up," he quipped with a smile. The lighthearted statement helped to levitate some of the tension in the room.

Mike wasn't through yet. He looked to the man across from him. "John, we'll need someone of authority to facilitate things from this end. Someone may need to make a decision in the event things don't progress as we plan."

It didn't need vocalizing; the short man was in no shape to do much physical activity. John was chief of the Bethany complex so Mike's suggestion played well into his hand. His jowls jiggled, nodding his affirmative. "My thoughts exactly." Felicia struggled to hold her musing. She succeeded but her contortions were almost comical.

Things quieted for a moment until Mike finished. He turned back to Lois. "As far as the rest of us go, I'm not sure except to say only one of us should leave. For one reason, we need someone on this side to keep things secure and two, if this team doesn't succeed, one of us'll need to take care of two facilities until a replacement is found."

Mike shrugged his shoulders and glanced around the room. Lois reacted quickly to Mike's comments. "I can help with that. You stay here, Mike, and I'll accompany the team. We're equally capable in both places and I don't have a family to worry about."

Mike frowned at her statement and began to reply but Lois beat him to it. "No arguments. It makes sense and you know it. If anyone else here disagrees with that I'll listen, but otherwise there is no more discussion."

Ray folded his arms and smiled. "Looks like you're out voted, Mr. Grotto."

Everyone signified the statement true and Mike threw his hands up in defeat with a smile on his face. "OK, OK. Those are my thoughts, Lois."

All eyes were on Lois. It had no effect on her composure as she sat back and allowed silence to dominate while she deliberated. After a minute, she began by thinking aloud, looking miles from the room. "That leaves us with Jesse, Felicia, Ray, and Craig to choose from. I'm a given so we must eliminate one of the other four." Lois examined the room once more. "First thing we'd better take care of is if we're going to allow Ray to participate in this. If he is or not will determine if we need to discuss this anymore." She scanned the room inviting any comments.

Ray decided to speak on his own behalf. He had the same crooked smile as his older brother. "I realize that I'm the black sheep here but there're a couple of things to consider. I've been there. I know well the layout of the place. As far as being recognized, two of us are going in by the back door, so to speak, and I'm not apt to run into anyone of concern. Don't forget; Sonya's there to help and she'd be more inclined to assist if she sees me. No one's mentioned it out loud but I know you're worried about my loyalties. After what I've done, I'm certain I'll never be able to work for the NMA again. They'll be looking for me and I'm not going to fool you people. I'm not convinced of your religious beliefs, but I've learned to respect them. It's wrong for the government to stop you from living the way you do. I'll understand if you don't wish me to help but believe me, you're the only friends I have now."

Red spoke up for the first time. His deep voice was soft, matching the look in his dark eyes. "He's right. After the NMA finds out what he did, Ray will be a hunted man. They've already considered he defected. What he did only gives them the proof to any suspicions. It won't matter to them. Ray's simply given someone the opportunity to move up."

Lois asked for other comments. When she received none, a vote indicated that Ray should be considered. Lois was back to square one. She heaved a small sigh and proposed her next question. "I know this isn't the most flattering way to put it, but which one of you four is the least useful?"

John began with an observation. "It seems we've successfully eliminated anyone who is good at electronics and teleportation. Everett's not going but neither is Mike who's good at that stuff. As far as I know, Felicia is the only other one who's had any training in that area."

Felicia flashed John a surprised expression at the compliment to her abilities. Murmuring and muttering elevated as they began talking amongst themselves over the dilemma. Felicia nodded her red head for the idea of her role in that capacity. She spoke up about it to Lois. "I might be able to handle it with a lot of tutoring from Everett first, but it's a subject I finally dropped to pursued other areas of interest."

Lois listened as the noise level began to rise. She readied to jump in and stop it when Kayla spoke up over the noise. "Just a minute."

Silence evolved as all waited for Kayla to enlighten them. "You wouldn't ever know if I didn't speak up. I need to because I want this to work more than anyone here. Red's a whiz at that kind of thing. He's told me he was preparing to enter either that field or medicine. He was hacking a secret from the government when the NMA busted him. He only got caught because a friend involved turned him in. Red could probably do it without Everett's help."

People turned to the newest member of the Bethany facility with surprise. Embarrassment washed over Red's face. "It's true. I'm probably the first choice after Everett to do the job. I'd be glad to help."

Lois saw how things were shaping up and tried to hurry it along. "I believe after Ray's speech and this revelation about Craig that we're down to choosing between Jesse and Felicia."

The latter pair looked at one another. Felicia finished the process. "I gladly bow out. Jesse's stronger if the situation warrants it and he has a closer connection to this. Kayla's one of his best friends. I know he'd like to help." Jesse didn't say a thing but gave Felicia a smile of gratitude.

Lois continued before others could throw a wrench into the way things came out. "Good. We have as the team: Craig, Jesse, Ray, and myself. All we need to do is plug each of us into the best place within the plan we developed and talk over minor details. I see no reason why we four, Everett, and Mike can't handle the rest of this."

John, Felicia, and Kayla left the room to go about their daily business. John hurried to his office while the two women talked as they walked. Felicia was taller than Kayla and looked slightly down at her. "I hear you turned in your resignation."

"Yes. What I had Ray do was a real threat to the Network. It was later I realized just how dangerous it could've been if Ray had decided to turn things around on me."

"You probably made a mistake but it worked out well. I don't think anyone is going to hold it against you. Have you heard anything yet?"

"No, Mike told me that Ryker has his own problems."

Kayla filled Felicia in on Ryker's daughter, Erica, and continued. "Mike's kind of upset. Ryker's decided to work out his problem alone. He's not listening to anyone. He says he has an idea but he's not going to tell a soul. No one knows what Ryker has up his sleeve."

Maneuvers

Silent scream. The dark cell. Snakes everywhere. Buck laughed as he released another serpent. Monica's dilemma demanded Ryker to do something but he couldn't. He was a spectator watching as the dream unfolded once more. This time, he didn't awaken as usual. Possibly his subconscious didn't want to leave. He watched as his wife fainted and sagged against the wall. She was still. The snakes ignored her and simply slithered around her. Ryker relaxed knowing at the very least his wife no longer felt her terror. As he relaxed, Monica changed and in her place laid Erica, unconscious. His attention turned to outside the cell. Buck slammed the box, which housed the snakes previously against the floor. The SS agent orally vented his frustration at Monica for depriving him of his fun. Buck yelled for answers asking who was in the cell. He never saw it coming but Ryker noticed it as a shadow first. A seventeen-foot python dropped from the ceiling and coiled itself around Buck before he could move. All Ryker could see of the man was his face that terror washed upon. For a split second, Ryker felt concern for his old childhood friend—then he awoke.

Slowly Ryker sat up from the couch and wiped his eyes of sleep. He couldn't bring himself to slumber in the bed that night. Fishing for his glasses on the coffee table he placed them on his head.

What was that suppose to mean? Lord, does it mean I could be successful in my attempt to get Erica back? I pray it's so, Lord. I leave the outcome in Your hands.

Monica and Julia came to mind but then he remembered Aunt Rose was caring for them. Monica was nearly out of her mind and was given sedatives to help. Today was going to be a stressful day. Ryker resolved to treat the day like any other day and prepared himself physically and spiritually for it.

It was late in the morning but he never met a soul on his trek to the office. He studied information on his terminal and found what he was looking for from Mike Grotto. After retrieving a few items from his desk drawer he left to begin his venture. The rickety elevator ride back down reminded him of the ups and downs in his life. The only lower time was when he lost Monica to the NMA many years earlier. He wiped a tear from an eye as the elevator door opened. No one was around to witness his departure, which only brought relief. A few more minutes of walking brought Ryker to one of the teleport stations within the compound.

Sadie Hampton perused logs at her post. Ryker chose this teleport and the technician working at it. He wanted his best for this operation. She greeted Ryker with a pleasant grin. "My my, don't we look spiffy."

Ryker wore an NMA uniform. It was cobalt blue with crimson trim. "Thanks. Not for the observation but for helping me with this."

Sadie liked her job. She was a natural technician. Her only regret was that she found out late in life that she excelled in the teleportation field. Sadie was several years older than the new chief. Ryker brought her to the Upper Room after looking into the recommendation of Pat Filmore. Pat told him Sadie was Ryan McDougal's discovery. She was his student and the little man's suggestion that she be placed at the Upper Room. Ryan wanted nothing to do with moving his career, but he was willing to sacrifice Sadie for the job. As Ryan told it, "She's the closest you'll get to having me right there." Sadie was as average as average can get in appearance. She had shoulder-length, straight, brown hair, sad-looking blue eyes, and a long face. There was nothing average about her ability. She was Ryker's first choice for this task.

Ryker gave her one of his amiable smiles. "Thanks for staying on your shift a little longer than normal. Do you think this has a chance of working?"

The puppy dog face was very endearing when the woman smiled. "You know how I feel about it but I'll give it a try if you insist. It's pretty tricky to teleport from one unit to another like that, but doing it with this one is a real challenge. Like I said, I give it only a fifty-fifty chance."

Ryker shifted to a grim smile. "It's better than no chance." He reached into his pocket and pulled out the disk that Mike prepared for him earlier. "Feed this information and let us get going."

Ryker stepped up onto the transport pad as Sadie dropped the disk into the reader and keyed the controls. She looked to Ryker. "You have that tracker, right?"

Ryker pulled it out of his pocket and showed her before replacing it. He spoke to himself but Sadie heard it. "This is the touchwood." The woman frowned at him, which made him realize he'd been heard. "Look it up. You'll understand."

Sadie said nothing and went back to her controls. After a moment, she looked back to Ryker. "Looks like you're being accepted. That's the first hurdle. Good luck. May the Lord be with you."

A couple touches to sensors and Ryker's adventure began.

White House

Few people had a chance to visit the White House. The grand structure had not changed in a hundred years—very converse to the rest of American heritage. Loren found himself strangely drawn by the physical link to American history. The edifice was off limits to the public, making Loren's opportunity a chance of a lifetime. He managed through his connections to get an audience with Sly Hawkins. Banking on his "understanding" with high-up officials of government, Loren was going for a large gambit to increase his ministry. The little man had convinced the head of the NMA that he had information worth Sly's attention. Loren agreed to meet Sly at his office if no one knew about it. Sly's interest peaked enough to grant Loren amnesty, only because he didn't know Loren's status. The worst would be if it turned out to be ruse.

Loren left the teleport from the main entrance and followed the guard studying the antiquity he passed. Many key government officials had offices in the building. Sly had the office of highest prestige, the old Oval Office. Disappointment came when Loren discovered he wasn't headed in that direction. Sly took advantage of the nice warm autumn day and set himself up outside. This day, Sly was giving a press conference and he was overseeing the setup. He thought a backdrop of the White House would give his speech a nostalgic punch.

Walking across the lawn, Loren arrived under the watchful eye of Sly. The small group surrounding him left as he talked to each. By the time Loren reached him, Sly was alone. Loren was in speaking distance when Sly smiled. "Thank you, Jackson. You may leave Mr. Richards and me alone." Jackson saluted, spun around, and walked back to where he came from leaving Loren and Sly alone.

There were trees on the White House lawn that weren't there a hundred years earlier. Oaks and maples obscured a view of the grand building from any walkway. The purpose was to keep the historic place from public view. Sly had several comfortable chairs set up under an oak tree at the edge of the small, planted woods. They sat with their backs to the building. The sun was warm and commodious, with a breeze lofting perfume fragrances from a nearby flower bed full of autumn blossoms.

Sly was relaxed as he turned to Loren and explained, "I thought this place might make things a little more private for our conversation." The deep, slow tones of his voice presented an amiable character. Loren studied the NMA leader's eyes for an underlining deception. The dead brown eyes worked well to hide any visible characteristics. Loren concluded that he needed to talk his way through this one.

The blonde Network agent smiled at Sly. "I'm not concerned about that. I believe our respect for one another is mutual. You'll be content to keep this to yourself so secrecy might be a smart move."

"I must admit, I find your audacity to contact me intriguing to say the least."

"Well Mr. Hawkins, I'm not easy and I'm not cheap, but you'll not be disappointed—I'm sure. Some of what I've to offer will cost you nothing. The other may pinch your pocketbook."

An odd twitch of his lips was the only facial change in Sly's features, leading Loren to believe he might have garnered some keen interest. Sly overshadowed the reaction well with lifeless eyes, leaving Loren with only a vague impression of that truth. The NMA head was a master at any type of negotiation. Loren knew he was up against the best and mentally prepared himself.

The pair sat in the shade facing one another. In the background, the White House was bathed in the morning sunlight demanding recognition for what it once stood for. Sly calmly handed Loren a cup of coffee from a small, nearby stand. "Sugar and creamer are right there. Please help yourself to whatever you prefer."

Loren smiled gracefully but never reached for the offered refreshment. "Thank you but I don't feel like coffee at this moment. I had my fill a short time ago."

Sly replaced the cup with no hint of the fascination he felt. He was rather enjoying the challenge this Rigid Christian dispensed. "Very well. It's wise not to over indulge in that which could cause one to be in discomfort." Hawkins' lips curled into a baneful smile as he directed his inanimate chocolate eyes to Loren.

The Network personality caught the double meaning. Timidity was not one of Loren's faults. Quickly he reacted to gain a more even playing field. A sly smile developed with his retort. "Experience is a grand teacher—don't you think?"

Sly's stone exterior never changed but he had enough of the verbal banter. He wished only to find out what this man had for him and get on with his other concerns. "Well said, Mr. Richards, but I'm a busy man. Please state your business."

Loren felt he gained a slight foothold and grabbed the opportunity to keep Sly off balance. "OK. One of your top managers of the NMA is in a precarious situation. There may be proof that he has roots deeply planted in the main family of the Network. Blood runs thicker than water."

Sly crossed his legs. Very apathetically he queried. "It is information I may be interested in if you have an engaging name and proof to back it up."

The ball returned so quickly to Loren's court it took a moment for him to realize the major move upon him. Sly enjoyed the stall he had caused. Loren recovered quickly. "The name is Alanson Shanach."

For the first time, the head of the NMA showed himself. Surprise washed over his face and as quickly was replaced with a confident smile. "You have my interest but the question is do you have the proof?"

With confidence, the little man pulled a pocket computer from his jacket. Before he handed it over, Loren keyed some information into the unit. "It's all there. Take a few minutes to study it. Of course you realize the information will last for only a few minutes before it's permanently erased. But don't worry. I've a hard copy in safe keeping if you find it of interest." With a satisfied expression, Loren sat back in his seat anticipating several minutes before Sly digested all he had. The Network agent knew that the genealogy charts and the information about Buck's dollar bill, along with the other incriminating evidences, would be more than enough to capture Sly's attention.

Sly surprised Loren when he read only a few seconds and turned his lifeless eyes up to Loren with a response. "Is this some kind of joke?"

Sly turned the computer to Loren to read. The blonde man's face turned horrified as he read the lines: "Sorry, Loren, but what you are doing is wrong. Please understand that I do this for your own good. Holly."

Many seconds passed before either man realized the position he was in. Without his expression changing in the least, Sly picked up a small communication device from the stand next to him. "This is Sly Hawkins. Security on the double."

Loren stood and smiled at the high official. "Sorry to waste your time but I have to leave now."

He rudely pushed Sly aside and ran for the small woods. As he began weaving in and out of the trees, he heard Sly hollering to someone. "Hurry up, you idiot. He's getting away through the tree cover."

Only seconds had passed before Loren ran up to an old fence. He began running along it in hopes of finding a way through. Loren heard Sly screaming more directions to his security personnel when he found a spot in the fence he could crawl through. Moments later, he was on the street and in a teleport. A few teleports later, Loren was safe from the clutches of Sly Hawkins but his conscience wasn't as relenting.

North Pole

Weaving its way around the larger snow dunes the sleek cargo snow sled bounced over a ridge facing Byrd Penitentiary. A large, orange sun hung low in the sky over the building like an ominous eye watching protectively. The heavyset vehicle approached the main door, which slowly yawned open. The whole picture appeared as an insidious invitation. Once inside and parked, a door to the snow vehicle lifted allowing occupants to step out.

Garbed in a ruby-colored jumpsuit, Lois led the small party to report. Jesse and Red followed her, dressed in similar fashion but in the color of charcoal. Velma Black was on duty. She had curled her auburn hair relaxing some of her stoic appearance but not her mannerisms. She impassively addressed Lois. "Main Point said you're from Teletron Incorporated. Please state your business."

Lois smiled and sculpted her amiable words. "Yes. We have a special delivery for Sonya Hamilton. If you would inform her we've arrived she'll understand. The security code to use is RD."

Velma understood. It wasn't unusual protocol for the facility. The teal-eyed woman dutifully fulfilled the task. In moments, Sonya's image was on the terminal. She seemed preoccupied with other business. "Hi, Velma. What can I do for you?"

Velma was as personable as the computer she used. "There's a cargo sled here and the person in charge says you're expecting them. I'm to inform you the security code is RD."

For a few seconds, Sonya ignored the intruding comment but then lifted her large expressive eyes to Velma. "Did you say my cargo from RD was here?"

Velma hesitated with a slight frown. "RD was the statement."

Suddenly, Sonya comprehended but was calm with a neutral expression. "Very good, Velma. Please show the driver to the loading dock and have the others report here please."

Velma tilted her head in respect. "Yes, right away." The screen went blank. Turning her attention to her visitors Velma took command, "Which of you is the driver?"

Jesse stepped forward. "I am."

Velma walked over to the cargo sled and studied the contents. There was one large, black, cloth bag and several small boxes easy to carry. All were labeled with "caution: handle with care" and had a special logo: Tested, Top Secret.

Satisfied, the penitentiary security officer turned to the threesome but focused on Jesse. "After you sign in, you may drive around back to the loading dock. You'll see a separate building with one door." She focused on the other two. "All of you step over to the counter. I'll process the driver first so he can proceed, then you two so you may report to Sonya Hamilton." They all complied as Jesse took a second to see his cargo was doing fine.

Things happened with a quick but concise manner. Lois and Red found themselves greeting Sonya at the bottom of the elevator ride. Sonya carefully used her professional demeanor under the watchful eyes of the guards. "Please follow me and I'll show you to my office where we can discuss this new project."

The two Network agents marched behind Sonya as she led them through the wide room and past the doors opposite the elevator. They were flanked by the compound's security until they reached Sonya's office. When the trio was safely alone, Lois informed the younger woman of their plans.

Above ground, Jesse steered his vehicle into the newly opened door of the receiving area. He was too late to see Lois and Red enter the elevator and descend, but he saw the glass-walled elevator unit. Upon entering the building, lights came alive and the door automatically descended. No one was in the large dock area as Jesse looked around with concern on his face. "I hope we don't need to use this sled again. There doesn't seem to be a way to activate that door from here anywhere."

The black bag in the back of the snow vehicle began moving. Ray poked his head out. "We shouldn't need to. Could you help me out of this thing? I can't loosen the tie strings any further."

Jesse teased Ray about his predicament as he assisted him. When Ray was free from his confines, Jesse thought about where they were. "What should we do now?"

Ray held a red helmet with a black face shield under his red-clad arm. An emblem on the red jumpsuit read: Teletron Security. With a smile he calmly replied, "We'll unload this cargo and wait for someone to come and get us." Jesse was rather sober at the thought.

The office of Sonya Hamilton carried a tense atmosphere. Red and Lois had finished their explanation and Sonya digested the information. If Ray had been there, he'd have tried to get a smile out of the woman. After some thought, Sonya broke the silence. "We'll try it. We have to now but let me handle the dealings at the holding."

Lois understood and gave Sonya one of her reassuring smiles. "Fine. You know best."

Sonya touched a sensor at her terminal. In seconds, she was giving orders. "Jimmy, run up to the loading dock. Show the two men waiting to the holding teleport. I'll meet you there." The unseen person replied affirmative. Sonya then took her pass card from her belt, sat down, and slipped the card into a slot at her computer terminal. For the next minute, she typed information and then finished by returning her special card to her belt. Sonya stood. "Let's get to work shall we?"

The Network duo agreed by following Sonya out. The special teleport at the end of the wide hall was soon occupying its normal quota after Sonya politely thanked Jimmy and sent him back to work. The door shut on the five as the last one entered. Sonya keyed in the special code. Ray donned his helmet concealing his identity, but Sonya knew who it was when he reached for her hand and patted it before releasing it.

In seconds they found themselves facing a green-clad officer holding a menacing weapon at them. Sonya stepped forward. Her small mouth drew a thin, tight line before she spoke. "This is a special project that has top-secret clearance. With me is Lois Green, project manager for Teletron Incorporated. She has two special technicians and a security officer with her. They're here to test a new security device and I have permission to watch and assist them in any way."

After the short introduction, Sonya handed the guard her pass card. A few moments passed as the security guard evaluated the situation and recalled the operating procedures for this type of circumstances. Through his clear face shield, the man's small, dark eyes revealed little. His badge indicated his name was Sid Spencer. Without lowering his weapon, he focused his attention on Ray but talked to Sonya. "Their security person is armed with a stunner."

The monotone statement was posed as a question. Sonya knew what to do. "It's all right. He's been given security clearance A-15. It's all here on my pass."

The green security officer recognized the clearance. The Teletron security officer had almost as much rank as he did. To confirm it all, he reached for Sonya's pass card and slipped it into his portable reader. He managed all this while holding his weapon up. Satisfied with his finding, the penitentiary guard lowered his weapon and continued with instructions. "All seems in order. Please wait while I inform the two entrance guards of your purpose. They'll be informed to keep an eye on your every move."

Sonya agreed with a simple nod and stepped back to talk to her companions. The two minutes seemed as hours to the nervous Network team but they handled it well. Given the OK to continue Sonya, Lois, and Ray stepped out of the teleport unit. Ray stationed himself just outside and stood at attention as Lois took a few more steps and turned to give her people instruction. "Jesse and Craig, you may precede with the installation."

Sonya made her way to the first guard's station and watched the team. Under the scrutiny of two green-clothed security officers, Red and Jesse took a panel off from within the teleport unit. They had all the tools they needed—a large electronic board and a few other pieces of electronic ware.

While the pair in the teleport worked, Sid came to Sonya with a question. "What should I expect when the new installation is complete?"

Her dark blue eyes shimmered slightly as Sonya struggled to hold her professional demurer. "The modifications will detect a marked, unescorted prisoner and if he hasn't been cleared from above to be in the teleport, he'll be directly teleported to our execution level below this one."

The reply produced a smile on the guard. "Very neat. That'd save us quite a few steps."

Holding to her neutral expression Sonya continued. "You'll be glad to know that we'll be testing the unit today. You'll have opportunity to watch it in action." A wider smile developed on Sid's face.

It took a little over fifteen minutes for Red, with Jesse's help, to install the special unit. When he finished, he informed Lois who had been watching. His deep voice echoed from the teleport unit. "Everything is ready, Lois."

Lois turned her determined face toward Sonya. "If you please, we'd like the assistance of your lowest security-risk-marked prisoner for a test."

It was the moment of Sonya's concern. There were limited choices of prisoners that were tattooed. She waited seconds feigning thought of her options and then turned to Sid. "Go get Mark Jacobson. The guy wouldn't dare run if we put him right outside."

The seconds passed with tension. Mark had special security that pertained to political prisoners. Sonya wasn't sure if the guard would stick with the correct procedures and deny the request or if her logic would make enough sense to warrant a bending of the rules. When the guard turned to the station counter and ordered Mark brought to the teleport, Sonya briefly closed her eyes in a moment of thankful prayer.

Red made some last-minute adjustments before he followed Jesse out of the teleport. They stood next to Ray. Time slowed to a molasses state as they waited. As he came into view, Mark's head looked newly shaved. Between two officers as escorts they guided him to Sonya. Without a clue to what was taking place, Mark looked wide eyed to the Network team. With the help of one of the guards, Sonya took Mark to the teleport. As he came closer to the team, Mark recognized Red from his brief encounter at Massena. A glimmer of hope rose up in him as he posed in front of the teleport.

Lois began her test. "Mr. . . . ." She turned to Sonya. "What was his name?"

The dark-haired woman gave a one-word answer. "Jacobson."

Lois turned back to Mark. "Mr. Jacobson, please step up in the teleport. Don't be afraid. Someone will retrieve you when we confirm the test was successful."

When Mark stepped into the teleport, his tattooed hand triggered the newly installed sensor and the door slid shut. Silence overtook the underground station as people waited to see what would happen next. When ten seconds had passed, the door to the unit opened revealing it was empty. Lois smiled and turned the expression to everyone as she commented. "It seems to have worked. Sonya if you'd send someone to the execution level to confirm the test we can go back above and discuss our results and the next step to this project. I'm sure you'll find Mr. Jacobson in fine health and ready to return to his cell."

Knowing time was very short Sonya hurried the team back into the teleport. "Very good. You four get back to my office. I'll be along in a minute. You have the pass code right Lois?"

Lois nodded once for yes. Everything worked like clockwork up until that point. Red, Jesse, and Lois, with Ray following behind began to file into the unit while Sonya turned to give Sid the instructions Lois suggested. A high-pitched siren drowned her first words. Accompanying the noise were red, flashing lights from every wall and ceiling. Green-clad security agents began converging to the teleport with drawn weapons.

Contemplating what must have happened Ray pulled his stunner and stood in the door to hold it open while he hollered over the noise. "Sonya, come. It's the only chance you have to get away now."

Ray stunned the nearest security guards before they realized there was opposition at the teleport. Sonya sprinted for the nearby passage as other guards began firing on Ray. The first two shots barely missed the Network agent. It wasn't stunner fire. Loud bangs accompanied small holes in the partly closed door and wall of the teleport. One bullet barely missed Red's head. These guys were shooting to kill. Ray stunned a few more guards just as Sonya was within reach of the teleport. It was then the woman noticed a guard had made it to the corner of the wide hall and was aiming at Ray who never saw the person. In the microsecond that passed, Sonya hollered as she threw herself between Ray and the penitentiary guard. Her momentum forced her and Ray into the unit, but not before she took a bullet in the back. The door closed and for two brief seconds pounding and thudding riveted the door before the teleport activated.

Velma Black did her job, which she did well. She noticed somehow a long-distance teleportation had taken place somewhere within the compound. Someone else might not have observed it or if they had, wouldn't know what do about information that seemed impossible. But Velma sounded an alarm. It was a calculation the Network team hadn't made. They thought it would be more than several minutes before the compound realized they had all escaped. They made it but just barely and at a cost they hoped they wouldn't have to pay. At the Byrd Penitentiary, officials secured the compound, dismantled the teleport modifications, and reported to Washington. It was all bad news, including the inability to determine the teleport's destination because programming erased it.

Saved at a Cost

Everett calmly studied the terminal but Mike wasn't as composed. He joined Kayla as she thoughtfully paced the floor. The three were the only ones allowed in the small transporter room at Bethany. Others waited patiently outside of the room to hear the outcome. John Ball poised his team ready to handle whatever the upshot was.

Mike was quite anxious as the time passed. "Shouldn't we be seeing something by now, Everett?" The older gentleman seldom seemed flustered. Lowering his eyes he drawled a reply. "Actually we're well within the time frame we set for ourselves. I wouldn't worry for at least another fifteen minutes or more." Kayla heaved a big sigh in frustration.

Quiet befell the room for another eight minutes. Heads snapped to Everett's direction at his placid comment. "Here we go. I have one transmission beginning. This should be Mark. I hope our teleport amplifier works as I planned."

The teleport slowly lightened revealing Mark with a surprised expression. Kayla ran to the unit and threw her arms around Mark before he stepped down. He was just beginning to grasp his good fortune when Mike ushered the pair away from the teleport. "Good to see you, Mark, but now we need to concentrate on getting the rescue team home." Mike tried to be as cordial as possible but in his excitement it came out with a hint of acid. Kayla and Mark quickly complied. In less than three minutes, Everett made his second announcement. "Right on time. Here comes the rescue team."

The teleport door slid into place and darkened. The first hint of trouble came with Everett's simple comment. "Oh, oh."

Mike trotted up behind the senior technician. "What's the matter?"

Anyone else would panic with excitement but Everett simply stated an observation as if having an evening chat with a friend. "There seems to be a lack of power. I'm holding them but I can't finish the transmission. They must have an extra person with them. I only programmed it for four."

Everett's fingers were flying across the complicated control panel. Mike felt a need to do something. "Can I help in anyway?"

Busy with the controls Everett directed Mike. "Yes. There's a panel below me to the left. Open it."

It seemed like minutes but in seven seconds Mike had the access panel opened. "OK now what?"

Everett continued touching sensors and sliding levers. "You should see an orange board with three dark blue slide switches?" Mike began scanning the area when Everett prodded him on. "We have to hurry. I can hold them for maybe another fifteen seconds before we damage their mass profile."

"I found it. Now what?"

Everett continued as if conducting a seminar. "Increase the first lever by moving it up two notches. After that, grab the second two and move them at the exact same time down two notches. Do it now." Mike finished his task when he heard the results from Everett. "Very good. I'm pulling them through now. If you hadn't done that correctly this panel would've blown up in our face." Anyone would have thought Everett stated a simple fact to a class of college students. Mike blew air from his lungs in relief and wiped sweat from his brow.

The teleport finished its work and the glass wall retracted. Red, Lois, and Jesse stepped over Ray who held Sonya in his arms on the floor. Lois was the first to speak.

"John, call medical and get someone up here right away. We've a wounded person."

The others went to the opposite side of the room where Kayla and Mark watched. Ray cradled Sonya's head in his lap. "Hang on, Sunny. Help's on the way."

Sonya's large, dark eyes glanced up at Ray's comment. She held a grimaced smile to her lips. "Did we make it? Is Mark safe?"

Ray smiled as best as he could. "Yes. We did fine. Now you be still until help gets here."

Pain washed across Sonya's face before a forced a smile. "It's too late for that. Don't worry about me. I'm going home to be with Jesus. Thanks, Ray, for everything. Please see to it that I find you there someday."

Ray tried to reassure her all was going to be fine when he saw her breathe her last breath. Sonya managed to leave him with one of her smiles.

Bob Gretchin burst through the doorway and ran to the pair on the teleport. Bob was Bethany's doctor. A tear fell from Ray's eyes and landed on Sonya's cheek as Bob leaned over to examine her. Ray didn't need to wait for the doctor's prognosis. His heart felt something he wished he would never experience. Only time was going to reveal what he would do about it.

As Through Fire

Zachary Forbes was on duty to welcome Ryker to the Washington DC NMA. He was very young and quite new to the duties of the security desk. It was a good sign to Ryker.

Lord, may his inexperience help me gain the time I'll need.

When the young officer smiled, Ryker felt prayers being answered. More mature NMA personnel refrained from using a blithe countenance when on duty. "Good morning, Mr. Button. What may I help you with?"

The Network Chief approached the main counter with an amicable but authoritative attitude. Leaning forward to read the badge, Ryker straightened to face the stripling with an air of lighthearted supremacy. "Well, Zach, as my telepass indicated, I'm here to transfer one of your prisoners to our facility in Canton, New York. This is by order of the vice president. Somehow he knows this person's a native to the area. The family has asked for visitation rights and this is the only way they'd have access to her. It's temporary. I believe it's for only one day. You may refer to security code T-20 if you have any questions."

Ryker's delivery was such that Zachary understood his position but there was no threat to his performance. A more proficient expression replaced the smile. Zach's curly blonde hair enveloped his face, giving his eyes a sparkling ocher appearance. He took a moment to refer to his terminal. After keying some information and examining the results, Zachary became even more professional. "It seems Mr. Button that I'm to inform Mr. Shanach of this before I can hand over someone with this criminal activity."

Ryker hoped he might not have to go this route, but had planned for it knowing it was likely. He used it to his advantage to intimidate the fresh SS agent. Ryker slowly drew a serious expression and with a monotone reply, simulating a computer personality said, "I should hope, young man, that you wouldn't have done it any other way." Changing his tone slightly he continued, "I am on a tight schedule. My only request is that you'd have the child brought here ready to transport while I wait for your superior to respond. He doesn't have much choice but to comply. I do understand the procedures just the same."

The ploy worked. Ryker stood back with his hands behind him and watched as his plan unfolded. Zachary stiffened, touched a sensor at his terminal, and gave orders. "Chuck, this is Zachary. Go to cell D-11 and bring," he studied the information he received from Ryker's telepass minutes earlier, "Erica Cuff up to the main lobby for a code T-20 transport."

After a short reply, Zachary fingered a couple more sensors and stood at attention to the terminal. "Ms. Pringle, would you inform Mr. Shanach that I have a code T-20 for a D-class prisoner." Angel gave a positive response. She must have signaled something else, because it produced a smile from the young man. He remembered what he was doing and dissolved it with an inert thank you. Zach turned his facial cast to Ryker. "It'll only be a few more minutes, sir. Please make yourself comfortable."

There were plush benches to either side of the counter on the outside walls. Ryker sat on a bench facing the door he knew Erica would be coming through. He used his idle time to silently pray, giving thanks for how things were working out and for intercession to positive results.

Two minutes passed when Zachary answered a terminal tone. He did everything but salute the image as the NMA director voiced his question. Ryker could hear Buck's voice. "I received your message, Mr. Forbes. Who's the prisoner in question?"

Stoically, Zachary replied, "D-11, Erica Cuff."

Oh Lord, things are going to happen fast now. Please orchestrate the next few minutes.

There was a moment of silence before Buck's acrid voice boomed from the intercom. "Zach! Don't allow anyone to leave until I get there. Call other security."

At that moment, an SS agent escorted Erica into the lobby. Ryker knew he needed to act fast so Zachary wouldn't overreact and shut the teleport down. On his way to the counter, he passed his daughter and gave her a look in which volumes of instructions became understood. Ryker and Monica had groomed their children over the years with knowledge if something like this ever happened. With a smile, Ryker approached the desk. "It didn't take long for security to show up did it? Sounds like a good man you have there as director. Very cautious. Not many would bother to involve themselves in such a matter. Don't worry; he'll find everything in order. You're doing a fine job, Zach."

Anyone could notice Zachary clearly relaxed at the compliment, though he changed his intonation little. "Thank you, sir."

Aware he had less than a minute left, Ryker worked to get him and Erica in position. He turned a worldly leer upon his daughter. "Not a bad-looking little girl, huh Zach? This may turn out not to be a bad trip after all." Ryker reached over and pulled Erica from the grip of Chuck and close to him. "You wouldn't mind taking a trip with me would ya, young lady?"

Erica played along and struggled greatly at Ryker's grasp. Ryker feigned stumbling at the resistance and moved the two of them within a few steps of the teleport. A surprised look evolved into a satisfied expression as Ryker worked to distract the SS agent and Zachary. "My my, she's a feisty little thing isn't she."

Zachary grinned and the SS agent folded his hands in front and shook with a delightful giggle.

Long, black hair billowed back from Buck's puzzled face as he burst through the door behind the SS agent. When he saw who was present, a baneful grin washed over his face. Buck slowed his pace to stand with his hands on his hips between his personnel and the Network pair. "Look who we have here—Ryker my old friend the head of the Network, and his lovely little daughter."

Behind Buck's back Zachary's face blanched with the horror he felt at his near tragic mistake. Buck continued with his arrogant cat verses mouse attitude. "You didn't really think you're going to get away with this did you? Finally, luck's graced me with good fortune. I have both of you now." Dressed in his customary uniform, Buck turned to the SS agent for assistance. "Give me your stunner."

Taking the opportunity Ryker dragged Erica across the floor at the teleport. One stride short of the entrance a blue flash filled the compartment, which stopped the couple in their tracks. Erica screeched as Ryker slowly turned to face Buck. His grim look caused Buck to laugh brutally. "You might as well come peacefully. The next shot'll still achieve my goals but there is no need in getting a large headache over it is there?" Buck posed the stunner threateningly at them both.

All seemed hopeless. Ryker weighed his choices and it didn't seem good—when it happened. Zachary's terminal chimed a short five-note tune. It was a special incoming message for Buck. Unwaveringly he talked to the security agent without turning from Ryker. "Put the message through right here, Zach. You two," he waved the weapon in a beckoning manner, "step this way please."

In hopes that the message would distract Buck, Ryker chose to ignore the command. All present could hear the communication directed to Buck. "Mr. Shanach, this is Sherman Bagnick from Byrd Federal Penitentiary. I'm afraid I've some bad news. Mark Jacobson has managed to escape with the help of some friends."

Buck's face dropped with shock. In reflex, he turned to the terminal in disbelief. "What? That's impossible!"

Ryker grabbed the opportunity and forced him and his daughter to jump into the teleport. Realizing his mistake, Buck snapped back in time to watch the door close. Sadie wasted no time and managed the next few minutes with great precision.

Buck screeched his next instructions. "LOCK THAT TELEPORT!"

The young agent frantically informed his superior. "I can't! It's been remotely activated!"

Buck jumped over the counter while screaming his orders. "ACTIVATE THE TRACER. I WANT TO KNOW WHERE THEY'RE GOING!"

Zachary succeeded to his and Buck's relief. "Good."

Pointing to the SS agent, Buck jumped back over the counter. "You come with me. They won't get far. We know where they're going."

In an unnamed town halfway between Washington NMA and the Network hideout, a teleport activated and deposited Ryker and Erica. Directly across the street was another teleport. Ryker took Erica's hand. "Come on. We have to hurry. Buck should be right on our tails."

They no sooner entered the new teleport when they saw the one they left activate again. Ryker felt pixilated about how things were going for him. "Look who followed me home for supper, Ma."

In the middle of his sentence, Sadie activated their teleport. The SS agent and Buck leaped from the first teleport while Buck fired but it was too late. Ryker and Erica slipped through his fingers again. Buck didn't possess the restraint common to others not as ambitious. In complete frustration, he screamed his rage. "NOOOOOO!" So angry at the world he turned his weapon upon Chuck the SS agent and dropped him. Then he threw the stunner on the sidewalk and crushed it under his foot. He unbelievably had lost to Ryker again.

Betrayed

Cerise streaks laced though the rose-colored skyline giving evidence to the late hour. Loren stood silhouetted against the colorful background seen through his large picture window. He faced the view with his hands behind his back. He was waiting and thinking, motionless at his home in Hollywood Falls. The small waterfalls rippled below the scarlet sky. It reflected the light, giving the impression of blood flowing from an open wound. Subsequently, Loren saw it as such and talked to the scene. "That's what I feel like. You've wounded me and I just don't understand why."

Tranquility broke with a reply from behind him. Holly's soft, puerile voice rolled gently across the small room. "It's not that way at all. I did it for your own good. What Calvin said is right. You're a good man, Loren. Your heart's in the right place but your logic is from wrong fundamental principles. We can still minister. It's just might be a little slower sometimes, developing the following."

Loren turned to face her. Holly sat comfortably in a large, soft, antique chair. The rest of the room held the same lavish furnishings. Loren wouldn't step toward Holly but said, "I'm afraid I can't live with that. I still believe all the good that's accomplished my way outweighs any erstwhile Christian doctrines."

Holly stood. Her long, honey-brown hair framed the concern in her hazel eyes. "I can't make you see it the Network's way can I?"

"I'll not compromise what I believe is the right way to handle things."

"I was afraid so."

The young woman attempted to continue but had a hard time forming her delivery. Before she could, Loren queried her. "Where's the evidence I'd entrusted you with?"

Showing her nervousness Holly bit her lower lip, then released it saying, "I turned them over to Vernon Cuff."

Loren seemed like a statue standing in front of his darkening windowpane. "I thought probably that's what you did."

He turned back to gaze once again out his window. Holly could see his determination so concluded her business. "The Network won't support you in your efforts any more unless you repent of your maneuvers." The sky phased from reds to violet colors. Holly saw the parallel taking place in Loren's heart.

The maverick was silent for another minute and then quietly gave a directive to his guest. "You might as well leave. Tell the Network not to worry about me. I don't need them anyway."

Having nothing else to say Holly saw herself to the teleport and had John transmit her back to the Upper Room.

It was a soul-searching time for Loren. Deep in thought he didn't move until the stars came out and the moon began to rise over the ridge. Only time would tell how Loren made out in his wrestling match with the Lord.

SEARCHING

"'And you shall seek me, and find me, when you shall search for me with all your heart.' Jeremiah the prophet repeated these words of God, recorded in the 29th chapter of his book. The Network is a living testimony to this fact. We must always remember we will not reach others with the gospel of Christ unless we strive to fill this truth on a daily basis."

Litton Cramer: in his journal dated 9/18/2076

Poised Cobra

Questioning, blank stares were all Buck could see and it made him even more incensed. It wasn't the question he asked that caused the reaction but rather his delivery. When Ryker escaped for the (too many times! Don't even mention it!), Buck snapped. It was a day later and he still ranted and raved like a lunatic. April knew if she didn't say something the man could very well do to all of them what he did to SS agent Chuck, but with more lethal consequences.

The young woman spoke in calm tones, soothing Buck's heightened excitement. "It's a rational, intelligent question, Mr. Shanach. We're lagging in your progressive thought process so if you'll give us a moment to think about your superior directive, I'm sure we may have the answer for you."

The comment and who gave it seemed to appease Buck. The color slowly drained from his tense face and a normal smile spread across his facade. "Thank you for saying something, April. I'm going to get myself a cup of coffee. I'll be back in a couple of minutes. That should give you enough time."

With his newly designed counterfeit calm, Buck walked out of the large conference room with various distinctions. It was modern but with a nostalgic flavor. You either liked it or found it very tacky. The characters present fit the same mold. Devon Damon seemed out of place with the others. Unconcerned with contributing, he relaxed out of the way in one corner. Buck had Devon there for one reason and one reason only. The others simply guessed what that might be. Also present were Klein St Denny, Cameron Axtell, Paul Egger, and Sally Diller. If tension in the room wasn't bad enough the antagonism between the two women was very visible. Klein was Sly Hawkins' head aide. Buck was glad Sly thought an aide was good enough for this meeting, but he also realized he needed to be careful. He didn't want any bad reports being sent back to his boss, which was the reason for the gaudy plastic self-composure.

As April handled the meeting at Buck's departure, Sally was quiet but her blanched eyebrows dived to shadow her blue eyes. New colors adorned April's stature. Verdant green with emerald trim enveloped her and accentuated the flowing cinnamon hair framing her face. With a promotion, Buck made her one of his department supervisors. The job was Cameron Axtell's a week earlier, which only added tension to the situation.

April worked to create a civil atmosphere. She looked from the door Buck exited and turned a serious expression to those in the room. "If you haven't figured it out already we'd better answer this man fast and with the correct response or he might find others who'll do the job to his satisfaction at our expense."

Klein smiled like he heard a comedian's sarcastic quip. Klein was a young man but mostly bald. What auburn hair he had circled his head and pointed to his large, sleepy gray eyes. "Sly said the man was ruthless. Mr. Shanach seems to have you people where you might hurt yourself if you move the wrong way." Klein couldn't help feeling ignored but it didn't seem to affect his satisfied demeanor.

April continued after looking at the man with a forced grin. "Al needs to push this effort. He feels the sooner the Cobra strikes the more effective our plans will be. He has reason to believe the Network is wise to us. So please don't take his attack personally. He just sees the goal closer than we thought and our move should happen soon."

The conference room was on the corner of the building on the top floor. Sunlight peeked out from around the thick clouds and came through one of the two glass walls. Paul Egger moved for the first time after Buck blew up at them. It was to escape the sun but as the others looked to him, he took the opportunity to say, "I'm not convinced our people are established in their positions well enough yet. This would accelerate the schedule almost two months. I can't guarantee what effects it'd have."

Cameron knew the continued success in his career depended on Buck. He felt the lateral move was temporary but his goal was still to move up. He wanted to appease the boss at all costs. "Now, now people." He was a soft-spoken person with a stutter he mastered well, but it still came through in tense times. His thin, fly-away mousy hair was parted on the left side. His pretentious smile was always present, except at rare times such as Buck's caustic explosion moments earlier. He quickly restructured it under his thin, blue-gray eyes. "I've worked long enough with Al to know he has a six, sixth sense when it comes to dealing with the Network. If he thinks Paul's people are re . . . re . . . ready then Paul must have done a better job than he, he thinks." Paul wouldn't argue around the compliment.

Sally spoke up for reasons others could only guess. She wanted to keep the conversation going in the current direction. Leaning back in her chair she crossed her legs. The woman knew it had an effect on some of the men. Impishly she played with a pencil, touching it to her smiling red lips. "I have to agree with Cam. Who're we to question Al? He wouldn't be in his position if he didn't take calculated guesses that worked."

April wouldn't acknowledge Sally but the comment was one she used. "True. Al will be back any minute. Are we in agreement that we can accelerate this operation without compromising it?"

No one would've said otherwise. They nodded their heads with varying degrees of commitments to the positive as Buck came back into the room. Intimidating neutrality was his facade. He sat down at the head of the large, odd-shaped plastic table. Swirling colors within it wrote the letters NMA across the length of it. "Well people, what kind of conclusion did we draw? Can the Cobra strike by the time five more days pass?"

No one said a thing for six seconds. Before April could react to dispel the silence, Buck smiled one of his wide, evil grins. His eyes sparkled with the self-satisfaction. "It's OK, friends. I already know. Maybe a little reluctantly, but I know you're with me. You don't think I really left you alone do you?" He laughed with a knee-slapping quality.

Almost everyone seemed puzzled until Sally allowed her pencil to point to the corner of the room where Devon sat. Unbeknownst to the group, he had donned his helmet when Buck left the room. The head of the NMA had watched them the whole time. Buck finished his meeting with a gleeful attitude. "Thank you all. I'll get us together again to coordinate the last pieces of information we'll receive in a few days."

He turned to leave and motioned April to follow him. Sally broke the pencil she held but calmly walked out after all the others left.

Debrief

Besides the auditorium, Central Library was the only place large enough to accommodate the people Ryker Cuff wished to bring together. The auditorium was too large and it might have stifled the interaction he hoped to generate. Several tables were removed and chairs used to fill the void. The library's backdrop of books, walls covered with patriotic documents, paintings, and the whiteboard made for a more sociable and serviceable place. So much had happened with the cooperation involving three of the Networks facilities that Ryker wanted to capture all experiences for immediate and future decisions. The Network leader demonstrated his role by facilitating the meeting. Calvin Katang silently wrote down all major information on the whiteboard. He fit it into categories the assembly generated. Kimberly sat to one side at a computer terminal, capturing things for the Network files.

An hour disappeared when Ryker felt he had achieved his purpose. "I'd like to thank you all for the great work you've done. Before we finish up, why don't we take a few moments to separate into three groups and make sure I've all we need? I'll give you ten minutes to study what we have up here," he pointed to the whiteboard, "and verify it or adjust it as you see fit."

They formed little cells in opposing corners as Ryker conferred with Calvin and Kimberly on some minor agenda details. It was a menagerie of personalities and varying ideals. Kayla Keating held onto Mark Jacobson and was very satisfied no matter what took place. Others contributing to this group were, Holly Tarbell, Red VanTimons, and Lois Green. The other two groups divided between Mike Grotto, John Ball, Ray Cuff, Everett Myron, Felicia Rederman, Jesse Bronchetti, Sadie Hampton, and Linda Paquin.

The ten minutes were up and additions made to the lists in closing. The room was silent as Ryker formulated his final assumptions. A serious smile grew upon his face before he began. "This is a momentous time. I'll remember it with mixed emotions. I praise God again in how He's worked in these last few weeks. We've been successful in thwarting the NMA in its endeavor to crush the Word and the works of our Lord. But it came at a cost." Ryker applied a grim expression and bowed his head as he glanced in Ray's direction before continuing. "What's accomplished was good but it's one of our areas of future concerns. How far should we go in our attempts to help a friend in distress? We need to closely consider this issue."

Shifting his load from one leg to another Ryker folded his hands behind his back and glanced to others as he continued. "We've learned much. The NMA has plans to undermine all our efforts. We'll alert others and help them to combat this. If there's any future subversive work done by us we need to realize the NMA knows we possess knowledge they never dreamed we had. They also will be working to neutralize any advanced technology we have. An example is our trackers. There's also a conflict from within our own organization we must remember. I don't know what Loren's intentions are. We need to pray for him. This fight is not finished and unless God intervenes, it won't be over soon. Again, thank you for all your inputs. Let's close with a prayer of thanksgiving and ask for wisdom in the days ahead."

After a few more minutes, the meeting was through. Most were not in a hurry to leave without greeting each other. Holly made her way to Ray and managed to corral him in the hall where they could slowly walk and distance themselves from the others. Concern permeated Holly's face. "You're pretty quiet today. Yes and no answers were all I heard you contribute. I'm worried about you. Can I help?"

Holly stated the obvious, which all had noticed. Ray wouldn't look her in the eye when he talked to her. "I don't think so."

"What're you going to do now?"

"I have no idea."

"Ryker's offered you a place here. Are you going to take him up on it?"

Ray stopped and leaned against the wall. After a moment, he put his hands in his pockets and distantly looked through Holly. "I can't. I don't fit. I'm not sure if I believe in this God of yours and if I did, I don't know as if I'd serve Him after what He's done."

It seemed as a photograph for many seconds as both digested the conversation conveyed. She didn't know if it was wisdom from above or mature insight. Empathy poured from her hazel eyes. "That's OK. God understands. He'll allow you to work through it. Just don't leave Him out of it entirely." An idea came to her. "Maybe the best place for you right now might be with Loren Richards."

Ray looked at Holly for the first time. He didn't say a thing at first but wrinkled his brow at her. The question came moments later. "Why?"

"You might be able to help one another. I believe you two could relate to each and balance one another out."

"That's kind of a wild, off-the-cuff idea, huh?"

"Yes."

Again, moments of silence prevailed. Taking his hands out of his pockets, Ray held one of Holly's. "Thanks for your concern. I don't pray often but maybe God just used you to answer one. I was going somewhere. I just didn't know where."

Holly smiled, putting a twinkle in her eyes, but before she could respond Ray continued with a sudden thought to the development. "I don't want anyone knowing what I do. Promise me that."

Reluctantly, she agreed.

New Information

Shortly after the meeting, Ryker made his way to Uncle Vernon's office. The pair relaxed comfortably in the sitting area.

After some other work-related discussions, Ryker switched gears. Between the couple on a coffee table sat a small pile of papers scattered across the surface. They were the reason Vernon wanted to see Ryker when time permitted. Ryker lounged back on the couch when he eyed them. He lowered his finger from his bearded cheek and pointed to the subject of his next statement. "This right here's what really blows my CPU. I would've never guessed the connection between Mark and Buck. It's really awesome that the head of the Washington NMA arrested his own brother. You haven't explained to me how Buck's connected to the Network, other than this," he said, still pointing at the information. "If Loren had been successful in feeding the proof he had, wouldn't it have ruined Buck?"

Vernon sat up and pawed through some of the papers. "Yes, it would've, but we shouldn't materially profit from it. I'm glad Holly brought this to me."

Finding the subject of his search, Vernon put it on top so Ryker could see what he'd learned. "I half expected it but never really figured it was true. Holly had these papers from her father, John Matthew Tarbell. It's a genealogy chart showing that he and Mary Ellen Tarbell, the mother of Buck and Mark, were cousins. Now I knew that but until these papers I never realized that Mary and John Tarbell's fathers were brothers to Alice Tarbell. The name Alice Tarbell didn't mean anything to me until I see here her husband was Algie Homer Eton. He's the one whose Bible we have. That's why Holly was so interested in it. She knew her great-great grandmother Alice had handed down a family heirloom of a special part of a one dollar bill, and none of them knew where it ended up. Working on a school project for college, Holly picked up the trail, which led to Mary Ellen Tarbell's story of giving up two sons for adoption. When Ray told Holly of the Bible you had and that it was from an Algie Eton, she began to put things together."

Ryker sat up and listened intently with a frown on his face. "I guess I follow to a point but besides having his Bible, how does Algie Eton figure into this?"

Vernon smiled deeper and pulled some more of the papers to the top of the pile. "I didn't know until this. Working her way back up the family line on the Eton's side, Holly found this."

He held the document so he could read it through his bifocals. "First, remember my father's name was Jesse Cuff. A daughter of Alice and Algie Eton, Louise, wrote a set of memoirs late in her life. Let me read a section for you. 'Jesse wished he hadn't of done it but at the time figured it was best to leave. Jesse was a "surprise" baby, born October 9, 1995 and may've been spoiled some by Mom and Dad. Whatever reason, he was the black sheep of the family and completely rejected our Christian beliefs. When the persecutions from the new NMA started, Jesse didn't want to be associated with his father's family. In 2019, he moved his family, wife Angel, and baby son, Henry, to Canada. Jesse was twenty-three at the time. There, he changed his last name to Cuff. He was always playing with words that way and must of thought he needed to keep his name consistent with clothing vernacular. I don't know what happened up there, but in 2023 the four of them (they had another baby) moved back. Keeping his new name, Jesse began working with the underground Christian efforts.'

"I'll stop there. Dad never told me he had changed his name and of course the other baby mentioned here, is me. Mother alluded to a secret in the family but I never paid any attention to it. See it all fits together. I'm going to say this slowly. Alice Tarbell is your grandfather's,

311

grandmother! Alice Tarbell is my grandmother. Algie Eton is your great-great grandfather."

Ryker's mind reeled as he took it all in. Without saying a thing, he began sifting through the papers and reading items here and there. After several minutes, he looked surprisingly to Vernon. "Buck and I are related!"

The older man chuckled. "Ironic, isn't it?"

Ryker was flabbergasted. During some more discussion, the subject of the dollar bill came up. Vernon displayed it. "Holly knew it was all true when she saw the second half of this in Buck's office."

Gingerly taking the green paper, Ryker looked at it again. He had seen it a few times before but now it seemed to hold a special interest. "She'd written on the back here. 'If in God . . .' What could the other half say?"

Vernon nodded his head back and forth. "I don't have the slightest idea."

Primer Set

Dried paper crushed within rippling fingers was the sound Sally's feet made as she paced back and forth in the fall leaves. A full moon hung high above her, giving good light considering the time of night. It was a desolate place but hundreds of yards down the walkway a street light gave some reference. Sally rubbed her hands together and blew in them, causing a billow of steam to float out in front of her. It was getting chilly. She wore her uniform with the coat to match but her hair wasn't long enough to help insulate her ears from the wind. Pacing, blowing on her fingers, and then putting them to her ears only made Sally more irritated.

Hearing something, Sally turned to face the dark forest before her. First, it was a twig snap, but then a shadow came creeping toward the young woman. Sally knew who it should be. "It's about time you got here! I almost froze to death. Why are you so late? I almost left."

Her voice stopped him for a moment. With a melodious quality, his voice came to her. "I was just making sure no one followed you. I'm not one to take chances. Besides, I knew you couldn't leave that easy. You've got too much invested in this."

Without saying anything, Sally signaled for the person to come to her. Each step crunched through the autumn leaves. Standing a few feet from Sally the moonlight washed across his face. He was a foot taller than the woman. It was John Sampson. His beard was longer and hair a little shorter but it was the ex-employee of Communiqué Incorporated.

Sally had waited long enough. She had reached impatience many minutes earlier. "You know what I want, John. I've the credits to pay for it. My only question is if you've the stomach for it?"

It had been a while since John saw Sally. His long face seemed chiseled with the emotionless expression he gave her. "Don't you worry. I don't know your reasons but if I do this, I'll see it as a plus for society. This isn't my first time. I've been doing this for ten years now."

Sally smiled. She did it well but John ignored it. "Yes. I was so surprised when I was given your name, John. You've turned into a regular vigilante. I like that. It does something for me."

The cold, hairy face hinted no reaction to the statement. John continued ignoring Sally's sexual suggestion. "You give me the credits and I'll take care of your wishes. The only other thing I need is the time."

The blonde lost her smile. She withdrew a disk from her pocket and handed it to John. "Here you go. The time is there with the payment."

As stealthily as he came, John left. Sally watched him go and then turned to walk from the moonlight toward the streetlight. Her pace increased as her happy countenance grew. "Yes. Yes, it won't be long now."

Celebration

Erica and Julia sat under the table giggling along with Gary Grotto and Luke Katang. The grownups were busy visiting and didn't realize the foursome was taking cookies and drinks almost as fast as Monica and Laura Grotto set them on the table. It was a get-together celebrating the safe return of Erica and Mark. Things had settled down after days of preparation and debriefing. They were ready for the repercussion expected. It was the lull in the storm and people took advantage of it. The Bethany and Jordan personnel were returning to their facilities the next day.

Mark Jacobson decided to make an announcement. With a large smile, he spoke over top of the noise until all eyes were on him. Before he started, an old nervous habit cropped up. He thoughtlessly tried to run his hand through his hair. He looked at his hand and laughed at himself. "Old habits break hard. Kayla told me to keep in practice because it'll grow back." Everyone laughed before Mark etched a more serious smile on his face.

"First, I'd like to publicly thank all of you involved in my rescue. If it wasn't for your dedication to the cause and our love for one another, I wouldn't have this great opportunity." He reached over and brought Kayla close to him then looked to all with a beaming face. "Kayla and I are to be married."

Congratulations burst forth from everyone. Ryker used the event to make another announcement. He gathered the engaged couple to him and brought a plain-wrapped package with him. In front of the small crowd he made a momentous announcement. "Tomorrow I'm going to make the official announcement but tonight you're getting the preview. It gives me great pleasure to give to this new couple something we hope to have in every family someday soon."

He handed the package to Mark who bestowed the privilege upon Kayla. She tore the wrapping off and surprise enveloped her face before she could speak. She held it up. "It's a Bible!"

Ryker explained, "This is the third one off our new presses. It took quite some time but we now have the privilege to produce God's Word without interference from the NMA. We've a small, networked computer system that is self-contained with our own developed software programs. It's going to be slow, but someday we hope to supply every family with a Bible like this one."

Someone started clapping and in seconds the whole room was full of the gaiety. While everyone turned back to conversations in small groups, Ryker queried Mark. "So what're you going to do now?"

The younger man took Kayla's hand. "Kayla and I are going to work at Bethany." Before he could continue, Lois stepped in standing between Ryker and Mark. She put an arm around each one's shoulder. Her light eyes danced with merriment as she sculpted her words. "Too late, Ryker. I managed to recruit him before you could. Mark's going to be working with Red on developing a secret system that'll work within the NMA teleport system. Not to do anything noticeable but rather monitor their movements."

The head of the Network nodded his head in agreement. "Sounds good. Keep me posted would you?"

Lois removed her hands from the two. "Wouldn't have it any other way." The conversation turned to more domestic subjects.

Even Him?

It was the dingy cell. It was full of snakes. Buck was at the bars pounding them in deep frustration. His wild blue eyes seemed neon against his scarlet face. "Where is she? Where in hell is she?"

The cell was empty of anything or anyone but the reptiles. Ryker knew it was his nightmare with an interesting twist. Monica and Erica were both absent, which lifted the immediate terror of the situation. On the floor lay the smashed box that had housed the snakes. It had been the object of Buck's first vented anger. Stepping back Buck spun his head around searching for someone in flight from him. His long, black, curly hair was as wild as he.

Again, Buck didn't see it but Ryker noticed the shadow as it grew over his old friend's head. It was too late for Buck to do anything, and then the seventeen-foot python had the frightened man in its coils. All Ryker could see of Buck was his head, one hand reaching through the large, constricting muscles, and his feet. Buck turned to Ryker with terror in his eyes and as loud as he could under the pressure of his predator pleaded, "Ryker! Help! It's going to kill me."

It was a shock. It was the first time anyone ever noticed Ryker in this dream. He tried to move but couldn't. Neither was there a weapon in his reach. Some of the panic and terror came back. With large, lime-colored eyes of concern he looked to Buck. "I can't move! I don't know what to do."

To the surprise of both men, the snake spoke. Bringing its head level with his victim, the python glanced from one than to the other as he hissed his message in glee. "It'sssss too late. Buck'ssss sssssoul isssss mine."

A pair of green and a pair of blue eyes stared in astonishment. Ryker sensed assistance in his being, which made him boldly face the intimidating foe. "It'd seem so but Buck could call upon help that you would fear."

The slithering beast tightened its grip in a defensive response causing Buck's eyes to open further. His voice was weak as he struggled to query. "What help? What could I possible do against this?"

Ryker didn't know where it came from but he held it in his hand. He raised the black, leather-bound book up as a shield. "It's all here in God's word. You've been fighting it. You've tried to eliminate it but the story of God's love and the simple way to Him is your salvation."

Sensing the need for a new strategy, the snake eased his strangle hold. Buck's face relaxed minutely as the serpent turned his carmine cat-like eyes to him. The forked tongue lashed out several times. "Sssssilly sssssuperstitions. Logic will prove I'm in control. You might ssssupose that you and I can make a better deal."

The fear in Buck's eyes was still very evident. "Deal? What kind of deal?"

Ryker seized the moment in order to redirect his old friend's attention. "See! He's revealed himself. The idea of a deal means you can earn something. Whether it is freedom or something for someone else, it'll cost you everything. God offers His grace, through His Son at no cost to you. He's more powerful than anything you may face. Even now, God waits for your call to Him, but you must trust Him and have faith in Him. You say you have no faith? Then take mine and use it. Know what God's done for me and ask it for yourself."

For a moment, Ryker saw calculating behind Buck's cold, blue eyes. The snake sensed the thoughtful hesitation and began to squeeze once more. "Don't lissssssten to him. Your life issss in my posssessssion. Deal with me!"

Ryker held the Bible up as a sword. "Buck, friend, please trust in this. You can make it a victorious weapon."

The scene grew dark and faded.

**

Ryker calmly sat up in bed. Next to him Monica slept quietly. Troubled, Ryker silently stood and dressed himself. It was morning and his alarm was ready to signal before he shut it off. The dream branded his mind as he made his way to his office. He prayed almost continually about what the dream meant and what his next move should be.

In Ryker's small sunlit office sat Mike, Uncle Vernon, and Calvin. Buck's secret was out. The Network needed preparations for what they knew was a fatal blow to their operations. They struggled with strategies that would counteract the Cobra strike. Planted double agents throughout the Network already hindered any avenue they took. In frustration, Vernon suggested they pray collectively for more direction. Each had an opportunity to vocalize and petition until Vernon said the last amen.

As an echo, Ryker's terminal beeped for his attention. He gave the machine a look of surprise. Kimberly had instructions not to bother the small group unless it was an emergency. The others could hear the receptionist's pleasant, professional voice. "I'm sorry to interrupt, but I thought you might like to take this special message from Mark Jacobson. You'll find it interesting."

Ryker made sure to indicate that Kimberly did the correct thing. "That's no problem, Kim. Thanks for bringing it to us. It could very well be an answer to prayer. I'll take it now. Patch it through to here."

After reading for only second, Ryker's face showed them something terrible had happened. When he finished, Ryker informed them of the news. "It's from Mark. There's been a terrible accident. Buck was almost killed last night."

Fire in the Sky
The Previous Evening

"Xerxes is not a name I'd want to give one of my boys. I don't care if it is biblical," Mark said with a laugh in his voice. Kayla had mentioned it in fun. It was a warm, autumn evening. Warm compared to the night before and what was coming. The young couple took advantage of the weather to sit outside and talk about their life change. Night time was the only time Network personnel felt comfortable staying outside. They knew it was moot because it didn't matter to the NMA, who could see whether it was night or day if they knew where to look, but chances were slim that the NMA was working offensively that late at night.

The moon lacked a sliver from being full. Thin clouds passed in front occasionally veiling it slightly, which gave it a surreal effect. The hillsides were at the peak of their autumn colors. In the moon's luminescence the reds, oranges, and yellows were almost fluorescent in shade. It was one of those rare, beautiful nights that seemed full of magic and possibilities. The couple discussed many subjects over the half hour. Kayla shivered, which caused Mark to bring her closer and wrap his jacket around her. "Are you cold? Do you want to go in?"

The moon seemed to have the same effect on Kayla's hair as it did on the foliage when she looked up at Mark. "No, not yet. Just a few more minutes."

An animal howled off in the distance. Mark leaned down and lightly kissed his fiancée on the forehead for reassurance. They sat there for some time when Mark vocalized his thoughts. "I hear Ray's skipped out. Nobody seems to know where he went. I wonder if that bothers Ryker at all?"

Kayla was quiet like she never heard him. Mark didn't think much of it at first, but then concluded he had made a mistake. "Hey, don't worry about it. I didn't bring his name up to hurt you in any way. What happened between you two was a mistake and you're sorry for it. That's good enough for me. Please don't fret about it." Placing a finger under her chin he gently lifted Kayla's face up to him. Her soft, blue eyes pooled, ready to spill the regret she felt. He pulled her into his chest and stroked her hair. "I've forgiven you. God's forgiven you. It might take time but I'll be here to help you forgive yourself." So thankful, the young woman squeezed him tighter and released the sobs that hung on the edge of her emotions.

It was minutes later when they heard it before they saw it. The distant explosion made both turn in reflex to find the source. Several miles away on the top of another small mountain a fireball rose in the air. It lit the top of the mount like a candle on a cake but died down to a less intense fire in seconds. Just the same, it wasn't going out anytime soon.

The young couple jumped to their feet. Mark stepped up on a small rock in front of them to give him a vantage. "Wow! What was that?"

"I don't know. Something just blew up. What could be out there in the middle of nowhere?"

"Same question I had. We'd better go inside. I want to get someone to help me and go investigate."

It wasn't the end to the evening the couple had planned but there was no time to think about it.

Demise
Fire to Come

Music filled the lavish home with a feeling of movement. It was a very informal gathering. Buck wore a jean-type pair of pants and a blue Prussian silk, long-sleeved shirt. His black hair lay loose, cascading around both shoulders. He was the most relaxed he could remember in years. The rest of the guests consisted of Klein St Denny, Cameron Axtell, and Paul Egger. Cam had a pretty lady with raven hair holding his hand. Her name was Lisa. Klein brought a friend named Cecil. He was a tall blonde with rippling muscles under his tight-fitting clothing. Klein and Cecil were holding hands also. The two couples were in conversation with Paul.

Buck wandered over to the entertainment center to adjust the music. April hung on his arm. She was dressed in a comfortable but appealing black pants suit. Away from the crowd she leaned up toward Buck and with a smile whispered, "You're in a good mood tonight. What does this, so I might know how to duplicate it?"

Buck smiled. It was a warm, inviting smile. In fifteen years April was the only one to see that side of the man. After feigning his musical adjustment, they sat down on a small love seat in the corner. Buck answered, "You're the main reason. I didn't know how much I . . . relied on you until you were gone there for awhile. I'm glad you're here with me again."

His sincerity convinced April as she hugged his arm tighter and laid her billowy brown hair upon his shoulder. Buck reached up and stoked her head lightly once before he continued. "The other thing is my plans are about to come to fruition. I've waited for this it seems like forever." For one of the few times that night, Buck frowned. "I wish Sally'd hurry up and get here. She said she'd be a little late but late and absent is two different things. We've some last minute adjustments and coordination to figure out and this Cobra project will be in full swing. She's holding us up and I want to get going."

April stood and smiled deeply with her petite mouth. It made her cheery eyes look bright and captivating. "Come on and mingle. Sally'll be here in a bit and then you can have your day. For now, let's enjoy ourselves." Buck smiled a little more plastic than the last one but agreed.

Almost another half hour went by and still no Sally. Among other subjects, the group discussed the project and pretty well ironed out most of the details. His good nature helped Buck take Sally's absence in stride. "Sally's missing all the fun here, but you know we might not need her input. If she just remembers to bring all the documentation with lists of people we could finish this without her."

April couldn't have been happier at Buck's announcement and the others all agreed. When the music paused in the lull of conversations, Buck stopped to listen. With faint meowing, Buck's cat, Mr. Tubbs, garnered his master's attention with a distress call. While the others continued their conversations, April followed Buck to his picture window.

He scanned the dark outside, moving his head back and forth until he stopped with a smile. Out past the gazebo Buck spotted him. "There you are, you naughty little thing." He turned to April. "He's stuck up in that tree again. That must be the third time he's done that. Listen, you have my security code. I'm going out to rescue the varmint. If Sally decides to come, let her through will you?"

Not waiting for an answer Buck went through the nearby door. The temperature was warm as Buck crunched through the leaves across his yard. There was a light on in the gazebo that illuminated his trek. He smiled to himself as he listened to the laugher coming from the house. They were probably making fun of him and his cat. At the edge of the light's extent, Buck looked up to his pet peering down on him. Mr. Tubbs gave one loud yawl before Buck lovingly reached up and plucked the animal from his predicament.

While he reached for his pet, Buck heard the teleport signal. He talked to his cat about it. "Mr. Tubbs, that must be the fickle Sally Diller."

Buck turned to proceed to the house. Scratching the cat behind the ears he heard the screaming. It was April! He stopped dead in his tracks to listen.

"OH MY GOD! RUN! IT'S A . . ."

She never spoke another word. If she did, the roar that filled Buck's ears effectively drowned them out. There was nothing but the consuming thunder and a blinding red and white flash. Everything went blank. Buck couldn't feel anything; he couldn't remember anything—until his vision cleared. He didn't have any concept of time passing. It seemed like a skip in his life and everything had changed. He thought at first he was looking at his own reflection. The nose, eyes, the shape of the face, all seemed so familiar, but it wasn't him.

It was Mark Jacobson. "Hold on. Help's on its way."

It was black again until many hours later.

Thinking

The first snow was always best for tracking. Most of the leaves had fallen and the dusting of snow made for a whitewash effect. It was late morning as Loren and Ray made their way down the trail back to the Ponderosa. It might have been against the law but no one could tell them. Hunting deer hadn't happened for over half a century. Ray and Loren prepared the camp deep in the wilderness for winter occupation. They were staying alone the whole winter season. Loren's round face was pink at the cheeks because of the cold. He wore a bright orange wool hat found in the attic. Ray wore only his hairy head and face.

They talked as they trekked. Ray had a thoughtful expression. "People really lived like this in the last century and before?"

"According to what I've read, yes."

"Do you think it'll do us any good?"

"I don't know but I believe if I'm to continue with my walk with the Lord, I need time to meditate and study what God's work is for me. Paul of the New Testament started preaching first thing in Damascus after his conversion. The people there wanted to kill him. Paul wasn't as effective until he spent time with God. I think that's what I'm supposed to do."

Almost in sight of camp Loren brought his arm up to stop his partner. Silently he pointed at a beautiful, rust-colored animal. Six long points glistened in the sun. Slowly Loren brought the antique gun to his shoulders and aimed.

The noise from the weapon made Ray jump a foot in the air. "Man! That scared the stuffing out of me. My ears are still ringing." He tapped at his ears when Loren got his attention.

"How do you like that? We got one." Looking at the direction Loren pointed; Ray could see the animal lying, a red stain forming in the snow around it. He assumed a perplexed expression. "Now what do we do with it?"

"We got our work cut out for us. That's food for the winter."

"Oh great. I hope you know what you're doing."

"Don't worry. I read about it in a book. To get back to our conversation, why did you agree to stay here with me?"

Ray looked back to the buck and then turned to Loren with a grin. "For two reasons I guess. One, to understand why you feel a need to seek your God so fervently and two, because you seem to learn well from books."

Loren smiled. "Ya, I think we can help each other."

Birthday Plans

November 17 was his birthday. That didn't matter to him. He would remember it for the day he decided to live again. He gave the credit to Ryker. No one visited, or at least almost no one. Sly Hawkins paid his respects a week after the accident but hadn't shown his face since. Sly did reassure Buck his job would be waiting for him, but the man seemed preoccupied and wasn't much company. Buck couldn't blame anyone for not coming. He didn't think he was very pleasant to look at. The hard thing to defy was no one cared about him. April was dead. That was the worst of it. His birthday was the day Buck decided Ryker was going to pay for that tragic loss in his life.

The next day, Buck was to go home. His private room was sterile but lavish. There was a communication port that kept him in touch with the outside world but he only needed to use it little. Until very recently, he was too self-absorbed to care about anyone or anything else. That had changed and for the first time in weeks he wondered how he looked. Standing from his hospital bed he made his way to the full-length mirror hanging on the bathroom door. The long, black curls of hair had fed the fire that took his home and friends. It was growing back but was too soon to say how. The scars were healing. His face and arms received the worst of it. Mr. Tubbs had landed on his face or it might have been much worst. Buck liked to think the cat gave his life for him. Seeing himself only made his anger inflame further. Sly told him that delivered papers pointed to an assignation attempt by an old acquaintance of his—a Craig VanTimons. Buck didn't say a thing to the story, because he wasn't sure. Besides, he was going to pin it on Ryker no matter who really did it. As far as Buck was concerned, it was ultimately Ryker's fault.

To his great surprise, Buck saw he had a visitor in the reflection. Turning, he welcomed Devon Damon and told him to sit down while settling back into the bed. "Good to see you, Devon. You always have been a loyal friend and employee."

Devon broke his code of conduct and smiled pleasantly. His voice was soft and deep. "I came for two reasons. Sly Hawkins is dead. Seems he had a massive stroke while in his sanctuary at home."

Buck was shocked. Almost immediately he considered his new options. He was still in thought about the news when Devon continued. "The second reason is that I thought you might want to be talking about plans or something. I'm here to give you a hand."

Buck felt touched but didn't reveal it. "Good thinking and great timing. I'd begun doing that and you're just the one who can help me. I'll tell you one thing. Someone is going to pay for these." He pointed to his face.

Devon's smile became a little more devilish as he reached up and touched his scar. "I know just how you feel, boss."

It took only an hour and the pair had a plan that Buck thought was fool proof. The crutch of it all depended if he could wait until the time was right. He learned one thing if nothing else. Timing was essential and anxious moves cost him much. He could—he must wait for Ryker's vulnerability to show. It hurt a little but when Devon left, Buck smiled one of his amoral grins.

Spring Changes

Yellow was the color of the day. Shades of it dominated the outside setting. Erica and Julia were both dressed in the festive color along with three-quarters of the other girls and women. Yellow daffodils, lilies, and other spring flowers were arranged around the deck and along the lawn of the Ponderosa. Sunlight forced its way through the thick, newly leaved trees that covered the hide-away retreat. Spring smells perfumed the whole area, making a pleasant morning all in all. Easter came late and spring approached early. The unbeatable combination made a glorious setting for a special Easter celebration. Loren Richards set up the special event and invited key personnel of the Network and almost one hundred other guests. After some investigation, Ryker accepted the invitation and encouraged the affair.

Serving as a stage, the deck of the Ponderosa held key people for the morning event. Ryker stood at the podium and waited for everyone's attention. Upon the platform along with him were Loren, Mike Grotto with Dove, and Dennis Prince. Ryker watched people sit in folding chairs or on the ground as they gave him their attention. His green eyes laughed, accentuating the smile within the hair upon his face.

"Welcome everyone. This is a great day to worship our Lord's resurrection. It's the main reason we're here this morning, but there are other things to be thankful for also."

The sandy-colored, thinning hair fluttered in the breeze as he turned to look at Loren for a moment before facing the crowd once more. "We can thank Loren Richards for this place. He's graciously donated to the Network this and all other possessions he's gained over the last few years. It seems the Lord has called him to minister by reaching out in cities and towns that have no Network influence. It's one of the items we'll be praying for this day. Loren's asked for a time to explain himself and help you understand where his prayer concerns lay. He'll be given that opportunity in a minute."

There was an alleluia in the crowd and Ryker concurred with it. A much more serious countenance washed over Ryker's face. "I just wanted a moment to remind each of us this is also a time to remember the late beloved Vernon Cuff. He'll be missed greatly by us all, but we know he's gone on to a better place." Looking down at Rose in the front row, Ryker watched as she wiped a tear from her eye. A sad smile graced the woman's face. Ryker continued. "Uncle Vernon had one thing to say to all of us and I need to convey that to you. He said something to me when I was a young man that I've never forgotten. It's something we need to remember when we endeavor to witness to others. I quote, 'We search and search for meaning in our lives. We seek that which will fill the void in our inner selves. We make it such a chore when all we need to do is sit still and allow ourselves to be found.' I find much truth in that. A gift is not a gift until it's accepted and used. I pray we'll recall Vernon as a man who helped us remember this. Let us have a moment of silent prayer."

Ryker said a quick prayer and then turned the service over to the others on the deck. Loren took the occasion granted to publicly apologize for his unfounded theological stand. His hair was longer, covering his ears with honey brown curls. His talk was a testimony, which was short but powerful. When Loren was through, he introduced Mike and the service began with music reflecting the joy and hope of the resurrection.

Dennis Prince gave a sermon that touched every soul present. When the service ended, Loren invited all to stay and share in refreshments he had setup inside. Groups gathered inside and out. Some left early by way of the teleport a quarter of a mile down an old path. An EFA station abandoned it decades ago and the Network modified, maintained, and monitored it. The unit was old but had been repaired to work well enough for the Network. It was the only way in and out unless one wanted to walk fifteen miles to the nearest settlement. Those who stayed enjoyed some unique food prepared by Loren.

Inside, Ryker found Loren and thanked him for the event. He then inquired on something he'd been waiting to ask. "I hear Ray spent the winter with you. Why isn't he here?"

Loren's grin didn't quite develop because he hid it behind a promise; however, Ryker thought he saw one. "Well, he decided to bug out. He had some other things to take care of. Don't worry; he plans on getting with you soon. He wants to talk to you about something."

Ryker pressured for more information. Loren wasn't giving any more so Ryker made a joke about it before he made his way to the front of the house, which was protected by a large screened-in porch. Kayla and Monica talked with Holly on one end, while Red visited with their two men. The two groups began with the same subject. Red and Holly had surprised everyone. Ryker took Red's hand and congratulated him. "I'm truly glad for you two. I didn't know you were seeing each other, say nothing about being married."

Red's hair enhanced the blush that came to his face. With a smile, his low voice defied the trivial words his attitude conveyed. "Yea, well everyone ought to do it once."

Some lighthearted jokes made them comfortable before the men turned to a more serious subject. Mark's hair had grown back slightly darker than before, though it had the same wave to it. With concern he said, "Yes, it looks more like Buck's this time around doesn't it?"

The three were silent for a moment until Ryker spoke. "Yes it does. I hear Buck's recovering well." No one said a thing so Ryker continued, knowing Mark could use what he learned. "It's a good thing you found him, Mark. Buck wouldn't be here today if you hadn't been in the right place at the right time. Things have turned out pretty well. The Cobra project was mostly stifled and one of the men responsible has been given a chance to think about it. Your brother has another chance." The young man smiled grimly and nodded an agreement.

Others came onto the porch and got involved in other varying conversations when Ryker saw him. Down the path through the woods Calvin briskly walked to the building. Stepping off the porch Ryker went to greet him. Calvin had a serious expression. Ryker wondered if something was on his mind or just the sunlight in his eyes. It was a little of both. Ryker greeted him. "I'm glad to see you made it. Where've you been? Kimberly told me you had some business to take care of."

The expected smile didn't develop, which gave Ryker his first hint something was wrong. "Yes, I received a special message through our contacts. Buck wants to meet with you. Says he just wants to talk to you. He'll even meet you alone."

They studied each other while Ryker digested the information. Before the leader could comment, Calvin offered some more information. "He's got it all figured out. Says he'll meet you any place of your choice as long it's near a teleport. I'm supposed to give an answer back within the hour."

Laughter burst out from the porch. Ryker turned to it in thought. *Lord, what should I do? Is this the time I'm to help Buck find you?*

Calvin watched as Ryker struggled with a decision. Neither the crowd on the porch nor Calvin heard Ryker's silent plea. He slowly turned to Calvin. His green eyes gained depth as He gave His answer. "Tell him I'll be at my parents' place at ten o'clock in the morning. If he's not alone, he won't find me."

Sensing something happening, Monica turned to watch her husband as he solemnly nodded his head at Calvin. She couldn't hear the pair talking, but something inside caused concern.

Decision

At zenith height, the cumulus clouds floated in the deep blue sky. It was another warm, sunny day. The old Cuff homestead hadn't changed much over the years. Inside, Homer and Judy were too nervous to enjoy what the day had to offer. Their son was taking the chance of his life and their minds focused on what their role was. The blue spot on Judy's cheek was brighter than usual because her skin was more pale than normal. "I know how this is supposed to work, but I can't help feel like something's going to go wrong."

Lowering his book, Homer looked to his wife across the room. He wore glasses now. His resemblance to Uncle Vernon came full circle. It was almost twenty years ago he sat and looked at himself through his uncle. It truly could have been a reflection. With hidden concern of his own, Homer ventured to reassure his wife. "I know how you feel, dear, but Ryker's determined. He feels the Lord wants this. We have to trust Ryker and the Lord."

Judy nodded her head but couldn't settle down just the same. "Monica's very concerned. She couldn't even be here if Ryker would've allowed it."

It was all nervous talk until the teleport signaled. Homer stood and waited with his wife while the teleport finished activating. As the glass partition slid back into the wall, Buck calmly stepped down. His clothes of simple civilian dress reminded them when he was a boy visiting. The black hair was growing back nicely covering the scars on his ears. The rest of his face showed only hints of the trauma it went through. The doctors had done a great job over the last few months.

Homer and Judy couldn't tell the smile was as plastic as most of his face. "Good to see you again, Mr. and Mrs. Cuff. You probably know I'm here to see your oldest son. Is he around?"

With no fanfare or pretense, Homer directed Buck. "Yes. He's waiting for you. You're to go out to the apple tree in the meadow and wait for him. Looks like you kept your word so he'll be there in a minute."

Without an utterance, Buck bowed his head in contrived respect and went through the door and to the tree.

Once Buck made it out of hearing distance, Homer spoke to the kitchen. "OK, come on before we run out of time." Ray trotted from hiding in the other room and joined his father at the teleport. Before they did anything, Homer directed a statement to Ray. "I still don't know why you don't want Ryker to know you're here but I'm glad you showed up. I'm not sure if I know how to do this or not."

Ray smiled. "Nothing to it."

He went over to the teleport unit and opened the main panel in the wall. Reaching in, Ray grabbed a handful of wires and yanked them out of the wall. Small sparks shot out into the room as the teleport controls went dead. An astonished expression evolved into a smile as Homer looked to his youngest son. "That was too simple for me to figure out. Like I said, I'm glad you showed up."

The three of them laughed as they settled down to see what would happen next.

The birds sang their song of joy because spring had come. The season also dressed the apple tree in blossoms of pink. Buck surveyed the area looking for his old friend. He had time to think about what was going to happen and it brought a smile to his face. The plan was so simple he knew it would work. Ryker was so gullible he wouldn't think the enemy could stoop to a level of deception involving a simple promise. Buck was still grinning with anticipation when he noticed Ryker walking up over the knoll of the hill. He came from the wooded area behind the house where the cave was. A minute passed before the two faced one another. Ryker held a very neutral expression. The wind was a bit stiffer than the day before, causing the hair on each to be blown about. Neither had enough to cause a nuisance.

Years seemed to flash back to a time when the two were very good friends. The thought of it made for a period of silence between them before Ryker broke it. "You wanted to see me. Here I am."

Buck held his smile. He intended to change it by giving Ryker one of his evil grins but something restrained him. He only succeeded in endearing the one he held. "Yes, you are. I knew you'd be. You're really quite predictable in most ways. I'd been surprise if you chickened out of the chance to talk to me."

Neutrality was the position Ryker was determined to keep as he conversed with the challenge before him. "I owe it to you. If the Lord sees fit to give you another chance, who am I to allow any prejudice to thwart it?"

Not expecting the response he received, Buck dropped his smile. "I thought you'd be full of all that gushy religious nonsense. You act as if I'm not worth it."

"Not true. It doesn't matter what I think anyway. God loves us all and wishes everyone to accept Him."

"That's your God. How do *you* feel about it?"

"Does it matter to you how I feel about you? If it does, then you can take solace in the fact that I can't help but feel concern for you. All the same, you're not a child anymore. You have some knowledge of what I and others like me believe but you've rejected any possibility of the truth in it. This moment is for you. There is a God. He loves each and every one of us. There's a heaven and a hell. God wants us to be with Him in heaven, but He's done a wonderful and very scary thing by allowing each one of us to make that decision ourselves. Because of that, there's evil in this world. Sin has entered in and we all deserve separation from God. The plan is very simple. So simple we find it hard to believe it's the way. Jesus, God the Son, came to earth, showed us what living a Christian life should be like, and gave His life willingly as the sacrifice, taking God's punishment for us upon the cross. The price has been paid. We either accept that, do our best to follow Jesus' example or—we walk ourselves straight into the hell prepared for the devil himself."

The armor was pierced. They faced each other for another minute in silence. A cloud blocked the sun for the duration and then moved on to allow the sunlight to fall upon them again. Ryker was so serious and sincere that for a moment Buck contemplated the idea. Then he remembered his plan. There was no stopping it now. Remembering his cavalry was coming, Buck painted his smile back on. "That's a nice little sermon but you see Devon will be here in a minute with a squad of SS agents to take you away. You didn't really think I'd let you go as easily as I did the last time we met this way did you?"

His green eyes softened as Ryker gave Buck a sad smile. "No, I didn't. I've come to know you pretty well and how desperate you are to run from God. But there's no one coming to your rescue today. I've had Dad see to that. You're here for a while. It's a long walk out of here unless you choose to wait for the repairs to the teleport. Then you'd have to know where to walk. I'm not sure you do."

Another high cloud hid the sun for a moment. It was like it wiped the smile off Buck's face and replaced it with a desperate appearance. It had never occurred to him that someone would damage a teleport. The new models worked flawlessly for almost two decades. You could count on them without thought.

Ryker offered more information, which Buck couldn't refute. "Devon will be here but it'll be quite some time. If he locates it, the nearest teleport is eight miles away. No one ever walks that far. He'll waste hours figuring out how to find a land vehicle of some kind and then getting it to the nearest equipment teleport, which is over twenty-five miles away. IF he finds one and IF he gets it there and IF he can find his way to here with it, the process will take him at the fastest—a day. I wouldn't expect him for two or three."

The truth of it was a slam in the gut. Buck stepped back and leaned against the tree they stood under. He didn't smell the fragrant apple blossoms. He didn't notice the bees buzzing around them or hear the red-tailed hawk screech way up in the sky. Ryker took the time to tell Buck all about his brother Mark, and that it was he who had saved his life. Not stopping there, Ryker continued to tell about what Holly Tarbell had discovered and that the two of them were distantly related. The dilemma consumed Buck to the point there was no fight left in him. He lifted his dull blue eyes to Ryker, readying for a simple sarcastic comment, but the concern on Ryker's face stopped him.

After a moment, Buck unconsciously vocalized what he was thinking. "You really care what happens to me don't you?"

Ryker's answer came naturally and sincerely. "Yes, I guess I do but it doesn't originate with me anymore. God's given this burden to me because He's the One concerned. He wants you to at least give Him a chance."

Not knowing how to handle the situation, Buck shrugged his shoulders in defeat and then crossed his arms. "Looks like I have the time. What do you suggest I do?"

It was more than Ryker had hoped for. It was a struggle not to show the joy he felt. Of all the things he wished to do he simply smiled. "Let Jesus introduce Himself to you. I've set the old cave up. There's a light, a comfortable chair, and the old Bible we found years ago. I suggest you start with the gospel of John. Then explore any other part of the New Testament, maybe Romans. No one will bother you. When you're ready, we can talk about it or I'll see that you get back. That's all I ask."

After a moment, Buck nodded his head with a thin-lipped grimace. "OK. I've wondered for some time about Paul Egger's concerns. Now's my chance to find out for myself."

Buck started to walk past Ryker when the latter put a hand on his shoulder. "That's all I ask. Thanks for allowing me in showing you this. I'll be praying for you."

With a snort, Buck gave a small grin. "I'll give you that much but don't expect any miracles." The SS agent continued his walked to a place where he'd see a new reflection of himself.

Ryker nearly skipped back to the house. The feeling reminded him of his younger days when he did it often. Inside he found a surprise. It made him stop dead in his tracks.

"Ray! What're you doing here?"

The younger brother laughed. "You just never know where I'm going to show up do you? I'm usually where you least expect me."

They gave each other a hug and a pat on the back. They took seats in the living room with their parents. Before any more could be said, Ryker asked his brother the question that had been on his mind for weeks. "Loren hinted that you may have plans. What're you going to do now?"

It was interesting to Ryker to watch himself through his brother. They were so much alike. Ray leaned back in the chair and cupped his bearded chin with a hand and rubbed it while giving his reply. "I've given that much thought. I feel I'm to be reaching the NMA in some way. I don't know how exactly. Somehow I think I can help bridge the communication gap between them and the Network. I've much to learn about this new faith. All I know for sure is that I'm to be battling at the front lines."

Ryker lifted his head in the direction of the cave out behind the house. "You might not be alone."

A huge smile graced his face.

EPILOGUE

Buck was never as nervous in Sly Hawkins' presence. It was six years since he had anything to do with Ryker Cuff after the mountain visit. That fact was the catalyst that resulted in his career taking off like an unburdened helium balloon. But now the SS agent felt the old emotions associated with the failures to those former times. Ryker Cuff returned to haunt him and he again faced those helpless feelings of ambiguity. Alanson S. Shanach was about to see who he was through the perception of someone other than himself. Someone he had questioned Ryker about before.

His eyes were the same vibrant blue but the face was softer looking under the short-cut, black hair. Buck sat in a darkened location, lit only with a crude candle found with some other primitive accommodations in the small cave. As the flame flickered subtly, the light revealed several scars on the weathered face and hands. Fingers trembled slightly as Buck reached for the . . . He stopped and thought first about how he got there. For the first time, he considered it might be his destiny to be where he was. After some contemplation, he decided to continue.

In the dim light, Buck noticed the lamp Ryker had left. He turned it on and reached for the Bible. Carefully opening it a half a dollar bill fell out. It had been placed as a marker to the gospel of John. Laying the book back down Buck picked the bill up and studied it. After a few seconds, he leaned back and fished in his pocket for his wallet. From inside he pulled out his half of the bill. Tenderly he took a closer look at it. His mother had given this to him. Until recently, he never knew who she was. Taking the two halves Buck laid them together on the table. The handwritten message left a clear message for Algie and Alice Eton. If IN GOD WE TRUST we will be ONE. The remark was a simple statement of faith between two people. Buck wondered if he could—if he wanted that kind of faith. He picked the book up and began to read the Bible his great-great grandmother had given to her husband.

AFTERWORD

This project started over eighteen years ago and was inspired by a college creative writing class, incorporated Sunday school teaching plans, and evolved into a reflection of the effects current events could have on our nation's future. Like many people, I love reading Christian fiction but find many times, as entertaining as it may be, I learn nothing new nor is my theological comprehension challenged. Either of these, I feel should be a major consideration when I determine my stewardship involving time spent reading something entertaining. That is me, and why I chose to write this work as I did. I hope my endeavors, at the very least, seem to target these goals even if the aim is less than desired. I hope others might be encouraged and challenged to realize the worth of evangelism and training, even in a work of fiction. What better place to achieve these goals outside the realm of just "preaching to the choir."

Richard Coller—July, 2010